LAST MISSION

Code name: 'Phoenix Rising'

JACK EVERETT
and
DAVID COLES

David Coles and Jack Everett have been co-authors for many years. They have written in a number of genres: Fantasy & Science Fiction, History, Thriller and Mystery. This is the fourth novel to be printed and there are several available as eBooks. There have also been articles and fiction, including a written soap and articles and short stories for pool & snooker and for golf magazines.

They write as Jack Everett and David Coles and – in F&Sf – as Everett Coles. The day jobs – to support the writing habit – are a sports bar in Jack's case and computer software in David's. Both live in God's own county - Yorkshire, England.

Visit their web sites:

David Coles – www.DavidBColes.co.uk

Jack Everett - www.JackLEverett.me.uk

ISBN: 978-0-9565342-1-7

Published by

www.acclaimedbooks.com

Acknowledgements

The Authors would like to acknowledge the help and support of their families during the writing of this novel.

They would also like to thank Joyce Minor for her invaluable help in proof-reading for American grammar and idiom.

PROLOGUE

Almost ten months after the 2006 tremor, the NOAA vessel was running a hydrographic survey along the outer slopes of the Septentrional fault zone bordering Hispaniola. Despite its being felt from Louisiana to Florida, there were no reports of damage or loss of life caused by the previous year's event. However the survey was looking for possible effects leading to instability that might cause further seismic events.

"Nothing?" Asked Robyn Madely, the senior scientific officer aboard the RV Thomas Harvey.

Philip Palmer shook his head and grinned. "Nothing special." Philip's specialty was vulcanology, he was running water temperature and chemistry experiments. Malik Rahn was surveying pollution effects on fish stocks and both took turns with Robyn to keep an eye on the hydrographics trace.

"Well, we'll reach Grand Bahama Island by midnight and that's it for the moment. I'll see you in the morning." Skip to her colleagues, Robyn was on duty until 2 am. The night time hours tended to be boring and she always took a book on watch with her – and so it proved, she got through three chapters of *House Rules* by Jodi Picoult and then sought her bunk.

In nineteen minutes, you can mow the front lawn or any number of other endeavors, according to the blurb on Picoult's – including stopping the world or even jumping off it. Robyn did none of these things when her phone beeped peevishly at her nineteen minutes after falling asleep.

"What?"

"Anomaly on the survey."

She could feel, now, that the Tom H, as they referred to the survey craft, was dead in the water. The diesels were running but idly, disengaged, the power generators were the only load.

"What sort of anomaly?" she asked, looking for something decent to put on.

"Like a long tube sticking up out of the seabed. Big, at least 200 feet."

"Okay, I'll be there shortly. Sounds like equipment malfunction." And when she reached the operations room, it did look like a long tube sticking up out of the seabed. "Yep. Equipment glitch I guess. We'll hang around until it's light enough to put a ROV over the side and take a look."

*

Robyn reached the deck at exactly five thirty. "So what have we got?

"A long tube."

"Sticking out of the sea floor?"

Cameron, one of the permanent crew of the Tom H, gestured at the picture being transmitted from the ROV – *the remotely operated underwater vehicle.*

"Weird. Have you been around it?"

Yup. I'd sit down if I were you. You're in for a surprise." Cameron chuckled as did the two interns – Pippa who was handling the ROV controls and Derren who was just there because Pippa was there; Philip was still awake watching the electronic traces for volcanic evidence.

"Go on then show me."

It looked like a giant grey finger pointing up out of the tumbled boulders close to the continental shelf. The picture drifted slowly as the mini-submarine paraded around the artefact. A bulge came into view, wobbled in a random current and cleared.

"A submarine?"

Cameron nodded then, to the operator, "Bring that registration up, will you?"

The cylinder swelled as the camera approached, the conning tower came into focus.

"And you're seriously expecting me to believe this is a U-boat? The World War Two U-boat, U-683? Nice and clean, the number as readable as it was sixty years ago?"

"Maybe it got buried in ejecta from a volcano." Philip said in a serious tone.

"There's absolutely no evidence for volcanic activity." Robyn pointed out.

"So it could be twenty, thirty miles away. Maybe it was a mud slide, that would seal it up nice and clean for years."

"That's true. Anaerobic conditions, no bacteria, no nothing."

2

LAST MISSION

"You see how it's sticking up, Skip? Bit of an angle, watch it long enough and it moves. I think it's been buried for those sixty odd years and it has only recently worked its way free of the debris down here."

"Go on."

"There was a bad 'quake along here, eight or so on the Richter scale, in 1946. Maybe that buried it and last year's September tremor loosened it and the air inside gave it enough buoyancy to bring it to the surface."

The observation vehicle had come almost full circle, back to where Skip had first seen it. She stared fixedly at the picture for a few moments. "Bring us in closer at this angle. Close as it's safe. Are we taping this?" she asked suddenly.

Cameron nodded.

After a minute or two, the hull plates could be distinguished.

"Look at that." Robyn tapped a fingernail against the glass. "Are those air vents, or something?"

"Sea cocks, I'd say."

"They're open."

"Yes, they are. Maybe it was sunk deliberately."

"Can we get in there?"

"Damn dangerous, Skip. We could cut a small hole, poke a camera inside."

"Do it."

*

Derren, an intern who had been with the Tom H for almost a year, pushed the camera through the neat circular hole and then the mini-floods. On the repeater screen in the operations center above, all that could be seen for five minutes or more was a drift of debris.

"Damn."The camera had reached into the air-filled space and Derren rotated it slowly. Almost the first thing they recognised was a skeletal hand; the camera tracked along the wrist bones – a watch, a moldering sleeve and quite suddenly, a skull. Below the survey vessel, Derren manipulated the lamps and then the camera once more.

"Get him out of there, now." Robyn snapped. "Now!"

Even as the intern climbed aboard the Tom H and the ROV was craned down onto the deck, Robyn was on the radio, sending a frequency coded signal.

The research vessel surged away, out to the deep waters of the Atlantic, a white panicky froth fountaining up from the bows. All the ship's 3000 tons and 270 feet were steaming at fifteen knots for the safest water they could find.

"That's right." Robyn was back on the radio speaking to her director, who had not yet finished his breakfast. "Huge. Big enough to blow the Bahamas out of the ocean."

She was silent as she listened to the voice on the other end.

"No, I know what a torpedo looks like and this is not a torpedo *and* it's been there for over half a century."

Again, she listened.

"Yeah," she said nodding heatedly over the mike. "Good idea. The Navy."

ONE

Crash!

Carl's fist hit the table with enough violence to make the dishes jump. Thin lips compressed to a tight, white line of anger, he glared at his wife.

Mai, too, was angry. She was often angry but rarely let her emotions surface.

"They are bad men Carl." She persisted in spite of the other's fury. "I will not have them in my kitchen again. I have seen their like before, back in the old country.

Mindlessly, she carried on with her pastry, rolling it out, automatically transferring it to the pie dish while her eyes misted with tears.

Carl ground his teeth together, he had hardly enough control to speak. It had been the first time that the cellar heating had gone off and he'd taken the two visitors from New York upstairs to sit by the stove. Mai had left them alone but had obviously overheard some of the conversation.

"I heard one of them call the President awful names, Carl. He said that he wished him dead. He is already crippled; it was a terrible thing to say." More American than the native-born, Mai had been brought up to a near reverence for the Presidency; to her, this was almost sacrilege.

"Woman" His voice was husky with suppressed anger, "Be quiet. This is my house; you hear me? I'll say who comes here and they can say what they want. That crippled President of yours helps the English; without him, there'd be peace by now." Carl was visibly bringing himself under control and pointed a still not-quite-steady finger. "You forget that your good all-American boys are pouring bombs down on the cities where you and I were born?"

It was a telling point. Mai originated from Hamburg. Last year it had been the recipient of thousands of tons of high explosive dropped in the course of a single night. Her lips were now as pale as her floury hands; for a moment, it seemed she was about to say something more but a faintly metallic sound from outside diverted her. She wiped her cheeks on her apron and peered through the net curtains.

"Paul." She said. "It's Paul. Now listen to me Carl. What you talk about with your friends is one thing but leave him out of it. My brother is American. He has a good job at Dyson's. I don't want him playing your silly games and losing the job he worked so hard for."

Carl said nothing. He gave one last, venomous, look to his wife and then smoothed his neatly trimmed moustache.

The front door opened, closed.

"Leave him alone Carl, or I'll tell the Police about your traitor friends."

6

LAST MISSION

Carl's fingers tightened on the chair back so that the wooden joints creaked but his face was beaming a warm welcome as the younger man came into the big kitchen.

"Paul!" They spoke together.

"Hi, folks." Paul unwound his scarf. "My, that smells good. What're you making?" He stretched a hand toward the big oven door.

"You keep your hands off, little brother – I'll smack your fingers."

He grinned. Mai persisted in calling him 'little brother' despite the fact that she barely reached his shoulder. There was a difference of almost nine years in their ages; a generation between their outlooks.

"Well, and how's everyone?" He peered at Mai's wan face, "you're looking – a little pale."

"Today I'm fine. And you?"

Paul patted his stomach. "I'm eating right, like you said. Not so many of Mama's pastries."

"No, I'm closer so you come here and eat mine."

Again, they chuckled. Mama Webb's cooking and Paul's partiality was a long standing joke. Mai would poke a finger at his hard, flat stomach and pretend that it was getting soft and flabby. If anything, her brother had lost a few pounds when he'd left home to move closer to work.

Mai was serious for a moment.

"You should always listen to me Paul. I know what's best

for you."

He planted a kiss on top of her head. "I know, liebchen, I do listen."

Carl cleared his throat and rattled the chair. "So, Paul. Enough of this woman's prattling," He smiled, teeth very white and even. "Let's go downstairs, boy. I'll get you some root beer." He winked and draped a heavy arm around Paul's shoulders. They headed for the cellar steps while Mai bent to inspect the contents of her oven. Her teeth clenching her lower lip.

Downstairs, Paul sprawled in an old overstuffed armchair while Carl crossed to a wall cupboard. Inside were several bottles of schnapps and some glasses.

His brother-in-law was a big man, bigger even than Paul. At forty four, his movements were still powerful, his increasing waistline not yet an impediment. Paul saw in Carl the man he would like to be: suave, assured and – most of all – mature. The crow's feet at the corner of each eye gave the impression that humor lay close to the surface.

"All right Paul?" He held out a half filled glass, Paul took it and held it up. "Deutschland." Carl dashed the neat spirit back and filled the glass while Paul drained his a little more slowly.

Carl had served with a Landsturm unit from 1916 to 1918 having suffered the ignominy of a wood splinter turning septic, the week before he had applied to become a fighting soldier. His uniform with its fully buttoned front and Infantry Battalion

8

number on its short turnover collar hung in a wall cupboard along with a very old 10.55 mm Reichs revolver- One of the first hand guns issued by the German army in the last century. His distinctive oilskin cap with the give-away Landsturm cross he had conveniently lost. He had never wished to be associated with a unit whose only claim to fame was Garrison duties.

There were various other military mementos on display as well as a map of present day Germany and a picture of the Fuhrer. To judge from the yarns he spun, Carl had been the only soldier doing any of the fighting; certainly, he dreamt of himself as a key figure in any action.

Paul was not certain what the older man did for a living. Sometimes he would vanish for days or weeks at a time; when he returned, it was with a bombastic swagger, a thinly disguised contempt for everything American and with a well-filled wallet.

"So, then. How is work?" asked Carl.

Paul shrugged. "Busy. We've started production on that twelve kilowatt transformer now; oil cooled. They've put me in charge of the line."

"Really? I'm pleased for you. It will mean more money, no?"

"A few bucks. I'm on forty one fifty now."

"Still not a lot when you are keeping your parents. I bet old man Dyson makes a lot more eh? With that fat wife of his and the two spotty daughters, he has to."

"Well, the raise makes it a bit easier."

"But you could do with more, hmm? Thanks to the Jews at the White House, your father will probably never work again."

"We get by."

"Of course you do." Carl held up the bottle enquiringly and Paul shook his head. "Still, now, you rent your own apartment."

Paul snorted. "It's only a room in an old walk-up, you know. I had to live closer to work."

"So? What did you come to see me for – or is this really just a social visit?" Carl was shrewd enough to guess that Paul was unlikely to pedal ten miles on a mid-week evening just to say Hi.

The younger man grinned sheepishly. "You know me too well, Carl, what I came for was advice."

Carl nodded, sure of what was coming.

"Remember the job down south."

" Remember?" Carl had given Paul the original advertisement.

"They've offered it to me. I guess they took the reference up with Dyson, he was looking at me kind of strange yesterday."

"Wunderbar." He filled the glasses again in spite of Paul's earlier refusal. "Knew you were right for it. You will take it of course." It was a statement rather than a question,

"I – I guess so. That's why I came." He paused a moment, looking around the room before continuing. "It's a hell of a long way, and there's Mama and Papa –you and Mai."

"You don't live with them any longer."

"No, but I see them pretty often. They can always call me."

LAST MISSION

"Those thoughts do you credit Paul but you have your own life to live, your career. Anyway, your sister and I are here; they can call us just as easily."

"I guess." Paul sipped morosely at his drink. "There's the other business too, that you mentioned before."

This was the crux of the matter. Carl had worked hard on his young brother-in-law. He had extolled the virtues of pre-war Germany, exaggerated its quality compared with the American way of life and then he had hinted that he worked for certain people in Germany. Fascinated, Paul had pestered him with questions. Carefully, he had allowed Paul to drag information from him; how he was an important agent in a German intelligence network, how he wrote coded letters and carried out dangerous missions.

Much of what Carl had said had been wishful thinking, nevertheless it sounded glamorous and exciting to an impressionable young man.

When he'd given Paul the job advertisement, Carl had, again, spoken of the network. At no point did Carl suggest outright that he wanted Paul to spy for the organisation, yet the implications were clear enough.

"Listen, how long have you known me?"

"Since you married Mai."

"Ja – ten years nearly. I helped you through college when you left high school, no?"

Paul nodded. It had been hard work and without Carl's

money, it would have been impossible.

"Have I ever given you bad counsel?" A shake of the head. "I want your success Paul, if you can help me – us – our country a little, it would repay my," he paused, debating a word, "my faith in you."

"What sort of help, Carl?"

"This place, this Los Alamos is connected with the war effort. We know this but we don't know how; any information you can give us will be helpful. You don't want this war to go on forever, do you Paul?"

"No, of course not."

"You see, if Roosevelt had not made this strange alliance with England, Germany and England would be at peace now; they would have joined against the Russians – they are the real enemy. When we know what is going on down there; well, perhaps we can use it to discredit the President before the election; perhaps there are other ways?"

"You make it sound easy."

"Easy? It is not so. There are so few of us soldiers of the Reich so far behind enemy lines. Your part will not be dangerous but it will be an important part."

"Just information?"

"Bitte?"

"You won't want anything- blowing up?"

Carl guffawed with laughter. "Paul, Paul. Such ideas. What would your sister say if I involved you in something like that?

So. We have to work carefully Paul. The reason that we have not been discovered is that we gather information only; none of us is an infiltrated agent – only our leader; the rest of us have been here most if not all our lives."

Somewhat reassured, Paul was anxious not to be thought of as a coward. "It isn't that I wouldn't do anything like that if it was needed Carl. It's just – well – that I don't know how."

"Of course not. We shall ask nothing of you that you can't do. If the chance to do something more active comes along – well, we shall see." He patted Paul's knee.

"I'd better go up and see Mai."

"Tell her nothing of this Paul." He warned, then, when the younger man had gone, he grinned, held his glass up to Hitler's portrait and murmured 'Heil Hitler.' to himself.

Carl had not yet said anything to the Major. It had all started some months ago with a bit of idle gossip picked up at one of the beer and schnapps parties he liked to throw. Someone had mentioned the huge site under preparation in New Mexico, Later, the name arose again. It was at a gathering of five of the field agents in the nondescript basement of a block of New York apartments; Piekenbrock was passing out assignments based on information he had gathered from a score of sources. These ranged from government secretaries and aides through cleaning women who could be bribed to inspect waste baskets, to newspaper items and radio broadcasts.

"– huge amounts of money have evidently been allocated to

this Los Alamos." the Major was saying when the name struck a chord in Carl's memory.

Returning home, he started checking through trade journals and was eventually rewarded with a job advertisement for electricians, Paul fitted the bill. The money that he had poured into the kid's education at Mai's chivvying, perhaps it might show some return.

Mai let the curtain fall again, turned to face Carl who was still sitting at the table. The look of loathing on her face was unmistakable; now that Paul had gone, she made no attempt to disguise it.

"If you get that boy into trouble Carl, I shall go to the Police." She went closer. "You hear me?" She whispered.

"Leave me be, woman." He muttered. "He's got a job down south now; I doubt we shall see him more than twice a year."

"Paul: Going away? Thank God for that."

Carl smiled, "Mai frowned.

"Did you have something to do with this? Carl? Tell me."

Carl said nothing; instead, he stood up. The movement was so abrupt that his chair crashed backward, skittered across the tiled floor. With, one continuing movement, he struck her across the cheek with the back of his hand; the force of the blow flung her head to one side. Without stopping to see what injury he had inflicted, he stormed off down to the root cellar.

Sitting at the old roll top desk, Carl settled down and began composing a careful letter. The incident in the kitchen upstairs

14

was already dismissed from his mind as he inserted another code word among the more mundane contents. His commanding officer would be pleased to hear of his penetration of the 'Hill' and Carl smiled as he addressed the letter to Mr. Charles Dingle, Rosewood Towers in Newark, New Jersey.

Dingle was Joseph Piekenbrock's cover name. Piekenbrock held the rank of Major in section six of the RSHA – Reichssicherheitsauptamt – which had its headquarters in Berlin. In New York he held the lowly position of janitor for the block of apartments but more than sixty volunteers reported to him, each one feeding information from widely scattered points throughout the United States. Most of his force was, like Carl, pre-war immigrants from Germany; several were native born Americans converted to the Nazi ideology.

The far flung net had been instructed to report on anything concerning the three centers of war effort research. The rumours generated by political in-fighting spoke of huge amounts of men, material and money being swallowed up at the sites; Piekenbrock, among others, was intensely interested.

Carl sealed the envelope, stuck a stamp on it and put it to one side; he tore the draft into shreds and burned them in an ash tray. He was well pleased with his efforts, a contact inside Los Alamos; add to that the fact that Paul was kin; he nodded to himself, he had done right to ask for more money, he had invested a great deal in the kid already.

Across the room, a movement caught his attention. Two

small red points reflected the dying flames from the ash tray. Reflexively, he hurled a letter opener, the eyes vanished.

"Goddamn rats."

TWO

The lady who met Paul at 109, East Palace Street in Santa Fe was a pleasant woman – in her forties, Paul guessed.

"Come in, young man." She opened. "I've been expecting you." She held out her hand; "Mrs. McKibbin," she smiled, "Secretary for the housing project. Do you have your details with you?"

Paul smiled back and handed her the letter he had received from the Albuquerque District of the US Engineers. It confirmed his appointment, told him that he was now on the payroll of the University of California and instructed him to report to this office.

Mrs. McKibbin's eyes swept over the sheet of paper with the speed of long familiarity; Paul was only one of many who came to see Mrs. McKibbin. She looked up. "Okay Mr. Webb. It all seems in order. Now, I have your pass and badge here – that's all you need until you get up there." She looked at her wrist watch and frowned. "You've only got ten minutes before the next service bus leaves; if that's too much of a rush you could rent a room at the La Fonda Hotel."

Paul nodded. "That's fine but I guess I'd like to get up there now. I've come so far – I might as well go the whole

17

way.Besides, I'm kinda interested to see what I've got myself into."

Dorothy McKibbin chuckled. "The times I've heard that. Well, you know best Mr. Webb so I'll wish you good luck. No doubt I'll see you again."

It was fortunate that Paul did not place the traditional reliance upon first impressions. The ride out from Santa Fe had started pleasantly enough but, very soon, the greener farmlands had been left behind as the bus climbed up towards the distant Los Alamos plateau. A dense cloud of dust chased them all the way until the bus pulled up to the main entrance.

He walked uncertainly towards the gate, holding back until the other passengers – more at home than himself – had passed through. Finally, Paul's turn came. He produced his letter of introduction for inspection by the armed guard.

The guard glanced quickly at the letter then back at Paul, "Webb?" The man had a mouth like a bear trap.

Paul nodded.

"Wait over there bub? Gotta get the office on the wire."

Paul leaned back against the springy wire fence and dropped his valise to the ground while the MP disappeared into his wooden hut. Whatever he said on the phone did not take long; he was back within seconds, looking fiercely down at the newcomer from the shade cast by the tightly cut peak of his hat.

"Won't be long bub. They're sending someone out now."

"Seems a heck of a lot of trouble, just to let me in."

The guard smiled grimly.

"Security's tighter than a rat's ass round here, fella. We even put I.D. tags on them."." A jeep screeched to a halt, bringing with it another dust cloud. "Here's the creeps, hope you gave 'em a good picture."

The formalities did not take long but they were thorough. One of the men that the gate guard had called creeps – an internal security man – checked his appearance against a photograph taken by the government people in the north. A photograph was fixed to the pass Mrs. McKibbin had given him and only when this was pinned to his shirt did the Military Policeman allow him inside the gateway.

Fifteen minutes later, still unsteady from the breakneck drive across five miles of roughly graded track, Paul was escorted into a prefabricated office where further security measures were taken. Fingerprints, his social security card, signature – all would be checked later to make certain that Paul Webb was who he claimed to be.

He felt subdued while he waited in the dusty little outer-room and not only from the strict security. The drive from the main gate had made him feel like an ant. Buildings and construction works played tricks with perspective; the area under construction was enormous. The jeep had threaded its way through piles of shuttering timber, mammoth bonfires awaiting a match, Paul had thought, skirting thoughts of sabotage. Bales of steel reinforcing rods, some already latticed and tied with wire had barred their way at one point, looking like a Brobdignagian child's construction kit. Above all, the din was indescribable; the noise of trucks, bulldozers, mobile cranes, dump trucks – all adding to the cacophony of construction on a scale that Paul had never experienced before.

"Hi there!"

The man who suddenly breezed in shut the door quickly behind him.

"Kinda dirty out there. You'll be Webb, pleased to know ya." He stuck a soft, pink hand out, smiled a baby faced smile. "Captain Bankhurst, Personnel."

Paul shook the limp hand, not quite certain what to say. Bankhurst saved him the problem of thinking.

"Care for a look round Webb? Gotta jeep outside…" The trivial chatter went on, and on.. It seemed the Captain never stopped talking, nothing could stem the flow.

The jeep bounced along rutted tracks, half hearted attempts at made up roads that washed out at the first rainstorm. Bankhurst told him the names of the buildings, showed him where the dormitory block was situated, the cafeteria, power house but Paul didn't hear half of what was said. Again, there were the haphazard obstacles of temporary power cabling, racks of high pressure piping and partly excavated trenches which soon had Paul lost as to direction.

Eventually they arrived back at the Personnel Office.

"Wow." Bankhurst put his hands to his ears."Let's get

inside, hey?"

"What's that?" Paul asked, pointing to a partly completed structure rising high against the sky.

"What?"

"Those buildings over there."

"Let's get inside, outa this noise."

They went into the office and Paul pointed again, through the window.

"That? Smart, hey? I guess you'd say that's the reason you're here, why we're all here." Bankhurst fingered his smooth chin. "That there is the Tech Area, the heart of Project Y."

"Okay then. Just why are we here?" He stared out at the massive hangar-like structures which, in spite of their incomplete condition, were obviously already in use.

Bankhurst grinned. "Let's go through to my office."

Paul followed him through a large open plan area and into a room at the rear. A phone was shrilling insistently as they went through the door, Bankhurst grabbed it on the run.

"Mm?" It was the first time Paul could remember anyone shouting that particular sound. "Yeah, Bankhurst here, Personnel." Whatever came through the earpiece could not have been complimentary, the officer's round face reddened with anger.

"'Kay. I'll pass it along." He slammed the receiver down. "Shit! Nothing works in this hell hole. Nothing but nothing – 'cept my damn phone. You know, we must have half the goddamn phone engineers in the States trying to make the goddamn system work and still we get nothin."

With an effort, Bankhurst calmed down looking at Paul, taking stock of the newcomer. Tall,180 or maybe more, blue eyes and dark hair. He nodded; good looking, he supposed, in a craggy sort of way but still a kid – not a lot of experience behind those eyes. He noted the cheap clothing, footwear.

"What they been paying you up North? Fifty, sixty?"

"Fifty dollars a week," Paul squared his shoulders. "and lunches."

"And lunches. Well, you're a bright one, Webb but let me give you a warning – don't be too curious. This place is kinda secret; half of those Washington types who proposed it don't know what they proposed yet. I'll tell you something, I sure as hell don't."

Bankhurst drew himself a cup of water from the cooler and emptied it in one movement, "Sarah," he shouted through the door, "nearly outa water. Yeah," he continued without pausing, "the official line – straight down from the top. It goes like this: Son, the job you have undertaken here is of vital importance to our war effort."

Paul chuckled, Bankhurst had imitated the fulsome, over dramatic government tones often heard on radio interviews. He shook his head, the guy had been talking so fast there had been no way of getting a word in. He had thought the Personnel Officer a bit of a drip when he first met him, now he was not so sure; it was possible that scatterbrained manner was all an act.

"Look." Paul reasoned, unwilling to let the matter go. "A big part of my job here is going to be riding herd on new labor - electrical engineers. These guys won't be stupid, you expect me to act as dumb with them as you are with me?"

"Yeah. Said you were a smart kid." Bankhurst's grin was a grudging one – the kid was maybe a bit green but he knew how many beans... "You'll find this whole place runs on a *need to know basis*. Our boss – that's General Groves – enforces that policy without exception. I can only give you more of the official line; FDR personally supervises our little project, we get to rate the highest priority grading possible – triple A, no less. An' I can say without fear of contradiction that success or failure here will directly affect the war in both Europe and the Pacific." He paused and looked at Paul who was wearing a slightly amused expression.

Bankhurst pursed his lips. "I guess you don't want to listen to that same line of shit. Anyway, it's that or nothing Paul – okay if I call you Paul? No, all I can say is that you've got one hell of an opportunity kid. Make a go of this an' your career'll take off like the proverbial bat outta hell, but..." he leaned closer – "you gotta be able to answer your own men's questions. You get my drift?"

Paul nodded. What the man meant was that anyone who worked for him would have to work in the same darkness as himself. No doubt the Army mind would be content but he doubted it would be so easy when more civilian labor came to Los Alamos – and it would. Well, it was a bridge he would have to cross later.

Seeing that the new section boss had realised that he would get no more information unless it was necessary – and that he had accepted the fact, Bankhurst relaxed. He stuffed a fistful of site plans and regulations into Paul's shirt pocket and, after a few pleasantries, detailed one of the military clerks to show him to his quarters as well as where to report for work the following morning.

With a lingering glance at Sarah – Bankhurst's stenographer – Paul followed the young private out into the noisy world of the 'Hill'.

The clerk didn't speak for several minutes, something was obviously exercising his mind.

"Not in the Army?" He asked at length.

Paul shook his head.

"Navy?"

"Reserved occupation." He volunteered, resenting the other's tone. "Heavy electrical industry."

The other nodded, withdrew into silence again.

"Thought you'd be on active duty by now." Observed Paul after a time.

After bedding down in what he later learned was temporary accommodation, Paul found his way to the cafeteria. Like his quarters, it was a prefab building similar to many more he'd seen

24

scattered around the sprawling site. The place was fairly empty; at eight p.m. most of the construction crews were still out working – as he would be doing from tomorrow on.

At the counter, he selected steak and salad. It came quickly, at least they'd gotten over the commissary problems that Bankhurst had described to him; at the beginning, they'd had to truck in hundreds of boxed lunches from Albuquerque.

Paul was carrying his tray to one of several empty tables when he saw her. The girl had her face buried in a book but what was on view was very appealing: a smooth sweep of honey blonde hair tied back in an almost adolescent pony tail. One tapering finger marked her place as she looked up at his approach.

"Mind if I join you?"

"Mm?" She glanced quickly from him to the wide choice of empty tables and back again. There was nothing adolescent about the amused – almost contemptuous glance she gave him. "Oh no, sit down if you wish." Her tone conveyed the fact that she knew all the lines he might be about to push.

"Not butting in on any studies?" Paul was surprised at her comparative youth, and he thought he detected an unusual accent.

The girl shook her head, bent to read again.

"Just arrived here." He offered then, as a sort of introduction, "Name's Paul, Paul Webb. New Chief of Electricians."

She showed an interest for the first time, condescending to push aside the manila folder of papers. "Really? Civilian?"

"Why yes, of course."

She laughed at this.

"Did I say something funny?"

"There's no 'of course' here. There're so many soldiers on this project, it's a bit of a rarity to run across a fellow civilian - especially one who isn't a Nobel Laureate. I'm Susan Millar, by the way."

"Hi." They shook hands. "What's a Nobel Laureate?"

"You know – a Nobel Prize winner."

The term was vaguely familiar to Paul. "Ah, yes – scientists. Are you one of those?"

Her eyes crinkled pleasantly. "A Nobel winner or a scientist?"

Paul shrugged, out of his depth.

"Sorry. I'm teasing you. Yes, I'm a physicist – at least that's what I'm told. I have a feeling that I'm really a gopher for the prima donnas of our profession."

"Bit temperamental are they?"

"You're not kidding. No – I'm exaggerating really, we've got a pretty good bunch. It's just the soldiers that're annoying – I have to fight them off."

"Me too."

She laughed. He liked what it did to her face and tried to think of more funny things to make her do it again.

26

"I guess I'm going to be pretty busy though, for the first week or two especially. Can I get in touch with you if things ease up a little?"

"Sure. Just ask for Doctor Millar at the women's hostel."

"Doctor Millar?" Paul thought he had the accent pegged. "English aren't you?"

"Yes." She stated simply.

*

The first few months after starting at the Hill, Paul buried himself in the work – or, more correctly, the work buried Paul. He memorised schematics and drawings by the ream and fell into his narrow cot at night with eyes that were red rimmed and sore. He tramped along miles of surface feeders, crawled passageways crammed with cable lays and grew to accept that the army personnel who worked for him were little different from their civilian counterparts. The fact that they worked longer and harder – though with fewer complaints – could be attributed to the threat of the cooler.

Paul had a natural ability to get along with most people, especially with work gangs. It stemmed, no doubt, from his willingness to jump into the trench with them and show them how he wanted the job done. Occasionally, it made for hard words – when the man in question was content to let the boss get on with it, but generally, the tactic worked.

However, Paul had no difficulty in maintaining the correct

distance between himself and the men. In this, he had received good practice during his formative years: he recalled how the other school children never admitted him to their circle, because of the accent and customs of his German parents. He had always been an outsider, stubbornly fighting his way through high school, studying when others more gifted than himself were out having a good time. He realised now that he owed his present post to his ability for hard work, and, furthermore, that he enjoyed the gruelling hours and responsibility. The desert sun of New Mexico had written new lines at the corners of his eyes, turned his skin a dark brown.

Since that first meeting with Susan Millar, he had fostered the relationship. It was not idyllic – they were rarely alone for there was nowhere to go due to security measures. Susan, as a scientist, was restricted to the site. Even so, Paul and Susan enjoyed each other's company, he recognised the potential in the relationship and they spent meal times together and breaks if they coincided. It was for this reason that he had turned down an offer to move to more sumptuous accommodation at Frijoles Lodge, the former Headquarters of the Bandelier National Monument.

One such evening, sitting on a wicker seat in an area of grassland not yet marked by the passage of earth moving equipment, Paul remembered Carl. He had been studying Susan's profile, making comparisons between her and his sister Mai. He supposed that he would have to make an effort and call

28

his brother-in-law, though what he could tell him, Paul didn't know; the prospect nagged at his conscience.

"I wonder." Susan whispered, looking at the hazy backdrop of the sierras. "If we're successful here, will the world still be the same?"

It was an idle thought, spoken aloud and, just as unconsciously Paul answered as he smoothed down an errant strand of her blonde hair.

"Successful at what, Sue?"

"Testing out the bomb."

"Mm. Don't know." His pulse quickened.and he felt sweat form in beads on his forehead. He wiped them away with his shirt then touched her hair. "Getting breezy, shall we go in?"

THREE

Herr Reichsleiter Bormann had never been one to brood over problems; rather, he thrived on them. Since the earliest days of his career with the Party, Martin Bormann had treated problems as stepping stones to elevate himself and engineer the downfall of those who stood in his path.

The last great problem he had used in this manner was the defection of his superior, Rudolph Hess, in May of 1940. Hitler had been beside himself with fury at the news, while Bormann calmly capitalized on the situation to plant further seeds of doubt concerning the loyalty of the Fuhrer's intimates. From that point, the Brown Mole – as his enemies called him – emerged more and more into the daylight, wielding an ever more powerful influence over Hitler.

One of the last of Hitler's few confidants, Bormann had advanced on the crest of a wave.

Now, that same wave threatened to engulf him. As events conspired to rob the Fuhrer of the vision which had driven him through these turbulent years, the Allies gathered like jackals around the still twitching corpse of Germany.

Bormann glanced around the office before returning his eyes to the pencilled list in front of him. It detailed the work he had to complete before flying to join the Fuhrer later that day at Bad Neuheim. He knew that Hitler would be inflamed with the success of his Ardennes offensive but, though he would outwardly share in his leader's euphoria, Bormann was quite certain that the German advance was the final effort of a Deutschland defeated in all but name.

He sighed and scrunched up the scrap of paper as he recalled the conversation of a few days before. Speer had been at the Chancellery attempting to temper the Fuhrer's scorched earth policy which was to be put into action if the Allies were not repelled. Klopfer had been having a whispered conference with Doctor Hupfauer, Speer's secretary, when Bormann had seen him; he called Klopfer into his office.

"And what did the Herr Doctor have to say with such urgency?" The tone was mild – far more intimidating than Bormann's normal brusque manner.

"He said – the Reichminister said – that the Fuhrer had overreached himself, he has stripped the Eastern front to bolster his attack in the west."

There was little love lost between Bormann and the Minister for Industry, the same was true of most of the inner circle of ministers and officials. At the same time, he had every respect for Albert Speer's intelligence and opinions – in private. In public however…

"And when did the Herr Reichminister become a general, hmm? How is it that he presumes to criticise the Fuhrer's strategy?"

Klopfer shifted uncomfortably, his gaze on the threadbare carpet unwilling to accept the amused contempt that would be in Bormann's eyes.

"Did he volunteer any more pearls of wisdom?"

"Only – only that the Reds would march into Berlin that much sooner."

"So. Not only is our Reichminister a critic of the Fuhrer's military genius, he is also an authority on the Russians' intentions."

Bormann frowned at the memory. He possessed no intelligence organisation like Himmler's but the whispers that reached him from his far flung net of informers provided a surprisingly clear picture of events. In general, they supported Speers' opinion.

"No." Bormann shook his head and clenched his fist around the ball of paper in his hand. The Fuhrer must be persuaded that it's in his best interests to listen to his contingency plans – the Reich could not afford to lose its leader. "But how?" he spoke aloud again. It was impossible to suggest such a thing to the Fuhrer at this moment; he simply would not believe that the fickle hand of Fate might now be turned against him.

Bormann sat hunched in his chair for several more minutes before evidently corning to some conclusion. Klopfer, he knew would be sitting at his desk outside the door. Bormann wished to go into the file room but could not do so while his secretary was in attendance. In fact, Klopfer would rush to assist him and help was the last thing the Reichsleiter desired in this matter.

He depressed a button which sounded a buzzer in the outer office; the connecting door opened before Bormann had lifted his finger.

"You wanted me, Herr Reichsleiter?"

"Of course. I am in need of a bottle of wine – a good wine for... for a special person; hein?"

Klopfer nodded and grinned. He knew of course, that his superior was due to fly out to meet with the Fuhrer that afternoon. Who else could it be for?"

"I shall try my best Sir. Do you wish that I go now?"

"Naturally Gerhard." Bormann waved his hand in dismissal then, seeing the look of surprise on his deputy's face. "Don't worry about me, Klopfer. I expect no one this morning – in any case, you will not be gone for long, will you?"

"I'll return as soon as possible."

"That is so and – Klopfer..."

"Sir?"

"I'm still waiting for those two forecasts I asked for – the Fuhrer's and the one for the Reich itself."

"They have not yet been traced Sir."

"Get on to it as soon as you return." Bormann dismissed him with a nod and leaned back in his chair as the other left. He relaxed as the door closed, running his hands up his face, knuckling eyes that were sore from too much reading.

The Reichsleiter was a heavy-set man, his most distinctive feature being the great bull neck. Physically, despite his lack of stature, he possessed an intimidating arrogance. It had not always been so; in the early thirties, as manager for the Party's insurance office, he was remembered as a slightly built man. Conscious then, of his shortness, he brushed his hair upwards and back to make himself appear taller. As his status grew, however; as he achieved power and responsibility he left this phase behind. Bormann was secure in the knowledge that his power was second only to that of the Fuhrer.

As soon as the outer door had closed, Bormann crossed to the window which looked out on the road. He started to open it but remembered the bitterly cold December wind and refastened the catch.

A moment later, Klopfer came into view, wrapped up tightly in his leather coat. He crossed Vosstrasse and the Reichsleiter went into the outer office, satisfied that his deputy's errand would keep him away for some time.

With a bunch of keys from Klopfer's desk, Bormann opened the steel safe-like door that had been set into the room's concrete inner wall. Inside, blue metal drawer fronts lined the small space; Bormann knew precisely what he wanted and where it was filed. He withdrew three grey cardboard folders from a cabinet and, locking the door, returned the keys and took the folders back to his desk.

Each one bore the same title: appointments 1942; each,

34

however, was stencilled with a different name on the front cover. He spent several minutes examining the contents of each before finally selecting one of the three. Nodding to himself, Bormann opened it to the first page and smoothed it out.

Unconsciously, the decision had been made some hours ago. The brief recap on the private lives and careers of the three men he had short-listed was merely to satisfy the logical part of his mind. He settled back and turned slowly through the pages where the life of Kurt Walther Schroeder was dissected in detail.

Schroeder's father, Dieter, was a Lutheran. Bormann frowned but shrugged – an almost imperceptible movement – no one could choose his parents. He read on: Dieter had been commissioned in 1915 and later been awarded the Iron Cross Second Class after the third battle of Artois. Promoted to Leutnant in September 1936 after Hermanstadt, the elder Schroeder died in action in Picardy, March, 1918.

The Reichsleiter turned the page.

Maria Schroeder, nee von Epp. Again the woman was a member of the Lutheran Church. Born in 1894, daughter of a Prussian aristocrat, she had married Dieter in 1913 in Berlin. At the time the dossier had been made up, Maria was still living in the family house in the Friedrickstrasse. Kurt was her only child.

Page three gave a similar list of details on Anna Schroeder whom Kurt had married in 1938 at a Catholic church in Munich.

There had been a son, he saw, but both he and his mother had been victims of the recent allied bombing in Berlin.

Bormann shook his head, he took care to stay below ground when those terrible rains fell but he had, nevertheless, seen the awful fire-storms that raced along streets after a wave of saturation bombing. The flames seemed to be borne on the arid air, consuming anything in their way like so much paper. He had looked at the bodies after the fires had passed, charred, unrecognisable; bundles of barbecued meat.

Bormann pursed his lips. The rows which must have taken place within those two families when the young Kurt and Anna had announced their intentions – a marriage between two such faiths! Suddenly interested, he looked at the two lines which summarised Anna's parents. There was nothing there; both had been dead for some time." At least, Kurt's father-in-law had had the good sense to die before he could make a fool of himself; a better sense of timing than his own wife's – Gerda's – father had.

The following pages were devoted to Kurt Schroeder himself. A full face formal portrait of the man: the picture was not a good one, it showed graininess from being blown up from a section of a larger negative. On the next page was a far better photograph; it showed a smiling Schroeder receiving his Iron Cross First Class from Field Marshal Rommel. Words had been scribbled across the foot of the picture, Bormann peered closely:

"For excellent fighting in the retreat to Fuka."

A signature followed, it was hard to be certain but the Reichsleiter suspected that it was Rommel's.

A sound from the outer office alerted Bormann. He swept

the folders together, placing them neatly in a drawer, closing and locking it before going to investigate. It was Klopfer, he was just taking off the heavy coat.

"Ah, Gerhard! You have the wine?" A bottle shaped brown paper parcel stood on the desk. Bormann rubbed his eyes, feigning tiredness.

"Oh yes, Herr Reichsleiter. A beautifully rich Mosel, I had hoped for champagne but..."

No, no, this is so much better, A German wine, I could not have asked for better." He closed his eyes tightly and then opened them, blinking rapidly for a moment. "I'm tired, I wish for some coffee."

"At once, Sir."

Bormann nodded and retreated to his own office, Klopfer entered a few minutes later bearing a tray with coffee pot, cup and saucer; his superior was inspecting the label on the bottle of Mosel,

"It is suitable, Sir?" Klopfer poured coffee into the Dresden china.

"Quite satisfactory." He sipped from the cup and pulled a face. "Strange," he said ruminatively, "the sad state we are in. Still it is possible to find a bottle of good wine but, instead of coffee, we must drink the juice of acorns – like hogs in the forest." He took another mouthful of the ersatz brew, grimaced. "What will we do when the Allies' shells have torn down all of our oak trees? Eh Gerhard?"

The aide shook his head evading a reply, Bormann in such a mood was unpredictable.

"And while I think of it, Klopfer." The Reichsleiter grew brisk once more, "I must go to an appointment, call the car and then check that the aeroplane is ready. Oh, and by the way – those two forecasts I want; leave them to me, I have learned that Uncle Heinie has the files in one of his research offices. I'll see him myself."

FOUR

The black Mercedes skirted several heaps of rubble in the street outside – mute testimony to the previous night's bombing. At one point a white Chancellery pigeon flew above the car, its home demolished by the blasts. Bormann did not notice the impromptu emblem of peace.

He took Schroeder's file from the case and opened it at the photographs again. He assumed that the smile was due to the award but in this, Bormann's character assessment was faulty.

Kurt Schroeder was singularly unimpressed by medals. He knew that for every one of his own awards, a dozen, a score of other men had acted just as heroically; a thousand had given their very lives for the Fatherland. Before the start of the war, Kurt had made a characteristic decision: studying classics at University, he had left to join the armed forces without sitting his finals. Like the medals, the parchment and the graduation robes were of no interest to him.

Steadying himself as the car detoured past a bomb crater, Bormann glanced out; watching the old men who had been detailed to clear the debris – virtually the only labor available in Berlin. He sighed, what were things coming to? He turned back to the first of the written reports, a standard form showing a brief summary of his appearance and one or two other details. He skimmed quickly through this: birth – 1914, March 9 at Friedrichstrasse 159; blue eyes, black hair; a metre 70 in height and 85 kilos. The only distinguishing marks were scars from combat wounds. The last date on the resume was February of 1942. The following report had a dateline of July of that year. Bormann's staff had been unable to secure files covering the intervening months.

The July, 1942 item read merely: el Alemain – see Appendix A.

Most of the other entries read similarly, with a place and date and an appendix reference.

The car came to a stop as Bormann leafed through to the first appendix.

"Now what is the matter?" He spoke into the communication tube. The driver replied into the flared horn in the front compartment.

"Unexploded bomb, Reichsleiter. We shall have to detour through side streets."

Bormann looked at his watch, "As quickly as possible." He returned to his reading.

Schroeder had seen action in North Africa from mid-42 through into the following year attached to the Luftwaffe Ramcke Parachute Brigade.

Unlike the man he was considering, Martin Bormann had never been in action. Reading the tersely written reports, he

40

found Schroeder, the man, staring at him from between the lines. Unable to imagine the filth, the despair, the degradation in front line action, Bormann could only see the romantic, courageous picture presented by the reports. Bormann's war was endless inter-departmental manoeuvring; he was a man of papers, of office memos and decrees, thus the Schroeder he came to know was only half of the full man.

Bormann's interest had been aroused when a letter came to his office for Hitler. The Fuhrer's secretary scrutinised all mail and reports addressed to his superior without exception. The letter had been written by an Oberst Krudemayer, it recommended Major Schroeder for a decoration. After reading it Bormann enquired the Oberst's whereabouts and, finding that he was still in Berlin after convalescing, he decided to interview the Officer and hear, at first hand, of the contempt in which Schroeder appeared to hold his own safety.

They were commanded by the Herr Generalmajor Bernard Ramcke, Krudemayer told him across the table – they were at Marta's, she had an apartment no more than ten minutes from Bormann's office in the Chancellery. Its convenience made it almost a pleasure to return to Berlin after a few days on the Obersaltsburg where his wife and children lived.

"We'd been posted to Africa to bolster Rommel's forces. It was just before el Alemain and Leutnant Schroeder – as he was then -was third in command of a rifle battalion, backing up the advance of our Panzer Division. The Fifteenth."

41

"Your cigar's gone out Oberst." Bormann lifted the candlestick and offered his companion a light. "Do you remember the date?"

"The date? Mm, end of August – thirtieth or thirty first. Important?"

"Not especially – I just want to review the field reports for the time."

"Anyway, Rommel was advancing into a minefield – we thought it was a lot shallower than it was. We'd gained – oh – twelve kilometres by dawn and then the British were on to us, pouring in high explosive."

"You were as close as that to the artillery?"

The Oberst shook his head. "Air Force. The Division was very exposed but we continued with the advance well into the afternoon and by then we were in artillery range, close to Alam Halfa Ridge. We took heavy losses among our infantry."

Bormann wrote the name down next to the date in his notebook. "But what of Schroeder?"

"I was coming to him. We – Schroeder too – had taken cover behind some Panzerwagons; we were pinned there for the rest of the day as well as most of the next. A schutzenpanzerwagon took a direct hit, the armour split like tin plate, you know?"

Bormann nodded, wishing that Krudemayer would get to the point.

"Decapitated one man, laid another's head open so badly,

that he died right afterwards.

"Now Schroeder recognised our predicament – he was about the only one of us on his feet, Major Buchner was unconscious, I was little better, Schroeder left his own cover, carried Horst – the Major – out on his shoulder. I crawled after them."

"You were lucky that he was with you."

"I have told myself this: why do you think I wrote the recommendation? The men had already started to retreat – without orders. I was delirious a lot of the time but I remember Schroeder rallying them – used some of the worst language it's ever been my pleasure to hear. Anyway he kept us hanging on until the official order to withdraw came through."

Bormann shook his head and nibbled a mint. "If only there were more like him, eh Krudemayer? It is the Fuhrer's one lament – brave men are so few."

The Mercedes jolted back on to the main road and brought the Reichsleiter back to the present, "So," he muttered to the photograph in front of him, "Leutnant to Major in less than two years. Careless of his own life when Officers of the Reich were in danger: what would he not do to save the Fuhrer himself?"

With a sigh of gratitude that fate had placed such a man in his hands, Bormann replaced the reports in his case and locked it as the car swept into the gateway of the Charité hospital.

The driver got out and opened the rear door, standing stiffly to attention as Bormann exited. He returned the straight-armed salute and gathered his coat about him against the chill wind.

Inside, people milled about like disturbed ants, oblivious to Bormann's presence. Indeed, it was doubtful that more than one or two would have recognised Hitler's aide. Knowing, in advance, which ward Schroeder occupied, he followed the signs, elbowing through the throng – it became more like an airport departure hall every time he visited the place.

Bormann stopped inside the doors. The beds were close together, double the number that the place had been designed for; it seemed as chaotic as the hall outside. He walked up the narrow aisle slowly, scrutinising each patient in turn, each bundle of bandages, until he recognised his quarry. The Major was leafing idly through the pages of an out of date magazine.

"Major Schroeder?" The other looked up. "We meet at last." Schroeder's eyes met Bormann's. In one glance they seemed to appraise the Reichsleiter and catalogue everything about him; Bormann felt as naked as a skinned wurst. Nevertheless, that piercing glance told him all he needed to know about Schroeder's strength of character: supply the right motivation and this man would be immovable.

The Major was thirty according to the files, he looked older. There was a dusting of grey in his hair at the temples with a smattering of startlingly white strands through the prominent widow's peak. The black eyes shone – almost fever bright, the sockets were dark and overlarge. Schroeder had seen too much of life, too much of death? For a moment Bormann knew what it was to be in action with metallic death raining about him.

44

"Sit down Sir. Please." And suddenly Bormann was aware of another facet to Schroeder: he retained a spark of humor, something lacking in so many soldiers returned from the front,

"Thank you Herr Major. I didn't wish to sit on your feet."

Schroeder seemed to be completely at ease. He was evidently not disturbed by his visitor's rank.

Bormann wondered how to start the conversation and an awkward silence was about to descend when he remembered the package he carried.

"A bottle of wine Herr Major. For you. A celebration bottle if you like."

"Celebration Sir? There is something for celebration?"

Bormann looked at the patient sharply but there was no hint of a double meaning in the words.

"Oh, I'm quite certain that there will be something to celebrate before I leave here. For the moment, just put it somewhere."

Schroeder, who was still holding the wrapped-up bottle, nodded. "Of course, Sir, My thanks." He reached across to the small, steel bedside cabinet, lowered the bottle carefully into the bottom.

"Good. I'd like to have a talk with you Herr Major. An informal chat. How are you progressing?" He indicated the bandages that were bound tightly around Schroeder's chest.

"Pretty well. Since the doctors took the twenty or thirty kilos of shrapnel out of me, I feel much better. They say that I should be out of here for Christmas."

"That's good news. You will stay with your Mother at Christmas?"

It was Schroeder's turn to look at Bormann. Undoubtedly he knew his Mother was a strict Lutheran; it was likely that, whatever reason the Reichsleiter had for coming to see him, he would certainly have looked at his dossier. Schroeder shook his head. "I shall go at New Year."

Bormann went on. "Just how did you get yourself into such a mess?"

"A mess? Yes, I suppose I did."

"Will you tell me about it?"

"There's little to say. I was in conference with other senior officers; the tent we were using was supposed to be behind the firing lines." Schroeder lifted his hands in dismissal. "One moment, the Oberst was speaking; the next, all hell let loose. I think that we must have taken a direct hit."

Bormann smiled, a mere thinning of the lips. "And that was all? What about the men you carried to safety?"

"That was nothing."

"Oberst Krudemayer disagrees with you Herr Major. He considers it a great deal more than nothing, he considers that your actions saved three lives – important lives too. What is more, both the Fuhrer and I are in agreement.

Bormann sat back and watched Schroeder who seemed to be at a loss.

46

"In fact," he leaned forward again, lowering his voice to a confidential level, "were it not that our Fuhrer is at the front directing the Ardennes counter stroke, he might well have been here instead of myself. As it is," Bormann reached into his pocket and removed a brown manila envelope, "it is a pleasant task to show you this." He passed the envelope across.

Schroeder, puzzled, took the proffered package and took out the parchment inside. He read it, stony faced.

"The Knight's Cross is not- conferred for mere nothings, Herr Major, but for immense gallantry. You will realise, of course, that this is in the nature of a preview; the Fuhrer himself will make the award at a suitable ceremony as soon as he returns."

Schroeder handed back the citation and its envelope.

"I am not ungrateful, Herr Reichsleiter, believe me. But do you realise how many men died on that day?"

Bormann shook his head.

"Neither do I. But I do know that, in dying, those men gave their all for the Fatherland. I gave a few minutes of my time and was fortunate enough to escape. Why do you not give a Knights Cross to all those who cannot come home, Herr Reichsleiter?"

Bormann sat very still. There were tears in Schroeder's eyes now. It was several minutes before either spoke. The injured man opened his mouth to add something further but the other held up his hand for silence.

"Herr Major. Believe me when I say that I understand your

passion. However, a Knight's Cross is not awarded just to one man, it is given to every soldier of the Reich; in this case, you have been chosen to receive it on behalf of those others. To exemplify to the living the pride and the gratitude that Germany bears the dead."

Bormann had not been gifted with the silver tongue that Goebbels used to such effect and the unexpected eloquence surprised the Reichsleiter as much as it did Schroeder. There was a certain amount of truth in what he had said and Schroeder was inclined to believe that Bormann was sincere.

"Let us talk of other matters, Herr Major. You will be rejoining your Brigade, when you leave here?"

"What Brigade? There is no more than a handful left. The Russians did not allow us to hold Gumbinnen without exacting a price."

"Mm. I see. Do you wish to seek revenge?"

"Would a single man make that much difference?"

"In the right place, he could make all the difference that mattered. Obersturmbannfuhrer Peiper is making a tremendous difference in the Ardennes. The Fuhrer fully expects to be occupying Antwerp before the New Year."

Schroeder leaned back against the pillows and looked Bormann straight in the face.

"Herr Reichsleiter, you could have me shot for saying this but I feel as many men do – that the war is now lost. The soldiers know it, most of the generals know it; it only remains for the

Fuhrer to know it. When that happens, then the Reich will fall."

Bormann was overwhelmed though it did not show in his expression. This, though he had not admitted it, was precisely the frame of mind he had hoped for. Now, if he could only convince Schroeder that his own plans were far more important than anything that could happen at this eleventh hour.

"I have no intention of ordering a firing squad, Herr Major. I suggest, however, that you keep such opinions to yourself. Tell me though, is there anything you feel might make you change your mind?"

Schroeder shook his head.

"I can think of nothing short of some kind of miracle. Perhaps the Fuhrer will really announce one of these super weapons that everyone whispers about. Perhaps then, we can really win this war."

Both men chuckled; Schroeder, however, sobered first.

"No Sir - the Third Reich is finished. Nothing can change that."

Bormann stroked the bridge of his nose with his forefinger.

"Suppose, Herr Major," he paused to pick a piece of lint off his brown uniform, "suppose that you commanded the mission to lay the foundation of the Fourth Reich?"

Schroeder regarded the Reichsleiter dumbly.

The Fourth Reich! His mind screamed at him. *Had he heard correctly? The Fourth Reich?*

Bormann knew that he had him; he also knew that he must

tread very carefully.

"Yes, Herr Major, you heard me correctly. The Fourth Reich!"

In low tones and rapidly, Bormann told the Major certain of his plans. Not the whole truth yet, the man was not ready for it.

"Paraguay." Repeated Schroeder when Bormann was through.

"Exactly. We have reached this decision after very careful thought, believe me. The country has tremendous potential, their political structure is already National Socialist in principal; it is beyond the grasp of either Roosevelt, Churchill or Stalin, it is of no interest to them. Ninety five per cent of the country is still undeveloped."

"Can you imagine the Fourth Reich being built there?"

"Like the Phoenix." Schroeder murmured, almost reverent at the vision in his mind's eye.

"The Phoenix. Oh yes, of course; I'd forgotten your classical education Herr Major. It's a marvellous analogy – I must mention that to the Fuhrer tonight."

"Tell me, would you be interested in such a project – No. That's the wrong word, it is a cause. *The Phoenix.*"

Schroeder nodded. "Yes, Herr Reichsleiter. I would be interested in such a cause, it would be a cause worth fighting for; a new beginning for me – and for Germany. If this war cannot be won then this must be the next best thing."

Bormann smiled his thin-lipped smile again. Contriving to

look both frank and secretive at the same time, he leaned close, placing his hand on Schroeder's. "I think you are the man I – we – have been searching for, Herr Major. You are one alone though, where shall we find others like you, eh? This war has robbed Germany of too many sons."

Schroeder looked at the other for several seconds. "Der sei ein? Mensch der menschlich Ansehn tragt." He quoted at last: He must be Man who bears a mortal form.

Bormann was silent. It seemed obvious to Schroeder that the Reichsleiter was struggling. Then the heavy brow cleared, he smiled.

"Of course, the classics again, Herr Major. Goethe is it not?"

Schroeder nodded. "Torquato Tasso IV."

"I confess that the implication escapes me."

The Major eased himself back on to one elbow. "A quarter of an hour ago, Herr Reichsleiter, I believed myself incapable of fighting any more. I could think of no reason strong enough to convince me that it would be worthwhile. You have given me that reason." Schroeder fell silent; Bormann could see thoughts moving behind the dark eyes and waited. "A man – every man – needs something to believe in, a cause, an incentive, I believed in the Fuhrer until very recently, the last few weeks killed my belief; I could see no reason for what he was doing."

"And now you can?"

"Of course. You have told me. The Fuhrer is trying to buy time for this glorious..."

"Exceptional, Herr Major. In a few seconds you have seen to the heart of the matter, I congratulate you. Now, your quotation; explain it to me."

"Now that my own cause has been renewed, I could probably pick a hundred soldiers at random, in a hundred days I would give you giants."

Bormann considered the other's words and then questioned Schroeder again.

"You mean that any man could help in this task?"

"Any German."

"You may be correct, Herr Major. Certainly you have an unusually high opinion of your fellow soldier. However, it may be that we shall not have a hundred days; at this point, we do not know. Recruit some men Herr Major, about twenty or so, and make them as near giants as you are able. That way we start nearer to our goal. I may be able to help by suggesting an odd name or two."

Bormann stood to leave.

"This is an order, Herr Reichsleiter?"

"You may consider it an order, Herr Major."

"It will be my pleasure Sir. I shall need some form of authority though; I can hardly relieve men of their present duties without such."

"Consider it arranged. A letter of authority will be delivered by messenger as soon as you leave this hospital."

"Thank you Sir."

52

"Thank you – Kurt.

Bormann flung his coat about his shoulders and strode as far as the end of the bed. "Enjoy your wine." And he was gone.

FIVE

The rain fell without respite for three days and nights. The temporary accommodation on the 'Hill' which had to house a steadily increasing work force, allowed water to leak in with little more than passive resistance. Complaints within the military were met with a gruff 'make a man of ya' for all that mattered to the higher ranks was the project and its progress.

Dry gulleys became turbulent creeks; unmade roadways, rivers of viscous mud.

Paul was one of the happier few. When the Government had decided on the Los Alamos site they had been aware of housing needs -although seriously underestimating the final population at the Hill, they had annexed many of the small ranches and farm houses in the vicinity.

When one of these had been offered to Paul, he seized the opportunity eagerly, his first consideration being his developing relationship with Susan.

In addition to the bedrooms, it boasted a dining room with kitchenette and a larder with a functioning 'fridge. Finally – the absolute last word – a bathroom with a tub and fully functioning faucets. His salary was now over a hundred dollars a week – a vast improvement on his income at the Transformer Works – and he had furnished it with second hand furniture bought in Albuquerque and shipped up in a colleague's truck.

A phone extension had been brought in from the project's installation which was convenient when it worked: about forty per cent of the time. It seemed that the local termites and other wild life were rather partial to the insulation that the phone company favoured.

On the third evening of the rain, Paul's supper was interrupted by the telephone's ringing. At least the rain hadn't gotten in the wires.

"Hello, Webb?"

"Yes." Wondering what was the matter at this time of day.

"Peabody." Paul knew the man by sight, he worked out of Nichols' office, the general administrative organisation, and had only been at the site a couple of months.

"What's the problem Mr. Peabody?"

"Rain of course. It's flooding the lower cable ducts and we're getting blackouts all over the place. The most important thing is the damage we're getting in the feeders to the Cockraft-Walton building.

Paul nodded, then realised that Peabody couldn't see him. "Yeah, I can guess." The ducts carrying power cables to the building were all of seven feet deep and nearly as wide. "A lot of the jointing in there was pretty rough; I can remember mentioning it to someone, always dry up here, they said."

"Well it's not dry now."

"No. I guess not. Have you got pumps on that section?"

"Yes. We're just about holding our own. We've got to have repairs done as fast as possible though."

Paul sighed. "You're asking the wrong man Mr. Peabody. My clearance doesn't include the Tech. Area – up to the fence, yes, but not underneath the walls which is where your main trouble will be. You'd better get hold of Sergeant Dawson."

"I know all about Sergeant Dawson." There was a sound that made Paul think of teeth being ground together: when he spoke again Peabody's voice was restrained, "Well, look, the fact of the matter is that Dawson was the guy that supervised the original installation, Doctor Fermi is a little disillusioned with the great US Army, "…Reckons they shoulda done a better job to start with."

"I just said that."

"Fermi asked specifically for you."

"I see, that puts things in a different light. I'll be right over." As associate Director, Enrico Fermi's word carried a lot of weight.

"Thanks Webb. Thanks a lot."

But Paul wasn't right over. It was about two miles from the main gate to the center of activities; the security guards at the gate had been warned of his arrival and opened up with the most cursory of inspections. Half a mile further on though, the road surface had been washed away by a miniature but nonetheless powerful torrent of rain water. Temporary repairs were already

56

under way but it was nearly forty minutes later that he drove the jeep over the rough boulders that had been tipped into the break.

When he got to the scene of the trouble, Paul counted three mobile pumps at work. Suction hoses, vibrating across the rain soaked ground, discharged streams of murky water into a fast growing lake some hundreds of yards away. Paul recognised Wilson, his deputy, and several of the electricians from the Army Engineering Corps who had been assigned to him.

"Hi John. Looks bad."

"Yeah. They don't get no easier."

"Insulation at the joints?"

"Looks like it." Wilson pointed to a section of the duct where the lowered water level had exposed a cylindrical junction box. Steam or smoke was being ejected in two long plumes. "Don't know where else it's happening but I guess we'll have to take a look at all of them."

Paul nodded. "Why the hell haven't they switched the supply off. I'm not working on hot wires with all this water around."

"We've cut out the main feeders but Doctor Fermi says he can't have a complete blackout, he's got experiments running."

"Shit! All we nee –."

"This is Doctor Fermi, Paul." Wilson interrupted hastily. "Doctor, my boss, Paul Webb."

"Evening Webb. Sorry to seem uncooperative but I've got a series of tests running that I can't close down – it would be disastrous. I asked for you particularly, heard you're a good man. Can't you come up with something?"

Paul peered through the rain at Fermi's face. Worry lines furrowed his forehead; he wore a raincoat but had thrown the hood back and the water ran in steady streams from his receding hairline down across his face. A fierce light gleamed from Fermi's deeply recessed eyes.

"Well Doctor- seeing as how this is our first meeting, I'm pleased to make your acquaintance though I wish to hell it was a bit drier for it." Paul stuck out his hand and carried on in a gloomy tone. "I don't know if you're aware of the gravity of the situation. You see," he pointed to the junction box which was still sizzling loudly, "each one of those things is a potential trouble spot. "The normal daytime heat has melted the pitch inside; probably the shells were never tightened down right or else they've buckled and the stuff's run out. You can see long strips of it on the cable-lays below it. At any moment the cables inside could melt completely. If it shorts while the power's on, well, we'd have problems clear back to the substation and right up to your equipment."

It had been a long speech for Paul, and throughout Fermi's face had seemed to collapse in on itself.

"If I send a man down there, it's a dollar to a dime I'd be signing his death certificate. Anyway, I wouldn't send a man. I'd have to go down myself."

"There's no other way?"

"I'm sorry Doctor. If it had been drier…"

"Do your best then Webb, do your best."

"I will Sir. We'll let you know." Then to Wilson, "Get it switched off John."

The water was still chest deep and bitterly cold when Paul lowered himself into it. He wore an elasticised seal-skin outfit and had two powerful flashlights: one strapped to the hard hat and the other in his right hand. Looking back up at Wilson, he grinned ruefully. "I want two flasks of black coffee waiting, John. I guess I'll be out in an hour. Do the boys know which way the ducts run?"

"Sure, their job's easy enough; we got all the covers off. You just take it easy under the building, you hear me?"

Paul threw a mock salute and turned to where the water ran blackly and broken by raindrops into the square hole beneath the sheet metal wall.

"I'll have the coffee laced with rum, John."

"Do that."

Paul pushed the improvised raft ahead of him. It carried a small selection of tools and a supply of temporary sealant and spare cable.

It was cold and creepy beneath the concrete and steel flooring, he wanted the job over and done with. He could already feel water seeping in at his waistband.

Paul followed the color-coded cables, ignoring junction boxes on the lines which could remain switched out until the emergency was over. He came to the first and examined it carefully. The joint seemed to be waterproof. He unscrewed the clamping bolts and checked inside; it was dry. He spread the sealing compound around the edges and re-clamped the cover. Now that he thought of it, the odds were pretty good that damage beneath the huge project building was minimal or nonexistent; it would remain cool down here even at mid summer. The heat which had affected the boxes in the duct where it had been cut through open ground would not have penetrated here and, therefore, there would not have been as much deterioration.

Half walking, half swimming, Paul proceeded methodically. At one point he dropped a wrench and spent several minutes, fully submerged, groping for it. Finally, he found it in the slimy mud at the bottom of the trench and came up muttering watery curses. He moved on, the beam from his head light picking out the gray concrete walls; the endless lines of cable, looping slightly from one support to the next; empty cigarette packs floating on the scummy water.

How far had he travelled? Paul wondered. Fifty yards, eighty? It was hard to estimate in the hollow, echoing chamber; with luck he might be half way along the subterranean pathway.

There had been no noise other than that of his own making for the twenty five minutes he had been down there. He started with surprise at the unmistakable sound of a generator starting up. Suddenly, the roof above him lit up with thousands of tiny lights. Startled, he looked up at the ceiling – no more than a foot above his head. Each of the lights was a small diamond shape, it was several seconds before he realised that what he was seeing was the criss-cross of a steel lattice which formed a floor to the room above. He switched off both flashlights and, with that, things swam into focus; he could, if he wished, push up one of the gratings, lift the others and explore the length of the duct from above: it would be quicker and more comfortable. Paul was just about to do this, his fingers already in the diamond shaped holes, when he heard the murmur of voices from somewhere nearby.

He strained his ears but was unable to catch more than a word or two. Still, the direction was clear and Paul moved through the water until he passed beneath an overhead partition. At once, the desultory conversation became clearer; the group – for there were evidently several people above – could be discerned through the diamond gratings.

Suddenly conscious of his position, the possibility of listening without being observed struck him. For months, Paul had worked like hell for up to twelve hours a day. Caught up in the enthusiasm which pervaded the 'Hill' despite the inevitable conflicts between military and scientists, Paul had never given more than a passing thought to espionage. Now, in the silent waters below the Tech Area, he realised that it was unlikely that another such opportunity as this would be offered him. He must make the most of it.

Carefully, to keep waves to a minimum, Paul waded through

the water which was now noticeably lower. He pulled his raft along below the center of activity and stood on it. The raft disappeared below the water but gave a solid enough footing when it rested on the bottom.

Now, he could see a little through the lattice, enough to recognise faces. One of those present was Dr. Fermi, two or three other faces were familiar, though he didn't know the names to go with them. Several more were there – one of them with a bad cough – but all were unknown. Fermi was speaking as Paul started to eavesdrop.

"…warm up the accelerator as soon as we get main power on. Guisely and I have several more test runs to do. Harrison, you and Peters get yourselves off to bed; you're going to have to carry on later today because of this delay. We've just got to keep to the schedule."

The terrible cough broke in again and then a second voice – evidently the owner of the cough – complained. "Aw, c'mon Doc. This is a natural hazard, they got to take it into account."

Fermi's feet moved sharply above Paul's nose. He could hear the ice in the older man's voice.

"Perhaps you'd ring Adolf up then – let him know that we're stopping work 'til the rain shower's over, hmm? I'm sure the Krauts'll down tools on their own atom bomb 'til we're clear here."

Paul stiffened but continued listening.

"No, Faber. You get your ass up to that control cabin and

start calibrating. There's no way I'm going to tell Oppenheimer we can't make it for the tests. If every one of us has to work twenty five hours a day, the boys in the Alberta division are going to have that material on time. Okay?"

The Cough grumbled some half hearted reply.

"I dare say that both Clinton and Oak Ridge have had their problems but we got their test samples on time. It's up to us to do our bit. The tests have to be made on time."

Fermi moved off, waving a pair of colleagues to go with him. Others departed for other areas of the lab and, when only two were left – working on some piece of apparatus – Paul stepped off his raft.

"Hope FDH drops the bloody atom bomb bang in the middle of Berlin," rumbled a deep baritone voice.

"There'll be plenty," answered the other. "One on Berlin, another on those shitty little Nips and we can all go home."

Paul moved out as fast as he could. All thoughts of checking any further junction boxes gone.

Atom bombs? An atomic bomb on Berlin, where the Fuhrer was. God in Heaven! Outside the gates, Paul had heard all sorts of speculation about what was going on inside Los Alamos: the rumors ran the gamut from a new sort of submarine to a P.O.W. Camp. Until now, Paul had not had the slightest inkling of what he had been helping to create.

It had to be stopped, he saw that now; Carl was right. Even in his cold wet clothes, Paul was sweating.

Mai answered the telephone on the fourth ring. Paul's mouth twitched at the corners at the sound of his sister's voice; he was pleased to hear her speaking and waited until she'd given the area code before replying.

"Hi, big sister."

"Paul."

"The same. How're things?"

"Oh – fine," the little pause was too obvious and there was a tone underlying the few words she'd said.

"Hey, you sure now? Sure you're okay?"

"Of course. I feel a lot better now I've heard from you. What've you been doing lately?"

"Nothing very special, really. Last night I was bathing in rain water; good for the complexion."

He got the expected laugh and they chatted for a minute or two. Finally, he asked to speak to Carl.

Again there was a pause, some of the life went out of Mai's voice. "I'll get him for you Paul. And – Paul?"

"Mm?"

"I'll see you soon?"

"Sure you will sis. Sure you will."

Moments later, Carl's usual confident voice boomed through the earpiece.

"Guten abend Paul. Vie gehts?" – Good evening and how are you.

Paul thanked his lucky stars that he had waited until he had gone into Albuquerque before ringing from a pay phone.

"Oh, I'm fine Carl, you?" He fed more coins into the slot.

Then, without preamble; "They're making big bombs down here Carl. Special ones, atomic –."

Carl interrupted.

"Come up this weekend Paul; no matter what it takes, come."

He found he was listening to a dead phone. He replaced it on its cradle and went back out to the jeep; he drove north slowly, not seeing the countryside, driving automatically. He thought a great deal about what he'd learned.

SIX

Bormann had not looked forward to the long flight; the later stages were in darkness and the small Storch staff plane rocked steadily with the constant squalls. In addition, the cabin was anything but warm.

Wrapped in his well used leather coat, he concentrated on other things and succeeded in putting the discomforts and potential dangers of the flight from his mind for much of the time.

Now that he had Schroeder: the keystone to his plan; he must concentrate on finding suitable transport. There would be a considerable cargo; not only the Herr Major and the small task force he would assemble, there would also be himself and the Fuhrer together with a significant amount of negotiable wealth.

Bormann's mouth twitched in a half smile as he thought of the wealth. Against the soft glow of instruments outlining the pilot's head and shoulders, he saw the color of gold. Gold coins and plate, the gold for which old masters, sculpture, tapestry could be exchanged.

The source of this wealth was the Linz collection.

Hitler himself had conceived the project. Linz – a nondescript little town in Austria – had always been regarded by the Fuhrer as his home town. He had planned to transform it into the Western World's cultural center by constructing a series of public buildings to house huge collections of artwork ranging from armour to paintings.

The Reichsleiter himself was no lover of art, the intrinsic value of a lovely sculpture had as much effect on Hermann as a magnificent concerto on a tone deaf listener. However, the project had been the Fuhrer's brain child and Bormann had taken over its management as long ago as 1939, seeing this as one more way he could ingratiate himself with Hitler. Sadly, construction was postponed and postponed as manpower and materials were siphoned off for the war effort and the exhibits were stockpiled. Recently, Bormann had performed some siphoning off on his own account. With an eye to Germany's uncertain future, he had arranged for quantities of small high value items to be transferred to Berlin; no more than a fraction of the Linz collection's value of twelve hundred million deutschmarks disappeared but, in the world outside of Germany, the artwork and the gold coins would provide a sound financial base for the Fourth Reich.

A particularly violent squall sent Bormann lurching against the safety straps, shattering his visions.

"Idiot." He shouted. "Can you not pilot this thing steadily?"

"The weather, Reichsleiter."

"Then climb man. Climb above it."

With a barely perceptible shrug, the pilot pulled back on the stick and commenced a slow climb. The weather deteriorated, the rain turned to hail that struck the windshield with a continuous crackling.

A few minutes later the pilot said, "It looks as though it'll be like this all the way up to our ceiling, Sir."

"Then take it down man. Taxi along a roadway if you like, just stop bouncing me around."

It was not the first time that Martin Bormann had searched for a clandestine route out of Germany. Months before, after the too-nearly successful attempt on Hitler's life in July, the Reichsleiter had made discreet enquiries concerning the use of a submarine. Had he been able to take a U-boat commander into his confidence, he was certain that a crew would have been only too willing to transport the Fuhrer. As it was, his vague enquiries were met only with excuses. Bormann would have preferred to take Doenitz into his confidence but the Admiral, he felt certain, would relay any conversation back to Hitler and Hitler would have refused, point blank, to consider deserting Germany. Even when – if, Bormann corrected his thoughts – the Ardennes offensive was to fail; the task of convincing the Fuhrer of the necessity of escaping would be to risk his own fall from favour.

Time went by and his fears for Hitler's safety dwindled. The present offensive had already driven well behind enemy lines and the German forces now occupied a front eight kilometres long and almost half as deep into Allied territory. There were signs enough though, that the German military would be driven

68

back by sheer weight of numbers and although the Fuhrer was optimistic, Bormann wanted his plans for possible flight well in hand by the spring.

"The Fuhrer needs me alive and well – not with my brains battered all over the inside of this infernal plane."

"We're almost there, Reichsleiter I am in communication with ground Control. A few more minutes.

The pilot was as good as his word. Bormann heaved an immense sigh of relief as he felt the bump of solid ground beneath the landing gear. From the airstrip, it was a short ride to 'Eagle's Nest', the Fuhrer's headquarters at Bad Neuheim.

Bormann had left the bunker three days before but it seemed as though weeks had passed since he'd watched the steady glow, listened to the regular thunder of shells falling on both sides of the front. He hastened inside, walking briskly along the sweating concrete corridors to the operations room where Hitler was talking animatedly to several staff officers. He paused as he caught sight of Bormann.

"Martin! How good to see you again. You have heard of our success? Young Peiper is carrying out the offensive exactly as I planned it. It is full speed to Bastogne now."

Bormann smiled, embraced his leader.

"How could it be otherwise my Fuhrer? You imbue our army with the determination it needs. To think that you must come here in person to stiffen our weak-kneed officers: it exposes you to terrible dangers my Fuhrer…"

"Ach! Martin, You are always so concerned about me. Look, I enjoy the best of health. Right here is the turning point of the war. Today we advance; tomorrow nothing will hold us back."

Bormann took a step back and looked at Hitler. He did look better. His leg still dragged but the trembling which had so afflicted his left arm seemed to have gone. His face, pale and puffy a few days ago had undergone a change for the better, his eyes were bright and shining with barely suppressed enthusiasm.

"Tell me, how is Heinrich coping?"

A flicker of annoyance crossed Bormann's face which he did well to cover before he replied. Heinrich Himmler had been made Commander in Chief of Army Group Rhine on the tenth, on the Reichsleiter's recommendation. "Not well, Sir, at the moment. However, he expects the situation to improve shortly, I have certain changes in mind which should aid the Reichsfuhrer Sir, perhaps we can speak later."

"Of course."

Jochen Peiper's advance ran into difficulty. Severe fighting checked the offensive at both Bastogne and Laroche and Hitler and his entourage returned to Berlin to find the Reich Chancellery uninhabitable. They moved into a series of bunkers beneath the Chancellery which was now open to the winter elements. Bomb blasts had stripped the roof of tiles and smashed windows, left doors hanging at crazy angles-

In the face of imminent disaster, Bormann clung to

optimism. It was only a matter of time, he felt, before Hitler became so disgusted with the disheartening efforts of his armies that he would agree readily to a new beginning in South America.

... Our unshakable faith in ultimate victory is founded in a very large measure on the fact that he exists – Bormann wrote to his wife. He intended to make as certain as possible that Hitler would continue to exist even though Germany certainly would not.

Soon after the failure of the Ardennes offensive, Hitler received bad news from Poland. One hundred and eighty divisions of the Red Army bad broken through the dangerously exposed eastern front and some means of hastily blocking their advance had to be found.

Bormann had already engineered Himmler's appointment to command the Army Group Rhine. This had two effects: one, it exposed his incompetence in the field and, two, it kept 'Uncle Heinrich' well out of the day to day affairs. Himmler, of course, botched his assignment and Bormann again used his influence with the Fuhrer to get him assigned to Army Group Fistula to be responsible for checking the Red Army's advance to the east of Berlin.

So – Uncle Heinrich was disposed of, at least, for the foreseeable future. The Reichsleiter felt free to once again turn his mind to the business of Schroeder and the eventual removal of the Fuhrer to the safety of South America. Since rejoining Hitler at Bad Neuheim at the time of the ill fated advance through the Ardennes, Bormann had had no time to pursue the matter with his superior. Hitler's mood of the moment was, understandably, a dark one. His trembling had returned; his tempers were frequent and prolonged and accompanied by vitriolic outbursts directed at those who surrounded him.

Bormann was virtually the only confidante in whom Hitler would trust. Carefully, he fanned the flames: fostered the Fuhrer's dependence upon himself. He waited patiently for the right opportunity to broach the matter with his leader.

SEVEN

Carl replaced the telephone receiver, studiously examined the wallpaper pattern for a few seconds and picked up the instrument again. He called a New York number, waiting while it rang six times and rang off. He watched the second hand on his watch turn through three hundred and sixty degrees and dialled again. The man at the other end picked his phone up before the first ring had finished.

"Yeah?" The voice was pitched low, quiet.

"Charles?" Carl used the code name,

"Yeah."

"Richard." It was Carl's own code.

"Well?" Charles- Herr Pieckenbroch – spoke economically on the telephone.

"It's important that I see you."

"I know of nothing that important. Wait 'till the next meeting up here."

"It can't wait. It concerns the eggs you enquired about. Remember? The large ones?" Carl heard the intake of breath and continued. "The salesman will be through here Saturday."

"You are absolutely certain? – I mean, he is reliable?"

"Naturally, the man is related to me."

"Very well. If I cannot make it, I'll call."

"Very good Charles. See you Saturday and – Goodbye." But Pieckenbroch had already gone.

In the kitchen, Mai was washing linen in a tub. Carl came in, glanced distastefully at the dirty clothing piled on the table. "Can you not wait until I'm out before you do this?" He kicked a grimy sweat shirt out of his way. "Paul will be here at the weekend."

As he expected, Mai's face lit up with pleasure.

"Another gentleman will also be coming from New York but I don't know whether he'll be staying overnight."

This time, Mai's smile was fleeting. She dropped the garments she was working on and straightened up.

"For God's sake Carl, do not involve Paul with your friends, please – I did say please, Carl." There was a new note of hysteria in her voice though, if he noticed, her husband ignored it.

"We have already had this conversation woman. Now get me some food and stay out of the affairs of men." Carl sat at the table and swept the washing on to the floor. "Paul is a good German. Unlike that snivelling Father of yours, he takes pride in serving the Fatherland."

"Carl..."

"Enough." Changing- his mind, he stood up. "I'm going to change. I shall go to see Franz, he's maybe too old to do anything, but at least, he remembers Germany with love. I'll eat when I return."

Carl left the kitchen and was part way up the stairs before he realised that Mai was only a few steps behind him.

At the landing, she began again. "No Carl. Not my Paul. If anything were to happen to him it would break Mama's heart – and Papa's." First entreating, then threatening to go to the Police, Mai failed to notice how rigidly Carl was standing.

Suddenly, he whirled. His eyes were blazing, his cheeks tight over bunched jaw muscles. Reaching out, he took hold of Mai's shoulders, his thumbs digging painfully into the flesh beneath her collar bones.

Slowly at first, punctuating his words, Carl shook her.

"I warned you Mai. Do not threaten me. A wife should be seen, not heard." His voice rose to a scream. "I tell you to stay out of my business, I serve the Fuhrer. Your only purpose is to provide for me and to share my bed. You understand?"

He released her, suddenly seeing how grey with pain her face had become. Mai swayed, her face the color of paper ash, her eyes blank empty pockets. She lost her balance and took a step backward, involuntarily trying to stay upright.

For what seemed like long seconds, her right foot searched for a nonexistent floor before she fell to one side and her head cracked solidly against the half newel post. Like a poorly stuffed rag doll, Mai plummeted down the stairs until she lay in an untidy heap in the hall. A trickle of blood stained the brown and black terra cotta tiles.

Carl had not moved. His face was still twisted with anger as he walked slowly down the steps; the expression never altered even as he bent to look at his wife's broken body. He turned her over with a foot then stooped to pull her arm from under her.

He held the wrist, feeling for a pulse. There was none; his expression became a frown at this awkward development then, standing, Carl rubbed his chin, contemplating the still warm corpse like a workman considering an unpleasant but necessary task. With a distasteful expression on his face, Carl opened the door to the cellar steps and tugged Mai's body to the top. A casual push with his foot sent the corpse rolling down into the root cellar. Closing the door, Carl returned to the kitchen to get a bottle of bourbon which he took into the lounge.

The bottle was a new one; he broke the seal and methodically consumed all the liquor. It had little, if any, effect on his empty stomach; he considered going to fetch a second bottle but finally decided against it. Eventually, he went out the back and returned with a sharp bladed spade which he took down to the cellar.

The floor was no more than packed dirt but the surface was as hard as concrete. Carl was soon sweating and discarded his shirt; beneath the hard surface, however, the earth was softer and soon the trench was long enough and broad enough for a grave. He swore softly.

In his native tongue; barely eighteen inches below the surface – less in places – he hit bedrock. Throwing the spade to one side, he scooped out as much dirt as possible and laid the

76

body in the shallow grave. It fit, barely, a sparse covering of soil concealed Mai's remains.

This task completed, Carl wondered what to do with the earth still heaped around the edges. If he bagged it and carried it outside, inquisitive neighbours would be watching, agog with curiosity. A moment passed before he shovelled it beneath a long workbench, deciding to dispose of it later – after dark. Tired, aching from the unaccustomed labor, he sat down at his desk, rolling back the top and reaching for a box of biscuits.

"Ach!" He looked in disbelief at the drop of red blood welling from the end of his middle finger. There was a brief rustle of paper and a grey shape darted away; the rat landed on the floor with a small thud and was off into the shadows at the far end of the cellar.

Cursing again, Carl extinguished the naked light bulb and headed for the medicine cabinet in the kitchen.

Deprived of its quiet meal, the rat watched Carl's hurried departure; its bright eyes glowing redly in the dim illumination from the stairs. A tiny pink tongue darted out, licked at the salty taste of human blood on its whiskers. Sitting on its haunches, the rodent washed its fur, savoring the new taste of blood.

Suddenly, it stopped, sat up rigidly and sniffed the air. The scent was there again, quite strong. With several small darts in apparently random directions, the rat discovered the source of the odor; it was almost overpowering now.

Tentatively, it scratched at the loose soil.

EIGHT

Kurt Schroeder was more than happy with his quarters. The front window had a view that was truly magnificent; to the right and above him towered the mountains and the Berghof – the Fuhrer's retreat on the Obersaltzburg; to the left, a long valley swooped down to the picturesque village of Berchtesgaden.

He sighed. It was wonderful, no doubt of it, but he could not help remembering what Bormann had told him: that the Reichsleiter himself owned the whole Obersaltzburg complex, all eighty seven buildings worth over a million and half marks. As such, it was merely an extension of the Government, a place where the Fuhrer formulated new strategy and Bormann hatched still more Machiavellian schemes. Schroeder was worried about Bormann who, since his visit to the hospital had communicated with him only in brief notes.

At first, with all doors opened for him by Martin Bormann's authority, he had enthused over this eleventh hour bid to resuscitate the ailing Reich. Now, after a mere two weeks into the preparation stages, the calm and analytical Schroeder was entertaining doubts. Despite the deference with which he had been treated by all who came in contact with him, despite the

78

fact that Gerda Bormann and the children vacated two rooms in Haus Goll to give him temporary office space, he wondered if he was as important as he appeared to be. Schroeder felt, somehow, inadequate to the task; how, he wondered, could a stolid career soldier believe himself to be the saviour of the Reich?

A knock at the door interrupted his reverie, snapping his attention back to the present. "Come."

The SS Scharfuhrer who responded was immaculate; the early spring sunshine sprang from the silver runic flash on its background of black cloth. Boots gleamed with the dull sheen of constant attention.

"Excuse me Sir," he began, "the first group of interviewees are here." His voice was even, respectfully correct, yet Schroeder felt that scorn lurked in the dark eyes – a hint of the contempt the SS held for every other member of the armed forces.

"Very good Scharfuhrer. One moment..." Kurt strode to the desk, heels clicking on the hardwood floor. He took a list of names from the desk and glanced down at it. "If there are officers amongst them, I shall see them first. Otherwise, you may send them in, in descending order of rank. Understood?"

"Sir." The officer turned with a click of perfectly polished heels and left.

That was another thing, thought Kurt, frowning then smiling at the dried mud on his own boots. His past dealings with the SS had convinced him that they, at least, considered themselves a race apart. These men here, merely guarding the property of

Reichsleiter Bormann, had obviously received very strict instructions. More surprising still was the fact that they were members of the Leibstandarte – the elite division of the SS and normally answerable only to the Reichsfuhrer SS Heinrich Himmler,or to the Fuhrer. Unaware of Uncle Heinie's present fall from grace – thanks to Martin Bormann -Schroeder chased away his misgivings with the thought that either the Reichsfuhrer or the Fuhrer himself must know of his activities; only Hitler could have coined the phrase Bormann had used, what was it? 'The Fourth Reich'."

Again a discreet tap on the door broke in on his thoughts. Schroeder sat down behind the desk, composed himself. "Enter."

It took three days to complete the interviews. The task of winnowing the wheat from the chaff was a wearying one for, in fact, the twenty six men discarded from the original fifty six were all of them, good soldiers. In addition to the nucleus that he, Kurt, had suggested, the Reichsleiter had picked a further forty two; all exceptionally fit and in most cases, battle hardened.

Kurt's intent was to select a final twenty. He reasoned that this would not be too difficult; he planned an intensive training program which would tax those chosen to the utmost. There were two for whom he felt reservations: the SS officer, Dietrich, who had, like himself, been discharged from hospital shortly before, also a Panzer Grenadier named Hoeckle who must have been fifty if he was a day though the man would not admit to it. Hoeckle was a giant of a man and loyal to Germany; Dietrich,

80

Schroeder decided, had suffered wounds more mental than physical: of the two, the SS man would bear the closer watch.

"Ah well." Kurt sighed tremendously and leaned back. "The next few weeks would tell."

Four weeks passed, of the thirty chosen, four had fallen by the wayside. Neither Dietrich nor Hoeckle were among them. Three of the four had been injured though not seriously; the fourth man had thought that his skiing ability was better than it was; he was now in hospital with a ruptured spleen.

That ski exercise had caught them all by surprise. Kurt had warned them that they would next see action in an arid country – Africa was the logical conclusion, even though the Allies had overrun that continent. All the men had had previous experience with skis and Kurt, wishing to evaluate their judgment rather than skill, had set a dangerous assignment. Only the one man had failed to assess the situation and use due caution.

Six weeks of intensive training lay behind the group. It was now formed into three sub-groups so that the final selection of a single unit would not disrupt the esprit-de-corps Kurt had labored to bring into being.

At six that morning, Schroeder had supervised the departure of his men. The final exercise lay before them. Until now, he had been with them every step of the way; he had bunked with them, messed with them and labored alongside each one. Today was to be different; today he had a bird's eye view.

After watching the start of their ascent along the steep and tree-studied valley, Kurt had taken a half track to the elevator which had lifted him in minutes to the summit. At Kehlsteinhaus – the mountain top eyrie, he had donned skis and made a fast survey of the snow and ice fields at this height. Conditions were perfect.

Back again at Kehlsteinhaus, a servant brought him a hot drink.

"The Reichsleiter – he is coming."

Kurt nodded and the servant left. He expelled a great sigh of relief that plumed into the cold mountain air. At last – Bormann was coming, the first time they had seen one another since the Charité. He took the hot drink out to the balcony, looking down on the pass below; now the Reichsleiter would tell him of the progress that he had made as well as assessing the mettle of the men now climbing the ice-filled pass.

Before leaving, the men had been warned to take nothing at face value, to take whatever action they deemed necessary.

It was cool and still at the moment, the light wind occasionally ruffled his camouflaged jacket which he wore in preference to the white parkas worn by his group. His hands, ungloved, clasped the mug – drawing warmth from the drink while he continued to scan the panoramic landscape below. The dots that he had first observed at the foot of the pass had now taken on the proportions of ants and were rapidly increasing in size; it was nine fifteen and Kurt unzipped his jacket to take out the high powered field glasses. Checking their position once more, he put the glasses to his eyes and adjusted the focus.

The men leaped into view and he began to examine each one, recognising them easily despite the hoods and tinted snow goggles. In his absence, Kurt had placed Dietrich in charge in deference to his more senior rank. He watched the latter's gestures, guessing, for the most part, what the orders were. Each carried a small pack of provisions to which was strapped a short handled trenching spade and an ice axe.

Something had obviously caught the men's attention below, their progress slowed, stopped, they all looked down and to one side; there was something there as yet outside Kurt's field of view. He knew, however, what was coming, the little drama had been carefully worked out a week before.

"Good morning to you, Herr Major."

Schroeder concentrating on the ice field below, looked round. "Good morning Herr Reichsleiter." He made to stand up.

Bormann signalled otherwise. "Please don't. I will watch with you."

Kurt nodded his acceptance.

*

"Panzerwagons." Shouted Dietrich, training a small pair of glasses down the pass. "Come on, dig in."

Metz guffawed at the suggestion. "For what? You think that the Herr Major is going to have them run us down after all the work he has put in to this unit."

83

"Dig in, I said." Replied Dietrich grimly. "That bastard is capable of anything. Those panzers will be here in fifteen minutes; now dig in, that's an order."

Hoeckle set an example, dumping his pack, the huge man took the ice pick and set to, breaking the ice beneath its thin covering of snow into glittering fragments. Others – including Dietrich, joined in, one man wielding his axe, a second using the spade to clear the debris. There were several who, like Metz, seemed to think the whole thing an elaborate joke; they struck a few blows then leaned on their implements. Metz even went so far as to light a cigarette while the grumble of diesel engines grew louder by the minute.

At nine thirty-one, six minutes later than the time agreed with Schroeder, an explosion shattered the still Obersaltzburg air. A cloud of smoke hung in front of the lead vehicle's gun muzzle, there was a brief whistle overhead and a cloud of ice and snow leaped into the air fifty metres ahead of the men.

This convinced the laggards that Dietrich had been right. Two more shells bracketed the group and it became obvious that those who had dismissed the exercise as a hoax were going to be left exposed.

Hoeckle turned from the panzers and, as if some sixth sense had warned him, looked up to the just visible parapet above. Kurt saw him quite plainly, his hood had fallen away and his hair – only two shades darker than the surroundings – made recognition sure, the grin which split the man's features was quite plain too.
84

Schroeder nodded to himself.

Whining now, on the steeper grade, the six tigers advanced. Another salvo of shells shrieked upward, one burst perilously close to the men still desperately digging into the ice.

"Tell them to use the shell craters." Shouted Hoeckle to Dietrich but Dietrich was rigid with fear, safe in his own trench, hands gripping the edge, he watched the approaching panzers through wide eyes.

Hoeckle cupped his hands into a megaphone. "Get in the shell holes." He shouted. "Spread out and use the craters."

It was too late for one man. Six more shells exploded, the lead tank was at almost point blank range. The figure was tossed boneless into the air as his fellows dashed for the holes already excavated by the shells.

A second man was hit by a tiger on the outside of the phalanx. His screams, as his legs were crushed beneath the tracks, were drowned by the howling Diesels.

A burst of gunfire rattled from several fox holes. Mausers were worse than useless against panzer armour, as a vehicle rolled over Dietrich's refuge, the small calibre shells ricocheted and whined off in all directions.

Dietrich had retreated into his own personal hell. Before the first shot was fired up the pass he had been more than half way out of touch with reality. At first, the SS officer had refused to believe his eyes and ears. Only when Hoeckle had muttered 'Tigers' did he really comprehend what was happening.

Mouthing obscenities, Dietrich dropped into the trench reliving memories be thought had been buried beneath weeks of careful therapy at the hospital.

As the six fifty-five tonne monsters – Tiger I Panzerkampf wagons with their F.62 millimetre armament and 110 millimetre armour plating – lumbered towards him, Dietrich could only crouch and peer over the lip of his fox hole. He strained to scream the orders that Hoeckle was shouting, to tell his men what to do but his lips froze, his blood ran thin and icy: rather than consciously willing himself to seek safety, he felt his body collapse into the hole and scrabble mindlessly in the bottom.

"The bastard." He whispered. "The bastard forgets I am SS"

"A very interesting and rewarding experience Herr Major," began Bormann looking sideways to where Schroeder stood, still examining the slopes below. "And this, I take it, is all part of your toughening up process."

"It was to be the final one Reichsleiter but I think there is still some work to be done." He turned away from the blood stained snows. "However, I could pick twenty men now; it all depends on your own plans."

Evading the question, Bormann said, "Shall we go inside? I am not dressed for these heights."

Bormann preceded Kurt in through the French window and took a glass of schnapps from the tray he had ordered.

"Help yourself Major then we will sit for a while and talk."

For the next half hour or so Schroeder listened to the news,

86

as Bormann saw it, from Berlin. Schroeder was pleased to hear these things having felt a little cut off in Austria but secretly he was more pleased that the Reichsleiter had at last come. And, had passed no comments about the unorthodoxy of his training methods.

"I had a dual reason for coming here," put in Bormann, as though reading Schroeder's thoughts, "I wished to see you, of course, "but I also wish to visit my family, this will be the last opportunity I shall have for some time."

Schroeder nodded having exchanged pleasantries with the lady once or twice in passing. He smiled politely.

"About my plans. There are problems as yet unresolved but," he emphasised, "as soon as these matters are clarified you will be the first to know."

Realising that he was to learn nothing more at that time Schroeder consulted his watch. He stood up. "With respect Herr Reichsleiter I must be getting back to my men. I have enjoyed the discussion. I hope to see you later." He brought his heels together firmly and executed a perfect salute.

Bormann nodded. "Yes. I shall be staying a little while longer. See to your men, that gives me the opportunity to convince my wife that she is safer here than in Berlin. It will probably be the morning but we will talk again."

*

When the group of men finally straggled back to their quarters, Kurt was waiting for them. He noted their obvious

87

weariness, the slovenly way they came to attention. Though understanding the Cause of their fatigue, the attitude, Kurt could not let it pass.

"Call yourselves men?" He snapped. He looked at his watch, "Three hours, what are you going to do when you have to put in a full days work?" His voice, initially rough, became smooth. "Perhaps you think of your comrades? Eh? Is that why your shoulders droop, why your bellies stick out like old men?" Schroeder's eyes raked each man from head: to foot; as he spoke, he watched backs straighten, heads come erect. He regretted the death, the other one who would never walk again, but they had treated the exercise as a game; it served as an object lesson to those who would be left in the group, none of them would be tempted to play games again. He looked at the two other injured men; one had suffered severe chest lacerations from shrapnel while the second had fallen into a shell crater and broken his arm.

He nodded to these two. "Fall out. There is an ambulance outside to take you to hospital." If the men wondered how he knew of the debacle on the Obersaltzburg, he decided to let them wonder. "Moel and Geblen, Metz, pack your kit, you have fresh orders. The rest of you may go back to your quarters."

The men relaxed again and began to drift away.

"Oh. Obersturmfuhrer Dietrich.

"Sir?"

"I wish to see you in my office in one hour." Dietrich

nodded, replied quietly. "Very good Sir." Kurt turned away, went back to the room in Haus Goll. Here, he sat down and went over the training program of the past few weeks. All had performed well in the mock combat situations; in hand-to-hand they were good – very good, utilising all manner of weapons from knives to rolled newspapers. On the final test though, some had failed: another might have expected and accepted the fact but not Major Schroeder, in Kurt's view there was only one person responsible Kurt Schroeder. He determined to be yet more merciless on himself; the failure had to be rectified.

NINE

Wolfgang Dietrich wondered about Schroeder's obvious knowledge. He did not believe in extra sensory perception and assumed correctly that his superior had spied upon their activities. How much of his, Dietrich's, actions had he seen? No matter, Dietrich shrugged his shoulders and adjusted the collar on his uniform; there was a guardian angel who would take care of everything, his mentor had been instrumental in his recruitment to the SS three years earlier; since then, obstacles to his career had vanished with remarkable smoothness.

But for Sepp Dietrich, the younger Wolfgang would not now still be in the SS ranks, Wolfgang had been an Untersturmfuhrer commanding a Tiger of the 1st. SS Panzer Division at the time. The previous day, British and Canadian troops had taken the town of Tilly-la-Campagne; Dietrich and his comrades had the job of regaining the French township. Completing encirclement, the panzer group had moved in, utilising every piece of natural cover available.

Dietrich loved the feeling of power this gave him, the throbbing Diesel motors, the effortless ease with which the machine could brush aside a wall, demolish a house. At Dietrich's orders the driver had come in behind a church and then chosen the shortest route to their objective; at the last possible moment, the driver had spotted an Allied tank through the observation slits. Too late, far too late; Dietrich was not to forget that fateful whisper.

"Sherman." Breathed the driver.

The world had seemed to end as the shell made a direct hit on the tiger's turret, the most vulnerable part of the armour.

Again, Dietrich broke into a cold sweat – it happened every time the incident came to mind. Metal slivers caromed from side to side inside the panzer, cutting and slicing their way through his colleagues leaving him wounded but still alive, buried in a charnel house.

Somehow, someone had dragged him out and seen that he was ferried to a field hospital where his wounds had been dressed. Dietrich had been catatonic for nearly three weeks and only technically conscious for as many months. Skilful therapy had restored him to a semblance of normalcy; Sepp's intervention assured him that a suitable position would be found for him.

A suitable position had been found. Wolfgang would carry the SS banner onward.

"Close the door Obersturmfuhrer," asked Kurt quietly. "I thought it better that we should speak together."

Dietrich closed the door and waited for Schroeder to go on, expecting the Major to offer him a seat. The offer was not forthcoming; Kurt waded straight into the matter."

"I have to inform you that you will be returned to your regiment." He began, choosing words with care. "This decision may appear harsh to you, Obersturmfuhrer, however..." Kurt gestured aimlessly, "my methods and those of the SS are different. I feel that..." He shook his head, not knowing what to say yet knowing that he had to finish his sentence with something.

In the event, Dietrich saved him the trouble.

"Herr Major, you know my name, perhaps you do not know that my Uncle is Obergruppenfuhrer..."

"Sepp Dietrich. Yes Herr Obersturmfuhrer, I'm perfectly aware of the relationship." In an odd way, Kurt was grateful for Dietrich's transparent attempt at name dropping. It made things so much simpler. "Nevertheless. The order stands." Kurt placed his hands on the desk, preparatory to standing up.

Dietrich on the other hand, was confused. Schroeder – a mere Major dismissing an SS Officer like a naughty school boy. Something snapped then, it was doubtful that Dietrich knew just what he intended to do but his hand slid the Luger from the gleaming dress holster.

Kurt watched in disbelief as the muzzle rose, as Dietrich looked down at the weapon; it wavered a little, rose a little higher. He watched no longer but moved like a cat; he covered the three metres from his half sitting position in a single leap. His right hand struck Dietrich's wrist a stunning blow and as the sidearm clattered to the floor his left hand was raised for a

92

second blow.

It was not needed. The other's eyes were focussed far beyond Schroeder's face; the Major had seen the expression before, in victims of shell shock.

"Come now Dietrich. Germany still has need of you, perhaps not here but there are many other tasks." Kurt spoke sternly but quietly. When he had finished, those far away eyes were coming back.

"Scharfuhrer." Shouted Kurt. "Come in here quickly."

The door opened and the soldier on guard stepped smartly into the room to falter as he saw the frozen tableau.

"Take him to his quarters, Scharfuhrer. Inform the estate doctor."

Schroeder sat down again as the two men left. He spun the gun on the desk. Committing suicide? He asked himself, or homicide?

Had Schroeder seen the hate in Dietrich's eyes as he went outside; he would have known.

Bormann sat behind the desk in his study at Haus Goll – the same room that Schroeder had used as his office over the past month and a half. He perused Schroeder's list, clicking his teeth with a pen. At length, he looked up at his protégé, sitting on an overstuffed leather couch across the room.

"Excellent, Herr Major, excellent work. You have forged a fine battle group here and I congratulate you."

"I thank you, Herr Reichsleiter. May I ask if any progress

has been made on transport yet?"

Bormann shook his head slowly, smiled. "You must learn to contain your impatience, my friend, I told you but yesterday that that is not yet settled nor, indeed, is the date set for the Fuhrer's departure, The Fuhrer will certainly wish to stay until the last possible moment. It is even possible that you will have to leave Germany first and leave the Fuhrer to follow. I do not know."

"However," Bormann looked up suddenly, "I foresee trouble ahead."

"Sir?"

"One of the men you deleted from your original list Herr Major. SS Obersturmfuhrer Dietrich," Again, the Reichsleiter shook his head. "We shall see Kurt, we shall see, but his Uncle…"

TEN

Paul's present earning capacity had allowed him to open a savings account from which he intended to pay back his brother-in-law the money he had provided for college; in addition to this, there were times when he mailed a check to his parents. Mama usually wrote him back within a few days to scold him and thank him at the same time,

The work was hard – as often as not, Paul would put in twelve hours a day with little more than a snatched lunch and yet his life was strangely satisfying. Far from his parents for the first time, a steady girl for the first time and real responsibility: it had quickly forged a man from the boy. Sun and weather had deepened the lines written into his face by the new life- Paul had gained two years maturity in the few months.

To a point, the fact that he was now running to Carl with a few shreds of information made him ashamed of himself? Twice in as many days Paul had almost called the man and cancelled the meeting only to find that his loyalties were too divided to allow a decision to be made.

As he treated himself to a cab from Des Moines bus station out to the old brownstone, Paul resolutely thrust the troublesome thoughts from his mind, concentrated upon enjoying himself. It was only now, on this final leg of his journey that he realised that he was quite looking forward to the weekend away from work. Apart from those weekends with Susan, he had taken no time off since joining the Los Alamos staff. The prospect of forty eight hours away from the organised chaos was invigorating.

He tipped the driver a quarter, the extravagance made him feel good, warmed him against the unremembered chill after the accustomed New Mexican weather. Paul had stopped the cab at the corner, two blocks away; he could just imagine Mai lecturing him on the sins of squandering money on luxuries.

The few minutes walk left him, not exactly shivering but, hoping that Carl had a heavy sweater that he could borrow. On the steps, he stopped and sniffed the air: pity, Mai didn't seem to have any baking on the go.

Inside, Carl heard the front door open. He left the pan of schnitzel simmering and glanced through into the hallway.

"Aha, come on in little brother." He returned to the stove, testing the veal before turning to face Paul. "A seat, Paul." He pointed with the fork. "Dinner is nearly ready; you must have smelled it all the way from the station. Butter some rolls, will you?"

"Sure Carl. Is this your new hobby?" He split some of the hard crusted Vienna rolls and spread butter.

Carl flashed a dazzling grin. "Hobby? No. Your sister, she is on an errand of mercy. My cousin Freda – you remember her? Milwaukee? That big oaf of a husband has finally made her

96

pregnant but she is not so well." Carl shrugged and tipped the veal on to two hot plates. "There was no one else to turn to and I asked Mai to help."

"Oh, I see." Paul was disappointed; he had wanted to tell Mai about Susan. "She been gone long? I see you haven't suffered from your cooking yet."

The other laughed as though the joke had been tremendous. "I used to cook for my comrades in the trenches. None died from my food – only English bullets."

Paul pulled his plate closer. "Mm, this smells pretty good anyway. What about Mai?"

"She went yesterday. Perhaps she comes back by next weekend, who knows? In any case, it is best she is out of the way for our meeting."

They chatted between mouthfuls.

"So what happens at this meeting? Who's the man you want me to meet?"

"Ch – Joseph. Ja, a fine friend – you will like him, I know. He is very clever, works hard for our Cause." Carl sliced his schnitzel and piled sauerkraut on to his fork. "You know of the Abwher?"

Paul nodded. "A little."

"That is the best way. Joseph is Abwher. He will ask you many questions, he will miss nothing. I think… that we may both be heroes if what you told me is correct."

"Great! I just hope I am right."

"Oh, I am certain of this. Still, Joseph will know: he hears a word here, a word there and puts them together – suddenly," Carl waved his knife, "Joseph knows. Ah yes, a clever man."

"When the simple meal was over, Carl put the dishes to soak and they went through to the living room – dusty and strewn with newspapers and used ash trays. If Mai had only left yesterday, Paul thought. Carl must have had a bit of a stag night last night. The older brother handed Paul the, by now, traditional cigar, and poured schnapps for them both; the liquor relaxed Paul and Carl lost some of the forced cheerfulness he'd been exhibiting. They talked about inconsequential things, neither mentioning the main purpose of the visit.

Outside the brightness had faded from the sky and big oily drops of rain began to fall. A flash of lightning dimmed the room lights and heralded the start of a downpour. Carl got up to draw the curtains and throw another pine log on the fire. Pine logs would not have been used before Mai left; she would not have tolerated the mess and the stink from the pitch.

"Good thing I brought those in this morning, getting quite chilly."

"Sure is, must be twenty degrees below what I'm used to. Is this Joseph from down South?"

Carl didn't reply for a moment, a frown creased his forehead. For a second, Paul thought he was going to ignore the question, he shook his head eventually. "No. From the East, he'll be used to this," he nodded towards the window where the

98

rattling told of hail amongst the rain. "Mind you, he may be held up, taxis will be scarce in this weather."

He quickly changed the subject, telling a lewd joke about Roosevelt having to satisfy his wife with his crutch. Paul didn't like sick jokes like that but laughed for appearance's sake. Conversation lapsed and Carl descended into a brown study, he seemed nervous for some reason; Paul guessed that he might be uneasy about the coming meeting – to some extent, he was correct.

The storm had drained the afternoon light away and it was quite dark before the knock on the front door made Carl start nervously. Almost bounding from his cracked leather chair, he disappeared into the hallway. Moments later, he was back, ushering in a figure swathed in a heavy woollen coat; a hand knitted scarf and a pull-down flap hat completed the visitor's armour against the weather.

Paul watched with interest as the man shed his outdoor clothes, allowing Carl to take them into the kitchen to hang in front of the stove. He saw a man in his early fifties, gaunt of frame, of average height, sparse light brown hair and a face no more than ordinary. Someone who would go unnoticed in a crowded room, a person one passed on the street every day. Yet, to Paul's thinking, there was something about him that marked him out as uncommon, something that eluded him for the moment.

As soon as Carl had taken his clothes, Joseph crossed to the

99

blazing fire and spread his hands to warm; this done, he turned and stood with his back to the fire, looking at Carl with an amused expression.

Paul stood up, advanced. "Hi." He opened. "I'm Paul Webb."

He offered his hand. The man turned his head, peered from beneath beetling brows; a corner of his mouth lifted in the beginnings of a smile.

"Well," he said taking Paul's hand in a cold, hard grip and glancing at Carl, "and what name am I today?"

Carl smiled his familiar disarming flash of white teeth.

"Told him "Joseph." That and no more."

"Very well then. Joseph it will be." He turned back to Paul, withdrawing his hand and clasping it behind him. "I believe you have a lot to tell me, young man."

Paul nodded, watching the watery blue eyes with fascination; now he knew what it was that made Joseph different, the smile never reached his eyes, they were expressionless – untouched by emotion. He shuddered and looked away.

When they were sitting down round the table, Joseph looked expectantly at Carl, obviously waiting for him to start the ball rolling. Carl took the cue, started to speak; the words came out as a whisper. He cleared his throat and started again.

"You recall my report about Paul getting- work at this Los Alamos place?" Joseph nodded, a single inclination of the head. "Well, our watch has finally been rewarded, he has – perhaps
100

LAST MISSION

you should carry on from here Paul."

"Sure." Paul took a deep breath and started to relate the events he had overheard from the cable duct beneath the Tech. Area building. He related the official line given him by Captain Bankhurst and, lastly, what Dr. Millar – Susan – had said about the world never being the same and about her reference to the bomb being tested.

Joseph Piekenbrock remained silent when Paul finished. He stayed this way for so long that he wondered if his information was, in fact, worthless. Carl was fidgeting restlessly by the time Piekenbrock spoke again; he looked at Carl first who stopped shuffling immediately, then he began to fire short staccato questions at Paul. Paul did his best but was sadly conscious of how little he knew..

"How large are the bombs?"

"I don't know."

"What do they look like?"

"I've never seen them. They must be stored in another section."

" The Security?"

Paul admitted that, aside from the internal security guards at the gate, he had never paid it much mind.

"Are the guards from G.2 Section?"

Paul shook his head, "Used to be. They have their own organisation now."

" – How many scientists are employed, what are they?"

He didn't know how many, so he said, "certainly over a hundred, physicists, chemists, metallurgists."

"Nuclear physicists?"

He nodded.

At each point, Joseph either nodded or remained impassive according to the answer. Paul was surprised by the man's lack of impatience with him for each question only served to enlarge the area of Paul's ignorance about the 'Hill'.

The session lasted nearly four hours, ranging from highly pertinent matters such as military numbers to items like marital relations which Paul could see no reason for. When Piekenbrock finally sat back and stretched, Pail felt drained and terribly aware of his inadequacy. He started to apologise but the senior agent cut him short.

"Don't apologise," he said, shortly. "For someone who has not been trained, you have done surprisingly well. However, there is some information which I must have. I would like to know much more but the matters I shall mention are most important – would you get a glass of water, Carl?"

Carl went into the kitchen: "And bring my coat." He brought back the water and the coat. Piekenbrock took a huge swallow of water and then delved into the capacious coat pockets, be brought out a camera and several rolls of film, he gave them to Paul.

"You can handle a camera, I trust?" Paul nodded. "Then I want photographs of the interior of this – what did you call it? -

Tech. Area. Pay particular attention to machinery and apparatus, particularly those types which are unfamiliar to you. Most important, I need to know the entire security set up: the number of men, their stations, when the shifts change and so on. It's a pity that G.2 does not still operate at Los Alamos. I have an operator with them."

Now, he turned to Carl. "I want a light aeroplane, one that will not draw attention – a crop-duster or some such. It is to over fly Los Alamos once, taking shots of the site and surrounding area. One slow pass, mind you – get it right the first time, a second will be too dangerous; I want nothing that might cause the Americans to be suspicious.

"Yes Joseph, it will cost money though."

Piekenbrock managed a thin lipped smile. "The money will be delivered as usual. Can you do it?"

Carl's chest swelled as he sat up straighter. "Of course, Sir."

So, thought Paul, the man must be an officer. "Carl tells me that you work for the Abwher, Joseph. I'm honored to do what I can for you."

Joseph frowned and looked at Carl who dropped his eyes. "The Abwher," he said slowly to Paul, "was disbanded some time ago. My section now reports directly to Reichsfuhrer Himmler. Your brother should have known that, he should also know better than to discuss such matters."

"I – I apologise, Sir. It was a slip of the tongue."

"A slip of the tongue which could kill us all – and do not

call me Sir. Now, once more to the matter in hand. The pilot of this plane must deliver the exposed film directly to an address in Mexico."

"Mexico?" Carl queried.

"There is much that you do not know about my network Carl. Much that it is better you do not know; however, in this case –," he shrugged his indifference, "one of my operatives holds a good position in a newspaper office; newspapers have radio links with other countries."

Carl nodded, anxious to please. "They also process film."

Joseph nodded.

Paul, listening to the interchange, began to have doubts about his brother-in-law. Carl had always been at pains to emphasize his importance to the Cause, to hint at the amount of sensitive information he dealt with, the number of men he directed...

"Your glass, Paul." Paul started and looked up. The others had their glasses raised.

"Germany!" Proposed Carl.

"Heil Hitler." Joseph added after drinking.

Shortly afterwards, Joseph prepared to leave although Carl was effusive in his offer of a bed for the night. Before he left, however, he drew Paul to one side, gave him a written address and an envelope. "Memorise this and send your photographs there – don't develop them of course. Other information, you may relay through your brother. The envelope contains money; I

104

suggest you buy a car."

"Brother-in-law." Corrected Paul, ignoring the money.

"Ah, in law, I see. Yes, for the time being, send your information through him. The photographs may be marked for the attention of Senor Alvante." Piekenbrock spelt the name for him. Finally, the German agent left with a 'Good luck, Herr Webber," to Paul.

As Joseph disappeared into the rain, the clouds lifted from Carl's face and he beamed as though he had, already, successfully carried off some important coup. The two men sipped schnapps and smoked; Carl regaled the other with stories of his youth and bravery but, though Paul tried to nod and laugh in the right places, his mind was more than halfway occupied with the tasks he had been set by Piekenbrock. How was he to secure the photographs – did he really want to? If he were to be caught, there was little doubt about his fate, he would be shot as a spy; come to that, could he get out of it? Probably the fish-eyed Joseph would have him shot if he tried to back out.

The part of his thoughts still with Carl, considered the new light shed on his brother-in-law's character. The tales he told were far too polished to be true, a large percentage of imagination had certainly gone into them, Paul was certain. The man who had shaped his adolescence shrank in Paul's estimation; inside the shell of braggadocio hid a small, mean personality that craved attention and admiration. Paul wondered why he had not seen this before, had it been naivety or immaturity?

There was a silence, Paul realised that he had been addressed directly.

"Sorry. What did you say?"

"You are thinking deeply. Worried about the photographs?"

"A little." Admitted Paul. "Probably Mai being away too, I was looking forward to seeing her again; after so long you know."

Carl showed no especial reaction, he merely glanced at the big oak clock on the mantle shelf.

"It's late too. The journey and the interrogation, they will have tired you. Perhaps it's time we were both to bed."

Paul agreed and, after covering the fireplace and putting out the lights, Carl led the way upstairs carrying a. nightlight, " a short fat candle on a saucer. Half way upstairs, Paul paused, his hand on the half newel. "I hope I don't fall down on this job Carl."

Carl turned and, looked down. The feeble flickering candle glow failed to reveal the sudden rush of blood from his face. In place of Paul, he imagined he saw Mai, her head swinging towards the smooth round post, striking it. He sucked in a gush of air, turned to hide his confusion. "I hope so too, brother." He whispered.

ELEVEN

Joseph Piekenbrock at first enjoyed the train journey back to New York; it gave him time to think without interruption. Despite the lateness of the hour, he was surprised to find that three other passengers shared his compartment; when he had got on, the whole car had been deserted. Two of the travellers were women laden with heavy baskets – probably returning from a family visit, he surmised. The third was a man who disturbed him more than the women who never raised her voice above a complaining drone; the man coughed incessantly, using a badly soiled handkerchief.

To distract himself, Piekenbrock listened to the women's conversation – a monotonous list of prices and shortages punctuated by an occasional 'shocking' or 'outrageous'. Piekenbrock fumed inwardly; he was familiar with dreadful shortages which had long ago become normal on the other side of the Atlantic, He felt like shaking the pair of them, telling them that there was a war for world supremacy going on but the gesture would make no difference besides drawing attention to himself.

Piekenbrock sighed and looked out at the meager lights of the ineffective blackout; the great American public, who had

107

never been invaded only felt the war as an inconvenience, as a drain on their pocket books. He remembered when he had last been home, when Hitler's blitzkriegs had won vast tracts of Europe from a totally demoralised enemy. Piekenbrock smiled, there had been champagne then – straight from the conquered vine-yards, caviar too before the Russians had changed sides. The smile faded and the German stared again at the emptiness outside the window, a reflected movement caught his attention – the man, sitting across the aisle from him had struck a match, a bright spark in the dim lighting.

Disbelievingly, Piekenbrock turned to look across the car. A crumpled pack of Lucky Strikes lay on the seat beside the man with the cough, he was in the act of lighting one. The man inhaled, coughed explosively one last time and chain-smoked the rest of the journey in silence.

It was cool in New York when the train got in, in the early hours. It was dry though and Piekenbrock wrapped the heavy coat around him as he left the station, keeping a sharp eye out for a cab. Ten minutes later, he successfully flagged down a cruising vehicle.

"Night club?" Asked the stubbled face from the front.
"Thank you, no." Piekenbrock gave an address a block away from his apartment building. Twenty minutes later he entered the basement apartment.

He switched on a desk lamp and then lit the kerosene heater. Despite the wave of warmth, Joseph shivered. There was no
108

doubt in his mind that the Americans possessed an atomic bomb and he dare not delay in passing the information on to those at home; fuller information could be sent later by the regular – and lengthier – routes but the bare facts had to be transmitted by radio.

Joseph Piekenbrock wrote the message out in clear then, using a double transformation with the key phrase 'spring is in the air' broke the message down into a string of apparently meaningless letters. Finally, he split these into groups of five to facilitate the use of Morse code and burned the originals.

He left his apartment and climbed the steps to the first floor to take the elevator.

There should have been no one about at this hour – soon after four thirty in the morning but, as luck would have it, Mrs. Granger stepped out of her apartment as he slid the door closed. Curlers in her hair, her incontinent poodle on its leash, she waved to him through the grill as she went to the other elevator. Piekenbrock bared his teeth in a smile.

On the top floor, he unlocked the door to the roof and climbed the short flight of steps. Outside, it was drizzling and Joseph trotted across to the small building housing the elevator gear. Again the door was locked, he opened it and dodged out of the light rain; kneeling, he reached down beneath the edge of the shaft, retrieving the transmitter. The German kept it hidden there except when a maintenance call was due and, conveniently, the Company always notified him, as the janitor, of the visits.

Sixty seconds later, he had committed the message to the ether.

As he returned to the basement his thoughts switched back to Carl. He was without a doubt a buffoon with a big mouth, he determined to do something about that.

Joseph Piekenbrock had good cause to worry about Carl's mouth; in June, 1941 he had sat sweating in that exact same basement listening to the news that thirty three of his colleagues had been arrested. In September, 1941 he had heard the news that they were to be executed as saboteurs. From that day forth he had lived in constant fear of being discovered, through three long years he had built up a new network, new contacts, new routes to Germany. He had been promoted and had received medals that his family had accepted on his behalf. Piekenbrock had far more to lose now than he had ever had, now – now that he had something tangible. And he knew it.

*

At the top of the Rockefeller Building in New York an antenna turned, stopped, turned once more and stopped again. Below, on a floor half way down the lofty office block, a tape recorder wound the second repeat of Piekenbrock's message. It was passed on to the decoding section within fifteen minutes of transmission.

Gerald Carpenter arrived at the S.O.E. offices promptly at nine a.m. By half past, he had disposed of the signals which had awaited him on his desk and was already going through the

110

night's search of the radio waves.

"What's this?" Carpenter held up the transcription of Piekenbrock's signal.

"No idea. It's not one of the Enigma ciphers. It isn't possible to decode it without knowing the key. Far too short even to guess at it."

"Transformation code?"

The other nodded.

"Guess you'd better file it then."

TWELVE

Empty windows gaped silently onto rubble filled streets. Fire weakened stonework crumbled away as pigeons sought familiar roosts. Smoldering timbers crashed in sudden showers of sparks as heavy trucks threaded a precarious course along the rubble strewn Vosstrasse.

The Old and the New Reich Chancelleries were fire gutted skeletons.

Deserted by their former tenants, they still shielded a semblance of Government. Fifteen metres below the foundations, a warren of damp, grey concrete corridors and cells housed a population of less than seven hundred men and women. Surrounded by moldy walls, breathing stale air, shaken by the nightly rain of high explosive, they charted the remaining days of the Third Reich.

To one side of Martin Bormann's office was that of Dr. Goebbels to the other was the power house. Doors opened to both of these though normally they were closed. Beyond, a third stood ajar, giving a glimpse into the telephone exchange and communications center.

Two men were on duty; one was dozing while the second sat, chin in hands, headphones clamped over his ears.

Occasionally, this one would move, sometimes to light another cigarette from the stub of the old; at other times it was to fine-tune a transmission and to write out a signal flimsy.

The night time hours passed slowly, marked off by bomb blasts which would shake a constant fall of gritty dust from the bunker roof. The single lamp swung slightly, moving shadows on the sleeping man's face. A particularly violent explosion woke him; unconcerned, he stretched, looked at his watch, yarned.

"I'll take over now Helmut. It's nearly time anyhow, you get some sleep."

"Okay – if those bastards up there let me." He hooked a vicious thumb upwards, nevertheless, he stood and took off the headphones. There was a plaintiff beep-beep from the phones as he dropped them on the desk.

"Hold on." And he picked them up, pressing one to his ear while scrabbling quickly for a pencil. He wrote furiously for a few seconds as the Morse hammered in from the ether; a swift acknowledgment and he checked the document as the message was repeated. A final reply and he put the phones down.

"I'll get this over to Ciphers right away. Come in from New York, top priority coding."

The other man nodded and Helmuth left the room. In due course, he returned holding a buff envelope, sealed and holding the decoded message from America.

"I suppose the Eminence is around somewhere?" Scorn in

his voice. "Not next door is he?"

The other shook his head. "Just looked in, desk's cleared; he'll be in his bed now."

"At this hour? He's usually awake until the Fuhrer goes to bed. I'll look around, he's maybe on the prowl."

Helmuth left only to return fifteen minutes later with the envelope still in his hand. "You realise what time this was transmitted?" He asked and shook the offending message in front of his partner's nose.

"Sure, a little after midnight."

"Five a.m. local time in eastern America. Five A.M. What the devil's that operator doing at that time? Tell me that. Thirty minutes earlier and the Reichsleiter would have been at his desk; now I have to wake him."

Bormann, the 'Brown Eminence' had turned in early. Troubled by a persistent cough he had slept badly all week and had taken the rare step of going to Stumpfegger for a sleeping draught. Despite his distrust of Hitler's personal surgeon – the latest of a line – he was pleasantly surprised to find the stuff worked. At one o'clock in the morning, neither a direct hit above nor any ordinary knocking on the door was going to rouse the Reichsleiter this time.

Helmuth Stern banged loudly and long and, at length, succeeded in waking Bormann. The door opened slowly, the Reichsleiter stood there fogged with sleep and blinking unwilling eyes into focus. He tugged at a fold in his nightshirt.

114

"What is it? Who is it?"

"Obershutz Stern, Sir. An important message just came in from the American network, I thought you would want to see it straight away."

Bormann took the proffered envelope, held the door wider.

"You'd better come in while I look at it. When do you say it came?"

"A half hour ago Sir, I took it straight to Ciphers but spent a few minutes looking for you – I hadn't realised that you'd…"

"No matter." His superior waved a silencing hand and switched on an overhead light. He sat on the edge of the narrow cot to read the signal. He became visibly agitated as the import reached his awakening brain.

"Bad news Sir? Should I inform the Fuhrer?"

"The Fuhrer?" For moments, Bormann could think of nothing, his mind was a blank. "The Fuhrer. Yes." He said at last. "I shall have to wake him; you had better get his valet up first."

Stern turned and headed for the door. He stopped at an almost inarticulate roar of rage from Bormann.

"Obershutz!"

"Sir?"

"What do you mean – coming here like that?"

"Bitte? I – I don't understand Sir."

"Look at you." Bormann pointed a shaking forefinger. "Collar undone, you're unshaven. An absolute mess"

"Sir, I've been on duty since six o'clock last evening."

"So? This is no excuse. No excuse at all, I frequently work sixteen hours a day – I don't let myself get into a state like that. Perhaps you think the war's over?"

"No Sir." Stern was standing to attention, more puzzled than alarmed by the sudden outburst.

"Well believe me Stern, it isn't – despite this signal. You have read it?" Bormann bent his face close to Stern's.

Stern shook his head. "Not in clear Sir, I only took down the coded signal."

"Ah!" Bormann straightened up, he smiled. "Good. You may go Obershutz, and Obershutz…"

"Yes Sir."

"Tidy yourself up. It doesn't help the Fuhrer to see men getting sloppy."

"Very good, Herr Reichsleiter. It will not happen again." Then, as an afterthought. "Do you wish me to wake Heinz Linge?"

"No, no. I'd better see to Herr Linge myself after all."

As the private left, Bormann bathed his face in cold water then began to change from his night attire. He was satisfied that Stern knew nothing of the signal's content – there would only be the clerk in Ciphers to take care of. He was determined that nothing of the matter must be leaked, only those who absolutely had to know must be informed.

He shaved carefully, groomed his hair then, immaculate, he

strode hurriedly through the Fuhrerbunker and roused Hitler's valet, Linge, in his turn, went to wake the Fuhrer. Thirty minutes later, he entered the sitting room where Bormann waited.

The Reichsleiter was shocked at his Leader's appearance. It seemed that he looked worse each time he saw him. A constant twitch afflicted his left cheek. His eyelids were puffy and great bags of grey flesh bulged beneath each eye. Hitler now kept his left hand clenched tightly in a pocket or grasped the wrist securely with his right hand; still the muscular trembling was evident.

"Ah, Martin. Heinz tells me you have urgent news." The Fuhrer stopped at a cabinet, bracing his left leg to stop this, too, from shaking.

"This is so, my Fuhrer. It came in around two this morning, from the New York cell."

"From your expression, I take it that it is not good news."

Bormann started to speak but a colossal explosion from overhead drowned any sound. Both men ducked involuntarily and in the silence that followed, the Reichsleiter handed over the deciphered message. Hitler glanced at it and shook his head.

"An atom bomb?"

Bormann nodded.

"Just what is it, Martin? What does it mean?"

"I have been told that such a weapon could be a hundred times more violent than the most powerful bomb we have, perhaps a thousand times."

117

Hitler started to pace the narrow confines, dragging the unwilling left foot behind.

"Why Martin? Why? Even at this stage I was confident that Fate had not deserted me, that relief would come – somehow. But this is just the excuse that our spineless officers are looking for, they will start surrendering in droves." He stopped, rounded on Bormann. "Who knows of this so far?"

"Just the cipher desk. I broke the seal on the envelope myself."

"It must not get out."

"Rest easy, my Fuhrer. I shall have the man moved; probably give him sole responsibility for these signals only. He'll be incommunicado."

Hitler nodded. "And we must have more information…"

Bormann. suppressed a cough. "You will see that photographs and a fuller report are to follow shortly – by the usual route."

"Of course but it is not what I meant. I want to know what our own scientists have to say about this – also, what they've been doing all this time. I want to know how the enemy has stolen a march on us."

"I shall have a scientist from the Institute here for when you wake in the morning, my Fuhrer. In any case – I really should not have troubled you at this hour; I've taken some sleeping medicine, I wasn't thinking clearly."

"Nonsense Martin." Hitler stopped his uneven pacing and

sat down at the writing desk to reread the message. "Who else should you go to? No, I was unable to sleep anyway and now is as good a time as any – get that man over here right away."

"Immediately. I'll order you some coffee."

At least, when Dr. Hertz was brought into the bunker, he made Bormann feel better. The physicist had been dragged from a bunk in the Kaiser-Wilhelm Institute's air raid shelter. He had had to dress hurriedly, leaving off his tie and unable to find his braces, the poor man had to hold up his creased and shiny trousers with one hand. Bormann felt several degrees more elegant.

Dr. Hertz sat across the conference table from Bormann. The Reichsleiter had already let the silence stretch into long minutes while the scientist nervously held his eyes on his clasped hands.

"Well, Herr Doctor." He broke the silence at last. "What can you make of this?" He slid the single piece of paper across the table.

Eager for something to do, the physicist seized the paper and scrutinised the contents. When he had finished, there was a smile on his lips.

"Impossible."

"That is all you have to say?" Bormann was amazed.

"There is nothing more to say. Your informant is mistaken."

"I think not. Herr Piekenbrock is most astute; his information is always impeccable. I suggest you take the message more seriously."

"Perhaps it is an oil refinery."

Before Bormann could reply, the door opened and Hitler entered with Blondi, his Alsatian, following his dragging heel. The Fuhrer crossed to the head of the table.

"Heil Hitler." Bormann stood to rigid attention, his arm at full stretch, his eyes on the scientist.

The doctor rose, holding his trousers in one hand and saluting with the other.

Hitler nodded perfunctorily and eased himself into the chair. The other two also sat down.

"Now Herr Doctor," Hitler began, "I wish to know why Germany has no atomic explosives while the Americans seem to have a manufacturing plant covering hundreds of kilometres." Hitler seemed to be more interested in the failure of his own scientists rather than in the success of the Allies.

"I deny that the Allies have succeeded Sir. Our own physicists are on the threshold of building a self-sustaining uranium reactor but our experience shows that many tonnes of heavy water are necessary to make it function. This message – ," he pushed diffidently at the paper with a forefinger, "indicates nothing of this. An installation of hundreds of hectares would obviously require gigantic storage tanks to hold the fluid."

Hitler shook his head. "Do you think that I would have been awakened at this hour if the report was not accurate? That Martin here would have gone to the trouble of bringing you here in the

120

middle of an air raid?"

The Fuhrer thumped with his fist.

"No Herr Doctor, Now, answer my question. I want to know when you will be supplying my hard pressed forces with a suitable counter weapon."

He stood up, his face becoming suffused with red blotches. "I will not have my enemies gaining technological ground on me in this way. I demand – Germany demands hard labor from her scientists."

Concerned for his very life at first, Hertz slowly relaxed in the face of the growing tirade. He knew that while Hitler was ranting on in this fashion, no reply was required beyond nods and mumbles in the right places. He glanced at the Reichsleiter.

Hermann was busily making notes of his Fuhrer's speech.

Hitler had called a situation conference for midday.

The small conference room-- situated across the passage that divided the Fuhrer bunker into two, was filled. Three director-scientists from the Institute were gathered at the foot of the table; Bormann was present as was Joseph Goebbels, Reich Defence Commissioner of Berlin.

The Fuhrer entered to a chorus of 'Heil Hitler'. He sat down, the continual trembling in his limbs appearing to have reduced overnight. Bormann remained standing and, after nodding at the stenographer to start, he opened the proceedings by reading the message and explaining the Fuhrer's requirements.

There was considerable debate between the three from the

Kaiser-Wilhelm Institute until Dr. Woermann, their elected spokesman rose.

"I think that my colleagues and I are agreed that it will take at least six months and several million Reich marks to prepare a uranium bomb. Also imperative is a directive to the I.G. Farben Works to increase their production of heavy water. Dr. Haushofer here believes it possible to use graphite in place of heavy water but the substance has already been investigated and its unsuitability proven."

Here, the scientist was being tactful, the idea of graphite reactors had been propounded by several scientific geniuses over the years – all of them Jewish, thus making further pursuance along those lines verboten; by Hitler's own edict.

"Six months is no good Herr Doctor." Husked Bormann, trying to stifle a cough. "We must have it..." The throat irritation won the battle and his words dissolved into a paroxysm of coughing.

"Here Martin." Goebbels spoke for the first time. "Take a glass of water."

"The time does not matter." Hitler spoke quietly into the silence following Bormann's coughing. All eyes turned to the Fuhrer.

"No. There is a cheaper and more effective way," He took hold of the original message sheet and waved it to and fro as though fanning himself."

The conference room in the Fuhrerbunker was silent, a hush

of expectancy.

Hitler drew it out to best effect. "We shall bomb this – " he threw down the paper, " – this place out of existence."

Still, there was silence though now it held incredulity.

The steady scratching of Frau Christian, recording the Fuhrer's words was the only sound in the room for long seconds.

Hertz shook his head. "Impossible." He muttered, lips scarcely moving.

"No," said Goebbels. "Difficult but not, perhaps, impossible."

"Magnificent." Rumbled Martin Bormann, scraping his chair across the floor as he lumbered to his feet. "Brilliant. Though I must agree to some extent with Josef." He inclined his head in Goebbel's direction, honoring the uneasy truce which, at this late stage, had bound them together.

"Obviously it is impossible." Repeated Herts. "I'm no flyer but even I know that Germany has no aircraft with the necessary range." He rose and crossed to one of the wall maps; it depicted the Atlantic Ocean. "Look, over 9000 kilometres at least. In any casc Allicd radar will pick it up, the plane would be brought down before it crossed the coast, even at night."

But Hitler merely smiled, his burning eyes drawing Hertz's gaze. Today, he seemed above the violent tirade and temper which normally would follow criticism. He smoothed the lank hair back from his forehead. "It would not be shot down if it was an American aircraft do you think? If it was painted as a hospital plane perhaps? Flying through neutral air space – in daylight?"

THIRTEEN

Returning to the Hill was like coming home; coming home with a new perspective. Up to a mere three days ago, he had had the feeling that it was just so enormous that one man's mind could not encompass the whole. Often, in conversation, Paul had said a man can only work in one place at one time.

That had changed, perhaps the talk with Joseph had somehow condensed his view, perhaps the time away had given his subconscious time to recover from the battering that the enormity of events had given it. Whatever, he began to spend time just getting the feel of the place, looking as much at the New Mexican countryside as at the installations themselves.

For Piekenbrock, he noted the army sentries, where each was situated, the arms they carried. He looked down the hundreds of gulleys and chasms which bordered the site, reviewing those most likely to offer ingress. Too, he fabricated excuses to work in and around the Tech. Area, even to the extent of attending a colloquium. These regular meetings were normally the preserve of scientists and senior technicians with sufficient knowledge to offer something useful to the Project.

At the Colloquium, Paul found the word security was

meaningless. Every one there accepted that everybody else was entitled to be there; their purpose was to get problems into the open where they could be solved. During the course of the evening, Paul heard words and snippets of conversation which were so much gibberish to him. Nonetheless, he committed as much as he could to memory; such things as present stocks of U235, will Kistiakowsky perfect the implosion method, Little Boy device, electrostatic generators, accelerators, cyclotrons – he could only remember a portion of the list but, in two hours, he found out more than he had during all the previous months he'd been at Los Alamos.

He had been meaning to make casual remarks about the strength of the staff in the hope of getting unofficial estimates. But the information was freely offered before he left.

" – Water shortage." Someone complained. "It gets no better; here we are with over forty thousand construction workers on the Hill add that to about ten or twelve thousand military and God knows how many of us egg heads. They must have the figures so when are they going to bring in adequate supplies?

Paul missed the answer, he was too busy exulting about this and other useful titbits. By the time they had finished, Paul's brain had reached bursting point. He had hoped to see Susan there so he could have walked her back to the single women's quarters but there were too many people. She might well have been present but looking for her would have been hopeless.

He drove back to the stockman's place he was quartered in

and made notes on all he had heard in the book he was now keeping for the purpose, A shower – necessarily cold – and a vigorous towel-down refreshed him and he decided to try calling the women's dormitory. Susan was there and a minute or two later she came to the phone.

"Paul?"

"Hi English Rose. How are you?"

"I'm fine thanks. You been trying to avoid me lately?"

"Lord, no. Sorry 'bout that but I've just been so busy."

"Just as long as you haven't got another girl hidden away."

"With you, Sue, there's no contest. Hey, let me make it up to you. I've got a really great house here, how about coming out to dinner some time?"

There was the briefest of brief pauses. "I'd love to. When?"

"Tomorrow? Around seven?"

"I'll be there."

Whistling at his success, Paul hit the hay and slept a solid eight hours. The following morning, the sun was only marginally ahead of him. Bright eyed he gunned the protesting jeep through the checkpoint. At his office, he checked out the day's work sheets and left various instructions for the work crews that would be along in the next half hour. By that time, Paul was already deep in the wooded area screening Project Y from the possibility of outside scrutiny. He made a mock salute to the sentry box halfway through the woods and added him to his mental list.

Out of sight and earshot, he stopped the jeep and checked

his map. He was well away from any of the buildings and storage sheds; still in the woods – he made his preparations.

He had rolled the camera in a piece of oily cloth to hide it from curious eyes; not that a search was likely, both he and the noisy jeep were too well known. Nevertheless, mandatory inspections were sometimes made at irregular intervals, so Paul had taken only minimal precautions against discovery. Now, he concealed the camera in one pocket of his loose jacket and a pair of heavy duty wire cutters and thick gloves in the other.

Above Paul's head hung temporary catenary cables, supplying – he had ascertained – several new items of equipment within Project Y requiring isolated and fluctuation-free power. The success of last evening's invitation to Susan had left him confident and he strode without a second thought to a tree through which the cables ran, a pine tree, the lower branches long since dropped away, leaving short stubs. Paul climbed the rough trunk without difficulty- and thrust his way through the yielding foliage until a cable appeared above his head.

He disliked hot-wire work intensely but in this instance, could see no alternative. So, donning the gloves, Paul clipped a jumper lead on at convenient points piercing the outer cover, and tightened down thumb screws at either end. The wire cutters were a trifle small for the cable diameter and he had to sever individual strands before the conductor parted and snapped taught against the jumper lead. There was little he could do to hide the effects of deliberate sabotage beyond fraying the fibrous

128

insulation and hoping that the untidy cutting would mislead a first glance. Paul pinned his main hope on the fact that he, himself, would be doing the repair job and would later report that the failure was due to chafing. A few turns on one of the thumb screws and the longer length of free cable sagged and fell to the ground. A small flash as the electrical connection broke told him that power was being drawn up to this point. As he released the other end of the jumper he heard the beep-beep of the pack radio in the jeep.

He dropped the last six feet to the ground and sprinted to the vehicle pulling the hand set free.

"Chief Electrician Webb." He announced.

"Hi Chief, Reubens here." Paul nodded to himself, he knew the man well enough; dark skinned, Latin extraction.

"Hello Reubens. What can I do for you?"

" There's trouble in the test area Chief. Supply's just gone off on one of the auxiliary supplies."

"Oh? Anything important?"

"Kind of. It's the isolated supply to the computing machines. I'll bet it popped a dozen valves when it dropped out."

"Hmm. Okay, you leave the supply to me, you'd better get on to the equipment itself, you're more qualified than I am. Let's see now, those wires're overhead aren't they – run in under the roof?"

"Yeah, I'll have schematics ready for you."

The rest was as easy as he had hoped. The supply failure

provided the perfect excuse to go crawling along the cat walks beneath the roof of the laboratories. Nobody thought to look up and, even if they had, it was doubtful that Paul could be seen beyond the glare of the powerful overhead lighting. He exposed five rolls of film; the combination of wide angle lens and fast, fine grain emulsion would secure far more detail than his own unaided eye could pick out.

When he'd used up all the film, Paul drove the jeep slowly along beneath the overhead cable, ostensibly searching for a break. Once again out of sight, he used a hand winch to pull the severed ends together and reconnect them.

Back in his office, he made out the report on the 'repair' then filled out an envelope to the Mexican address for the film, expecting to mail it later in the day. For a moment, he toyed with the idea of waiting until he could buy the car that Joseph had suggested to him and deliver the film to Carl; still, the mail would be faster and his instructions to mail it to Mexico had been explicit.

It was a pity though. Mai should be home soon, it would have been nice to see her. It had been a hell of a time since the last time and – come to think of it, he hadn't heard from his parents for a month or two despite the check that they should have received more than two weeks ago.

Before leaving the site, Paul stopped outside the PX to get some postage stamps. The store was pretty busy however and he put it off until tomorrow – another twenty four hours could make
130

no real difference and more than enough time had been spent on illicit activities for one day. No: he returned to the jeep and headed home, there was a dinner to prepare for a special lady tonight; there was more than enough food in the fridge. Preparations for the evening were far more important than worrying about Carl and his fish-eyed friend; it was unlikely that they'd be giving much thought to him.

At the time, Susan had accepted Paul's invitation without thought; only now, as she changed for the occasion, she paused to consider what her feelings were.

She liked Paul, was fond of him without a doubt. Did her emotions run deeper than mere affection? It was difficult to decide. He was so different from the men she had known before he came to the Hill: the soldiers, flaunting their healthy young lust; her own colleagues living in a world of high energy physics, conversation bounded by neutron emission rates and gas diffusion processes.

Susan had more than an inkling of what was likely to happen that night – given half a chance. She looked at the Susan who gazed back at her from the mirror, traced the laugh lines etched into her skin by the New Mexican sun. She wasn't old at twenty eight, was she? Most women of her age at Los Alamos were married – many of her female colleagues on the scientific staff were married to other physicists and chemists. Somehow, she had never gotten around to marriage, only rarely spent time socially with men since coming to America despite frequent opportunities.

At the University, a younger Susan had given little thought to passing years. It had been a time to learn, an opportunity to join an elite.

They had been exciting years, full of exciting new knowledge, crowned with a first class honors degree. But pre-war Britain was a disappointing place for a girl.Even a shiny new B.A. was only a passport to a job as a technician in a metallurgy lab. After the outbreak of war, a former lecturer took the trouble to trace her and offer her a place on a team engaged in vital war research. Susan accepted instantly and went to the I.C.I, laboratories as soon as she was able.

The work was absorbing, in the forefront of nuclear science. When the team was transferred to a subsidiary of the Imperial Chemical Industries: Tube Alloys, she was required to sign the Official Secrets Act. Perhaps it was unconscious gratitude to Mike Holderness – the one time lecturer – that brought it about, perhaps not, but the transition from colleague to friend to lover seemed no more than a natural progression. The relationship didn't last long; Mike was a blitz casualty and when many of T.A's scientists were sent to join the Americans' parallel organisation – the Manhattan District Engineer Project – Susan was an early transfer by choice.

First, at the Clinton Engineer works and then later at Los Alamos, she worked indefatigably; escaping her memories in sheer exhaustion. Eventually, her regrets became a part of the
132

past; something to be taken out and looked at occasionally but the habit of hard work stayed with her and gained Susan a large measure of respect from the predominantly male staff at the 'Hill'.

Mike's faded image passed before her mind's eye as she finished brushing her hair. Would Paul make a determined pass at her tonight? There had been a number of opportunities which he had passed up before. Why should he start now? Susan shrugged and started to choose her outfit; it must have been something in his voice, she decided as she began to dress. Any move he had made before – even the goodnight kisses and his gentle caresses could almost have been interpreted as brotherly affection; not quite, but almost. Somehow, his words over the phone had lost the diffidence they had held before.

With an annoyed frown at herself, Susan put a determined stop to the train of thought. Tonight would take care of itself. She appraised her appearance before the mirror; yes, she had chosen the right dress, the blue one suited her best.

FOURTEEN

Paul could find no candlesticks; after a moment's thought he found two cork drink coasters and dropping melted wax onto them he stuck the candles upright and placed them on the table. They were the final touch to his careful preparations. The meal: turtle soup followed by roast lamb, beans, sweet corn and baked potatoes was either simmering on the stove or in the final stages of cooking. The dessert was a fruit flan from the PX, it waited, together with a bottle of Californian Riesling in the fridge. One thing was missing: a carton of cream that he had intended to get when he had stopped for the stamps; instead, a jug of evaporated milk would have to do. A glance at his watch and he decided he should set the plates to warm.

Paul stood still. There was just nothing else he could find to do and with the inactivity came the first wave of nerves. He went back to the kitchen and opened a box of cigars – a present from his Father two Christmases ago. He cut the end off one and lit it carefully, then blew great clouds of smoke into the air. Like his father,

Paul smoked occasionally; when he was with Carl, he used more of the things.

"Oh well." He muttered. "It'll drown the cooking smells."

134

His mind turned once more to Susan and the next few hours. Was this evening going to turn out like previous occasions….? There, despite his good intentions the thought had come through defeating his attempts to sidetrack it.

Paul rarely thought of sex and Susan at the same time; he rarely thought of sex if it could be avoided – not because the idea offended him but, really, because of his lack of knowledge on the subject. It often arose with the men, up at the 'Hill' and Paul coped with the dirty jokes and half serious questions by returning an amused smile – as though his experience with the female of the species was so wide that the men's jokes were kindergarten stuff. At least, that was the theory; whether it worked or not, he didn't know.

Paul's actual experience of sex had been surprisingly limited for a man of his years. The first time had been with a freckle-faced teenager on the back stoop of her house; he remembered how the girl had giggled when he ran his feverish hand up the inside of her leg. She'd closed them together then, forestalling any further exploration and told him her father might come out, Paul couldn't have cared less at that point, he continued up the front of her thigh, stopping when his fingers touched the mound where her legs came together. The bull-like roar of her father's voice had frozen him; even when she twisted away and disappeared round the corner, Paul was still paralysed with shock until one hard and heavy boot lifted his backside off the step.

There had been two more occasions after that, with different girls. The events were hazy with time, by now all he could remember was the last had been at a movie. He could remember the film clearly enough: a comic spy thriller starring, he thought, Mickey Rooney. That thought brought him up cold, the film had been funny then but he couldn't raise a chuckle now.

"God. "That didn't seem so long ago. Was I really as stupid as that? Just a goddamn groper?"

Was he any more mature now? He would know the answer to that before the evening was out, anyway. Since he had taken to dating Susan, Paul had been trying to impress her as a man of the world; it was high time he started believing it himself.

FIFTEEN

Susan knew the way; at least, she had driven out with Paul on previous occasions. Driving herself though, in a friend's Buick, was different; she drove slowly, the approaching evening uppermost in her thoughts.

She was no prude, she thought to herself, hardly a dried up old spinster but it had been so long since she had thought of a man from this point of view – sexually, she made herself admit. Was she looking forward to it? Did she want to go to bed with him?

Susan postponed the answer, looking fixedly at the road so as not to miss the turn off. It came up and she turned to the left, bumping across the ruts and into the twisting track that wound between clumps of mesquite and creosote.

She bit her lip as the persistent train of thought surfaced once more. Their backgrounds were very different: where Susan had come from a comfortable middle class English home, Paul had had to pull himself up by his bootstraps; she knew of the four thousand dollars his brother-in-law had given him but the sort of education this had bought could not be compared with a British University. He had changed of course, since he'd first come to the 'Hill'; responsibility had been thrust upon him and he had matured tremendously – he wouldn't still be here if he hadn't. Come to think of it , she herself had altered since crossing the Atlantic – the differences were more difficult to pin down because she saw them only from the inside; nevertheless, Susan knew that they were there.

A grin spread across her features as the little house came into view. Perhaps Paul had nothing more than a platonic dinner in mind; what then? Chuckling now, she switched off the engine and got out, slamming the door closed. In that case, she would just have to dust off her technique and seduce the man.

She was five minutes late. Paul, hearing the car had the door open and she entered in a cloud of some soft and elusive perfume.

"Hi," Said Paul.

"Hello yourself. I guess I'm a bit late, not keeping anything waiting am I?"

"Nothing that'll spoil for a few minutes."

"Great, I'll just fix my hair – Bound to be a mess."

She skipped by him, into the bedroom. Paul looked at the swiftly closing door, she seemed – what did she seem? Nervous?

Inside the bedroom, she stopped abruptly and let her breath out in a long sigh. "My God," she whispered, "I haven't felt like this since that first dance at the Church Hall. She patted one or two stray locks of hair into place and repaired her lipstick. "There now, that'll have to do. I really am being stupid."

138

Back in the long, raftered dining room, Paul had put out the soup, its aroma filled the air and reminded Susan that she hadn't eaten since lunch. She sat down and consciously relaxed.

"Okay?"

She looked up from the table, smiled. "Mm. Soup smells good, what is it?"

"Turtle."

"Really? Can we start? I'm ravenous."

"Right away, wine?"

"I'll have wine with the main course if I may."

"Very sensible."

The meal was a huge success. Conversation centered on Paul's culinary achievements and when he disclosed the only disaster – a minor one in which the sweet corn had been burned – Susan laughed, delighted.

"You had some more then."

"'Fraid not. I was going to serve it on the cob so I stripped the kernels off and served them like this, in a dish.

"Well, it's a whole lot better than the cafeteria. I could be persuaded to make a habit of this."

"I'd be very pleased if you would."

"It's a pity I can't return the invitation but I don't think the women's dormitory would have quite the same ambience – d'you?"

"Maybe not." Paul stood and collected the empty dishes.

"Mind you – if you've got something better than a wood

stove out there, I could come out here and do some cooking."

"You be careful – I might take you up on that."

"I mean it, really. I'll give you a hand with the washing up."

"You certainly won't. These'll keep 'til tomorrow. It's drinks time now."

"Shall I mix them?"

Paul fiddled with the radio and, thoughtfully, took the phone off the cradle before sitting with Susan on the old sofa. The music was soft and dreamy, its mood fitted well.

"Tell me some more about yourself Paul, I don't know much about you really; not about your childhood, your home."

Susan had meant it as no more than a conversation opener, prompted by idle curiosity but Paul's mind froze for a moment. Once again, he realised how careful he had to be; he must say nothing that might reveal his ethnic origins. He said: "It's kinda hazy now, I guess – we used to live in Chicago when I was younger, I can remember the tall buildings, the narrow streets. The kids were pretty rough too. When we moved to Des Moines I was into my teens -I was pretty surprised, you know? Things were so different. I guess I must have thought everywhere was like that – closed in, paved over. My Pa got a job right off, I can remember Mama singing in the kitchen." He stopped, realising who he was talking to, Susan had sidetracked him a little – Paul turned the tables.

"Tell me about you. I bet Oxford University was a lot more interesting than my old college."

140

"Another time, maybe." She touched the back of his neck, gently. On the table the second candle guttered and winked out.

At first, they kissed as they had done before – lightly, affectionately, A moment of this and Susan parted her lips; without quite realising what he was doing, Paul responded with an enquiring tongue. He kissed her lips again – hard, her eyelids – softly; nibbled at the lobes of her ears, the nape of her neck, her throat.

Susan, in her turn, all but writhed as his questing tongue flicked the sensitive skin she presented to Paul's eager mouth. She lay back, pulling him with her and he planted eager kisses between her breasts. When the deeply cut neckline frustrated his efforts, she twisted her shoulders so that the smooth fabric slid lower until he was able to take one of the hard nipples between his lips.

"Let me." She whispered as he tousled with a zip that was tangled in the folds of her dress. She stood up and the dress rippled to the floor, her underclothes followed quickly, then she knelt and undid Paul's shirt buttons. Nervously, he touched her thigh, caressed the smooth flesh; Susan put her hand on his fingers and pressed them before she continued with his clothes.

For a few seconds, Susan sat on her heels, content to watch the play of firelight and shadow across the muscular body before her. Then she leaned forward, her head on his chest, her hands running slowly across his stomach, his thighs and closing upon his private parts.

"Shall we go nearer the fire?"

Paul nodded and, together, they moved the cushions on to the rug.

Now Paul paused and looked at the lovely body. Touching lightly the smooth breasts, nipples dark in the red light of flames; the soft skin of her stomach, downy hair and the moist flesh that pouted between her legs.

It was all too much; he straddled her then, as her legs parted, lay between them while she guided him into her,

"So long," Susan thought, "so long – ah," the half remembered sensation of invasion, the tongue upon her nipples, the weight of hard straining muscles on her body. She felt it start, knowing there was nothing she could do to stop or delay it; Susan trapped his waist between her thighs and opened herself to the rush, feeling him spasm into one uncontrollable thrust.

Then he was still, his weight, heavy on her stomach.

"I'm sorry." He whispered. "I just couldn't…"

"It's okay." Susan held him tightly, their bodies still together – his within hers. "I know how it is. Don't mind about it now."

Paul lay within her, feeling himself go flaccid, knowing instinctively that it shouldn't have been like this. He stayed like that a few seconds longer before pushing himself up; their skin – stuck together with perspiration – peeled apart and he got up.

Dejectedly, Paul crossed to the table and poured himself a bourbon. "Drink?"

142

"Okay." Susan sat up and, finding a poker, pushed the smoldering logs apart so that they blazed up. Paul came and sat by her and sadly stroked the golden cascade of hair.

"I'm sorry." He said again.

"Don't be, darling." She took a sip of liquor; it ate a fiery path down her throat. "This was the first time, wasn't it, mm? First time, all the way."

Paul nodded.

Susan smiled and ran a cool hand over his chest. "I suppose it has to be this way round sometimes. I just wish that it had been the first time for me. Do you mind – that it wasn't?"

"No." It had never entered Paul's head to wonder if Susan had been a virgin. He just regretted that he'd let his first girl down.

"Come on then cuddle me a bit, I'm cold."

Paul placed an arm around her and emptied his glass then pulled her head into the angle between his shoulder and head. She turned her face towards him and began to nibble his ear; a warm breast swung against his chest, he could feel the still erect nipple rubbing against his skin. He touched it tenderly, lifting it, feeling- its weight and, as he did so, so he felt his desire rising again.

"Oh oh. Soldier boy's on his feet again." Susan had realised what was happening.

Paul pushed her down to the pillows again, determined to take the initiative this time, to lead instead of being led. He

143

explored every inch of her body with lips and tongue until she quivered to his touch. Only then, did he allow himself to enter her and moved with long, slow thrusts, the urgency of before entirely gone.

Susan awoke sometime later. She lay still, considering her lover. She hadn't realised how much sex had meant to her, shutting herself away from it all these years. Turning her head slightly she could see Paul, watch his breathing. Somehow the fact that he had been a virgin stirred her; she determined not to lose him.

One side of her body felt warm where Paul lay against her, asleep. The other side, now that the fire had died to ashes, was cold and clammy. Gently, she extricated herself from his sleeping embrace and groped in the darkness for a log to put on the fire; the slight noise awoke Paul.

"Wow, I'm cold; are you?"

Susan nodded then, realising that he could not see her: "Mm. It's turned a bit chilly."

Fully awake once more, they dressed, then sat before the rekindled fire, talking aimlessly as, outside, the night turned grey with approaching dawn. They took an early breakfast after sharing a shower and Paul followed Susan's Buick onto the Site, both of them stopping outside the PX store. Laughing at the coincidence, they went in together.

"Cigarettes." She explained.

"I didn't know you smoked – not in all this time."

"Not me. My boss, it's his birthday and he chain smokes like anything. What do you want?"

"Some stamps. Got letters for some relatives up North."

"Careful what you say. All the mail's censored you know."

"Really?"

"Too true. You'd be surprised at some of the things they ink out before they let the mail go."

Back in his office, Paul let out a long, whistling breath as he put the stamps with the letter in his pocket. He'd almost dropped Carl's letter in the box at the store; how stupid could one man be?

SIXTEEN

When Hitler made his proposal, it was impossible to decide whether the idea was the product of careful thought or if it had been dreamed up as he spoke.

Bormann's immediate reaction – despite his ready agreement – was much the same as Woermann's. Within seconds however, he had changed his mind, the plan had merit, it was just such an unexpected coup that would succeed, and its success would have the same demoralising effects as Hitler's tremendous blitzkriegs in the earlier part of the war. Too – his quick brain was already probing other possibilities – the crew: Schroeder's crack team, he could suggest them. The Fuhrer he was sure, would accept. They could then go on to Paraguay after refuelling in Brazil. Once there, the beginnings of the Kamaradenwerk would be sown; a safe refuge for the Fuhrer, a safe refuge for himself for Gerda and the children.

Mm! The Reichsleiter's mind worked furiously.

The meeting broke up rapidly then. Bormann mistrusted the club-footed Goebbels and he waited, shuffling papers as Joseph clasped Hitler's arm warmly and congratulated him before he followed Dr. Bormann out into the corridor.

Bormann marvelled at the miraculous improvement in the

Fuhrer's health. In the early hours of that same day, the man had been visibly coming apart. Now, he was calm, spoke quietly and with assurance; he smiled a secret sort of smile.

When the two were alone, Hitler sat back in an empty chair. He patted his knee and Blondi padded across to lay her head on his leg.

"It came to me as I lay in bed this morning, Martin. Perhaps that hour or so of sleep after midnight did me good, eh?"

The Reichsleiter grinned, crossed to another chair, patting the Alsatian's head as he passed.

"You remember those horoscopes I ordered? The one for myself and the one cast for the Reich?"

Bormann nodded, frowned; ready to make apologies.

"Well Joseph picked them up for me. I knew you had been busy."

"A moment my Fuhrer, I had ordered coffee as soon as the conference finished." Bormann was on the point of rising to press the servant's bell when the door opened and a thin, pale girl entered with a tray. "Tea." Hitler continued when she'd left; he accepted a cup. "Both horoscopes forecast a tremendously bad time in the early months of this year- They were correct of course."

Bormann sipped, made his habitual face which relapsed into a gloomy unfocussed gaze as he thought of the forecasts. He should have got them. He said in agreement, "Of course." Though he had not seen them.

"Exactly my dear fellow. Both prove that we have simply reached the darkest hour before the dawn." Hitler paused for a moment then continued, "Joseph sat with me last night, after the meeting. I couldn't get back to sleep – no, do not blame yourself Martin." Hitler misconstrued the look of concern on his companion's face. "Joseph was reading to me from Frederick the Great – Carlyle's work. You are surely familiar with it."

Bormann nodded and was about to reply when a shell exploded nearby, drowning his voice. Both men shielded their cups from the falling dust, it was a habit of some standing.

"That man's indomitable will is a source of strength to me, Martin. Always, Frederick was on the point of perishing, always in danger and now, now that Konigsberg is fallen; like him, I await the miracle." There was much more said after that but finally they parted and made their way to their beds.

*

There was much for Bormann to do over the next few days. Quite apart from the colossal amount of work he reserved to himself, there were various tasks to be accomplished in connection with Major Schroeder and his small battle group. In some cases, Bormann had had to use the Fuhrer's authority to have men detached from whatever their current duties had been; a crusty General who had lost his best adjutant was demanding a replacement of similar calibre. The Reichsleiter wrote a second letter imploring the General's patience and then put that matter

148

from his mind. A second problem had arisen over Schroeder's dismissal of Dietrich, as Bormann had accurately forecast; the problem was a difficult one and appeared to have only one solution; nevertheless he ordered his new aide, Willi Rattenhuber, to arrange an appointment with the officer in question.

The final problem – that of transportation – had been solved in principal by Hitler's directive; there still remained the practical difficulties of locating a suitable aircraft and the vast amount of fuel it would require to carry it across the Atlantic,

Like the Fuhrer, Martin Bormann rarely sought his bunk before four or five in the morning and not infrequently, the Reichsleiter worked the clock around. There was simply no one else – not even the faithful Goebbels – to whom Hitler would entrust what little government was left. Bormann would not have wished it otherwise, indeed he had labored to arrange that all routes to the Fuhrer lay through his small, three metre square office. It was from that little concrete walled cell that the power of the dying Reich was wielded; here, all intelligence, all communiqués came together; from here, all orders – civil and military – were issued in Bormann's hand.

SEVENTEEN

Once again, the rashly proposed mission to bomb the American's atomic installation was under discussion. Hitler sat at the head of the table; he had the shakes again, like a man suffering the effects of malaria. Although still reasonably calm, the others could sense a rising tension in his small frame.

Bormann, sitting to the Fuhrer's right, radiated his usual air of massive, unruffled calm. Dr. Woermann looked at him from time to time, wondering. The Reichsleiter was by no means a tall man but Woermann always felt as though he had to look up to him. Joseph Goebbels was present, sitting hunchbacked across from Bormann and toying with a fountain pen.

Two other men attended the situation conference: a Luftwaffe officer from KG 113 Flight where an Allied B24 had been located and a communications officer with aerial photographs which had come in from Mexico by radio the previous evening.

All were in subdued mood. The US Ninth Army had crossed the Elbe, the information had spread through the bunker's labyrinth like an insidious plague.

"So. The vultures gather." Hitler's voice was quiet, "I see this operation as a turning point, gentlemen. Once we have

150

attained this objective, the Allies will be so stunned that their organisation will fall apart; they will find that we are not yet carrion."

The Fuhrer looked down the table at Woermann. "Now, Herr Doctor What of our own atomic research? Is it possible to have our own weapons ready at short notice? If they are used at the moment the Americans are robbed of their own success, it will carry a maximum psychological effect."

Dr. Woermann shook his head. Why should they ask him about weapons? His team, occupied themselves with basic research at the Virus House.

"I'm sorry," he began, "there seems to be a misapprehension here. The people you should be speaking to are at Kummersdorf. Doctor Diebner is in control of new weapons development. I do know a little about their work."

Diebner, as Woermann knew, had no atomic weapons either in the development stage or in production. Nothing was even planned beyond some rather optimistic notes on the subject. Not only was atomic weapons research largely a figment of imaginative reports prepared to keep the scientists involved from being drafted but Himmler, himself discouraged the work. The Reichsfuhrer continuously redirected their efforts into schemes which he deemed to be of greater importance.

Hitler's tension was visibly increasing at Bormann's delay in answering. His face grew blotchy, fingers tightened around his pen.

"Go on. Dr. Woermann." Bormann tried to forestall the Fuhrer's imminent outburst of recrimination."

"Diebner is considering ways of adapting present weapons before developing a completely revolutionary one. Not conventional explosive, you understand. No, no. This more like, mm."

Sweat ran down his temples as he tried to think. "Like, err. Chlorine perhaps. Mustard gas, you remember? That's a poor example – ah, rat poison. Yes, rat poison."

"Rat poison?" It was Bormann's turn to wonder if the other were insane.

Suddenly on surer ground, the Doctor stood up straighter, assumed a lecturing manner.

"Atomic metal – that is uranium – is exceedingly poisonous; especially in the finely powdered form we have been using. It emits invisible rays that cause a burning of the flesh; severe cases are always lethal."

He glanced at Bormann, the Reichsleiter nodded once? His gaze, one of approval, of tacit understanding of the deception.

"We propose to fill shells and landmines with this metal dust. When the conventional explosive is detonated, clouds of finely divided uranium will shower the enemy. It will be impossible to avoid breathing it, they will die –."

"Like rats." Terminated Bormann, firmly. Then, to the Fuhrer. "I knew our scientists would not fail us. He turned back to Woermann. "And how soon can this be put into effect?"

152

"Our supplies of atomic material have been moved to Echingen to safeguard the extremely delicate work necessary. A few weeks, perhaps, should see the first armaments ready."

"Excellent, Herr Doctor. My Fuhrer?"

Hitler nodded, looked down at his agenda. "Now, the Operation requires a name, one that will give some inspiration." At that moment, Blondi who had entered unseen, poked her nose into the Fuhrer's hand. He looked down, smiled; sitting beside the bitch was Wolf, one of her puppies. "Yes. Operation Blondi, what is more inspiring than a mother's devotion."

Woermann sat down suddenly, weak kneed with relief that the nonsense he had spoken had been accepted but he must start doing something. If there was time.

Steinmetz rose to report on the preparation of the B24. Lightweight, long range tanks would be fitted inside every spare centimetre of her fuselage. These could be removed as soon as they were at journeys end. Armour and armament were being stripped to reduce weight as were seating and most other removable items. Apart from the crew all the men would make the journey on latex foam mattresses. All that was possible to allow the journey to be made in a single, uninterrupted flight was being done.

The bomb racks were being modified to carry a specially prepared three thousand kilo bomb. Other modifications were being made to the Herr Reichsleiter's specifications.

Hitler listened, nodding attentively. Bormann too listened,

153

though most of his attention was inward, upon his own plans for this flight.

The Reichsleiter's orders, which had been glossed over by the Luftwaffe Officer, included foamed latex to seat a dozen men in addition to the flight crews. There was also to be some space left to carry the art treasures diverted from Linz and for weapons and ammunition, all of which would help to smooth Major Schroeder's path in South America. It was well into the afternoon when the meeting finished and Hitler invited both Goebbels and Bormann to his sitting room for tea and cakes. Dr. Goebbels excused himself reluctantly. As Gauleiter for Berlin, Goebbel's duties above ground were inescapable.

Noting Goebbels' departure, Bormann gave an inward sigh of relief and also declined the invitation. He returned to his own office and ordered a car to meet him at the entrance to the Fuhrerbunker.

"I have to go out, Willi," he told Rattenhuber. "I shall be at Templehof looking over the Fuhrer's wonderful aeroplane."

"When shall I expect you back, Herr Reichsleiter?"

Bormann shook his head. "Before the air raids start – I hope." And with that he closed the door and made his way along the central passageway where a small crowd was gathered.

It was a motley assembly; grey haired pensioners, whey faced youngsters with dark eyes that had seen too much too soon. This was a sample of the 'Feldgendarmerie' or Battle Group Mohnke to give it its official title; a rag-tag crew of barrel

154

scrapings consisting of the remnants of the Hitler Youth and men too old to be conscripted into the regular army. Major General Mohnke had been charged with the dubious honor of defending the Citadel – the Government Quarter; Bormann wondered at Mohnke's private thoughts when he had first seen his force.

They awaited a brief decoration ceremony. Bormann would have given them no more than a passing thought if their presence had not reminded him of yet another small task. He put his head back round the office door,

"Willi?"

Rattenhuber looked up, surprised. "Sir?"

"Find out the time for tomorrow's award ceremony. "Phone Major Schroeder at my house on the Obersaltzburg and make sure that he can attend. Failing that, make it as soon as possible. Remind me to speak with the Fuhrer about him first."

EIGHTEEN

The car turned into Vosstrasse and picked a careful route through the ever present debris in front of the Reich Chancellery. Token attempts were being made to keep the street clear but, often, the pieces of masonry were too heavy to be moved by muscle power alone.

"Where to, Herr Reichsleiter?"

"Templehof. It is still possible to get there?"

"Oh yes, at the moment. In a few days – perhaps not."

Bormann grunted and sat back.

It was later than he expected when he reached the secured hangar at the Templehof aerodrome, the roads far worse than anticipated. Bormann had intended to make a complete inspection of the American aircraft that had crash landed near Wesel. In the event, he had to content himself with a short talk with the engineer in charge and a brief look into the hangar itself.

One wing had been removed from the fuselage and new sheets of duralumin were being riveted to the framework. The rest of the plane had already been burnished and a huge red cross adorned the side he could see.

On leaving, Bormann took with him such items as the

identities of the crew who had baled out or been killed in the crash. It was a pity they had burned their flight orders but there were other things like a British magazine, snapshots, the contents of the crews' pocket books. All might give up valuable information when collated and compared by those experts employed at the Dulag Luft; Evaluation Center West at Oberursel near Frankfurt-Am-Main.

Before the car took him from Templehof, Bormann spared the time to check the small, guarded warehouse set aside for the B24 cargo. Here were the oil paintings – canvasses stripped from their frames and rolled in oiled silk, small sculptures, gold and silver plate and solid gold and silver which would be used to buy fuel – probably in Portugal.

The bullion itself had been diverted at the beginning of April when the Nazi gold reserves had been moved from Bad Gastein to a secret salt mine. The Linz collections had been dealt with similarly earlier in the year, the bulk of the artwork ending its journey at various other salt mines near Saltzburg.

Dusk was falling when the Mercedes was halted by a pile of bricks and timber spilling into the main road. A gasthaus had taken a direct hit from shell fire and the rubble effectively blocked the way to all but pedestrians.

"Can you find a side road?"

"I'll turn back and pick up another way in," replied Marstein, the chauffeur.

It took an hour and a half to reach the center of Berlin only to find their way blocked once more. A stick of bombs exploded straight down the street in front of them, the nearest landing no more than two hundred metres in front of the car. The windscreen shattered immediately and when Marstein got out to investigate, he discovered that the radiator had been damaged by a long shell fragment; only the bulk of the engine had saved himself and the Reichsleiter from its being driven straight through the vehicle.

They were forced to proceed on foot, sheltering frequently from the steady rain of death from the Eighth Air Division overhead. It was well past midnight when Bormann turned out of the Vilhemplatz; the Chancellery buildings had received another direct hit from incendiaries and were burning furiously though what, Bormann wondered, there was left to burn was past understanding. They struggled along the cooler side of Vosstrasse.

Within the bunker, Bormann's anger at the Allies evaporated, turned to puzzlement. Perhaps the Reich had won the war while he had been outside dodging flying bricks! He pushed on through the men and women who were drinking beer, laughing and joking.

He tossed his old leather coat onto the desk in his office; he noticed several places where it had been singed. Inside the door to the Fuhrer's quarters, he was surprised to find Albert Speer; Speer disliked the Reichsleiter intensely, the mystery only deepened when the Minister smiled at him.

"Martin!" Unmistakably, it was Hitler's voice but stronger, full of good humor, Bormann saw him standing on the far side of the small crowd, he was holding a champagne glass. Wonderingly, he crossed to the Fuhrer's side. "Just as I predicted Martin," he grinned. "This war is not lost – not by Germany, anyway."

"Please, my Fuhrer. I have just returned, I've spent the last few hours ducking Allied bombs."

"Roosevelt is dead!"

"What?"

"Fate has removed the greatest war criminal of all time. Now we can go into the future with a sure step."

"Roosevelt dead. I can't believe it."

It seemed as though a brilliant light was shining in Bormann's head. Heedless, he took the champagne glass that a servant was offering to him, he slowly became aware that Hitler was still speaking.

"Bitte?" He offered.

"Los Alamos, Martin. Operation Blondi. I've had second thoughts about bombing the installation."

Bormann nodded. There was something important about Los Alamos, something of importance to him, what was it? But the fumes from the champagne on an empty stomach fogged the memory.

"It will end the war at a stroke, Martin. Without Roosevelt

to incite them, the British will conclude a treaty and the old races will triumph together. All I need is a good leader – someone who is still loyal to the Fatherland – and a few brave men."

"What do you wish these men to do?" Bormann smiled as he saw the opportunity he had waited for.

Hitler told him. There was a short silence before the Reichsleiter spoke again,

"The men are to hand, my Fuhrer. An exceptional leader and men, all trained, ready, waiting impatiently – you see how your Fate fits all the pieces together?"

Later, Bormann shook his head. To actually steal one of the American atom bombs and then to blast their own capital. The idea was...

NINETEEN

A little after five a.m., they crossed the Main river and Schroeder, at last allowed himself to relax a little. The Junkers tri motor – known affectionately as the Old Aunt Ju – had sounded rough to his untutored ears at first but, now, he had grown accustomed to the steady roar. The sound's somewhat tranquillising effect and the constant vibration eased his hard muscles until, to all outward appearances, the Major slept. He realised that this could also be explained by the brief cessation of stress after forty eight hours of wakefulness.

Whatever the reason, Schroeder welcomed the sensation and allowed his mind to stray back over the past few hours that had started with the telephone call he had received the previous evening.

The time was seven forty and Kurt was just getting ready to take dinner. He found little pleasure in the meal these days; he took all his meals alone, preferring not to allow the general relaxing of discipline that eating with his men would entail. This was contrary to the SS custom where fraternization was encouraged but his father had instilled into him the belief that an officer should keep himself apart from the enlisted men, should maintain his dignity in all situations. "Show neither fear nor favour," had been the old man's maxim.

The telephone call was from the direct line at the Berghof, just above Haus Goll. The operator had asked him to accept the message from Berlin personally which meant his driving up to the Fuhrer's residence.

He rang the kitchen staff, telling them to delay dinner and then ordered a truck for his own use. Schroeder shrugged into outdoor clothing and left the house.

Kurt was flagged down twice on the undulating approach road but the men, unrecognisable in their Alpine garments waved him through the check points with minimal delay, A few minutes later, he was glad of his deliberate choice of the heavy truck in preference to the staff Mercedes, it had studded tyres.

Rounding a bend, Schroeder was suddenly confronted by a squad of Schutzstaffel using the road for drill purposes; their grey-green field uniforms seemingly an inadequate protection against the chill wind of evening.

He stood on the brakes and slid to a halt to wait until the squad had cleared the road. Twenty minutes later, his papers inspected at both gate-houses, he entered the magnificent white, three-storey house and was escorted to the telephone office.

At least they hadn't bothered to keep the line open. The white-coated operator introduced himself as Scharfuhrer Most; he handed him the written message, chatted inconsequentially while Schroeder read it. The orders were simple. He was to return to Berlin with his ten best men. A plane would be waiting

162

for them at four the next morning at the Saltzburg airstrip. Reichsleiter Bormann's name and title were appended at the bottom.

Most took him along the terazzo passage towards the entrance hallway. As Schroeder turned to bid the man good night, he caught a glimpse of movement further along the corridor. A pale faced woman, brown haired and moderately pretty emerged from a doorway; she was wearing a silk dressing gown, plum colored. For a moment, their eyes met and then she was walking away from them.

Most saw the direction of his attention. "Fraulein Braun," he explained. "Another day and she might have travelled with you to Berlin. She intends to visit the Fuhrer though he would prefer her to stay here."

Schroeder nodded. A telephone operator, no doubt, would have many opportunities to overhear gossip; with times as they were, there would be few who would ignore a chance to glean such titbits of information which might prove useful somehow. At the least, she is safer here than in Berlin." Most nodded and the Major turned to go. "Heil Hitler." He saluted.

Within three weeks, the Herr Scharfuhrer was to remember those words. Hitler's beautiful retreat above Berchtesgaden was bombed into ruin on the twenty-fifth of April.

Schroeder, unaware of having dozed off, was awakened by the words: "A drink Herr Major?" Immediately he was back in the present, the old Prussian, Hoeckle, was standing there, a steaming mug in his hand. "Little more than lemon flavoured water sir, but it's hot."

He accepted the mug with a twitch of his lips which almost shaped a grateful smile. He sipped the scalding brew. "Thank you." Then, as a sort of excuse, he added "My eyes are tired."

"Of course Sir." Hoeckle agreed with tact.

The hot liquid served its purpose, nullifying his fatigue and Schroeder looked around at the men he had selected. He was disappointed that he had been ordered to bring only ten from the full compliment and wondered what would happen to the remainder.

The thought was a momentary one and quickly dismissed; war was more fickle than a woman, he did not doubt that Bormann would see to such. "The choice had been a difficult one because all twenty-six were excellent; these were the best, he assured himself though only future events would test his choice as being correct. In fact, he might never find out; their mission was a passive one after all, they would act only as guards – Germany was not at war with Paraguay.

The Junkers' seating arrangements were such that three men sat facing three more across the central aisle while the other four occupied seats facing the front of the aircraft. From where Kurt was sitting alone in a double seat at the rear, he could see the faces of but three of them. As he inspected the features of each one, their names and what he knew about them slid easily to mind.

164

LAST MISSION

Otto Hans Kiebel, a Berliner like himself; aged thirty with blonde hair and a red meaty complexion. Uncomplaining, perpetually happy with whatever fate dealt him, never questioned an order – obeying instinctively, He had served under Schroeder at Korosten on the Eastern Front and was the second man he had requested for transfer to this unit.

Alongside Otto sat Gunther Weber, another veteran of Korosten and Schroeder's first choice. He recalled the night he had asked Gunther to lead a patrol into Red held territory. The instructions were simple and clear: "Go in fast, get me a man – preferably an officer. Any trouble, get your men and yourself out. No heroics." Gunther, dark haired and dark eyed, thirty one years old at the time, affected a careless attitude which made his exploits appear incredibly easy. He had gone with a four man patrol and returned with – not one – but four Russian officers. Schroeder could hear his laughing words still echoing in his memory: "Sitting there, drinking like they were at home. I couldn't bring myself to break up the party." He had recommended the man for a medal after that, for a full debriefing had exposed the fact that Gunther had killed two guards silently and by hand to effect the kidnapping. He nodded to himself; one man who didn't take life too seriously was good for morale. How Reichleiter Bormann had complied with his request for these two men was beyond him. Almost, it had him believing in miracles.

The third, sitting closest to the window, was an enigma. All that Schroeder knew of him when the man came, was his name,

Oskar Fachinger – like the mineral water, His file said that he was twenty three and had fought on the Eastern front prior to joining the unit at the Obersaltzburg. One of Bormann's choices, Schroeder had included him in the final selection solely on his performance in training. He was a quiet, studious person with intensely blue eyes, hair of a light brown shade and little else to distinguish him from the crowd. In physical combat, Fachinger had bested everyone bar the huge Hoeckle and was without peer in knife work. His speech was heavily accented Schwyzerdütsch and, perhaps because he was self conscious over this, he rarely chose to enter the others' conversations. Schroeder, however, knew that his colleagues had developed a great respect for the fellow as a person as well as a fighter.

The plane's navigator chose that moment to appear at the head of the aisle. He walked back and squatted down next to Schroeder, speaking into the Major's ear.

"We should be touching down at Templehof in about an hour, weather permitting. I can't guarantee the quality of the landing, we had to dodge shell holes when we took off."

Schroeder nodded to show he understood.

"The accursed Americans are bombing the place during daylight now, they make holes faster than the work crews can fill them in, But, provided the RAF didn't hit the field last night, we should be all right. There's a camouflaged runway, when that gets hit it's only by accident."

"That bad?" Kurt was out of touch after his weeks in

166

Bavaria. "What's the Luftwaffe doing?"

"Bad? Worse than bad. It's those thousand bomber raids – the sky's black with them. Our lads do their best of course but they're short of planes and fuel."

Schroeder made a sympathetic noise. He recalled a shellshock victim in his ward at the Charité. He would whine like an animal and literally shake with fright at the sound of an aircraft overhead. "Let us know when to strap in?"

"Of course, Herr Major."

His consideration of the three men's pasts led his mind to look at his own. Schroeder found, to his surprise, that he could remember his wife and child without the expected hurt and anger; it was a subject he had schooled himself to steer clear of for many long months because of the emotions it stirred.

Anna had been a gentle soul and, like himself, interested in the classics. They had met in the reference library at Berlin Central and, by the time they discovered the disparity in their religious upbringing, it was too late to do more than ignore it and agree to differ. They had married in haste, not for the more usual reasons of unplanned pregnancy but because it seemed that each had waited their whole life to find the other. Kurt had proposed marriage suddenly, on impulse, fully expecting disappointment and literally amazed when Anna had accepted.

At this point, the couple's parents made strong objection to the union, objections that united Anna and Kurt more strongly than ever. Both sets of parents were, to a certain extent, estranged from their wayward children and the couple spent more and more time together, more often than not, searching for somewhere to live.

Eventually, they found a single floor apartment for rent at the top of a three storey house in Friedrichstrasse. Married, they transformed the dingy, poorly furnished apartment into a home where children could be raised. Their first child was already stirring in Anna's womb and was born a scant eight months after their marriage.

He was plump and pink and he was beautiful and, as his newly born features settled into more permanent lines, Anna could see her husband's face in the infant's more clearly every day.

Passionlessly, Schroeder remembered the day he had heard of the death of Anna and his five year old son. He had been on the Eastern front then; the news had been shattering, stunning, his world had crumbled about his ears.

Anna's letter telling him that their second child had been conceived, burned with the house. Fate had been merciful.

Schroeder had wandered off into the tree studded hills of the battle-field and had stayed away all night, lying on the damp turf, stricken with grief. He returned in the grey light of early morning, emptied of emotion, shaking with cold and fatigue. His superior officers had left him alone, aware of the news and understanding that this was a battle in which they had no part. They neither rebuked him for his absence nor offered

168

condolence; either would have been futile.

Remembering like this, the first time he had allowed himself to grieve made Kurt Schroeder come to know himself a little better. "The actions in which he had involved himself since then, the acts of so-called courage which had earned him commendations and medals, had been the product of a death wish – or so he had told himself until now. In fact, it was nothing so positive; it was because Schroeder had felt that there was nothing left to live for, the parallel death of Germany, served only to underscore the point.

It was apparent, with hindsight, that Bormann's visit to the Charité had marked a turning point in his mental convalescence; the Reichsleiter had thrown him a lifeline.

The sun was shining, albeit a watery one, as they approached the Berlin air corridor. Lining up on the Fuida beacon with his radio compass, the pilot passed over it and watched the indicator reverse itself through 180 degrees to point straight astern. Two hundred and eleven miles to go. Beneath the plane, the wounded countryside was swathed in foggy bandages; he hoped that the sun's warmth would have burned the mist away by the time they reached Templehof.

Schroeder watched Berlin appear ahead of them, he looked down at the city of his birth and at the devastation wrought by Allied blanket bombing. Buildings reached skyward in despair; sometimes no more than a single wall left standing, others exposed rooms and staircases like dolls' houses with the front opened; many of them had no right to still be erect.

Templehof came into sight as the Junkers banked to correct its direction on the glide path, ahead was the path through the middle of the ruined crater-scarred runways. Schroeder wondered how the pilot would pick his way through the cancerous growths of warfare. Templehof, once the world's finest airport, was nearing its end.

"Strap yourselves in please. The navigator stuck his head through the door to the flight deck. "We'll be going down in a minute."

Kurt fastened his own straps and tensed his muscles as he checked that the others were complying with the request. He heard the engine note change, watched the flaps start to extend and then the ground came up to meet them.

The pilot knew the aerodrome's layout like the back of his hand. He had flown for Lufthansa before the war and had taken off and landed here a thousand times. Confidently, he went through the checks, cleared the landing with control and dropped down along the center line of the runway. He expelled an unconscious breath of relief as the main landing gear touched the surface, adjusted the flaps, cut engine speed. Looking across at the navigator, he grinned, gave a one handed thumbs-up. "Here we are…"

The ground crew had been at work all night, filling in and compounding the bomb damage. Had the Junkers weighed a little less than its 4000 plus kilos or if there had been perhaps only five or six passengers, the weak spot might have held. The point was academic. At a speed slightly above seventy knots the starboard gear hit a hastily patched area of runway; the wheel sank half a metre, up to its axle.

At that speed, the struts buckled like straws and the main pillar sheared off. The plane swung in a tight arc, tilting over and burying its wing in the soft turf. It careered sixty metres before coming to a bone jolting stop.

The pilot and navigator were uninjured although shaken up. The pilot immediately clambered aft to check on his passengers. Schroeder was the first to recover his wits and, as always in a crisis, his judgment was cool and dispassionate.

"Out. Everybody get out." He shouted, releasing the safety webbing.

The pilot kicked the door out, adding his voice to the Major's. "Outside. Don't worry about the drop, get away from the aircraft as fast as you can."

One by one, the badly shaken occupants filed up the canted deck past Schroeder and the pilot and climbed through the door. When the last man had dropped to the ground, Schroeder glanced swiftly along the interior. A passenger was still in his seat, his head hanging at an unlikely angle.

"Dead, Major. Broken neck. We should go quickly, before she explodes". They scrambled through the door and slid across the swell of the fuselage to reach the ground.

Schroeder was annoyed, not with the accident or the death

but with himself. He could not recall the dead man's name.

Several vehicles came racing up, churning furrows in the wet grass as Kurt sprinted towards his men, most of them were fire tenders. There was no doubt as to their efficiency; men were leaping from the tenders before they had come to a stop, hoses appeared as if with some vast sleight of hand and in moments rather than minutes, were discharging.

There was little time allowed to consider the fire details' technique. A voice spoke behind him. "Major Schroeder, your transport, Sir." Minutes later, Schroeder and his team – all but one – were at the far side of the airfield, nearing a hanger liberally covered with 88 millimetre anti-aircraft guns. The Leutnant who had accompanied them spoke again. "Your men are to remain here, Herr Major; they will be billeted in the hanger for the time being. My orders are to get you to the Fuhrerbunker as quickly as possible."

Schroeder nodded but ordered the driver to halt when the following truck stopped. He had just remembered the dead man's name; it was Klaus Haller, he wanted to give the news to the others, personally.

"I shall not be long." He spoke curtly to the young Leutnant. He watched as the Major strode towards the truck which was carrying the nine men.

"Everyone all right?" He asked.

"Yes Sir," replied Weber, "except for Otto here, I think his ankle's broken; did it when he jumped from the plane."

172

Schroeder began a curse then, remembering himself, spoke to Kiebel "I recall that your wife lives here in Berlin?" Kiebel nodded. "If I did not know better, I would think you planned this." Chuckles ran the length of the truck. "I'll arrange medical care but I think that your war is finished."

He continued. "I have also to tell you that Haller was killed in the landing. The best I can arrange.for him is a funeral, I'm afraid. The rest of you will stay here until I return. I don't know how long that will be but, until then, Feldwebel Hoeckle will be in charge."

"Sir."

Schroeder saluted and returned to the lead vehicle, climbing in and apologised to the waiting Leutnant.

The journey to the Fuhrerbunker was tedious and lengthy. When Schroeder was last in Berlin, he had then thought that conditions could not have deteriorated any further; in this he was obviously wrong. In all but the major streets rubble from the ruined buildings all but blocked the way; pathways had been cleared, though most were only wide enough for two pedestrians to pass.

Organisation Todt vehicles were being loaded with debris by women and old men supervised by Arbeitfuhrers.

At least, the important roads to the airport and other public services were being kept clear. Apart from a detour along Haupt Strasse and Potsdamer Strasse to avoid an impossible Braunauer Strasse the driver was able to keep moving, if slowly.

The vehicle drew up at last and Schroeder stepped down, securing his small pack of clothing and personal items before saluting the young Leutnant.

At the entrance to the Fuhrerbunker, Schroeder found himself face to face with an Obersturmbanfuhrer who had been invisible until he entered. He gave the stiff armed salute, it was returned by the SS Officer, immaculate in silver and black. The SS Colonel smiled laconically.

"You are…?"

"Major Schroeder, Sir", Schroeder straightened the Waffenrock uniform while the other checked a clipboard of expected visitors.

"Ah – the Major. Herr Reichsleiter Bormann expects to see you before the award ceremony. May I extend my own congratulations Herr Major? The Knight's Cross is a singular achievement." Schroeder bowed slightly. "Will you follow me?"

Well, thought Schroeder, at least we shall have that over with very shortly. If only the Herr Reichsleiter would clear up a few other matters.

As these thoughts ran through his mind, Schroeder was being guided through damp concrete corridors and down flights of steps. He had never seen so many SS Officers in one place and all of them from Liebstandarte Adolf Hitler, the Fuhrer's personal bodyguard.

Eventually, his guide halted before a door no different from any other. Opening the door, they passed into a small but busy
174

telephone office: across this was a second door at which the officer knocked.

A muffled voice bade them enter.

"Herr Major Schroeder," announced the Obersturmbannfuhrer, gesturing Schroeder past and then closing the door behind him.

Bormann's face seemed greyer, more lined than the last time they had met. Nevertheless, he got to his feet and shook Schroeder's hand with vigour.

"Sit down Kurt." He indicated a chair. "Sit down, I am told that your pilot made rather a rough landing. You're all right?"

"I've had worse, Sir. However…" He went on to tell Bormann about Haller and Kiebel. "Can we get a plane through to Obersaltzburg, do you think?"

Bormann looked thoughtful, steepling his fingers and frowning. "I'm afraid not. Time is now of the essence, we shall have to find some other way to make up the complement.

"What is the time? Nearly nine forty five. Have you eaten yet?"

Schroeder shook his head.

"Then do so now, the ceremony is to take place at ten thirty and I am not able to brief you at the moment. You will find that the plans we spoke of are changed, the Fuhrer has conceived something far more brilliant than anything you or I could have dreamed of. There are seventeen men that our Fuhrer wishes to honor, he will speak privately with you after the awards are made. Question nothing at that time; he is far too busy to bother with details. In any case, I am sure that I have covered most of them. You will find the mission you are to fulfil – awe inspiring; it is best that you hear it first from the Fuhrer's own lips."

A phone rang on Bormann's desk. "Excuse me." He lifted the phone, listened for a few seconds, replaced it. "That was the Fuhrer's adjutant, he wishes to see me now. Until ten thirty, Herr Major."

Washed and with a meager breakfast inside him, Schroeder asked directions to where the awards would be made, A young, white uniformed member of the Liebstandarte barely sixteen, Schroeder guessed, took him to a small room where a number of other officers waited.

Apart from himself, Schroeder saw only one other field grey uniform, the rest wore either the black of the SS or the blue of the Luftwaffe Major who acknowledged his presence with a curt nod. The group waited in silence, self conscious shuffling betraying the tension that all seemed to feel. The minutes grew longer and longer and when, at a quarter before eleven, the door opened; almost everybody jumped at the sudden noise.

There were three rows of seats and the waiting men filed out, with the front row leaving first, to follow the Officer who had beckoned them to follow him. The second row passed in front of Schroeder and, with a slight shock of surprise, he recognised one of the SS – Dietrich – but a Dietrich subtly changed from the man he'd known; now, he wore the more self

176

assured – almost insolent – expression common to members of the Schutztaffel, regardless of rank. There was no mistake, however; this was the Dietrich who had nearly killed himself – or Schroeder – a few weeks earlier on the Obersaltzburg.

They marched into another room, slightly larger than the previous one and furnished more comfortably. Schroeder guessed that they might be in Hitler's private suite. The only decoration was a portrait of Frederick the Great.

Without conscious effort, the awards group made up two ranks and came to attention. Two Generals were already present together with a Fieldmarshall and an Obergruppenfuhrer SS and several lesser ranking officers. Moments later, Reichsleiter Bormann came in followed by Reichsmarshall Goering and Propaganda Minister Joseph Goebbels. They looked over the assembled ranks and apparently satisfied, Bormann crossed to another door and tapped lightly.

Hermann had already returned to his place when the door opened and the most powerful man in Germany entered.

The Fuhrer was dressed in a grey double-breasted coat with the German eagle on the left sleeve. He wore no hat, there was no need of insignia to spell out to everyone present who this man was. The Fuhrer did not look well, he seemed somehow shrunken inside the greatcoat, yet Hitler's personal presence reached out and touched every officer there. Schroeder felt the impact like a physical blow; it caused him to stand straighter, grow a centimetre taller.

"Gentlemen." Again Hitler's voice caused a stiffening of backs. "Today, we are here to honor our heroes. It gives me great pleasure to award, these tokens of Germany's esteem. I do not see your ranks, I see only the one thing that is common to you all – heroes of the Reich.

He turned to Bormann and whispered something; Bormann nodded and called:

"Hauptman Albrecht. For bravery in the field, the Iron Cross First Class." The Officer stepped forward, snapped his heels and saluted.

"Heil Hitler."

The Fuhrer fastened the ribbon about the man's neck and whispered some private commendation. He shook the Officer's hand and smiled. The Officer returned to his place in the line.

This pattern was repeated twice more and then a third time with Dietrich who received the Iron Cross Second Class and a wound badge. Bormann then handed a small package to Hitler who unwrapped and held up a SS ceremonial dagger beautifully decorated with oak leaves and acorns worked in silver. The Fuhrer spoke louder this time, so all could hear.

"Your Uncle sent you this gift with these words, "do not fail your Fuhrer." I repeat his message and add that where Sep has faltered, you can redeem the name of your family. Make it shine with honor, Obersturmfuhrer."

When Schroeder's name was called, Bormann again said something to Hitler in a low voice.

"So then, this is the immortal Major Schroeder," Hitler began. "This time it is the Ritter Kreuz I am presenting. I am certain that you will soon have the oak leaves and swords to add to it."

Schroeder was at a loss for something to say, so he kept his silence; smiling slightly, he bowed and returned to his place in the rank.

A little later, the ceremony was over and they began to disperse. "Major Schroeder." Said Bormann. "Remain here please." Schroeder stood against the wall as first the heroes filed out and, then some of the onlookers including Goebbels and Goering who left last of all.

Finally, there were six of them left and Reichsleiter Bormann decided to introduce the others to Schroeder. He found himself shaking hands with Fieldmarshall Keitel, Chief of OKW, Obergruppenfuhrer Fegelein, General Oberst Koller – the Luftwaffe Chief of Staff together with a Luftwaffe Oberstleutnant Reinicke who Schroeder guessed was a lot older than he appeared at first glance. Fegelein, Schroeder knew, might someday become Hitler's brother-in-law for his wife was the sister of Eva Braun.

Scarcely had Schroeder got the names fixed in his memory when Keitel ushered them from the room and across the corridor to a conference room. Most of the wall space here was taken up with maps of Europe to different scales; at both ends were map tables carrying more charts, maps, diagrams and other

179

miscellanea. The Fuhrer stood at one of these now and the others grouped themselves around the other three sides.

"Gentlemen," he started, his voice quiet, "many are the operations that have been born in this room and launched upon the Ausland with terrible success. But never has there been an operation which could have so great an effect on Germany's future as the one which will be outlined today,

"I am not proud to say that, at this moment, there are many who speak as defeatists." Hitler looked up, thrust his hands deeper into the coat pockets. His eyes blazed. "I shall never give up. This operation will turn the tide of war in our favour; it has had to be held back until now – until the warmonger Roosevelt was dead. In this way, it will have its greatest impact."

Several of the men were used to the Fuhrer in this vein, his 'historic decision' mood, and remained unimpressed. Schroeder, however, had never felt Hitler's power at such close quarters before; the effect was similar to the feelings created at a rally or when the Fuhrer used to address the army earlier in the war but it was magnified a hundredfold, a thousandfold. Almost, the Major was hypnotised by those feverish eyes.

"This will crack the Alliance so wide open that it can never be patched up again. England will see the Americans for what they are – bourgeois, with neither honor nor tradition. The British will join with us against the common foe, the Russians."

For the first time since Hermann had warned him of a change in plans, Schroeder suspected that Paraguay was not to be

180

their destination and that something far more dramatic was in the offing.

Hitler continued. "When I first heard the news that the Americans had started to test a totally new weapon, it was my intention to destroy the manufacturing plants immediately so that our own idle scientists could be given enough time to equip our arsenals with similar weapons.

"However, the death of their president has played into our hands. We – or rather, you – Major Schroeder, will steal one of these bombs and use it to bring about the reaction I mentioned earlier."

Schroeder nodded. The idea certainly had merit.

"Gentlemen, I am assured that an atomic bomb will destroy a complete city."

"One bomb!" Breathed Schroeder, incredulously.

"Yes, Herr Major. A single bomb. The city that will be destroyed is Washington."

There was a pause while the Fuhrer waited for the name to sink in. A few moments and then there was a series of short gasps quickly terminated by a brief round of applause, led by Reichsleiter Bormann.

The Fuhrer silenced them with a glance. "I have put the concept to the Reichsleiter," he nodded to Bormann and then towards Koller, "and to General Koller who have worked out the details. I think that the operation itself is quite as brilliant as the original idea.

"General Koller will now take you through the operation stage by stage."

All things considered, Schroeder was pleased with what he had heard. The plan could be made to work, he was certain. When he had asked pertinent questions at the end of Koller's discourse, he had received crisp answers; not the evasiveness that went with so many of the half thought out.missions he had been involved with. The fact that there was a local organisation with an inside man at this Los Alamos pushed the operation from the far fetched to the distinctly possible.

Photographs of the plant interiors were freely available, well drawn maps had been prepared. The plans had been drawn up with such thoroughness; it put Schroeder in mind of a film-script.

It was while the Major was lost in these thoughts that he felt a hand on his shoulder. Looking round, he found the Fuhrer regarding him with those penetrating eyes. "Would you come over here Major? I wish to speak with you."

Schroeder bowed and followed Hitler to the far end of the conference room where they would not be overheard. Hitler turned and looked him straight in the eyes.

"The Reichsleiter selected you to lead this mission for Germany, Herr Major; a mission more important than any that have gone before. Tell me please, why I should trust you. What is it that makes Martin trust in your abilities? And how can you assure me that you will not let me down like the Generals I have had to rely on in the past?"

182

Schroeder did not know what he could say, yet he had to answer somehow – and convincingly. Suddenly, inspired, he remembered the oath that every individual in the armed forces had taken upon the death of President Hindenberg in 1934. He repeated this now.

"I swear by God this holy oath, to obey unquestioningly Adolf Hitler, the supreme military leader, Fuhrer of the German Reich and its people and to serve as a brave soldier even unto death." He paused a second, then added; "There can be no greater thing that I can promise, my Fuhrer."

Hitler was obviously delighted with his response, He nodded, took Schroeder's hand and shook it. "Well said, Major. Martin convinced me of his own faith in you and now I can see why. From this moment you are promoted to Oberst – though you will have to earn your new rank; you understand? Failure cannot be tolerated." The Fuhrer smiled, diluting the severity of his words. "Tell me Herr Oberst, why did you not join the Schutztafel?"

"Family tradition, Sir." Answered Schroeder without hesitation. "All of my family has fought with the Wehrmacht. Even so, my honor is no less my loyalty, my Fuhrer."

Hitler laughed openly this time; to have the SS motto quoted to him on top of the Wehrmacht oath. "I'm certain it is not Oberst. Fine words but remember, you still have to prove them to me.

"Next week is my birthday. I would like news of your success to be my greatest birthday present."

Bormann chose that moment to approach, clearing his throat as he came. "There is one small matter that the Major has probably not mentioned yet, my Fuhrer."

"I see. The Herr Oberst has mentioned nothing, what is it?"

"Two of the men he has trained and brought with him were injured on the way here; one, in fact, was killed, There is not sufficient time to replace them with others from his group since the schedule calls for the aircraft to leave early tomorrow morning."

"This is unfortunate but it is not a problem. Three hours ago, we had a room full of heroes, did we not?" Do you still have the list of names?"

Bormann did and gave it to the Fuhrer.

"Ring for Albrecht, will you?" Hitler held the paper close and peered at the names. When the Adjutant arrived, Hitler spoke to him at some length, pointing at names on the list, while Bormann turned to Schroeder.

"I gather you have just been promoted. Allow me to offer my congratulations, Herr Oberst. So then Kurt; what do you think of the Fuhrer's plans?"

Schroeder was enthused with the prospect; it showed in his face and manner. "If it means that this war will be ended, it is nothing short of brilliant."

184

Hitler, who had been conversing with Koller, broke off as Bormann's brother, Albrecht returned with two officers in the SS black. He brought them across to Schroeder and Bormann.

"Here are your two heroes. Herr Oberst. Martin, will you introduce them?"

Bormann did as he was asked. "Herr Oberst, may I present Hauptsturmfuhrer Bergerud and also, Obersturmfuhrer Dietrich. Gentlemen, Herr Oberst Schroeder." Bormann lifted a quizzical eyebrow in Schroeder's direction. Dietrich was familiar to both of them.

Hitler spoke once more. "I have followed the careers of both these gentlemen with interest, Herr Oberst; it is why I chose them to accompany you. The Hauptsturmfuhrer has fought with the 28th Panzer Grenadiers under Stormbanfuhrer Degrelle and distinguished himself on many occasions. Dietrich here," Schroeder noted the use of his surname rather than rank, "is with my own Liebstandarte; he knows why I take such an interest. These are the Officers who will share in the rising…" and here, he used Schroeder's own word, "… of the *Phoenix* with you."

TWENTY

Sunday and Paul was exhausted.

Running several gangs of electricians had its problems, not the least of these being the long hours and early starts. It was six am, and his internal clock had awakened him half an hour before with the feeling that he had forgotten something important.

At first, Paul assumed, that it was the unaccustomed luxury of not having to get up and he tried to relax, to doze off once more – This was the first Sunday – the first day, in fact, that he had had off in a month.

He had just about reconciled himself to the fact that he was not going to fall asleep when the thought emerged and woke him fully: Mai! She had not telephoned, even with his being out on the site and unable to be reached, there had been no message taken by the switchboard for over a month. Normally, if Paul was unable to ring her then his sister would telephone to let him know that she and his parents were okay,

Paul got up, rubbing his bristly chin ruminatively. What had Carl said? She had gone to see his cousin or something – a difficult pregnancy. Even if the baby had not been born yet, there was no reason why she should not have called.

Reaching a decision, Paul felt for his slippers while putting on an old bath-robe. In the kitchen, he threw the coffee pot on the stove, switched it on and then dialled long distance.

At this early hour on a Sunday, the call went through quickly. It rang a long time before Carl's voice answered.

"Hello." His voice betrayed a yawn.

"Carl. Paul here."

"Hello Paul. How are you?" The tone was more awake; Paul thought to detect a hint of wariness.

"Fine Carl. How about you and Mai?"

"Fine. We are both fine."

The tone seemed false and Paul decided to take the bull by the horns. "I'd like to speak to my sister."

There was a pause, "But she is still asleep."

"It's urgent. I want to speak to Mai, now."

The pause was long – very long. He thought the connection might have broken,

"You still there Carl?"

"Er, yes. There is no easy way I can tell you Paul."

"Tell me what?"

On the stove, the coffee was boiling furiously, unheard.

"She has left me Paul. Mai has walked out on me. For good, she said."

"Why would she do that?"

Paul could almost imagine Carl's look of puzzlement.

"I cannot say."

"Was this before or after the baby was born?"

"Baby? Oh, the baby. After she came back. A few days ago, else I would have called you." Carl's voice took on a plaintiff whine. "I haven't got over it yet Paul. I – I was very -fond of her. Do you think maybe she met someone else while she was up there?"

Paul bit his lip. It wasn't like Mai to walk out like that, she had never been secretive or devious – and she hadn't rung him, Paul.

"Do Mama and Papa know?"

"I couldn't bring myself to tell them, it would upset them so."

Paul was at a loss; twice he opened his mouth to say something and twice thought better of it. How did he finish this conversation?

Carl solved his problem. "Paul," he said anxiously, "this won't affect things between you and me will it?"

"Well, of course not. We'll still be friends unless there's something you haven't told me."

"That too, certainly but I meant what we're doing for the Cause."

"I can't think about that at the moment Carl. I'll be in touch." He slammed the receiver down; angry that his brother-in-law should bring up the matter at such a time.

Paul sat down and scalded his tongue with the coffee. Two cups later, he rang Susan.

"Could I come round to see you? I've got a bit of a problem, you're the only one I can talk to about it."

"Come right away. You'll probably find me in my rags – I'm not much of a glamour puss on a Sunday I'm afraid."

"What? Oh, don't worry about that. Fifteen minutes?"

"Fine."

"Better make it twenty, I still have to shave."

Susan tilted her mouth up to be kissed as Paul came into the lobby He touched her lips perfunctorily and went through into the lounge of the women's hostel.

"You know about my sister," he started as soon as they'd sat down, "back in Des Moines. Usually one of us rings the other every week or so – well, it's been over a month now and I haven't heard from her."

"You were up there on your last weekend off."

"I know, she wasn't there then either. My brother in law told me she was away helping some pregnant relative of his that I'd never heard of before."

"Well then, there you are."

"But, even so, she'd have called; left a message. Anyway, I spoke to Carl not an hour ago; said she'd left him – run away."

"Just a minute." Susan got up and crossed to an old leather chair. She felt between the cushion and the arm and brought out a small hip flask.

"I don't think Lois will begrudge you a shot."

Paul took it, his hand shaking. "Thanks." He took a

mouthful. Another. "Emergencies?" He asked, holding up the flat bottle,

"Medical emergencies only. Lois has quite a few."

Paul smiled; the joke had relieved his tension a little.

"You don't believe him, this Carl?" Susan asked, seating herself again, "You think he's thrown her out?"

Paul raised his shoulders, dropped them dispiritedly. "I hadn't really thought. Could be. But she hasn't rung me, don't you see? That's what has me worried."

"Well look, I know you two are close. Why don't you go up there yourself, now, and sort it out, I know I'd want to if I had a brother or sister."

"I'm back on duty at five in the morning. I need two days to get there and back.

"So take an extra day. You're a civilian, not a soldier."

"I can't do that."

"Of course you can. I'll have a word with Personnel for you; I'll not promise you'll get paid, but you won't get fired. All I have to say is that you had to go home for compassionate reasons. They're a lot easier on personal travel since last November when Security let up a bit."

"You'd do that?"

"Certainly."

Paul reached across and squeezed Susan's hand.

"You can do better than that, can't you?"

Smiling, he kissed her lengthily. "You know Sue; you're the

best thing that's happened in a long while. When I get back, I'll bring you a present. Maybe we'll get drunk and who knows…"

"Hey, hold it there! What's this 'who knows'?"

Paul grinned wickedly and gave Susan's bottom a playful slap as he left.

It was getting quite dark when Paul pulled into the kerb outside the house; there were lights in two of the windows. He slammed the door and ran quickly up the steps. The lights were misleading, the door was locked and nobody came in answer to his knocking.

Looking to right and left to make sure no one was watching, he reached up and felt along the narrow ledge above the door lintel. It was still there, a spare key, rusty from long exposure. The key fitted and turned stiffly in the lock.

The house smelled empty and unused. An aroma of stale cigar smoke and booze hung heavily on the air. Across the hall, the sitting room was ajar; a wedge of light splashed across the floor and lit the bottom of the stairs. Inside, the overhead lamp cast a baleful yellow radiance on the dusty table littered with empty schnapps bottles and full ash-trays.

It was easy to see that Mai hadn't been around for some time, thought Paul, remembering the pride she took in a clean and tidy home. Always flicking a duster here, a long handled cobweb broom there; it was as though her invisible presence was looking over his shoulder with disapproval at the unkempt scene.

The kitchen was cluttered with dirty dishes and cutlery and

empty food cans, some of them already growing mold. He backed out and, one by one, opened doors into other rooms – all of them in need of a good airing.

Stopping for a moment at the door to the cellar, he considered checking Carl's den but decided to look around the bedrooms first.

Like those downstairs, the first three rooms smelled musty. They were empty of course and Paul then went into the large main bedroom. He screwed up his nose in distaste at the pile of dirty clothes which had been carelessly tossed on a chair and overflowed on to the floor. He stepped over the garments and tried the doors to the large wardrobe. They opened with a faint creek of un-oiled hinges; inside there were a number of dresses that Mai used regularly for walking out. Handbags and shoes lined the bottom shelf, tidy stacks of feminine underwear filled two more.

Closing the wardrobe, Paul went back downstairs in a thoughtful mood. That Mai had left with no more clothing than what she stood up in was uncharacteristic, even if – as Susan had suggested – Carl had thrown her out, it seemed unlikely that he would not have let her pack a bag. Perhaps she had not come back from – where was it? He frowned, trying to remember, going into the living-room and absently going to the sideboard for a drink.

Milwaukee. That was the place. Paul remembered Carl bluffly serving him with food and telling him about Mai going

192

off to Milwaukee. The sideboard was empty of drink; Paul shook his head in annoyance and went back into the hall to the head of the cellar steps. He knew where Carl kept his 'put by' drinks.

It was extremely dark beyond the doorway and he had to descend the three top steps before his groping fingers located the light switch, He had never understood why the electrician had put it there, if it had been himself… Paul halted the thought with a rueful grin and went on down.

Startled by the light and the footsteps, the rat had scurried away from its grisly banquet and was safely hidden beneath a bench when Paul came in. Sitting there, it watched with tiny pink eyes, cleaning its fur with quick agile motions.

There was an almost full bottle of spirits leaning against the back of the chair where Paul usually sat when he came here. The wall cupboard where Carl kept his supply hung open and bare, his brother in law must have drunk his way through every drop of alcohol in the house except the one he now held.

Paul flopped down into the chair and wiped the neck of the bottle on his shirt cuff. Lifting his feet off the floor, he crooked them over the arm and tilted the bottle up, taking a small mouthful letting it trickle down his throat. His gaze roamed around the cellar while he wondered where Carl might have gone and for how long.

The picture of the Fuhrer was covered, as usual, with a piece of old bed linen; Carl uncovered it only when Paul or some sympathiser with the Nazi cause joined him. The various worktops were still littered with the dozens of little jobs that Carl had started and not completed: a three-legged stool with one leg broken, a baby's cradle that had been lying there since Mai's miscarriage almost three years ago.

There was something new over by the far wall, a big packing case that Carl was either dismantling for second hand lumber or was converting to some other use. Paul got up to take a look and discovered what was behind the box.

Six or seven seconds passed while his brain refused to believe what his eyes registered. Finally, a strangled moan escaped him and he sank to his knees.

It was the glint of gold that had attracted his gaze, a gold wedding ring. It wasn't the ring that had caused Paul to cry out though, it was the skeletal fingers that protruded stiffly from the dirt floor and around one of which the wedding band was fitted.

For long minutes, Paul stared in horrible fascination at the white bones which seemed to beckon him.

Tears streamed down his cheeks. Certain as to what he would find, Paul scratched at the soil, it was soft and moved easily. He discovered the head and hair a second before his lungs drew in the terrible smell of decay. It had been in the air all the time, he realised, although diluted and masked by the stale odors of food and smoke.

He steeled himself and forced unwilling hands to uncover more of the head. The bloated features were unrecognisable but the fair hair with its remembered fringe was. As he knew

194

already, it was Mai and... He swiftly covered her up again. Just as he was climbing to his feet and still bending over, Paul felt his stomach contract and throw up. There was nothing he could do; his body was entirely out of control, gripped in one spasm after another until there was nothing left to vomit. Even then, he was racked with dry retches for long minutes. Finally, he straightened up, his stomach and chest sore and bruised from the unfamiliar exercise.

The smell and taste of bile was strong, regurgitated food particles were lodged in his nose and mouth. The nearest thing was the bottle of schnapps still standing on the corner of the packing case; Paul took it and used the spirit as a mouthwash and then blew his nose vigorously several times. This failed to remove the smell completely but was good enough for the time being.

Paul went back to the chair where the grave was hidden from view by the packing case and upended the bottle. No short swallows now; he drank the raw liquor down until the bottle was empty.

Later, Paul had lost track of time and may have been asleep but he heard the street door open and slam shut. A voice followed quickly.

"Paul! Can that be you boy? Is that your new car outside?"

Hard leather soles walked the length of the tiled hallway.

"Paul, where are you? Is it you, no?"

"I'm down here. Carl." A stranger spoke the words.

"What you doing down there, hey? Come up here in the sitting room. I have some bottles here."

Paul remained in the chair, ignoring the other's words. Eventually, Carl descended the stair with, heavy steps. He came in, narrowed eyes surveying the cellar's confines. His nose twitched.

"What's the smell, Paul? You been sick or something?" Carl bustled about, ignoring Paul's silence. Eventually, he contrived to move to a position where he could see behind the packing case; he looked back at Paul who was watching him intently.

"Now don't make the wrong connections Paul."

"Carl..."

"All right, I lied to you, I'm sorry. Mai, she had a heart attack, I didn't know what to do. I couldn't call the doctor, he would have reported me." Carl walked towards Paul, his arms outstretched, pleading for understanding. "I would have been interned Paul, the Cause would have been finished."

Paul never heard what Carl said. His words were no more than a distracting drone. When the drone ended he acted without thinking. He launched himself from the depths of the armchair straight at his brother in law, his fingers fastened like steel bands round the bigger man's throat. The rush sent Carl stumbling backwards until his shoulders came up against a wall and stopped him. He growled with surprise and struck upwards with both hands fisted together.

The blow knocked Paul's hands away and carried on

upwards to take him beneath the chin. He staggered back, bemused for a second. A second, no longer; he was young, strong and filled with anger; he came forward again, swinging his fists. One struck Carl behind the ear, the other glanced off an upraised arm.

Paul threw punches from all directions. There was nothing scientific about it, just a grim determination to punish the man who had desecrated his sister by hiding her corpse in unhallowed ground.

Paul's fists were powerful. Carl was neither as fit nor as swift as he had once been and the blows made him stagger as each one landed. Again, the bigger man stumbled, flailing his arms to regain his balance; somehow, a hand caught at Paul's shirt and suddenly, Carl had his hands on Paul's neck. He began to squeeze, his thumbs on the windpipe; the pressure increased as Paul's punches lost their force.

Locked together they lurched and reeled across the cellar floor, Carl intent on strangling the other. Paul could feel his head beginning to spin, his vision becoming fogged. Desperately, he tried to break the grip but failed. His foot caught against something on the floor and both men fell over, Carl uppermost, his hands still squeezing, squeezing. They had fallen across a bench; Paul's spine was pinned painfully across the hard edge.

The pain had a momentary effect, clearing his mind for a few brief moments. His hands, groping for some leverage to pull himself to his feet, touched something cold and hard and heavy.

197

Unthinking, he grasped it and swung it at Carl's head with all the force he could muster.

Paul's hand had found an empty bottle, it fractured when it hit Carl's head, making him release Paul and stagger backward. It was a short respite, a quick shake of his head and Carl came in again.

Paul was weak from lack of air, he had hardly enough strength to swing the bottle but he tried anyway. It came up, the sharp corners glinting in the light. Carl saw but could not stop in time,

The jagged end caught Carl in the neck, his own momentum thrusting it home. Carl collapsed on top of Paul, blood flooding across his shirt. Carl slid off, sinking to his knees in an attitude almost of prayer. Blood ran from the lacerations beneath his chin; he opened his mouth to speak but blood, not words, escaped.

With a sob, Paul pushed himself away from the bench and Carl, robbed of support, fell forward, his face only inches from Mai's grave. Paul made the stairs in a rush, stumbling along the hallway and outside.

He pulled into the kerb some miles away. His hands were shaking so much that driving the car was a danger. The cigars he'd bought were still on the dash where he'd tossed them – what seemed like days ago.

The fourth match struck with a flare that startled him and he got the cigar started. He sucked the smoke deep into his lungs, it

198

was like a fist hitting him beneath the heart, Paul coughed until his eyes watered; it had been a week since his last cigar. He drew on it again, more cautiously this time and then exhaled slowly.

When his heartbeat had slowed and his hands ceased to have a will of their own, Paul reviewed the recent events with a measure of detachment. The facts were few but clear: Mai was dead, Mai had been avenged; the only thing left was to decide what to do. In his hurry to leave the house, he had forgotten that his shirt was stained with blood; he needed to change and to get washed up. The solution, of course, was simple; his parent's home was only another two or three miles away, Papa was smaller than himself but that wouldn't matter.

Still smoking, Paul got out and went round to the trunk. He opened it and got an old gabardine raincoat out; he had kept it there, together with gumboots since the springtime storms and the flash floods they brought. He put the coat on then got back behind the wheel to drive to his old home.

For a moment, Paul thought that he had taken a wrong turning but there had been no mistake. The house was boarded up; the doors, the windows including those upstairs. "What had happened here? Fleeting thoughts of Mama and Papa, dead and rotting like Mai skipped before his mind's eye but he thrust these away and went round to a neighbour's.

He knocked twice and the door opened slightly. A pinched face peered out over a security chain.

"Okay, what do you want?"

Paul did not recognise the sharp, middle-aged features of the woman. It was not surprising though; people were always coming and going in this neighbourhood.

"I wanted to see the Webbs, next door. Can you tell me where they've moved to?"

"Gone where all filthy German's should go, young man." Her voice was scratchy and thin, like an old phonograph record. "Been taken to an internment camp, that's where. Thought they'd got away with it, didn't they? Keeping quiet and using an American name but the Government got 'em in the end. They want to drop 'em off over Berlin with all them bombs – back where they come from."

Paul backed away from virulent hate spitting through the gap in the door. Turning back to his car he resigned himself to his new status: alone, no family, no ties, no home.

Fifty miles south of Des Moines, he realised that he had been wrong. He did have ties and a home; both of them were in New Mexico, at the 'Hill.'

It was a long time before the rat left its hiding place; the violence had thoroughly frightened it but everything had been quiet for a long time now.

Cautiously, it raised its head and sniffed. There was that scent again; rich, salty. Tentatively, it pattered out onto the floor.

The blood was sweet and thick but failed to fully satisfy its hunger. The rat moved closer, started to chew. The meat was still warm.

TWENTY ONE

Schroeder stopped short and looked from the aircraft to Reinicke and back again. "Just what is that?"

Reinicke grinned, "That's an Allied B24 Liberator, formerly owned and run by the 389th. Bombardment Group of the Eighth Air Force."

"I had the idea we'd be using a B17, a Flying Fortress."

"Don't let this old girl's appearance deceive you. She was one of the Sky Scorpions. Saw action in Africa in '43 and Europe the rest of the time. They're tough, Oberst, believe me; you should hear some of the stories I've been told."

"Where did you get hold of it?"

"The Wesel area. Her crew was making a supply run on March 24th to their ground troops. We got the whole story from one of the crew at the Dulagluft: they were supposed to stay on the east side of the Rhine but a navigator seems to have erred in his calculations, four planes crossed over to the west side. They were flying low, tail heavy with the weight they were carrying."

Reinicke chuckled again. "Battlin' Banshee" here had a fuel blockage, too low to feather the prop. All the pilot could do was to bring her down."

"Very convenient."

201

"Could have been worse. They were over marshland, the pilot belly-landed her without dropping the wheels in the hope she would sink with all that weight."

"But she didn't."

"Not in time. "We managed to tow her out; there was only slight damage to the underside, nothing that couldn't be fixed. Come on, let's take a closer look."

They walked across the hangar's concrete floor, watching the men who were stripping the last of the paint from the fuselage.

"You mentioned one of the crew, did they parachute out?"

Reinicke shook his head. "Too low. They managed to burn their documents though, before our boys got there. It would have been nice to have some recent call signs; still, they'd probably be out of date by now, anyway."

They were under the port wing now and Reinicke leaned against the wheel. He swept a hand from front to rear.

"Quite a lot of alterations though most don't concern you directly. The ones that do are these – seating and armament. We've had to save weight; the only seats are those on the flight deck, you and your men will have foam rubber to sit on – I'm afraid it's the best we can do."

Schroeder shrugged his shoulders. "What about the armament?"

"There won't be any, nor armour either."

"You mean we're defenceless?"

"In the air, yes. Remember, we're a flying ambulance, nobody's going to be shooting at us."

"I hope to hell you're right."

"What about the other changes then?"

"Extra fuel capacity. Most of that's in the rear of the aircraft, it'll make her tail heavy to start with so you're all going to have to crowd forward until we get her trimmed after take off. We've also had to make a fairly hefty structural change." The flexible bomb doors were open, rolled up along the outside of the fuselage; Reinicke ducked down and up into the open bays, "Come in here, Herr Oberst," then, as Schroeder joined him on the inside, "my name's Pieter by the way – much easier than Oberstleutnant."

Schroeder considered the brisk overture of friendship. He would be travelling half way around the world with this man, it was essential that their relationship should be a smooth one. He held out his hand. "Kurt, Pieter. Though not in front of the men, you understand?"

"Perfectly." He pointed to the main structural frame which divided the two in-line bomb bays. "You'll see we've modified this to accommodate the bomb we're supposed to pick up. By all accounts, it's a whopper and we have to get enough of it inside the fuselage for Joachim to work on the fusing mechanism while we're in flight."

"Yes, of course. Joachim?"

"Joachim Neuper. Luftwaffe. Oberleutnant Neuper's been

attached to a bomb disposal squad for the last nine months. Instead of defusing them now he's got to work out how to do the opposite."

"I suppose you can fly this thing?"

"You worry about your end of things, Kurt. For the past three years I've flown nothing else but Allied aircraft." Unconsciously, Reinicke puffed out his chest. "I flew the first Bl7 ever captured, December, "42 in France. Since then I've flown most of the models that we got our hands on, advised the High Command on their strengths and weaknesses."

"And what are the Liberators like?"

Pieter paused a moment, calling up the data from memory.

"Pretty effective, carries a big load, phenomenal range by our standards, Pilot vision is poor – especially on the ground, stability can be poor with a lot of tail weight like we shall have until the fuel's been used in the rear tank and I'd be happier with a single tail instead of this twin affair. Don't let it disturb your dreams though, Kurt; we'll handle all that."

Schroeder nodded. Reinicke seemed to know his airplane though he was anything but modest about it. "Very good, I'll take your advice. How long do we have before we leave?"

Reinicke checked his watch. "A little over three hours. If you want to catch an hour's sleep, I'll wake you."

Schroeder shook his head. "Thanks but there isn't time. I'll take a look inside then I have to see to my men. I'll sleep later, it'll be a long journey."

"And that's another weakness of the B24. You can't sleep without ear plugs and it's draughty. It gets damned cold at seven thousand and some metres so we have electrically heated suits. I suggest that you inspect the aircraft later, the ground crew still have work to finish inside. Your lads are billeted in what used to be the changing- rooms – off to the right as you came in."

"Thanks Pieter. I'll see you later then."

Some of Kurt's men were asleep on the cots which lined one wall of the room. The few that weren't dropped magazines and hastily put down their cups of tea or coffee to stand to attention as he entered. Dismissing them with a perfunctory nod, he indicated those asleep. "Wake them, would you? I've a few things to tell you."

When all eight were paying attention, Kurt started. "Three hours from now, we shall be embarking on a journey which, if we're successful, is going to alter history."

"We know about that, Sir." Put in Duensing. "We've been told that we've got a special job to do and that we'll be leaving in the American plane out there."

"Thank you Erich." He had not expected it to be a secret at this stage but he wondered just how much had been revealed, "The purpose of our mission then is probably known already then?"

"Er, no Sir."

"Good. Security demands that I do not tell you this until we reach our destination. What I can say is this; everything you have learned at the Obersaltzburg will stand you in good stead."

"The skiing too Sir?" Asked a voice that Kurt could not identify.

"Except the skiing, I believe I warned you before that we would be operating in near desert conditions?"

"Yes Sir."

"Very well. The Fuhrer himself has planned this mission personally, he has code named it Operation Blondi."

At this news, the men gave a ragged cheer. Kurt held up his hand and the noise died away, Kurt hardened his features.

"The Fuhrer has also selected two men to replace Haller and Kiebel. Both are Officers of the SS. Need I say that you will accord them both the respect due their rank."

Weber lifted his hand.

"Weber?"

"What kind of SS are they Sir? Soldiers or…?"

"Hauptsturmfuhrer Bergerud and Obersturmfuhrer Dietrich are both Waffen SS. Bergerud was with the Wallonishe Legion who – as you probably know – were originally Wehrmacht. If I say that he was one of the survivors from Cherkassy, it may tell you something of the man.

"Dietrich, you already know as a former member of this group. He was recalled to Berlin, you may remember, some weeks ago. Today he received a decoration from the Fuhrer."

Kurt moved towards a bench and sat down. "Now, if there is nothing else, would someone offer me a drink? I could do with a

206

moment's rest..."

He had wanted to tell them about the two new members and to see what reaction there would be to outsiders being brought in at this late stage. His eyes had told him little; sitting down and listening to the men's conversation while he took a cup of ersatz coffee might tell him more. Kurt leaned back and closed his eyes. Warming his hands around the hot drink against the chill air of the small hours, he listened.

"The Wallonies are volunteers." Said someone, Kurt could not yet identify the voice. "They fought at the Dnieper bend alongside the Wiking division. If what I heard was true, they held an escape corridor open though it cost them nearly fourteen hundred men."

"Ja. But aren't they Auslanders?"

"Biggest part of them are but that doesn't worry me so long as this Bergerud's a soldier. If he can fight and is willing to die, he's one of us."

"Dying? Who's talking about dying?" That was Weber. "You don't think they'd train us like they have if they intended us to die, do you? Dying's for the old men and boys these days."

This was greeted with a murmur of agreement and Kurt almost smiled. The talk drifted on to other things for a while: girls, where the aircraft had come from, how much fuel had they scraped together. Then someone spoke of Dietrich in a lowered voice.

"I thought we were well rid of him." Kurt had to strain to

hear what followed. "Can't understand the Old Man wanting him back."

"No choice perhaps. You remember he said the Fuhrer chose them." No choice indeed, thought Kurt, remembering the scene when Hitler had led the two SS Officers across and introduced them. He had mumbled a greeting without giving away the fact that he knew Dietrich. He had wanted to protest but how could he? When the Fuhrer had presented the man, it was a fait accompli; there was nothing that could be done.

Since then, Kurt had thought about the matter on and off all day. He had half convinced himself that Dietrich had been ill before and that, now he was recovered, he might well be easier to get on with. Even after the meeting, when Reichsleiter Bormann had offered him coffee in that tiny cell he called an office, Kurt had tried to have the man replaced.

"Take him Kurt, he is the Fuhrer's own choice. If anything goes wrong, use him for a scapegoat; this young man is under careful observation, his uncle has blotted his copy book with our Fuhrer." Bormann chuckled momentarily. "Uncles have a habit of doing that. I think."

The reference to Onkle Heinie – Himmler – who had been relieved of his command with Army Group Vistula, was lost on Schroeder.

"No, if he disobeys a direct order, shoot him but you cannot go against the Fuhrer's wish."

Well, perhaps he couldn't. But Kurt resolved to keep

Dietrich under just as careful observation as the High Command's.

Kurt pantomimed waking up, professing surprise at the coffee still in his cup. Standing up, he asked about equipment.

"Over there Sir. We stacked it at the end."

Schroeder went over to inspect it.

There were enough guns and ammunition to start a small scale war of their own. Twelve MP 43/1 assault rifles with screw on grenade launchers were standard infantry issue. Two MG 42 machine guns with 7.62 ammunition – both boxed and belted. A Panzerfaust anti-tank gun with arrow bombs and six boxes of grenades. Lastly, there were several ten and twenty shot magazines for the Mauser hand pistols.

"Silencers?" Asked Kurt, looking around, "For the Mausers?"

"Here, Sir, and some new plastic explosives."

"Good. Everything is here. I want everything field stripped and checked out now. Remember, your lives depend on these so get to it, I have to check our transport."

Kurt left them to it and was half way across the floor of the darkened hanger when a Mercedes staff car crept through the slightly open doors; the narrow slits of the black-out masks on the headlamps were next to useless. Someone cranked the huge doors shut and overhead lights came on.

Two figures got out of the rear door and came towards him. It was Bergerud and Dietrich who had changed into combat strip since he had last seen them.

Both Officers saluted together. "Heil Hitler!"

"Heil Hitler." Returned Kurt. "Follow me gentlemen. I'm just going to have a last look at the aircraft before we embark."

The two men fell in behind him as Kurt turned and walked briskly away. He had deliberately asked them to join him in order to prevent any friction with the others before take-off. Hopefully, once they were airborne, the operation spirit would weld them into a single unit and blur any distinctions between SS and Wehrmacht.

The Liberator- he now noticed- had been given her disguise. Two large red crosses had been painted on the bare metal of the fuselage and two slightly smaller ones added to the underside of the wings. Code numbers had also been painted on.

Pieter met them as they scrambled into the bomb bay and helped Kurt up on to the deck. As the Luftwaffe Officer noticed the SS. insignia on Bergerud's and Dietrich's collars, Kurt thought he saw a hint of amusement in the other's eyes.

"Welcome aboard gentlemen. We are almost ready. You can see where you will be sitting and, at the same time, I can introduce you to my navigator and wireless operator. Oberleutnant Neuper will be with us shortly."

Kurt performed the introductions and Pieter returned a sloppy salute to the SS Officers.

"You have explained the accommodations to your Officers?"

210

Kurt shook his head, "Not as yet."

"Then allow me." Suggested Pieter with relish and went on to explain the more uncomfortable aspects of the journey. "Now, where is Willi?" he finished. "A moment while I fetch him."

Pieter went forward and returned a few seconds later with a disreputable looking character whom he introduced as Herr Major Willi Braun. Kurt was surprised, to say the least; the SS men could hardly believe their eyes. Pieter, quite evidently, was amused at the situation.

Willi Braun wore a cracked leather flying jacket which, if it had seen better days, must have been many years ago, it carried neither insignia nor medals. He nodded, disdaining the Nazi salute and grinned at the three soldiers.

"Welcome aboard the Flying Eightball, Herr Oberst, gentlemen.

Kurt lifted a quizzical eyebrow.

"The name the Americans gave their aircraft." Pieter looked at the blank expressions. "A game," he explained further, "something like billiards I understand but they call it pool."

"So?" Asked Dietrich.

"I can tell you no more." Willi shrugged,

"And this," said Bergerud, changing the subject and looking down at the foam rubber padding underfoot, "is the seating you mentioned?"

"Correct." Pieter pointed to twin lines of straps hanging from the overhead spars. So that you can walk about if the weather is rough. Gets more like the U-bahn by the minute, no?"

Kurt smiled. "And toilet facilities?"

"One, a chemical toilet just through there. It should be enough for the fifteen of us provided we don't drink too much; if that gets filled we shall have to crack the bomb bay doors for the incontinent ones – which reminds me.

"Liberators have slight fuel leakage problems from the wing cells. Any one who wants to smoke – get it over with before you board. One of my crew will come back from time to time to open the bomb doors a little to drain any fuel that does run down."

Kurt nodded, he had never smoked, he was more interested in practicalities. "And you, Major Braun, can you get us where we have to go?"

The sudden question, fired at Willi, caught him unawares for a moment.

"I am only human, Herr Oberst but I shall find the way. If anything goes wrong with the compass, the radar or anything else, there is always Arcturus." He pointed roofward. "We shall navigate by the stars."

Kurt was satisfied but he turned to Pieter Reinicke with one last question. "Only three of you to fly this aircraft, is that enough?"

"Normally there are eight but with weight an important factor, we three can fly it. Willi can fly the plane, I can navigate also. Joachim will take the job of flight engineer. Why do you think we were chosen, Herr Oberst? We three are like six."

212

"You did say it needed eight." Reminded Kurt mildly.

"No, I said that the normal crew was eight. Another advantage of the B24 over the Flying Fortress; it can be flown in an emergency by a single man. In any case, several of the usual crew would be gunners, we have none."

"I see, and Willi – Herr Major? He will double as bomb aimer?"

"Not so. Friedrich Haas who will also double as radio operator. You see – already we are up to eight."

"Thank you Herr Oberstleutnant. I can see that everything has been thought out very thoroughly. Perhaps you will give me a last check on the time?"

Pieter consulted his watch. "I have fifty two minutes to take off, if you would assemble your soldiers in, shall we say thirty minutes' time?"

"Very good. In thirty minutes then." Kurt saluted – more for the benefit of Dietrich and Bergerud than for any other reason.

Once outside in the vast and echoing hanger, Bergerud spoke in impeccable German. He asked what his and Dietrich's duties might be.

Kurt's first thought was to bawl him out for impertinence but a moment's reflection told him that the man was perfectly correct. He stopped, looking at Bergerud's almost white hair and classical features; the blue eyes looked calmly back at Schroeder.

"Until we arrive at our destination, I cannot reach any decisions.

"You will realise from our final briefing last evening that we do not know enough about the site to determine the best means of ingress. When I have conferred with Major Piekenbrock, I can reach realistic conclusions; he will have a far better appreciation of the site layout."

"Piekenbrock." Broke in Dietrich, "he is no relation to the one who was at Prince Albrechtstrasse, is he?"

"The old Abwehr? I don't understand."

"A coincidence, them being in the same line of business."

"Just so. Herr Obersturmfuhrer…" Kurt turned back to Bergerud, "Oberst. You are an explosives expert, I believe."

"This is correct."

"And, like Obersturmfuhrer Dietrich, you speak good English?"

"Yes, I studied at the University of Oslo – before 1940."

"I am already acquainted with the Herr Obersturmfuhrer's qualifications. I think that I can promise both of you interesting and leading roles in this exercise. At the moment, I can say no more."

"Er, Herr Oberst? May I have a private word, please?" Dietrich asked.

"Of course, give me a moment. Obersturmfuhrer." Kurt looked up at Bergerud.

"Perhaps you would introduce yourselves to the men? Tell them also about the smoking.

"Most certainly, Herr Oberst."

214

LAST MISSION

Kurt checked his watch, subconsciously aware that his was three minutes slower than Reinicke's. "I can spare you five minutes."

Dietrich bowed formally. "I shall not keep you that long, Sir. It is good of you to give me the chance. I would like to assure you that the incident at the pass was one that I deeply regret. I have had time to reflect on the matter and I realise that I was still suffering from shock."

Dietrich spoke rapidly, as though he were frightened that, should he stop, he would not be able to will himself to start again. "However, I am now fully recovered, I assure you I shall serve the Fuhrer and the Reich honorably.

Kurt could see how hard the apology had been to make and took the intent at face value. "Thank you Dietrich." He said, deliberately omitting the title. "The matter is forgotten. We have difficult and glorious work to do for the Reich. It will be easier if we act as a unit." Schroeder added a mental qualification to his acceptance, knowing that it was a man's actions under stress that counted. He would follow Reichsleiter Bormann's advice.

*

With ten minutes to go before the Liberator took to the air, all of the men, with, the exception of Major Schroeder, were settling themselves as far forward as possible. For the time being, some arms and other equipment was stacked and tied down on top of the life rafts beneath the wing spars. The remainder was stored in the nose compartment, which would remain unused until Haas required it for bomb aiming. Everyone was dressed in the padded suits and, for the moment, they all sweated profusely.

They were waiting for one man: Oberleutnant Neuper was late.

Kurt was watching from the port waist window and was eventually rewarded as not one but three cars, followed by a Kubelwagen, swept into the gloomy hangar. The lead vehicle, a Horsch staff car pulled round to within a few metres of the aircraft. Reichsleiter Bormann stepped out as the driver came round to open the rear door. He was followed by a small man in a Luftwaffe great coat.

Neuper – Kurt assumed it to be him – went forward to join the crew through the nose wheel opening. Bormann simply waited and Schroeder hurriedly unlocked the rear hatch and scrambled out to meet him.

The Reichsleiter had to shout to make himself heard over the roar of the four Pratt and Whitney radials which Reinicke was now running up.

"Kurt." Exclaimed Bormann. "I came to wish you luck. The Fuhrer and I are relying on you to carry this mission to a successful conclusion. The air crew will be picked up by Herr Kapitan Reinhardt. A U-boat is already on its way to ferry you, Kurt, to Paraguy, Pieter Reinicke will arrange the rendezvous."

"Thank you, Herr Reichsleiter."

"One more thing." Bormann handed a small pouch to

Schroeder. "These are diamonds, Herr Oberst – enough to finance your operations in South America."

"Thank you again. For your confidence in me."

"Heil Hitler." Bormann threw up his arm.

"Heil Hitler."

Bormann watched the Liberator taxi out of the hangar, moonlight glinting dully on the smooth metal surfaces. A few minutes later, he ordered the doors to be shut.

When Schroeder and the Allied Aircraft were irrevocably set on the Fuhrer's mission, Bormann had bethought himself of the treasures from the Linz collection. They would never, now, be used in South America and with the Russians a mere thirty five minutes by air from Berlin, Bormann had no intentions of leaving them in a store room at Templehof,

The Kubelwagen was driven to the rear of the hangar when the lights were switched on again and the men started to load the unpainted wooden cases from the inconspicuous store room.

"They're damned heavy." He heard a man say. "I wonder what's in them."

*

Momentarily, as the Liberator lifted from the patched-up runway, Kurt remembered the abortive landing of twenty four hours ago. The workers had certainly repaired this stretch carefully, he thought, there had been no more than the usual bumps from the landing gear before the four 1,200 horsepower engines started eating into the sky,

Forward, Reinicke killed the lights as the landing gear rumbled into the wings and concentrated on altitude. Satisfied with one rectangular circuit with the airport at its approximate center, Reinicke shouted back.

"You can begin moving the weight back now, Kurt – Oberst. Do it slowly while I get us trimmed, okay?"

Kurt gestured to the men who, knowing what was required, began distributing the guns and ammunition boxes evenly along each side wall. Soon after they were finished, Kurt felt them start to climb again; six minutes later, he and most of the others were swallowing to accommodate the pressure drop.

From now until they finally landed in New Mexico there was little for them to do, they were literally no more than cargo. Kurt settled himself into an angle between the wall and a frame and made himself as comfortable as possible. Now would be as good a time as any to catch up on the sleep he had gone without but his thoughts at first refused to settle;

There had been some talk – even at the late stage of the penultimate briefing – of putting down in Spain to take on extra fuel. However, General Franco's two-caps policy towards the Reich and the Allies had seen the argument firmly tilted against the idea. Somehow, enough hundred octane fuel had been found to fill the tremendous capacity now built into the Liberator.

Although exact calculations were impossible, General Keller had stated categorically that their range would be more than
218

sufficient. The half way fuel situation- because of the gradual decrease in weight -would be well over half way across the Atlantic; Neuper, the flight engineer, would keep a careful watch and recalculate the rate of consumption as they went.

There were a number of contingency plans that Schroeder had to keep in mind. The first, of course, was fuel. Brazil was fractionally nearer on the 'great circle' route they were to follow and rather rushed and make-shift arrangements had been made to refuel there, clandestinely, if the need arose. Next most important was the choice of targets; quite simply, these were the White House, Washington or if this could not be reached, then they were to destroy Los Alamos itself. In the latter case, the conflagration would be enormous with an unknown number of atomic bombs, all of which might be detonated by the one they dropped

Finally, there was the matter of their destination itself. Piekenbrock was to set up three radio beacons which would transmit on the aircraft's radio compass frequency at a predetermined time. This would allow their navigator to solve his rector triangle and find the prepared landing area. If this failed then Reinicke would have to make a sighted land with Piekenbrock firing a signal flare which would be a risky business.

Kurt felt himself succumbing, at last, to drowsiness. A last few moments, he forced his eyes open to check on the soldiers' activities. Bergerud was chatting with Hoeckle, he noticed. No doubt, with them both having served with Panzer Grenadier regiments, they had found something in common.

He drifted off as the plane continued to climb to its intended altitude of seven and a half thousand metres.

Pain in his ears brought Kurt awake again some five minutes later. Hastily, he swallowed and yawned until it went away. Schroeder resolved to stay awake until the climb was finished, sleep was a little dangerous at the moment. He stood up, strap hanging to the nearest window and gazed out at the darkened earth below them. Down there and behind would be the outer suburbs of Berlin, ahead – Leipzig, the blackout left only a few sparks glimmering in the blackness. Far behind was the red glow of the fires that the R.A.F. had sown last evening; concentrating on the marshalling yards at Moabit and staying well away from Templehof for once.

Turning from the outside world to the inside one, Kurt's eyes flicked from man to man as he conducted a mental checklist.

Seated opposite to him were Bergerud, Hoeckle – still deep in reminiscences – Duensing, Weber, Furtner and Strauch. On his own side were Muller on his left with Schiff, Fachinger and Dietrich to his right. Most were obviously tense and, for a moment or two, Kurt toyed with the idea of asking Furtner to give them a song; Bruno had a fine baritone and, before the war, had been a professional singer.

The thought was gone as quickly as it had come as another

220

sprang to the forefront. Why, he wondered, if the Americans possessed such powerful weapons, did they not use them on Germany? A single bomb on Berlin would destroy the Fuhrer and what semblance of central government still remained, the Reich would fall like a house of cards.

Kurt nodded as the answering thought came to him. The Allies knew as well as he did himself; Berlin would fall in a matter of weeks anyway. That was the single terrible fact behind Operation Blondi; without the operation's success, the Russians – followed by the British and Americans – would soon be picking over the bones of Berlin. There had been a noticeable pattern in bomb distribution over recent months; it was not being cynical to assume that the Allies were purposely sparing the industries they would want when Germany surrendered.

Oberleutnant Neuper appeared in the passenger section. Crossing the cat-walk above the bomb bays, he came up to Kurt,

"Good day, Herr Oberst." He opened the bulging briefcase he carried. "The Fuhrer suggested that these might be appreciated."

Joachim took a package from the case and handed it to Kurt. "Cigarettes, French and American. From the SS store at…"

Response from either side of Schroeder was immediate; from the others, only fractionally less so. "Real cigarettes, I don't believe it."

Joachim smiled round. "Oh they're real enough. Enough for three cartons each – more if some of you don't smoke. Do you,

Herr Oberst?"

"Thank you – no." Returned Kurt and, suddenly, he was aware of a silence loud enough to hear above the engine noise. He looked around at the eight pairs of eyes fixed on him. "Something is wrong?" He enquired.

Muller replied, a trifle self-consciously. "We had not been notified of your promotion – Herr Oberst'

Kurt chuckled. "So, the grapevine did not extend to that." He looked round at his team. "My apologies, I'm afraid the matter escaped my mind, it has been a full day. However, you will find that it will make no difference; I shall be as hard a taskmaster as always."

Nils Bergerud spoke up. "Excuse me, Herr Oberst. I appreciate your feelings but I believe it does make a difference. Your promotion reflects on your men. They now know how highly their commandant is regarded. I for one am proud to serve on this mission."

There were sounds of agreement from the others and Kurt found himself unexpectedly affected. He was moved and he turned, lest his water filled eyes betrayed him. "Take your cigarettes. When this mission is finished with you shall have cigars."

Neuper handed the packs around, they were speedily broken up and distributed. "And remember – don't smoke them until we land tomorrow unless you want to blow us all up." Then he returned to the flight deck.

222

LAST MISSION

Reinicke was behind the starboard controls, "Another five, six minutes, we'll be at our planned altitude Joachim. You might keep your eyes peeled on this side for any hostiles. It's getting lighter outside, now, Friedrich, anything on the radio?"

"Nothing Pieter."

Willi Braun was kneeling on the co-pilot's seat, to give him a better field of vision. Friedrich Haas was listening on the radio, tuning up and down the dial to cover all the frequencies used by the various Staffels.

All Luftwaffe bases still operational –some, though fuel was desperately short at most – had received instructions to ignore the Ambulance plane. However, just in case an overzealous pilot became suspicious, Pieter Reinicke was leaving as little as possible to chance,

They met neither German nor Allied fighters. Despite this, the flight deck relaxed fractionally as they crossed the Rhine near Freiberg and ventured into French air space. The Liberator was now in level flight with thick cumulus below them.

"Do we go down and hide? Asked Neuper.

"It wouldn't be a bad idea, no sense in riding Lady Luck too hard, you'd better pop back and warn the men that things will be bumpy for a while – and check for fuel leakage, drain the bomb bays if you think it necessary."

At about four hundred kilometres an hour, they would cross the Iberian coast in another four hours. The Liberator would then change its bearing, holding to a great circle course across the

Atlantic, taking a further twenty four hours or so to reach their destination at about three a.m., local American time.

*

"We got notification of a B24 flight Sir?" Sergeant Crabbe; duty radio officer at the US air base in the Azores, handed a flimsy to his CO. "Rogers went out in the Hudson to investigate some wreckage at first light. They just reported a visual aircraft sighting."

"Whereabouts was that, Sergeant?"

Crabbe turned to the wall map. "Here. They're about seventy miles north of Graciosa. Apparently travelling about 260 magnetic."

"No response to radio request for identification. Operator was probably on a call of nature."

It was the end of a long and boring morning and Signals Officer Jamieson was looking forward to a hot bath. He frowned at the signal for a moment.

"On that heading, they'll be flying home for a little R and R with their girl friends. That or they've pulled duty dogging a U-boat. Anyway, log it. You can check with Radar Section later, send a signal off if it seems necessary.." Jamieson yawned. "Me, I'm gonna grab a bath and then work on my sun tan."

Crabbe snorted and tucked the signal into a file case. If Jamieson was planning on sun bathing with Sarah Joplin again, the only part that was going to get sunburned was his ass.

TWENTY TWO

Edward Roberts was the product of an American-German
relationship. The American side was represented by Edward's
father, a commercial traveller in fibre during the nineteen
twenties with much of his time spent in finding customers in
Europe. Roberts' smooth line went down as well with the girls as
it did with the clients; alas, he was to find that his success did not
extend to irate fathers. Following the shot-gun nuptials, Roberts
had little choice but to take his pregnant bride back to the USA,
though it was not long before he left to tour the European
capitals once more.

The pace of life took its toll, in November of 1929, five
years after their marriage, Roberts died of a heart attack in a
Dutch whorehouse,

Lotte did not mourn his loss. The 'land of opportunity' he
had described to her at eighteen was a bright picture which had
tempted her into his bed; the reality was an ancient clapboard
bungalow on the outskirts of Lincoln, Nebraska where she
struggled through the depression. Besides small sums of money
sent from Europe, Roberts contributed nothing to the household
before he died and very little in the way of a will afterwards.

Later, Lotte sold the land occupied by the decaying house,

having accepted her brother in law's offer to go live with his family. The situation was tolerable; she had the little money from the sale, she had Edward to bring up in her own ways and to exaggerate – as his father had done before – the qualities of her homeland.

Edward had only been sixteen when he had attended his first Bund meeting. It was, as his mother had predicted, filled with happy, exuberant people. Germans all; many of them despising their adopted country. His sixteen years of life had been neither miserable nor happy but, compared with other boys of his age and background, there was something lacking. Edward never realised just what was different, nor that there was anything missing; certainly, he never connected it with his absent father.

The Bund filled the void.

The Bund told him to be glad when Germany took Poland.

The Bund taught him how to shout 'Heil Hitler."

And it was the Bund that brought himself and Otto Schranz together.

Otto was German, not an emigré but a real German, sent to America to find support for Hitler and the Third Reich. He was looking for people who were prepared to do more than just cheer. Edward volunteered, severing his connections with the Bund at Schranz's orders. All members of the Bund organisation were automatically suspect by the United States security agencies and a close watch was kept on local meeting places until the organisation was banned.

226

At first, he was used as a messenger, running errands, taking messages. As he grew older and bigger, his size was used to coerce marginal sympathisers into donating funds to the Cause. Edward became expert at the work and retained the job until Piekenbrock took control of this and other groups in 1942.

Piekenbrock had entered the States from Brazil the year before with South American papers. At first, he reported back through the Sicherheitsdienst – the German Security Service – offices at Calle Gangallo 439, Buenos Aires. In the autumn of 1942, Piekenbrock was ordered to break his connections with the Brazilian network and report back solely to Herr Generalmajor Walter Schellenborg. Piekenbrock owed his continued liberty in the United States to an almost pathological distrust – a trait which his superior knew of and fostered.

After a certain amount of leadership training, Edward Roberts was put in charge of a cell of four and drew regular pay for the first time.

In November of 1943. Ed had his first taste of danger. He had brought two German spies up from Florida – fresh off a U-boat which he was disappointed at not being able to see. The agents were boarded with two of his cell members and seemed to occupy most of their time spending the Fatherland's dollars in bars or at cinemas rather than in any for-real espionage.

The situation went sour within three weeks, one of the Germans turned himself in. Piekenbrock, with an uncanny foreknowledge rang Edward and warned him; the cell leader left home hurriedly, sparing neither time to let his mother know nor to pack. He was given a new address to move to, a new name to contact; the name had been Carl's code identity.

Ed had, in effect, been demoted; a fact which he resented for some time but Carl was older, with tales to tell of the Great War and soon the younger man warmed to Carl's charm.

Carl was a great drinking partner and threw regular drink sessions for the other three members of his cell. Ed enjoyed these, they took the place of the earlier Bund meetings which had been declared illegal by the Government. All three happily travelled miles every month to meet together in Carl's root cellar.

To do Carl justice; these meetings were not all booze and reminiscences. Each of them had work to do which ranged from combing magazine articles and newspapers to surreptitiously covering army manoeuvres,

At the last meeting Carl had been brimming with excitement. He had dropped broad hints of a big operation in the offing, something to make them all nervous. Ed and the others had left sharing Carl's enthusiasm; the idea had appealed particularly to Ed, since Germany had declared war on America, he had blamed his long dead father for taking him away from his rightful homeland and the chance of fighting for the Reich,

Carl surprised him three weeks after that occasion by calling him and inviting Ed over for drinks earlier than the usual monthly interval. He was further surprised on arrival to discover

228

that he was the only visitor and that Carl's plump little hausfrau – who seemed to detest his get-togethers – was away. They had not bothered to go down to the cellar then or on the five evenings following. The pair had quietly consumed schnapps with beer chasers in the sitting room each night.

His cell leader had explained that he was waiting for the all important call that would send them on the way. Ed felt more inclined to believe that Carl was lonely with his wife away; he merely wanted company – something Ed was quite willing to provide in return for free drinks.

For the seventh evening in succession, Ed was on his way to a night's drinking. They would continue until the bottles were empty, they would sing a few German songs, talk about women and, maybe, the phone would ring tonight.

Ed nursed the ancient Dodge up the slight incline just as another car drew away from the kerb with a squeal of smoking tyres. He thought nothing of it; Ed liked to take off like that himself – when the wheels were up to it. He locked the car up and trotted briskly up the now-familiar steps.

The door was open and Ed walked in shouting Carl's name. There was no reply and he wondered if it had been Carl in the other car though, surely, he would have locked the street door. Perhaps he had left a note? There was none in the kitchen or the sitting room. The cellar? The light was on, he went down the steep stairs.

For a moment, all was silent then his eyes were drawn to a

229

half-seen motion as a fleeting form sought refuge beneath a bench.

Subconsciously, he knew it to be a rat but his attention was fixed on Carl's body sprawled out on the dirt floor. Ed cursed, though lightly, believing the other to be no more than sleeping off a real bender.

"Hey! You've tied one on, friend."

He bent over, shook Carl's shoulder. Nothing.

Grasping the jacket, he tugged, and turned the man over. Blood ran from the neck wound.

Ed's immediate reaction was one of disgust. He thought of the form scuttling away beneath the bench.

"Bloody rats!" He kicked Carl savagely. "Come on Carl, get up damn you. Bloody rats have been at you."

But there was too much blood already soaked into the dirt for the wound to have been caused by a rat's teeth. He looked at the gash again; then, glancing around, saw the blood stained bottle.

At the exact moment that Ed presumed his friend to be dead, a sound escaped from Carl's body – not from the mouth but bubbling from the gaping hole in his throat,

"Oh God – I'll get a doctor, don't move Carl."

Ed was halfway up the stairs before he had second thoughts. His training prompted his secrecy, there could be no doctor unless Piekenbrock knew of one.

Piekenbrock – that was the answer, could he recall the

number after all this time.

Joseph Piekenbrock was in his basement apartment. He chewed at the end of his pencil in annoyance as he checked off two lists against each other. On the left was the list which had reached him from Schellenburg as a microdot beneath the Swiss stamp. On his right was the list of items already acquired.

It was the number of articles still outstanding that worried him, that and the fact that he still did not know the operation date. All that the message told him was that it was 'imminent'.

He swore, an uncharacteristic gesture, and tossed the lists away in disgust. What was he going to do about three portable radio beacons if his black market contact in the Army supply business could not deliver? A further example of the stupid blind faith that the SD had in him was the specially tailored breakdown truck, what if it could not be finished in time? Piekenbrock made a note to remind himself to phone the Omaha operative who had this in hand.

Still muttering his annoyance, he took up the lists and started again. Another note – this time to check on Erich who had driven down to New Mexico two days before and who should have called him by now, Erich was a New York layer of bricks, the nearest he could find to an airfield engineer; his brief was to find a mile and three quarter stretch of flat, level ground. Would he know what to look for?

Piekenbrock lifted his shoulders in a shrug and picked up his coffee. It was cold but he drank it with a grimace of distaste.

He put down the Dresden china cup carefully and, right on cue, the phone rang.

It was not Erich. The voice was agitated, its owner obviously confused and Piekenbrock had to concentrate to ring some sense from the garbled words.

"I'm sorry", he said at last, his tone politely regretful, "I know no one named Edward. You must have dialled a wrong number."

"Don't go Charles. I'm upset, it's Peter here. I was forgetting.

"Where are you calling from? I presume that it is important?"

"Carl's. Yes, it is important."

"Stay where you are then." Piekenbrock put the receiver down, took down his overcoat and consulted his watch. He reminded himself that he would have to hurry in case Erich rang.

From the anonymity of a phone booth, Joseph made the call. The first ring was not complete before it was answered.

"Yes?"

"What is the trouble?"

"It's Carl. Someone's near killed him with a broken bottle. He's lost more blood than a stuck pig: I'm certain he'll be dead if we don't get him to a hospital."

"You haven't tried to get a doctor or anything?" Piekenbrock was suddenly very worried.

"No – of course not."

232

"Good. Do you know who did it, or why?"

"No idea who but I reckon I might know why. I had a good look round after I rang the first time. There's a body buried down in the cellar, it looks like it might be his wife."

Piekenbrock tutted to himself, that could explain a lot. "Can you clear things up? Dispose of the evidence?"

"No. Too much to do, too risky."

Joseph paused a moment to think. "And you say he's very bad?"

"Bloody terrible. His throat's been cut."

"You'll have to finish the job for me Edward. Then burn the house down, leave nothing that might come through the fire. Can you do that?"

There was a second's silence, then: "Yes."

"Very well. Is the bottle still there?"

"Mm."

"Then wrap it carefully, try not to smudge any finger prints. Okay?"

"Okay."

"Then this is what I want you to do…"

Ed walked slowly back up the street from where he had parked the car. Already he was certain that he could see the ground floor windows lit by the glow of leaping flames. When he was still a hundred yards distant, flames suddenly erupted from the lowest windows; the panes cracked like pistol shots and the roar of the flames brought faces to windows all along the road.

In seconds, there was a crowd of onlookers, some –
neighbours -wearing worried expressions and others who were
obviously enjoying the unexpected entertainment.

By the time the fire service arrived, neither Carl's house nor
those immediately adjoining it could be saved, Ed quietly walked
back to the car as the fire chief directed the hoses into the
windows of the two outer houses and on to the roofs of those
beyond.

The basement was thick with smoke. Since the root cellar
had neither doors nor windows to the outside, the fire burned
slowly here. When Ed had left after sluicing the place with
kerosene, the rat had come out of hiding again but the smell of
oil confused it; when it reached the still warm corpse, the
kerosene had spoiled the fresh, red meat.

Now, it scampered across the floor from one side of the
cellar to the other. Flames hid its bolt hole, licked over the
wooden roll top where it sometimes found biscuits. The air was
hot, depleted of oxygen: the rat panted rapidly as it searched for
some way of escape.

The rat's fur started to singe and fall away, its squeaks of
alarm sounding almost like a diminutive scream. Its skin flaked,
its eyes blistered. It could neither see nor hear the ceiling fall in
with a shower of hot, burning debris. The rat was not even aware
of being killed by the collapsing beams.

TWENTY THREE

"Sue – Susan Millar. Call for you."

Susan was not in the shower. Not quite. She came downstairs in a bathrobe and took the phone,

"Thanks." She said to Martha Longbury, house mother at the women's hostel, then into the phone: "Hello. Doctor Millar here."

"Hello." Said a weak voice. "This is Paul, Can you do me a favour, Sue?"

"Of course, if I can."

"I'll be home in a couple of hours or so, I've just reached Las Vegas."

"Back early, everything okay then?"

"I'll tell you later. Can you meet me at my place?"

Paul's voice sounded subdued. He had been right to be worried about his sister perhaps. "Sure. I'll be there. You all right, Paul?"

"Yes, I'm okay. I'll see you later, right?"

"Right."

"Bye then."

"Goodbye."

Susan completed her shower. Dressed in grey slacks and a

matching turtleneck sweater, she drove slowly south through the nondescript little township of Los Alamos and out towards Paul's house.

It was an April evening and the plants which had lain sticklike and dormant for most of the previous twelve months were bursting into bloom. Along one side of the road ran a dry wash. Once or twice a year, it ran with storm water which soaked into the subsoil almost as quickly as it came. The south western desert plants, adapted to their environment, drew greedily on the moisture when it was available and when spring arrived they burst exuberantly into bloom to carry out their perennial reproduction.

Susan knew many of the flowers that blossomed across the desert: honey mesquite, the blue and white paloverdes, the bird of paradise flower, tamarisk. Each one painted its own scrap of desert in pinks or violets, chromes, indigos, violent reds; each one vied with its neighbour to seduce an insect to bear its pollen away or to drop some other flower's grains. In among the flowers were equally attractive grasses and stunted shrubs: here and there was an occasional ocotillo, some standing taller than herself.

She smiled as, unconsciously, her foot let the gas pedal up and the car slowed to a crawl. Susan had fallen in love with this country and its ever changing scenery. Three hundred and forty days of sunshine against the dreary, cloud-filled sky of her native

236

island. A temperature that ranged from fifty through ninety instead of the months of cold, wet fog or drizzle that characterized the industrial heart of England. There was more to it than this, of course, but how could you explain in a letter, the special radiance of this Western sky, its constant clarity. Her parents and friends thought her crazy and asked in every other letter when she would be leaving 'that terrible desert'.

As a child, Susan had woken every morning to the sounds of blast furnaces and steel rolling mills, factory sirens and the peculiarly singular noise of trains clattering over points and junctions. Remembering back to childhood and early teens, she could only picture rain falling from a heavy grey sky, downpours that churned up the dirt yard behind their terraced house leaving oozing mud innocent of a single blade of grass. Here, Susan looked forward to the rain, warm and sensual against the skin after the desert dryness; it served its purpose and disappeared into the grateful soil. There were the occasional flash floods of course, sometimes more than the storm drains could handle, but they were minor irritants compared with the whole.

No, Susan thought firmly, treading on the gas and speeding up, they were two different worlds and she had no desire to return to that other one. Her mind meandered back to Paul, she wondered if he felt the same. If he did, they might well settle down here permanently.

With a start, she realised that this thought, or something like it, had been buzzing around her mind all day without her facing up to it. It had not seemed to fit in properly with work but out here, among the scenery she loved, it seemed the right place to explore her future.

Susan had promised herself on more than one occasion to steer clear of involvements of the heart. Paul was very different from Mike Holderness. Mike had been mature and totally self assured in every way, his career at T.A. in England had been firmly mapped out with a ruler until the Luftwaffe bomb doors had swung open above London,

What were the important differences, she wondered. Mike had not really needed her; she had been an accessory, little more. Paul, on the other hand, did need her – he was self confident enough with his men but, away from the job, he was another person; naive perhaps, a little awe inspired by the vastness of the world he found himself in, perhaps – again.

There was more to her feelings than affection. She grinned at the memory of their first night, when she had considered seducing him. Paul had certainly risen to the occasion – eventually – and on several occasions since then. It wasn't even that he was a skilful lover; in fact, now that she thought about it, maybe it was the reassurance he needed, the slightest little bit of help and guidance that he wanted at such times that made their lovemaking so pleasurable.

Paul was like a puppy growing up, feeling his strength for the first time and she might as well admit it, thought Susan; she loved him. She ought to start considering how to make Paul

238

realise that he loved her and to do something about it.

"High time he thought about making an honest woman of me." She said aloud as she drove up the rough track to the old bungalow and braked to a stop.

*

The sun was dropping redly behind the mountains when Paul drew up in a cloud of dust. The western sky was a blaze of orange and gold.

The long drive back, down through the heart of America had given him more than enough time to come to terms with what he had seen and found. More than enough time too, to decide what to tell Susan and what to leave out.

Susan was in the single living room listening to the radio when she heard Paul's car, smells of cooking wafted from the kitchen. She checked her hair and face on the way to the door and nearly collided with it as Paul threw it open from the outside.

"Hi." She said, expecting him to kiss her as he came in.

"Hi." Paul pushed gently past her. "Just let me get a drink first."

"Sure darling but..." This was not the way Susan had pictured his arrival.

"In a minute, Susan." His voice was dour, irritable. "I've got to have a drink, hon."

Three full fingers of Scotch later, Paul sank wearily into a chair. He sighed; in the car, it had all seemed so simple but now that Susan was sitting there, facing him, it was not simple at all.

Susan was puzzled by his manner but sensed easily enough that something eventful had happened and that Paul would tell her when he was ready.

He drained the last drops and set the glass down with a bang.

"I found Mai's body in the cellar." He told her at last.

Susan gasped with shock. "Oh God, Paul." Tears stung her eyes and she went across to kneel on the floor near his feet.

"Rotting there, buried in the dirt. My own sister." Paul's voice broke. "I loved her Sue, more than I did my parents." Tears streamed down his cheeks. "And they've been interned."

She put her arms on his knees. "Do you know what happened? With Mai?"

He shook his head. "All I know is that she's dead."

"God, I'm sorry darling. I don't know what to say. What did you do?"

Paul jumped. Susan knew that she'd touched a raw nerve. His expression changed in an instant; from grief to hate.

"I killed him. Carl. We had a fight down there, he was trying to strangle me and I hit him with a bottle."

"Are you sure? Maybe he was just knocked out."

"The bottle was broken. I hit him in the throat. Look."

For the first time, Susan realised that Paul had on an old raincoat. He opened it, his shirt was stiff with dried blood, it smelled awful.

"Did you check though?" She asked after a moment. "You

can't be certain you killed him if you didn't – check, I mean. Beside, it was self defence."

Paul wiped his face on a coat sleeve and turned to look squarely at Susan.

"It doesn't matter anyway." He said viciously. "I'm sure I killed him. If I didn't, I will next time I see him."

Susan could understand Paul, what she could not understand was herself. She was talking to a murderer, her Paul. She should feel horror at the deed, repugnance; yet this was nothing of that sort, it didn't seem real. She shook her head, hair flying, agitated by this same lack of feeling.

"What made him do it Paul? Why would a man kill his own wife like that?"

"I don't know, Sue, I don't know." He put his head in his hands. "I guessed she disagreed with his views about the States and Germany. Probably knew that he dabbled in spying; maybe she threatened to turn him in if he didn't stop. Mai was proud of being American, I know; she couldn't understand that Carl was still a German."

"But you could?"

It was a loaded question and Paul took his time before answering,

"I thought so once. He only wanted to stop the war, Susan, though how he expected to do that, I don't know. He reckoned America was ripe for National Socialism."

"You mean Nazism."

"I – I suppose so."

"God, Paul. You're as bad as that Kennedy chap. I suppose he asked you to help, didn't he? Don't I remember you saying once, that Carl encouraged you to take this job?" Susan's voice had turned hard; she sat back on her heels. She had added one or two facts together and come up with a full-blown plot.

Paul looked up, his smeared face, defiant.

"Yes. Just to keep my eyes open, let him know if I discovered what was going on."

"Not to mince words, you were spying?"

"Hell no – I'm no... Well, okay; I suppose you could call it that if you want to. Look, I keep telling you; all Carl wanted to do was to stop the war and, anyway, he's dead now isn't he? He's not going to do anything about it now."

Susan had climbed to her feet. Now she glared down at him, furious; her hands balled into small fists.

"You think that by telling him things about the 'Hill', you could really stop a world wide war? How gullible can you get, Paul Webb? You must be out of your skull."

Paul winced as Susan screamed this at him. Her words hurt; the long silence that followed while she just stood, glaring at him hurt even more. It made him think hard, he chewed his lip.

She was right, he admitted finally; he had been an idiot. The whole thing had seemed no more than a game, an adventure.

Eventually, he told Susan as much and she softened a little.

"You're a twerp, you know? You've worked yourself into a

242

good job here " you're very well thought of. Oh yes – I know," she said as he looked up, "they know we go around together. I get to hear quite a lot about you. And now you're throwing it all away – just like that."

"I'm not. I haven't yet, anyway."

Susan's eyes narrowed once more. "Do you know something that could hurt the Project?"

"Look, I told Carl what was happening here, before – before we got serious about each other. So the Germans know too, they've got photographs

"Good God." She threw up her hands in mock despair. "Snapshots of the most secret site in the country."

"Aerial photos." Said Paul, dissembling. "They used a crop dusting plane, I think," Paul paused a moment, "guess they know about some weak perimeter points too."

"Which you told them about?"

Paul merely nodded, ashamed.

"And there's my pot roast – burning." Susan dashed for the kitchen. "Well, what're you going to do about it?"

He thought about it until she came back, having rescued some of the meal. "Well?"

"I guess I could tell someone? Not anyone here though."

"That's a start. The Pentagon I suppose, though you're the native, not me."

"Okay, I'll do it."

"Then get a shower first. They'll be able to smell you at the other end if you don't."

Paul scrubbed himself clean and they both sat down to the burnt-flavoured food. They ate in silence, neither speaking until the meal was over

"Susan."

"Well?"

"I'm sorry."

The long distance operator put the call through to the Pentagon with only a slight quaver of surprise in her voice. It rang a number of times before it was answered.

"Yup?" The voice was tired, bored.

Paul steeled himself. "I want to speak to someone about a matter of National Security."

It was 0007 hours, seven minutes past midnight. The security office was manned by two G11 guards, one of whom was presently asleep on a couch. Corporal Foster who had lost the toss to take phone calls for the night could think of any amount of better things to do.

Calls regarding National Security were a dime a dozen. Fifth columnists seemed to crawl out of the woodwork after ten o'clock at night. Foster yawned, pulled a scratch pad towards him.

"You're speaking to an expert on National Security, buster. Okay? Let's start with your name."

Paul was struck dumb for a count of three, he had not

thought the man would ask that. "Er… Smith." He offered, his voice almost turning it into a question.

"Okay Mister Smith. What's the problem? Neighbours keeping you awake by singing Deutschland, Deutschland uber alles? Just sing the Star Spangled Banner right back at them. Perhaps your cleaning lady's got slanty eyes, eh? Talks with a funny accent?"

Paul was annoyed. "There's no need for sarcasm. I'm trying to tell you that there's a German spy ring that's showing interest in Los Alamos. They're probably cooking up some sabotage."

"Los Alamos? Where the hell's that? Makes a change from the White House anyway."

"Now look, there's no need to treat me like a crank."
"Gee, I'm sorry buddy. Didn't mean to give that impression. Now, can you tell me how and when this sabotage is going to take place? Oh – and by the way, there ain't no German spy rings in the States, they're all cleaned up. So where are they coming from?"

"I'm only trying to help."

"Help is it? Okay, let's have some facts." The Corporal injected some briskness into his voice. "First off, how many Germans are we talking about?"

"I don't know yet."

"Okay. How are they getting here – or there, land, sea or air?"

Again, Paul could not answer.

"Well, let's press on Mister Smith. Third, what precisely are they intending to do; fourth, how do you know all this; fifth, what's your job and just for the record, what's your real name. I mean, Smith went out with the Ark."

Paul had had enough. He slammed the receiver down. This was certainly not going to work; he would have to think of something else.

Foster chuckled as he heard the caller hang up. Another nut – he could tell after the first three words. He turned the diary around to face him; April 10th, 1945 said the printed entry. He entered the first item of the day:

0007: Male caller. Informed of German sabotage intentions at Los Alamos.

"Where the hell is that?" he wondered. "Sounds Mexican." He looked the name up in a gazetteer and completed his entry with state – New Mexico,

Susan read Paul's lack of success in his features. "No go eh?"

He shook his head. "No. They made me realise that I don't know anything. Every question he asked, I just didn't know."

"Well never mind. You said yourself, Carl can't do anything now. I expect it's all fizzled out."

Paul agreed. He did not say anything about the fish eyed Charles who had come to see him so many months ago in Des Moines.

As Paul was making his call, four of the agents he had tried unsuccessfully to report were no more than forty miles from his house. They had pulled off the road south of Santa Fe to drink beer and eat stale sandwiches from a late night diner. The car was thick with tobacco smoke.

Edward – the nominal cell leader now that Carl was no longer with them – and Errol a native American recruit, had arrived by car and collected the other two from outside of the railroad station.

"The Major wants us out at this guy, Webb's place." Ed told them between mouthfuls. "He takes the can back for Carl's death and, me, I'm going to put the fear of God into him. Carl was a good friend to me."

Ed drained the bottle and rolled the window down to toss the empty out. "'Nother bottle back there? Thanks. I've got to call Major P. when we get there, he'll give us the lowdown on what we do then."

"For Chris sake, shut that window. I thought it was supposed to be hot down here? What's he want us here for, anyway." The speaker was Frederick, one of the two who had travelled south by rail.

Ed shook his head and rolled the window up. "Don't know yet. With Carl taken out like that, I don't know nothing; he had all the details. Big job though, I reckon we'll make them fat asses sit up and take notice in Washington – that's for sure.

"Hey Ed, Errol said you burned Carl's place to the ground."

"Damn right I did." Ed chuckled. "Whole goddamn row was afire when I left. Nothing for anyone to find there, believe me, but nothing."

"And, Webb's sister – she was buried down there in that cellar too. Damn creepy.. She must have been down there while you were drinking Carl's booze, Ed."

"Me and you too. She'd been there a few weeks."

"I wonder who wiped her out. Reckon it was Carl?"

"Don't know. Could've been."

"Maybe that's why Webb took a bottle to him."

Edward turned suddenly to face Fred and jammed his beer bottle under the other's chin, pressing against his windpipe. "Now listen, Carl was a good friend of mine; just keep that mouth of yours buttoned – okay?"

"Okay." Fred husked as the pressure was released. "No offence."

"Right. None taken. Let's just concentrate on the job."

The four figures advanced on Paul's house from three sides. It was two fifteen a.m. and it took only two minutes to discover the place was deserted.

"So what now?"

"We go inside and wait, dummy. Now get that heap out of sight."

*

Joseph Piekenbrock was pleased yet unpleased. Reviewing his lists again and double-checking. Piekenbrock put a

248

checkmark against the final items. His black market contact had secured the radio beacons and parachutes, the most difficult objects to obtain. This was the reason for his pleasure. Adding to this was the fact that Erich had called him with news of a suitable place to prepare for an airstrip; however, the good news was tempered with Erich's information about several soft areas.

"Can they be avoided if we… mark them, do you think?" Piekenbrock asked from the phone booth.

"No. They're not big though, we could cover them with steel mesh – you know, the stuff they reinforce concrete with?"

"You're sure?"

"No problem. I'll need welding plant, someone to give me a hand, say two or three men."

"I'll arrange it then."

He had done so, but it was one more problem to contend with.

The other and more important reason for his displeasure was the orders from Schellenberg. On one day each week, a day fixed no more than two weeks earlier, Piekenbrock spent half an hour on the roof of the apartment block. Ostensibly, he was a conscientious janitor inspecting the ventilation ducts and elevator winding gear; in reality, he brought his hidden radio from its hiding place to listen for signals or, more occasionally to transmit. The radio was useless in his apartment because of the steel frames of the building and neighbouring blocks.

Today, Piekenbrock had received a message. Decoded, it

told him merely that the operation was on; the aircraft's E.T.A. was sixty hours away. The signal was signed 'B' which meant that it came not from Walter Schellenberg but from Reichsleiter Bormann.

Sixty hours – three days and two nights to draw all the threads together. The special breakdown truck, a fuel bowser from south of the Mexican border, the landing strip preparation and the focus – how far was that? Two thousand miles away? Eighteen hundred?

On top of these things was Carl's death. A braggart he might have been, but he'd had a lot of energy; he could get things done in a hurry when he tried. Almost certainly it was Paul Webb who had caused the man's injuries. Edward's description of the car he had seen leaving clinched the suspicion; Webb would have to be brought to heel, he hoped Edward would make him see sense.

A superman was needed, he thought; remembering a comic book a child had dropped in the lobby a few days ago. Was he one?

Sighing, knuckling his eyes; Piekenbrock began to formulate his plans.

*

Susan and Paul had closed the rift between them and were now sitting in the site cafeteria, open but somewhat deserted at this time of the morning. Paul had driven Susan back in his own car because she didn't like driving alone at such a late hour.

"I'll put everything down on paper then, you think that's best?"

"So long as you don't implicate yourself – or me, come to that. I'm an accessory to conspiracy or something by now."

"Right, I'll do it in the morning and you can type it for me tomorrow evening. Although I still think I should report in tomorrow."

"Give over, love. I told them you wouldn't be back until the day after. You've been driving eighteen hours or more, you can't do a proper job if you don't rest up a bit."

"Okay – I'm too tired to argue."

"You'd better get off home then, Paul. I've got to work tomorrow even if you don't. You're sure my car'll be all right?"

Paul got to his feet. "Certain." He kissed Susan on the lips. "Did I ever tell you I love you?"

"Not lately. I'll remind you sometime."

"Tomorrow then?"

"Tonight."

Paul pushed the door open, feeling for the light switch with his left hand. He didn't make it, A knee caught him viciously in the stomach; he doubled up, coughing and gasping for breath.

He had glimpsed the leg as a grey blur in the darkness. He never knew what hit him next – or after. He came round later, spluttering, looking up at a grinning man holding a washbowl.

"How come a little runt like you could take out a real man like Carl?" asked the face, swimming in and out of focus.

251

Dazed he might have been, but Paul understood the question. Not many moments passed before the full import flooded his mind. He knew, at once, who his assailants must be and refused to be cowed.

"That's my business – and I'd do it again if I had to."

A foot thudded into his ribs. "Don't get clever, sonny. Why?"

"Because the bastard killed my sister, that's why." Paul shouted.

"Yeah – I thought it musta been him that did it."

"I warned you before, Errol. That mouth'll get you killed one of these days." Then to Paul: "How do you know?"

"Why else would he bury her in the cellar?"

There was a concerted murmur of voices and Paul rolled over and got as far as his knees.

"Cut it out you three," He kicked Paul again though he didn't succeed in knocking him over. "Carl was my friend, Webb, and you killed him. You got any reason why I shouldn't finish you off?"

Paul thought fast, was this really happening – in his own home? "Your boss might not like the idea."

Edward bent down and breathed sour beer fumes in his face. "What do you know about my boss?" Another kick for good measure.

"If you leave the footwork out, I'll tell you." Watching the other carefully, Paul got stiffly to his feet. "I'm on your side, or I was 'til you got here. Who do you think dropped the word to the Major about this place? Carl was a personal matter – nothing to do with the Cause."

Paul staggered towards the couch and collapsed, pretending worse injuries than he had received. His ribs and genitals hurt like hell but he thought there was no permanent damage.

Edward looked at Paul, trying to gauge his frankness. Piekenbrock had told him to bring him into line; he had said nothing about Paul's involvement though the Major had been in a hurry.

"Hmm. What time do you have?"

"Four a.m.," offered Albert, smallest of the group.

"We'll give it another hour before we try the Major. Somebody get some coffee on, Webb and I are going to chat a bit more."

"Awe, come on." Paul felt on stronger ground now. "I've been awake for twenty four hours – I'm tired."

"Don't worry about it; you'll get to sleep when I'm satisfied, not before."

Paul thought back carefully. At no time had he indicated to anyone that he had had a change of heart. Provided that he trod carefully, he was sure that he could convince them.

"Just what do you do for the Cause?" Edward asked, drawing a chair up.

"I work at Los Alamos."

"What, in that dump – what is there to do there? Sweep the

side walks?"

"Where? In the town? For God's sake – you don't know yourself, do you? That's it, then, you'll have to wait until you get in touch with the Major. I'm not saying a word until he gives the go-ahead. Christ – I don't know you from Adam, you could be Federal agents for all I know." Paul suddenly wondered if he could be right. "You get in touch with the Major."

"The Major ordered me to question you, Webb. That's what I'm doing."

But the initiative had passed to Paul.

"Not 'til the Major says it's okay. I'm going to get some sleep until then. I'll be no use to him in this state."

So saying, Paul got up and went through to his bedroom and fell on his bed utterly exhausted. He heard a voice say. "Watch him" just before he lost consciousness.

Piekenbrock waited for the second sequence of three rings before lifting the receiver. He said nothing until Edward asked to speak to Charles and gave his own code name: Peter.

His watch on the hotel bedside table showed eight o'clock.

Edward told him of Paul's unwillingness to help them without the Major's authority.

"Put him on."

Errol had dragged Paul into the room as soon as the call was answered. They had been ringing Piekenbrock's number every half hour since five that morning.

"Good morning, my young friend. I was not pleased with the

254

news you left behind on your last trip north."

"I'm sorry about that, but you don't know why..."

"I have a shrewd idea. However, that is unimportant for the moment. I understand that my friend was not able to persuade you to help?"

"Not without your permission, Sir. He could have been anybody."

"Quite understandable, commendable even. You have my permission. Now will you put Peter back on the line?"

"Peter?"

"Me, you fool." Edward took the phone from Paul. "Yes?" He listened.

"Peter, you are to stay with your host, he may well be of help to us and certainly appears willing. You agree with this?"

"So far." Ed was grudging.

"I'll be visiting with you tonight, we'll talk about it then. What I want is this: your colleagues must visit Santa Fe this morning, an old friend will meet them there, outside the Palace of Governors. The reunion will take place at eleven this morning; his instructions must be followed exactly. There is construction work to be done and someone will have to drive a truck. This is understood?"

"Yes. What time do we expect you?"

"When you see me. Look after your host."

The receiver went dead and Edward replaced it on the hook.

TWENTY FOUR

Quite pleased with the results of his efforts, Joseph Piekenbrock put the phone down. Slowly, surely, all the pieces were falling into place. As long as they kept a firm hand on Webb, he was the secret to the success of the mission; other things were falling into place.

A contact, made when he worked for the Brazilian section of the S.D. had been able to supply a truck, rented through local contractors; welding gear was available from the same company. Two jeeps had been booked through a regular hire company and a fuel bowser – in reality, a sewage truck for purposes of disguise – would be waiting on the Mexican side of the border.

Even Mr. Scaporelli from apartment 137 had readily agreed to cover for him for the few days he expected to be away from his janitor's job. All that it had taken was the sight of a few bucks.

Bucks, bucks, bucks. They oiled the wheels of the American way of life. They eased everything from elections to espionage. Dollars – the key to America's downfall.

Barring accidents, everything would be ready at the appointed time. Joseph had procured every item required, made every arrangement called for. He allowed himself the luxury of a thin smile as he packed his valise before going downstairs to check out of the hotel.

Dressed unfamiliarly in a dark business suit, Piekenbrock left the hotel's breakfast room and walked casually into the lobby. He looked around at the occupants, his eyes coming to rest on an olive skinned Puerto Rican dressed in an old cotton windbreaker and reading a morning paper from the table.

"Mr. Enrico?"

"Yeah." The man stubbed out his seventh cigarette since arriving. "You'll be Maxwell?"

"Correct. Is your car parked close by?" The other nodded. "Then bring it to the entrance, I'll meet you there."

The Puerto Rican stamped on the gas peddle and the light green Plymouth shot into the traffic with a scream of smoking rubber.

"Mister. Enrico, take it more steadily. We don't want to draw attention."

"That's Enrico, mister. My first name, see. An' this is the way not to draw attention. If I slow down, they'll think I've got something to hide."

Joseph sat back. No doubt the driver was right.

"You do have everything. Mister Enrico?"

"The lot. Fifteen parachutes, fifteen army uniforms, three radio beacons. All courtesy of the US Army Airforce. I also got a Very pistol from my own stock with six Smith and Wesson.J58s and ammunition."

"I also ordered…"

"Ain't finished yet. Enough food for a siege and one very special winch truck."

"And fuel…"

"And fuel – hundred octane aviation spirit." Enrico looked at his chrome plated wristwatch. "Should be filling her up now. Driver'll be in Ciudad Juarez by this afternoon – one thing. They'll need a guide. You'll have to get someone to go down and meet it as it comes across the border. Okay?"

"All right."

"I'll give you the telephone number when we stop."

"You have done well. The price?"

"As agreed. All in at twenty five gees."

"And this also pays for your silence?"

"Hell, Mister Maxwell. What kinda question's that now? We done plenty black market business in the past."

"This deal is not just a camera or a few cases of cigarettes." This was all traceable stuff, thought Joseph to himself, this was the first time, they had met in person. Joseph had much preferred to use the ubiquitous telephone to preserve his identity. "What would you have to say if some of Mr. Hoover's little boys came around Mister Enrico?"

"Fuck Mr. Hoover's little boys. The F.B.I, don't know I exist." He grinned. "That's the way I like it."

For the remainder of the short journey, nothing further was

258

said until the car reached its destination: a large corrugated iron shed on the town's outskirts. Enrico searched his pockets and eventually came up with a set of keys.

"Mind opening the doors for me? I'll drive straight inside."

Enrico lit another cigar from the stub of the first and gunned the motor as his passenger slid the doors apart. When the car was inside, he closed them again and turned towards his purchase.

"Beaut, eh? The jib slides around in a circle so you can use it to lift stuff on board, also gives you access to the compartment under the floor. Take a look around." While he spoke, the black marketeer and sometime engineer took a hip flask out and poured a generous mouthful down his throat.

"Yes. I was told that you like a drink." Piekenbrock's tone was disapproving.

"An odd one, only an odd one. Kills the germs, see." Enrico laughed.

"Too many odd ones add up to trouble Mister Enrico. Is it gassed up?" The other nodded. "Show me how the jib works."

"Take out these two bolts here, see? They're dummies." He took hold of the hook which was secured to a cross brace and pulled. "Turns round real easy." The base plate moved and exposed the sawn end of an inch thick floor board. Jumping up, Enrico levered it up and threw it to one side. The remainder of the floor could then be folded up on hinges.

"There you are."

All the equipment was packed in to either side of a central, half cylindrical rack in which the packs of food were laid.

"Excellent." Joseph was quite satisfied, the standard of workmanship was all that he had asked for. "Now, the telephone number."

"Ah yes." Enrico fished inside his wind breaker and found a notebook. He tore out a page and passed it across.

"I'll just have a look in the cab." He went round to the front as Enrico replaced the floorboards and resecured the crane. "Ignition keys in the dash – oh, what's this, Mister Enrico?"

"What's what?" He came round and looked in through the door as Piekenbrock stepped aside and pointed.

Piekenbrock stepped behind Enrico and caught him by the throat with his right arm. With his left hand on the back of the other's head and a sharp jerk to the Peurto Rican's chin, the spinal column snapped with an audible click.

Joseph's expression, though grim, was a satisfied one. Just like basic training at Park Zorgvliet where he had been an instructor for almost six months before the war. So much quieter than a gun, so much less messy than a knife.

He dragged the small body to the Plymouth and arranged it behind the wheel. Joseph had no qualms about killing when it was necessary – and this was. The Government equipment was stolen, not surplus; eventually it would have been missed and inquiries would have led inevitably to Enrico. Like himself, those who would follow up would be professionals and Enrico had known him now by sight instead of a number in a public

260

telephone box.

The thought led to another one as he turned the ignition and pressed the self starter. So far, only Erich, Edward and Paul knew him but that would change when he reached Los Alamos; Erich and Edward would die, he knew, before revealing anything but, Paul Webb and the others? He would have to see.

Piekenbrock searched for the flask of bourbon and then Enrico's notebook. He put the latter in his own pocket and then checked the other pockets and car. There was nothing which shouldn't be there.

He poured the spirit into Enrico's mouth and down his front before closing the dead man's fingers around it. Finally, Joseph jammed the other's foot on the throttle and closed the door. Going to the other side, he reached in and jerked the gear shift into drive and stepped back smartly.

The car moved off, gathering speed from the racing motor and crashed into the far end of the garage, stalling as the metal sheeting buckled.

Joseph opened the main doors, quickly glancing to right and left before pushing them all the way. He climbed into the gleaming yellow breakdown truck and drove out on to the highway.

Piekenbrock pointed the hood south and put his foot down.

TWENTY FIVE

Alone in the house with Ed, Paul considered tackling t
he man. With the other three men gone, the odds were a little
more even but, looking at the overall size and musculature of his
keeper – for that was certainly what he was – the odds were not
that even. The man was a freak, all of six feet three with huge
bulging shoulder and chest muscles, arms that almost reached his
knees. Paul, if nothing else, was a realist in gauging his chances
against another man; against Ed, his chances were close to zero.

Evidence of his nature was written in every course feature: a
strong arm man. Paul imagined the pleasure Ed would take in
tearing his arms from their sockets and stamping all over him in
his brand new cowboy boots. It seemed best to take things nice
and easy and to try and get along with his guard until
Piekenbrock arrived.

He dealt another hand of gin and stopped suddenly – there
was a rifle in the kitchen! Nothing special, a gun he had bought
and used on occasions for shooting at jackrabbits but no, it was
hidden from thieves behind one of the ceiling joists. It would be
awkward to get out in a hurry and the ammunition was in a
drawer in his bedroom. No, he would have to forget that for the
time being.

LAST MISSION

Paul dealt out what seemed to be the thousand and first hand of gin.

Erich led the convoy of four vehicles out of Santa Fe, heading for the wooded country which concealed the valley selected for the airplane's landing. The elderly Ford and the two jeeps were tied to the best speed that the truck, with its load of wire mesh, could make. He calculated that it would take them a good two hours. He had left his own car at the truck depot to bring the driver of the truck back later.

He totted up the length of time needed to finish the job; two hours there, four more to lay the reinforcement, weld it and spike it firmly into the ground and a further hour to return to Webb's place. Unsure of the food situation, Erich had spent the last half hour before the meeting shopping in the main street stores.

Asking directions to the museum known as the Palace of Governors – probably Santa Fe's most notable building, he had nearly had a heart attack, seeing his three comrades cruising slowly along the street. Errol, who had more than just an eye for the girls was leaning out of the rear window, whistling and shouting obscene suggestions at every woman who had the misfortune to be on the sidewalk. If ever there was a time when they should have avoided attention, it was now and here they were creating the biggest disturbance the little town had probably seen since General Kearny retook it from the Mexicans.

Erich had left the old man pointing along the street and had dashed across the road, regardless of traffic, scattering fresh rolls

263

and sliced salami in the process. He had got Fred's attention by pounding on the bonnet and only just in time; a gum-chewing Deputy was giving the car earnest consideration; seconds only had saved them from a public dressing-down and official form filling.

Of course, if the Major had given more explicit instructions to his agents rather than expecting them to meet up this way, the incident would not have occurred but Piekenbrock had a pathological distrust of written instructions. He even hated the microdots which reached him through the Swiss or Norwegian and Bahamian mail lines.

Erich, as the Major's closest confidante, respected Piekenbrock's methods despite the difficulties they could lead to. Errol, in fact, was a prime example of why the Major exercised such care. A few beers and a willing woman and the man would spill everything. His appearance and fondness for women had given him his name. It certainly was not the one he had been christened with. Erich did not know the full story but he had gleaned so much. It seemed that Errol bore some little resemblance to an actor of that name. A young man known for his love of women and wine.

Well, he had no power to change Errol's nature but all that he and the others would spill today would be sweat.

When they reached the site, Erich started them off as he meant to go on. "You'll work like hell today if you want any supper. No time for smoking. Every one of us is going to pull his
264

weight here. Okay?"

Three reluctant groans were his only reply.

TWENTY SIX

Eight hours into the flight, the interior of the B24 was freezing. Although not warm, the men were not cold in their heated suits, though draughts seemed to penetrate every opening. The bumpy flight earlier had made them even more uncomfortable and adding to this, the fumes from the aviation spirit persisted even though Neuper had drained the accumulation in the bomb bay. The oxygen masks only partially protected them from the effects of the petroleum and Schroeder checked his team for any illness or nausea.

Unmoving, uncomplaining as yet, most were asleep or trying to sleep. Only Hoeckle seemed aware of Kurt's gaze, he winked above the mask. Kurt smiled, nodded, passed on. He was sure that if he had a dozen, no – less, six Hoeckles, then anything would be possible. The man was a veritable tower of strength. He was the only member of the team who Kurt would have liked to relax with but of course until the mission was over that was impossible. Seriousness was a mask Kurt needed to wear at all times.

Seated again, Kurt watched the damp grey fog outside; torn to shreds by the air screws and rushing astern. With nothing to occupy him, he began to think about the mission; was it possible? He began to entertain doubts, the first since leaving the Fuhrerbunker.

Would the aircraft make it, was there sufficient fuel? Despite the fact that he was looking at two huge multicelled tanks, Kurt thought to hear a lack of rhythm in the pounding engines. Could they possible get away with stealing a bomb from what must be the most heavily guarded installation in the United States? Were the scientists right in calculating an atom bomb's strength: equivalent to a thousand single one ton bombs? What would be the effects of such an explosion, surely it would blow the plane out of the air?

Suddenly beset with misgivings, Kurt released his safety harness again and made his way forward. On the flight deck, he tapped Oberstleutnant Reinicke on the shoulder. The pilot pointed to the jack plug dangling from his mask then to a socket; Kurt plugged it in.

"Herr Oberst? What can I do for you?"

"You know the power of this bomb we are to drop?"

"I know what the scientists say."

"Would the shock wave affect the aircraft?"

"Ja. It would. It would crush us to pulp."

"God in Heaven."

"But do not worry Herr Oberst. Immediately the bomb is released, I shall put the Liberator into a steep dive to gain speed. The shock wave travels at the speed of sound, this is fast but not so fast that we cannot run before it. When it does reach us, it will be too weak to do any harm."

"You are certain of this?"

"As certain as one can be But if current orders prevail you wont be on the plane when I make that run so why worry, your part of the job must be rough enough?" He shrugged, changing the subject. "Any how, how are your men taking the ride?"

"They do not complain."

The Liberator droned on. Beneath them, the Pacific was an expanse of tiny blue corrugations. The horizon was lost in haze and blended imperceptibly into the lighter blue of the dome above them.

Two soldiers opened tins of self heating soup, handing them out before taking four through to the aircrew. The soup was followed by more hours of inactivity. The twelfth hour passed and Willi Braun came back to switch from one to the other of the internal fuel tanks. He gave a quick thumbs up and went forward again, plugging back in to oxygen and communications.

"All right, Willi? Your sums are coming out right?"

"So far, so good."

"Better get our intrepid Oberst Schroeder in. I'll let him know. It can't be easy for them all back there, sitting around with nothing to do."

Willi opened the door, secured Kurt's attention and beckoned him forward.

"Yes?" He asked a few moments later,

"Thought you'd like to know that everything's fine. Had a

slight contretemps with an Allied spotter plane a while back. Wanted our identification."

"What did you say?"

"Nothing. We waggled our wings and left them to it. They will have to assume that our radio was faulty or tuned to another frequency – whatever they like."

"Our fuel is still all right? I mean, we still have enough?"

"I sincerely hope so, Herr Oberst. This aircraft is virtually a fuel tank with wings, we've stripped everything it was possible to strip. Don't worry, we'll get there – we shan't be doing any sightseeing on the way but we'll get there."

"I know arrangements have been made to get us back to Germany or, at least, to a neutral country. Do you want to go into details while I'm here?"

Reinicke shook his head. "Not if you don't mind, Herr Oberst. I'll say everything when you brief your men; save saying it twice."

"Very well, Oberstleutnant. Thank you."

"Not at all. Willi, take over now, eh? It's my turn for a few hours' sleep. Goodnight Oberst Schroeder."

The World turned beneath them as the B24 flew west. The sun overtook them and, ultimately, drew a blanket of night and stars over the lone aircraft.

Far beneath them were stars too; occasional lights where the blackout was incomplete or ignored. Ahead, outlined against the gleaming surface of the sea and edged with phosphorescence would be Florida.

A half hour previously, Willi had shot the stars and then worked for some minutes with pencil, paper and charts. He instructed Reinicke and, at the precise second, the pilot altered course a few degrees to the south. The unseen shores of the Florida peninsular edged round on to the starboard quarter as the Liberator left its great circle course. An hour passed and the plane turned west once more, then towards the north. The Gulf of Mexico lay ahead, Cuba to the south, Florida – now dimly visible – to the north.

Reinicke began to lose height while Willi watched the magnetic compass. They crossed the coast of the North American continent into the state of Louisiana at less than two hundred meters.

"Next stop, the Rockies." Said Willi. "I'll take a nap – and keep it smooth."

"At this height?"

"Wake me in an hour, I don't want you running into the mountains."

"Joachim." Pieter Reinicke looked round. "Check the fuel in the fuselage one more time. The wing tanks should be far enough down now so it shouldn't be a problem."

Neuper went back and nodded in Kurt's direction. Kurt got to his feet and took off his mask. "Nearly there?" He mouthed. Neuper pointed to his ear and Kurt shouted into it. "We're pretty low now. Will we be landing soon?"

270

The other held up five fingers. "About five hours." He shouted back. "Staying low in case of radar. Up again soon."

Kurt nodded and looked at his watch. "Soup?" He mimed drinking actions and Neuper nodded.

A few minutes later, Fachinger took warm cans forward and Duensing distributed more between his comrades and officers.

When Reinicke judged it safe, he climbed slowly back to an altitude of seven thousand five hundred metres. Friedrich Haas had listened intently on the radio, searching the frequencies; he had picked up local radio stations, a radio ham and – briefly – a police band but nothing which should concern them.

Suddenly, Haas sat bolt upright. "Pieter."

"Trouble?"

"We're being signalled by a US ground station, call sign KG830E. They want us to identify ourselves and to know our flight plan."

Reinicke shrugged. "Manufacture some static Friedrich. Tell them that we're an air ambulance on an emergency flight – you know the stuff."

Friedrich switched to transmit and started to speak, flicking the toggle switch every few seconds and making certain that important bits were covered by silence.

"Say again." He heard in his earphones. "You must have a problem on your radio."

"Fli... air ambulance... field." He returned. Most of the removable panelling on the radio equipment had been discarded

271

with the armour plate and other weighty items. Friedrich reached inside and pulled a valve loose, rattling the pins in the socket. KG830E would hear a medley of crackles, buzzes and other assorted sounds.

"Out of range, Pieter."

"Good."

TWENTY SEVEN

The hours had passed slowly for Paul. Despite his allusions to the Cause and to the Major as though he were a close acquaintance, his companion had continued to watch him with obvious distrust. Ed would neither play cards nor join in conversation.

Paul had tried to convince his keeper that his presence would be missed at the Hill. He had dozed off and on throughout the morning and prepared lunch for both of them: grapefruit segments, poached eggs on rye bread and the coffee which had been virtually on tap since he had been woken to speak to Piekenbrock.

"Well Ed, when do you think the Major will be here?" Paul asked between bites.

Edward shifted his huge frame until the wicker seat creaked. He stuffed half an egg into his mouth and spoke around it.

"Early evening. Said he still had a lot to arrange, driving down from Pennsylvania."

"Sooner the better. If I can't go into work, I want to know what I'm supposed to be doing. As the man on the inside of all this, I expect he'll have a lot for me to do."

If Paul had expected to draw Ed with this remark, he was

sadly mistaken. Ed grunted – the same response he had had since the other three left.

"What about your friends?"

"So what about my friends?" Ed was both aggressive and wary.

"What time will they be back? I'm just thinking of food. I could have got something if you'd trust me. They're going to be hungry and I don't have much in."

"Forget about the food, Webb. It's all taken care of. Piekenbrock will have seen to that. Now just shut that face of yours. I don't like questions, see?"

"Okay." Paul got up and started to gather dishes.

"Now what are you doing?"

"Washing up, of course."

"Forget it."

Paul became annoyed.

"Look, you object to my talking, you won't let me clear the table. Do you mind if I go to my room and lie down? I didn't get much sleep last night." At least, thought Paul, I can get the ammunition out. I may get a chance at the rifle later.

Edward's mind ticked over steadily.

"Let's take a look." He said at last.

They went through and Ed pushed past him and gave the room a good look over. He stepped back again into the short corridor. "Where does this door go?"

"Spare room."

Ed opened the door and glanced in, a two-high bunk bed was the room's only furniture. A metal gauze fly screen covered the window, screwed to the wooden frame.

"In here Webb. And if I hear anything I shouldn't God help you. Until the Major gets here and gives you the okay, I don't trust you an inch. Understand?"

Paul nodded and went in, closing the door as he went.

Ed slammed it open again. "And leave the goddamn door open." He turned and went through to the kitchen-cum-living room.

"Damn and blast the man." Paul cursed under his breath. "At least I'm away from him for the time being – he was starting to get to me and that's a fact." He lay down on the narrow bed which twanged musically as he did so. He tried to channel his mind along some useful lines. No ammunition; even if he could get the rifle, one was useless without the other. Perhaps if he stayed quiet for long enough, Ed would find some reason to go outside; he could then get both.

Paul remained there for what seemed an age, his thoughts chasing each other in a circle until, from sheer boredom, the very thing happened that he had not wished for. He fell asleep.

The sounds of a big engine awoke him just in time to hear it switched off. He looked at his watch, four o'clock. What the hell was he doing in bed? Suddenly everything flooded back, he remembered Edward and the others; without a doubt, the others had returned. He had fallen asleep and was now no nearer a solution than before, if only Susan hadn't kept him up late the night before.

…Susan!

The thought struck him like a hammer. She was coming round this evening – how could he stop her? Nothing came instantly to mind. Angry with himself and wondering what opportunities had slipped by while he was asleep, Paul got up off the lower bunk and strode hastily into the other room.

They were just coming in the door – all three, no, four of them. God, they were getting more numerous by the hour; how many more were still to come, he wondered.

"Hi Ed. How's the baby sitting going?"

Ed lifted his arm as if to hit the other, though he grinned as he did it. "No sweat, Erich. Had a hard day?"

"Has he had a hard day." It was Errol. "Ask us, not him, he's a bloody slave driver."

Erich grinned. "We had a job to do. I told you, sooner it's over, sooner we eat." He looked Paul up and down. "So this is Webb?"

"Yeah. Webb. Brother-in-law to Carl and also murderer of Carl." Ed spat on the floor. "Says he's one of us but I've got my doubts. Carl was my friend."

"Heard about it from the Major. Says you burned the house down after you found the body."

Paul's ears pricked up. This was something new.

"Too right I did. Somebody had to tidy up after the bastard

276

had finished."

"Carl killed my sister." Paul offered as a defence and then abruptly changed the subject. "If you're hungry I can probably fix up some beans, there's nothing else."

"Beans? No thanks. We've got plenty to eat in the truck outside. Got anything to cook steak on?"

"Steak? Sure. Bring it in, I'll put the grill on."

"And eggs." Added Errol. "Steak and eggs." He belched. "Been thinking 'bout them all day."

"Sure – if you've got the eggs."

"We've got 'em."

The 'phone rang just as Paul was laying the first plate of steaks on the table. Automatically, he went to answer it but, Ed, moving with the speed of a much lighter man, was there first. "Yes." He listened for ten seconds. "Right away, about a half hour."

He turned to look at the rest who were all standing, frozen in the attitudes they had been in when the phone first rang. "The Major. He wants someone to go and lead him here. He's in Santa Fe."

They all relaxed but no one volunteered, everyone was too hungry and loath to leave the smell of grilled meat.

"Okay." Said Edward, smart enough to realise the problem. "The man who goes gets to take two steaks with him."

Coming as it did after that long, long day, Piekenbrock's

arrival at the house was an anti-climax to Paul. He had spent so many hours worrying over events he could do nothing about that Paul had become resigned to almost anything. Even the bright yellow winch truck, streaked with dust and standing outside his door aroused only a slight interest.

Both Edward and Erich came to attention as the Major entered the room. "Heil Hitler." Roared Ed, throwing out his arm, fingers stretched flat, in a Nazi salute, incongruous in a man dressed in a brightly colored summer shirt.

Piekenbrock nodded in return and nodded again following his introduction to each of the cell members. "It's been a long ride." He said. "A cup of coffee would be welcome. A strong one."

"At once, Sir." Replied Ed. "Webb. Coffee for the Major."

"It is black, Major?" Paul asked, making an effort to imply a longer acquaintance than was the case.

Joseph Piekenbrock smiled with his lips, as he had done on the last occasion. "That is correct Paul." Then, turning to Erich. "The landing strip. Is it prepared?"

Erich told him that it had been, that he anticipated no problems,

Paul brought the coffee. His guess about the color had been pure luck, of course, a fifty-fifty chance; still, a small victory. So was the discussion now taking place; an airstrip meant aircraft or an aircraft.

"Good to see you again, Paul." Said Joseph as he took the

cup from Paul's fingers. "Soon, we shall have a long talk. First though, there are other matters to arrange."

"Ah, uh, fine Major. Look, um; I have a date tonight. I guess, under the circumstance, I'd better go around and see my er... date and put her off."

Again, Joseph smiled, chuckled and again, the humor didn't reach his eyes. "A date? She is coming here, Paul?"

"Yes. Around eight."

"Well then, let her come. I would like to meet her. You can show your young lady what fine friends you have."

Paul's heart skipped a beat but Ed was there, listening to every word; he grinned. "Sure, she'd love to meet you Sir."

"Good. Then it is settled. We shall not be staying late. We have a busy night ahead of us but perhaps we can be sociable; one of us will stay to keep you company." Ed nodded with satisfaction. His suspicions were all but confirmed. "Another cup of coffee, if you will and then you must excuse me."

"Right Major."

"Oh – and by the way – the telephone, it works at the moment?"

"Sure."

"Good, good. I remember your saying it is sometimes troublesome."

"It's mostly okay now."

"Fine. Now Erich; this valley of yours. How long to get there?"

"Thirty miles, Sir. Should take an hour or so. The last ten miles is pretty rough terrain."

"Mm." Piekenbrock consulted his watch. "Then we shall have to leave around nine. The jeeps and the truck – what arrangements are made?"

"Jeeps are on station Sir. The truck's still here. You probably noticed it when you came in. Whoever takes it back will have to pick my car up from the depot."

"I agree, the truck must be returned to Santa Fe and someone else must go to…" He paused. "The car you use Paul, is it the one we bought?"

Paul frowned and then suddenly realised what Joseph meant, it had been bought with the money that Piekenbrock had given him. "Yes it is." He noticed that Ed was back in the dark again. "You want the keys?"

"Yes please Paul. I need it for someone to go to the Mexican border in."

Paul watched as Joseph took a slip of paper from his jacket and then ask for a Ciudad Juarez number. When it went through he said: "Maxwell. What time?" There was a pause while he listened. "In that case, my man will be ready for you at six in the morning." He rang off and looked round for Edward.

"Edward. You have a man who speaks Spanish."

"Albert understands a little."

"Then Albert it shall be. Albert, when the rest of us leave for the strip at nine, you will drive south to, er," he clicked thumb
280

and forefinger, "to El Paso, to the border. Use Webb's car, check to see that there is plenty of juice in it. At six o'clock tomorrow morning a sewage tanker – which you should be able to smell – will cross over. You will pretend to thumb a lift. When the driver stops you will say

Lo mejor es no decir nada, "the best thing is to say nothing'.

"Okay." Albert repeated the phrase.

"The tanker must be brought straight to the airstrip."

"Now this I have to see." Remarked Erich. "A plane that flies on shit."

Joseph mimed a smile. "You all hear that? We move at nine. We may well have to wait quite a while, make sure you are dressed in warm clothing. If you have vacuum flasks, fill them with hot drink. There will be no lighting of fires."

Joseph appeared to have finished. "Shall I make something to eat?" asked Paul.

"What time did you say your girl friend is coming?"

"Around eight."

"And she will be expecting to eat with you?"

Paul nodded.

"Then we shall all of us eat together, it will help to fill the time. Ah – Paul."

"Sir."

"You will be meeting with a German Officer tonight – I should say – in the morning. He will want to know everything that you know about Los Alamos; perhaps you had better start to

281

put your thoughts in order while you cook."

"What are we trying to do?"

"That is something for you to wonder about until the appropriate time Mister Webb."

The use of his surname was a rebuke for his curiosity. Paul returned to the kitchen area, flicking a longing glance at the joist which concealed the rifle. What to do about Susan? He wondered. Meet her at the door and frighten her off somehow? How could he explain that to Piekenbrock? He shook his head and knelt to sort through the tins and packages that had come out of the yellow truck. There seemed nothing else to do but play along as long as he could, learn as much as he could. The more he knew, the more he could tell the authorities.

In the event, Paul had no chance to meet Susan at the door. The ever-vigilant Ed beat him to it by seconds.

"Hi Paul. Your car broken... down?" Dismayed by the six men looking appraisingly at her, Susan's voice ran down. "What is this?"

Joseph rose and took her by the arm, ushered her to the seat he had just vacated.

"Good evening." He said and Susan started at the sudden words after the long hush. "We are all old friends of Paul's, from Iowa, from Des Moines. A camping holiday – we decided to visit with him since we were so close."

It was the flat tone of Joseph's voice, accentless, almost devoid of inflection, that disturbed Susan most. She looked at
282

Paul, searching for some answer. Paul smiled but did not move to kiss her.

"And Paul is such an excellent cook." Joseph carried on, unperturbed by the atmosphere. "He insisted that we stay and eat together."

Mechanically, not knowing what else to do, Paul set out the dishes on the table while Joseph persisted with Susan.

"Now my dear; I must say, you are a most charming young lady. What do you do for a living?"

It was such a simple question that it caught her unawares. "I work for the Government."

"Really? The Government, Round here? What work is of such importance that the Government brings you to this dreary part of America, Miss Millar?"

Susan tried to play it down. What had he said and why had he not kissed her? If these had been friends, he would certainly have done so; he took a boyish enjoyment in showing her off to friends.

"Doctor Millar works in the medical unit." Interrupted Paul.

"Oh – I see. And what are your feelings for our Paul?" Piekenbrock changed the subject with a studied lack of delicacy.

"Nothing to do with you Sir. I can tell you that." Susan's forbears had Irish as well as English connections; she rose to Joseph's bait quickly, her ready temper showing in her color.

"Come now Susan – I may call you Susan? I'm like a second father to Paul. I meant no harm. I was only checking out

283

my guess – that you both think a lot of each other. Has he introduced you to his sister yet?"

"His sister's dead." The reply tumbled out without thought.

Joseph pounced. "Ah, he has told you of that. Did he also tell you of Carl?"

Numbly, Susan nodded.

"Paul told you how he avenged his sister, then?"

Again, she nodded.

"And obviously you have not informed on him." Joseph nodded slowly. "Highly commendable Susan, considering that the authorities would take a poor view of your conspiracy." He patted her sleeve. "You're a very lovely girl, Susan, and a high spirited young lady. English, aren't you?"

"And if I am?"

"Nothing. Nothing at all. I have a high regard for the English; despite their size, that country's tenacity is well illustrated by that British Bulldog, Churchill. Yes – English; educated at Cambridge, I would guess from your accent."

Joseph turned to Paul. "I think it would be useful for your young lady to speak with the gentleman who will be arriving later. Do you see any problems in this?"

Paul chose to take the question literally.

"Only if Susan is late for work. They will wonder where she is."

"Then Susan will telephone in the morning and tell them that she is ill."

"And what about me?" Asked Paul.

"You! Why, you are one of us Paul. When this over, you will not need to work here again."

"You're Germans, aren't you?" Susan asked, her voice level.

"I am German, Susan. The others are German only by birth – like Paul here. A good German soldier in the heart of America."

Piekenbrock abruptly dismissed them from his thoughts by telling both Paul and Susan to take a seat at the far end of the room.

It was almost nine o'clock and the agents clustered around him as he gave final orders and all but one of them went outside. Joseph stood too and spoke in their direction.

"Edward will be staying here. I suggest you get some sleep while you can. It will be an early rise tomorrow."

Piekenbrock left, closing the outside door carefully behind him.

"Come on. Let's go and lay down." Paul got up and followed by Susan, went out of the room towards his bedroom.

"Sorry to disappoint you folks." Edward was right behind them. "There won't be any nice soft double beds tonight. You'll be using this room." He indicated the spare room with its bunk beds. "Springs're pretty musical, I'll be able to hear every move you make."

Although the breakdown truck made easy work of the trip to

the airstrip, Piekenbrock experienced twinges of doubt when he considered the fuel tanker. There were several areas of rough ground and two points where the terrain lifted sharply and unexpectedly up steep grades. He put the thoughts to the back of his mind; it was no use worrying when he had no idea of the make of the tanker and, when Erich brought the truck to a stop, Joseph had other matters to occupy him.

The trail they had been following fell steeply into one end of the shallow valley and continued along the floor, two hundred yards at its widest point. Moonlight was bright enough to show quite clearly the stands of trees climbing the mountain slopes to either side.

Joseph nodded. "It's an ideal spot Erich, well chosen. You're sure that we shan't be disturbed here?"

"Nearest peublo is Santa Clara, all of ten miles from here. Kapo Indians. They have a few sheep grazing hereabouts but it's rare for them to be about. Usually range more to the North and East. In any case, even if they get wind of us, they're solitary types; be weeks before the local Indian agent knew about it."

"That may be so but I don't care to take the chance; I want guards posted. I guess we're a bit thin on the ground and I'll need you to help position the beacons but the other two – what were their names?"

"Errol and Frederick. Fred for short."

"Mm. Well, Errol and er – Fred can take up positions on either side of the valley. Up there," Joseph pointed, and there; as

286

high up under the tree line as they can get."

"You want them to stay there until the plane takes off again?" Erich was quite serious but Piekenbrock knew the quality of his recruits. The nights were cold, frosty in sheltered places; his agents were enthusiastic amateurs not Waffen SS. He smiled. "No. I presume that Schroeder will want to make his own arrangements but, meanwhile, we must remain vigilant. Give each of them a handgun out of the back and impress them that the weapons are to be used for signalling only in emergency. They are not to shoot at anyone, understood?"

"Understood."

"Nor at jack rabbits. I want no disturbance."

Errol and Fred, who had ridden up on the back of the breakdown, had already jumped down and were stamping the ground and swinging their arms in an effort to stay warm. Erich gave them their orders.

"Goddamn it, Erich. It's cold enough down here, it's going to freeze our balls off up there." Fred spat a wad of chewing gum on to the turf.

"Yeah – an' I still got use for mine."

"Get up there." Erich spoke low and fierce. "You can keep warm by running. Now get before I sink my boot in your ass."

Joseph ignored the interchange. They were menials. If they wished to serve the Reich, they must begin by following orders – unpleasant ones as well as pleasant. When they had gone, clutching a vacuum flask in one hand, a gun in the other; Joseph and Erich compared their surroundings with a large scale ordnance map.

"The beacons should be situated here, here and here. That puts the first up there, see that outcrop? You take a transmitter, put it on top; you're younger than me. I'll see to the other two; they want to be on either side. Over there and, the other one – there."

"Okay. Just show me how to turn it on again."

"Just a simple switch, see? I've preset the frequency." Later, when the beacons were operating; Joseph paced the length of the proposed runway at Erich's side. They stopped at each area where it had been deemed reinforcing was needed.

"Okay?" Asked Erich, anxiously when the inspection was complete. "I should think it will be all right. None of the soft spots are anywhere near where the plane should touch down."

"It's a pity we can't speak to them direct, we could talk them down then."

"Yes – a pity but…" Joseph coughed and cleared his throat.

"Excuse me, it must be the air up here after New York."

"I guess it's the altitude. I hadn't noticed it though."

"No, I mean that I'm not used to so much fresh air." Joseph returned to the previous subject. "No, it would be too dangerous to risk breaking radio silence. Always the chance that unfriendly ears may be listening."

Erich nodded, looked at his watch and then up at the brilliant scattering of stars. "What are they going to do when they do get

288

here?"

"I can't tell you."

He wondered if the Major meant 'can't or 'won't'. Did he know what their mission was and preferred to be secretive or was even Piekenbrock excluded from this knowledge? Erich did not enquire.

Time passed. The wind sighed in the trees on the hillsides and the stars wheeled slowly above them. The cab was getting cold and the engine ticked every few minutes as metal contracted. Erich pulled his jacket closer and looked at his watch for the twentieth time. "How long do you reckon?"

"Sometime just before dawn if they timed everything right. They could be later, of course, if something happened. If they're not here by full daylight we must use our own discretion, perhaps abort our side of the operation. One thing is certain, they can't turn back."

Piekenbrock switched on the engine. "Another hour at the least before they come. We'll park the truck at the other end; the headlights will light up the strip if it is too dark when they get here."

In the privacy of the spare room, Paul tried to apologise to Susan for the way things had turned out. She put a finger to his lips. She knew what had happened since she arrived and had reconstructed much of what had gone before; she knew that once things had been set in motion, he could have acted in no other way. She told him as much in whispers.

Paul told her about the aircraft that was expected; they talked about it in more whispers, concluding as Paul had already done, that they should bide their time. "They will need more information from me," he said, "and that is where I can mislead them. They have no way of telling if I'm lying. At the first opportunity, one of us must inform the creeps at the Hill. If you hear our friend go out, we can risk a phone call."

"I wouldn't bet on that big hunk going anywhere without being told. He looks one step removed from a caveman. Did you notice the length of his arms?"

Paul chuckled. "He's smart enough – don't fool yourself. But don't let him get to you, as long as they need me, they aren't going to touch you."

"I know," Susan nodded but thought; *how long will they need you for?*

There was not a lot of room on the bottom bunk, enough for making love and Susan thought of it once or twice but with Ed outside, alert to every sound they made, the idea died as quickly as it came to her. She satisfied herself by drawing Paul closer and kissing him long and hard.

"Don't worry darling," she whispered, "every dog has his day."

TWENTY EIGHT

He was not worried, Pieter Reinicke told himself.

His nonchalant manner hid the fact from the others but it was becoming increasingly difficult to convince himself. He was staring at fuel gauges that were turning towards the zero mark far too rapidly for his peace of mind.

"How far do you think?" He asked of Willi.

"Can't be far now. Say three fifty kilometres?"

"Could you say a little less?"

"I've been watching the gauges too, Pieter. There's a smudge on the edge of the scope, it could be them."

"I hope to God you're right."

From the hedge-hopping episode – or as near as one could safely hedge-hop a B24, Pieter had stayed comparatively low which meant that the fuel burned faster. However, it was more economical than climbing again if they didn't have too except that now the Rockies barred their way. "Time to take her upstairs."

"You'd better. I don't see what else it can be."

"As long as you're sure Willi. If you're wrong, I'm going to have to bring this thing in on fumes."

Willi's eyes swivelled from screen to gauges and back

again. "Take her up. It's got to be mountains, filling the top of the screen now. If I'm wrong, you can always court martial me when we get home."

Pieter laughed. "If you're wrong, Willie, there'll be no need of a court martial." He eased the control column back and the Liberator started to gain altitude gradually.

"I hope our friends down there have found us a nice flat landing strip. It's a certain fact we're not going to see the other side of the Rockies."

Willi didn't answer immediately, he was busy. "Level out at forty seven hundred metres, it gives us an adequate margin."

"Right. Four five now." A few minutes later: "Four seven… now." As he put the stick forward, Haas' voice filled his earphones.

"Beacons ahead on our frequency Sir. Approximately one ninety, two hundred kilometres. Alter course to the south by two degrees."

Pieter visualised the chart in his mind. "Hear that Willi? They must have found a strip up in the mountains somewhere. Joachim, tell Oberst Schroeder to start getting his men ready for landing. Bring them forward although they don't have to play at sardines like they did at take off. Oh – and just check that we don't have any fuel sloshing around still."

As Neuper went back, Pieter tapped Willi on the forearm. "Thanks for getting us here, Willi. I'll see if I can bring her down

292

now."

The sky above the eastern end of the valley shone blue-green as the dawn crept towards them. A shallow layer of mist floated in tentacles above the valley floor. An occasional bird still sang, a late reminder of the dawn chorus that had started an hour ago on the wooded slopes and died forty minutes later.

Suddenly, Piekenbrock wound his window down.

"Do you hear that, Erich?" Joseph put his head out into the cold air. "Engines. I'm sure I can hear aircraft engines."

They got out, the sound of slamming doors echoing across the valley. "Yes, I hear it now Major."

The B24 swept towards them and banked almost above their heads; both ducked involuntarily, despite the fact that the plane was several hundred feet above them.

"What's the pilot doing?" Asked Erich as the aircraft disappeared over the hills.

"I believe he'll be inspecting the landing area. He will have checked it for length and made a mental note of where he intends to touchdown. Listen." Joseph held up a finger. "He is coming back now."

This time, the Liberator came in much more slowly. From where they stood, the two men were suddenly blinded by the two underwing landing lights. As it came in, the beams passed beyond them and now they could see that the landing gear was down seemingly, almost brushing the tree tops.

Neither spoke, both held their breath as the huge bird settled. A wheel touched down and the whole aircraft seemed to rebound in a slow motion bounce. The wheel hit the ground again, the other one came down and the B24 careered towards them at a speed that seemed horrifyingly fast to the inexperienced onlookers. Seconds later, it was hurtling at them; the engine noise, magnified by the enclosing valley, was solid, physical waves of sound.

A hundred yards, fifty. The Liberator was slowing, dipping on the nose wheel suspension as the brakes took hold. The pilot swung the plane around with a final burst of power until it faced the direction from which it had come.

One by one the engines died, the lights went out. It was very, very quiet. No bird sang as the sun cleared the far end of the valley and followed the plane down the landing strip.

Reinicke flipped the switches, killed the engines, the lights. He arched his back in a long, luxurious stretch and exhaled fiercely. They were down, the landing had been rough; not the roughest he had ever handled but far worse than any on Templehof's pock marked runways. He turned suddenly, to find Willi smiling at him.

"Thought she was going to come apart, Willi?"

"Not exactly but don't make a habit of it."

"I've no intention of doing so."

"I don't think it'll be difficult to find something to do while

294

we're here. Do you?"

"No I don't. They'd have to be pretty close behind me before I'd chance a take off along there. Anyway, we'll look it over later; we'd better see to our passengers."

Despite the punishment his hindquarters had received, Kurt was first on his feet. As the engines died, he looked around. "Everyone all right?"

There was a murmur of replies, peppered with expletives but no complaints.

"Right. As soon as we deplane, I want the equipment out and checked." He paused again – there were no comments. "I'll issue additional orders as soon as our local contact has briefed me."

Reinicke came through from the flight deck at this point. "Herr Oberst? We have arrived. I apologise for the quality of the landing, the take off will be much better, I promise. Would you like to start getting your men off through the rear hatchway? They can then shift their equipment out from the nose wheel compartment."

"Thank you Oberstleutnant. I'm sure my men would agree that congratulations are in order."

Reinicke was embarrassed. "Thank you Sir. We all have our jobs to do."

Kurt nodded.

"I have to speak with our contact."

Pieter nodded and went forward.

As Kurt reached the ground – the first man from the plane – he saw two men waiting for him. He straightened up and stretched, breathing the cool fresh air gratefully. An awesome thought struck him, this was an immense achievement; he was the leader of the first invasion party ever to stand on American soil. The concept was overwhelming.

He walked forward and the taller of the two men came to meet him, hand outstretched.

"Colonel Schroeder." He spoke in English and shook the offered hand. "At your service gentlemen."

Piekenbrock, despite his wearing civilian clothes, came to attention and bowed. "Major Piekenbrock; a pleasure to meet you Colonel. This is one of my aides; Erich Grunwald."

Kurt nodded, shook hands and turned back to Joseph. "Where exactly are we Major?"

"As nearly as I can tell you, we're between thirty and forty miles North East of Los Alamos."

Kurt's brow furrowed. "Thirty, forty miles about – fifty some kilometres?"

"That is correct. This valley is fairly remote, the wooded area being pretty extensive. Erich tells me that the only occupants are likely to be a few Indians – little more than savages who now scratch an existence from the soil."

Joseph's off-hand description of the Indians brought home just how different this part of the world was from central Europe.

296

Savages; how long had it been since Europe had seen savages, then he thought of the war – not so long perhaps.

"South of here and West," Piekenbrock continued, "the country is quite different – large areas of flat desert."

"Is there a possibility that we may have been observed?"

"I would say that it's quite likely. However, do not concern yourself too much. You are not very far from the military flight path from Alamagordo. We have camouflage nets as requested and I have two men posted as lookouts at either side of the valley – not enough, I know but there are not many of us."

Erich broke in deferentially. "They're probably cold and hungry by now, Sir. They've been out there for close on six hours."

"Right." Kurt reverted to action. "As soon as we have our equipment off-loaded, I'll see that they're relieved."

"Thank you Colonel. I was wondering if there was a place for them in your plans."

"For them? Off hand, I can think of no reason I could employ them unless they are qualified as guides? Or are capable airfield builders."

"Not at all. But they can all use a shovel." Replied Piekenbrock quickly watching the combat clad officer closely,

He guessed at Kurt's age, putting him at ten years his junior. He noted the way he moved, a sense of controlled tension, an aura of absolute command in every gesture.

"The two men are second generation American,"

297

Piekenbrock continued; "either one or both their grandparents were German. They know of the Fatherland only through Bund meetings and second hand memories, what they see in books or newspapers. This operation is little more than exciting play acting to them; I'm concerned that their tongues will flap after a few drinks if I send them home now. I would prefer them to take an active interest in their little adventure a bit longer."

"Mm. I understand your problem."

"Rubbing shoulders with our soldiers may also teach them something, impress them too, perhaps."

"Very well. Let them stay until the mission is completed. There is plenty of work to do – stripping out the fuel tanks and so on. I will ask Oberstleutnant Reinicke to keep them busy. Do they speak German?"

"Erich?"

"Fred does a little. I don't think Errol can."

"Oh, Major. I am forgetting; I have a package for you." Kurt undid the four top buttons on his jacket, took out the small parcel and handed it over.

"Thank you Colonel. Perhaps you should come back to our base; in actuality it's the home of our informant on Los Alamos – Paul Webb. You will have to speak to him in any case and you can have a cooked meal too; snatch some sleep. There are certain things I must tell you about Webb, as well."

Kurt thought a moment, looked over to where the Liberator's bomb doors had been opened to unload more

298

equipment and supplies. "That would be most welcome." He replied at last. "Thank you. My officers should come too but what about food for my men? They need something more substantial than soup."

"I have several crates of food on the truck, here. Everything from tinned meat to fruit. I would guess," Joseph went on dryly, "they will find it very acceptable after the rations they will have become accustomed to."

Kurt nodded, thinking back to the last good meal he had had – at Berchtesgaden. "I'm sure of it Major, certain."

When the supplies had been taken from the truck and stacked beneath one of the wings, the camouflage netting was pulled across the B24 and pegged to the ground. Errol and Fred came back from their cold vigils, replaced by two of Kurt's men who would take a short first watch of two hours before their chance at the food Piekenbrock had supplied. Neither of the two Americans had any complaints about their orders to stay with the German task force; already, the glamour of foreign comrades-in-arms was taking effect and they watched with awe as Kurt's superbly trained men each casually shifted ammunition cases that would have had the pair of them straining, one at each end.

Satisfied that all was in order, Kurt climbed into the winch truck with Joseph while Reinicke, Braun, Bergerud, Neuper and Dietrich followed in one of the jeeps.

Hoeckle watched them go, his mouth busily masticating the first fresh apple he had seen in eighteen months while, around

him, the others opened tins of America's gift to the world –
spam.

By the time they reached the outskirts of Los Alamos, the
sun was beginning to feel warm through the windscreen while
Joseph explained Paul Webb's place in Operation Blondi, his
association with the girl – Susan Millar – and his, Joseph's,
suspicions concerning his informant.

"Excuse me. Will it get much warmer than this?"

Joseph nodded and sped through the small town already astir
at this hour. "Normally, at this time of year, it averages about
eighty degrees Fahrenheit, I believe. In the summer months it
gets considerably warmer."

"A change from Berlin. When I left they were still having
sleet and a few weeks ago, my men were training on skis."

"Then Berlin is not that different from New York, Colonel.
Yes, this is very different from the Northern States. A new
world, in fact."

It had not occurred to Kurt that Piekenbrock was as
unaccustomed to this kind of weather as he was himself. It
brought it home to him just how large America really was.

"It certainly is a new world Major. Let us hope that our
mission here will make it a better one."

Piekenbrock trod heavily on the brakes and they skidded to a
halt in front of the house. A pair of suspicious eyes peered
through the dusty panes of the kitchen window. He preceded
Kurt into the house to find the expected pot of coffee bubbling

on the stove. He introduced Kurt to Edward and then asked where Paul and Susan were.

"I put them in that little bedroom, Major. The window's secure and I'd hear it if they tried to get out. Coffee?"

"God in Heaven, Major. Can I really smell coffee? Real coffee?"

Joseph was puzzled.

"Only the High Command can get hold of the genuine article in Germany. I'd forgotten what it smelled like – and how it tastes."

"Americans live on the stuff, Colonel. You can have as much as you want. There are seven of us, Edward, by the way; are there enough cups?"

"Sure thing, a cupboard full. I've left plenty to wash up though; I don't see why the woman shouldn't make herself useful."

"I quite agree. Would you pour us all a cup before Colonel Schroeder dies of anticipation?" Joseph turned back to Kurt as the others trooped in, making the relatively large room seem positively cramped.

"Brought American uniforms in case you thought it wiser to use them, Colonel. Do you have any thoughts on the matter?"

"Why do you ask?"

"I ask because this is a Government property on loan to Webb. There is always the possibility that someone may call here."

301

"I see." Kurt nodded and explained to the other officers, speaking in German before asking: "What do you think? Bear in mind that if we are caught out of our own uniforms we can be shot as spies."

It was Bergerud who replied. "I'll wear it if you think it necessary for the Operation but I hardly think we need to worry about visitors. Surely, we can move to another room in that eventuality."

"Major?"

Joseph shrugged. "True."

"Right. There will be a necessity to wear them later on – with the exception of yourselves gentlemen." He said, nodding at the air crew. "Your job is to ready the aircraft and to fly it."

Peter Reinicke added: "And to do some work on the strip if we want to take off safely with the extra weight that we expect. It needs a bit of improvement."

"Well, you have Fred and Errol, for what they're worth," interjected Joseph. "There will also be a third man presently. At the moment he is seeing to your fuel requirements but he should be back here some time today. With Erich here, that gives you four extra pairs of hands."

"What about our friend over there?" Kurt nodded towards Edward who looked up from his coffee pouring.

"Edward? No. I'm afraid he is needed to look after our lady guest while the rest of us are away."

"In that case, Reinicke, you now know what you have to

302

work with."

"So be it. Can you give me any idea how long we've got?"

Kurt shrugged. "Today is Friday, how long do you need?"

"Two days?" Pieter looked hopeful.

"Two days then – provided that we don't have to move earlier. A lot depends upon what Mister Webb can tell me in the next few hours. In any case, I can't see anything happening before tomorrow evening. As well as developing our plan for…" he looked around, realising that there would be those who were not privy to the mission's objective. "… for the operation, we all need rest."

Ed came back with the coffee, handed it around. "Shall I get the lovers up? The woman can make some breakfast." He asked of Piekenbrock.

Joseph looked at Kurt, who nodded. "All right."

As Ed went through to the hallway, Kurt remembered the package he had given the spy. "Are you going to open your mail, Major?"

"Mail?" He looked blank for a moment. "Of course. Certainly. So much has been happening that I'd forgotten about it." He took the package from his pocket, opened it. There were four things: a personal letter, addressed to himself; a typed page of official instructions; a hefty package of dollar bills and finally, wrapped in a square of silk, a small black cross.

Joseph fingered the medal for long seconds before reading

the accompanying documents for it was the Iron Cross, First Class. Piekenbrock had been decorated before but always in absentia; his family in Germany held those others. This was the first time he had received one personally.

Eventually, he got to the letter and when he had finished, he looked up. "It seems I have been promoted to Lieutenant Colonel," he said mildly, "the decoration is for my services to the Fatherland. The letter is signed by General Schellenberg and countersigned by the Fuhrer. The instructions order us, among other things, to signal the S.D. as soon as your mission is a success and you have taken off."

Kurt translated Joseph's words for the benefit of those who spoke no English. There was a round of applause and Joseph found himself in the enviable position of being warmly congratulated by his peers. Another first time situation.

Paul, who had just followed Ed into the room saw humor reach Joseph's eyes – it made him look almost human. He noticed Paul's entrance and then Susan, who had stopped long enough to fix her hair, came through; it was sufficient excuse to miss out the speech that would be expected.

"Gentlemen," he began, "allow me to introduce Paul Webb and his young lady, Susan... ?"

"Millar." Susan supplied, taking in the crowd of people; the German uniforms.

"Of course – Susan Millar." Joseph smiled, it still infected his eyes. "We were wondering if you might cook some breakfast
304

for us, my dear. We are all hungry; no doubt you are also."

"Not really." She replied, glacially but, since she had only just promised Paul to do nothing that might antagonize the Germans, she acquiesced. "I don't pretend to be a good cook, if you're willing to take what comes...?"

"I'm sure we are." Joseph was at his most charming.

While this interchange was taking place, Kurt and Paul were weighing each other up. Paul noted a powerfully built man with keen eyes and a strong jaw. He imagined the other to be inwardly smiling at him but knew that he could be wrong. Whatever else, Paul knew that here was a man; forget the nationality, he knew integrity and loyalty when he saw it.

Kurt, however, viewed Paul very differently. Before him was a young man in his mid-twenties. There was obvious intelligence there, though it lacked the discipline that can only come from military service. He noted the signs of the arid desert climate; the hard coppery skin, the furrows at the corner of each eye and between them. He saw the obvious physical strength – again, untempered by military training.

At the moment, Paul was lounging with his shoulder against the wall, his arms folded and Kurt made an error of judgment. He decided that Paul's was a weak character, easily led by a more dominant personality. Eighteen months previously this assessment would have been quite true but Kurt did not know what the other's job was; Los Alamos had made not a few changes in Paul, most had been for the better.

Kurt moved across, his hand extended. "Kurt Schroeder; Colonel in the German Army and officer commanding this operation. I understand that you have much to tell me?"

"Yes, I guess so," nodded Paul. "Whether I can be of real help or not…" He let the thought hang.

"Your help will be invaluable, Mister Webb. However, breakfast first eh? There is plenty of time to talk."

After a meal of underdone bacon, burnt eggs and luke warm beans, Pieter Reinicke broke the silence. "Very nice my dear." He lifted his voice and spoke in English so that Susan would hear him in the kitchenette. Then, reverting to German he spoke to Kurt. "We of the Luftwaffe must leave now, Herr Oberst. There is much to do if we expect to be ready for tomorrow night."

"Of course, Oberstleutnant." Kurt rose, wiping his lips with a napkin. "I shall be returning to the strip myself as soon as matters here are cleared up. I shall be bringing Oberst Piekenbrock's man with me. In the meantime, you have with you his other two operatives – feel free to make use of them."

They shook hands and the air crew left. As the door closed, Kurt turned to Dietrich and Bergerud.

"I suggest, gentlemen, that you take this chance to get some sleep. There will be a full briefing for everybody later on and a second one for the officers following that. I need you fully awake on both occasions."

The SS Officers nodded in unison and were shown to the

main bedroom. Susan watched the silver collar runes flash in the sunlight with fascinated horror.

"Now Colonel." Kurt addressed Piekenbrock. "I would suggest that Edward shows the lady to the bathroom while he takes a rest in the other room. The fewer people who hear what we have to discuss, the better."

TWENTY NINE

The three men: Piekenbrock, Webb and Schroeder, sat around the table as Kurt withdrew a collage of aerial photographs from a slim packet. He spread the sheet out; it showed the Los Alamos site and a thin border of its environs. He pressed the creases flat with his fingertips.

Oh, my God, Thought Paul. *This is really it.*

"These," began Kurt, "are the shots taken by the crop duster that you employed, Colonel. They have been blown up, of course, and are a little too grainy for fine resolution, as you can see. No doubt Mister Webb will be able to fill in the details."

These were the first photographs of their type that Paul had seen, it took a minute or so for him to orient himself to the image. Part of his problem was that the photographs were a year or more out of date; more than anything else, they made him realise the tremendous changes that had taken place at the Hill since they had been taken. He put these thoughts into words.

"Describe these changes." Kurt demanded.

"The number of buildings, for example. Since these were made, all these areas here, here and here…," he pointed to two places where the ground had been cleared in the photographs and a third which was covered with trees, "have been built on. There

308

are over forty thousand workmen in construction, you know. They've been throwing up buildings everywhere."

"Then I suggest you draw them in and tell us what they're being used for."

"I can draw them in but I haven't any idea what most of them are for. Honestly, I just don't know."

Kurt looked up at him. "I find that hard to believe, Mister Webb. You sent us excellent photographs of one installation."

"That was different. I rigged an electrical failure as an excuse to get in. Everything at the Hill works on a "need to know" basis. My work is primarily on the outside – the main power supplies."

"I can confirm this Colonel Schroeder." Piekenbrock said. "Other sources back up the extraordinary secrecy observed at Los Alamos. I think Mister Webb is telling you the truth."

"I see. In that case, let's start at the beginning. Show me where the bombs are stored, which access points we can use and what present security arrangements are."

"I... I'm not sure about the bombs – nobody asked me to keep tabs on them but Project Y is still where they're working on them and that's where it always was, right here." Paul stabbed a finger at the photographs.

"All right. Access and security?"

"The access is still the same too." Paul scrutinised the layout again. "This is a narrow arroyo with steep rock walls and gives the best chance of getting close without being seen. Now, security. That's been changed a number of times. At the moment, there are two man teams patrolling the outer wire and inside, they've got mobile patrols as well as static guards."

"How many and exactly how often do they patrol?"

"I'm not sure."

Kurt looked at Joseph, then back at Paul. His eyes were hard, piercing. "You are dissembling. I do not think you really want to help us. However, Colonel Piekenbrock has something to show you, it may change your mind." Kurt nodded to Piekenbrock.

Joseph got up and went to the couch where a brown paper bag had been tucked behind a cushion. He brought it back and opened it, taking care that he did not touch it.

"Do you recognise this, Paul?"

Paul looked at the bloodied bottle; his face turned grey, his eyes opened wide, memories flooded back. Carl, lurching backward, clutching at his throat with blood pouring between his fingers.

"It is the same bottle, Paul. It has your fingerprints all over it. The Police will already have discovered the body, both bodies. They will be looking for a murderer, Paul."

"Which would be worse, electrocution or cyanide gas from your fellow Americans or a decoration from your rightful country?"

Paul shuddered.

"I might add too, that unless we get your cooperation , your girlfriend will not be seeing you again. Now, which is it to be?"

Dragging his head up, Paul looked wearily at the two men. He faced Schroeder's steady, intimidating gaze.

"I am telling the truth but you're asking me questions far too quickly. You'll have to give me time to come up with the answers." He pulled himself together. "For example, I told the truth when I said I didn't know where the bombs are stored; not now, anyhow. I know where some of them were but that was months ago."

Kurt sensed that this was not a lie. He sat back, his unfocussed gaze on Paul, while he considered the facts so far. What Paul had said meant that he would have to get into Los Alamos twice: the first time to locate the bomb stores and, a second time, to actually steal one. This was bad news; it could make the operation impossible.

The thought of failure was fleeting, instantly dismissed. There would have to be two sorties; it would have to be done.

Starting anew, the two Germans questioned Paul exhaustively until, eventually, Kurt decided that he could learn no more. "That will do for now. We will talk again, later." He glanced at Joseph as he got up and the other followed him outside.

"Well, Colonel; what do you think?" Kurt spoke quietly and in German, so that he could not be overheard or understood from inside the house.

311

"I think that we must now test his truthfulness. I will let Edward speak with him."

"No. There's no need for that; I know when a man is speaking the truth and when he is not. Besides, I would prefer that Edward knows nothing specific until he has to. As with Los Alamos – the "need to know"."

"Well, if you have that much confidence in Herr Webb, why not let him go into work today and find out what we don't know yet? We have that bottle – you saw the reaction it provoked; we have his girlfriend; he has no choice but to do as he is told."

"I agree that it is one way but, tell me, why am I so reluctant to take it?"

Joseph chuckled. "Perhaps, like me, you do not trust him as much as you think?"

Kurt smiled too. "Perhaps you are right. I shall have to consider other ways. He can stay here today and, if I don't come up with something else, Webb can go in tomorrow.

"For the present, I intend to take a closer look at this 'Hill' myself. I shall need a guide and I want to take one of my own men."

"I'll get Edward to wake your Officers."

"No, no. Just the man named Hoeckle."

"In that case, I will act as your guide. Edward can stay here with our guests."

When Piekenbrock and Schroeder had left and Edward had been given his instructions, Paul went through to the smaller
312

bedroom to find Susan. Ed made no protest, indeed, seemed happy to have him out of the way.

With the door shut, Susan embraced Paul, held him tightly.

"Oh darling, what the hell are we going to do? That man, Ed, positively strips me bare with those eyes; he really frightens me, Paul."

Paul stroked her hair. "Sweet Sue." He murmured, burying his face in the golden cascade. "Ed is a nobody, he does what he's told to. It's the others we have to fear; they threatened to kill you unless I co-operate." Paul made no mention of the bottle.

Susan stiffened against him. "Did you say you'd help?"

"Of course, what else do you expect me to do? They keep going on and on about those goddamn bombs. They want to know where they're stored."

"What bombs?"

"The atomic ones."

Susan paused a moment. "What did you tell them?"

"Nothing. I said I didn't know anything about them."

She thought furiously for several seconds. "Listen, let me talk to them when they come back. I may be able to stop them pestering you any more."

"Oh no, Susan. I forbid it. They think you're a doctor at the medical unit – let them keep on thinking it."

Susan nodded and relaxed.

But her mind remained active.

THIRTY

Albert Gross removed the old fashioned fob watch from his pocket and stared at the white dial in the light from the dashboard instruments: 3:10. It would, he knew, be around six before the sewage tanker got through the customs post.

Time enough for a nap. He pushed the seat back on its runners as far as it would go, settling back and easing his vast stomach under the steering wheel. Albert couldn't get comfortable: the.38 revolver Piekenbrock had given him pressed into the small of his back, the steering wheel rim chafed his belly. Cursing, he took the offending hardware out of the waistband and dropped it beneath the seat before sliding across to the passenger side and getting comfortable.

With a last look round at the dusty and empty streets of El Paso, Albert closed his eyes.

It was the insistent sound of a bell that woke him. He sat bolt upright and wiped a clear space in the condensation covered window. People were hurrying along the street in both directions, some were on bicycles and it was a cycle bell that had cut his sleep short. Albert extricated his watch and checked the time, it was now two minutes past six.

For all of his bulk – which was considerable – the man could

314

move fast when he wanted to. He left the car at a run, heading for the highway where he should have been almost a quarter hour ago. Ed's instructions rang in his ears: "Leave the car somewhere quiet, somewhere it won't rouse suspicion – and immobilise the damn thing so we can say it was broken down if anybody asks when we come back."

Well he'd done that last night, the rotor arm was in his pocket. He'd have to put the bloody thing back if he'd missed the tanker and go haring after it.

It was nearly four hundred yards from the parked car to Highway 66; he made it in two minutes, perspiring freely and tucking his shirt back into his pants. He hoped to God that the tanker was late or had been held up at the border for some reason – if he had to go looking for it, it would mean dumping the car along the way. There was no way he would dare to admit he'd been asleep to the Major; Piekenbrock would flay him alive or, worse still, he'd set Edward to the job; that man was a sadist.

Albert recalled going collecting with him one day. They were calling on the known German sympathisers, using a list that the Bund had made up and asking for contributions. One old man had pleaded penury, saying that he could hardly afford to eat, never mind helping someone else out. Ed had taken the fellow by the scruff and lifted him clear off the ground, shaken him like a dog would a rat. The look of pure malevolence, malevolence mixed with glee, that had taken hold of Ed's features would live with Albert forever. He was sick in the head, therefore deadly

315

and Albert was shit-scared of him.

Albert was waiting on the north side of the city since it made sense not to hang around or board the tanker where the Customs could see him, possibly remember him. But it was as frustrating as hell. Until the vehicle actually rounded the nearest bend, some two hundred yards away, he wouldn't know whether it had gone or not.

For the fifth time since his arrival, he checked the time. It had only reached 6:12 a.m., if it had passed, it must have done so in the two minutes or so after six, he had had the highway in sight since then.

"Christ – let it be late." He muttered and left his watch alone by sheer will power,

Albert called on God often – mostly in the name of the Son; not that he was especially religious nor especially deserving of the Deity's help. An inveterate gambler, often drunk and with a penchant for small thefts, Albert kidded himself that he was headed for the job of chief stoker for the Devil. It was unlikely, however, that he would ever reach such a responsible position.

Whether the Almighty was listening and had actually taken pity on Albert or whether that was just how it was, the fat little man's anxiety was eased. Around the corner, surrounded by the thick black smoke from a poorly adjusted diesel engine, came the sewage tanker.

As it drew nearer, the vehicle slowed, allowing its over-ripe aroma to sweep on before it and roll over Albert. For a moment,

316

he forgot what it was and truly believed it was the sewage tanker it was supposed to be. He wrinkled his nose up in disgust and stepped back a pace.

With a popping and sputtering from a broken exhaust, the vehicle drew up alongside. The driver, a ginger haired man of indeterminate age looked down.

"C' que pese, hombre?" He queried, showing broken teeth in a nicotine colored grin.

"Ugh! Oh yeah." Albert gagged and searched his memory for the lines.

"Lo mejar es no decir nada."

The driver grinned again. "Not bad for a gringo. Hop aboard." The transition from Spanish to English was sudden enough to take Albert aback but he breathed a sigh of relief. His oft boasted command of Spanish was largely in his own imagination; the few phrases and expletives he knew, he had learned from the Puerto Ricans in New York's West Side. As a youth, as a gang member, there had been occasions when he'd exchanged words with them – usually derogatory ones.

"Gracias." And made his way around to the far side of the cab.

The smell inside was only marginally sweeter than outside and, not knowing whether to mention it or not, Albert refrained from comment. The driver, however, was not so reticent.

"Stinks don't it, this shit?"

Albert had to agree.

"Had to dip the hoses in it and fill the bucket with it before I left. That's what stinks. Good disguise though; worked a treat, coming over." He slammed the truck into first and got on the proper side of the road again, working up through the gear box. As their speed increased, they outdistanced the stench of raw sewage and the cab's atmosphere became breathable again.

Having spent his whole life in the northern states of the Union, Albert felt he was qualified to comment? "You're an American aren't you?"

"Sure." The driver was matter-of-fact. "American this side of the border, that is. If I'm on the other side I'm Mexican." He shot a quick look at his passenger's face, laughed at Albert's scowl of puzzlement. "Name's Hank Garcia. Ma – she was born in the States. Had a small bar back there in El Paso. But my father, he was a Mex. Ma's best customer, she used to say. So – ," he released the wheel, spread his hands expansively, "up here, I'm an American."

"I suppose that helps with your job – driving for a Mex outfit?"

"Helps? I suppose. It's my truck though. Got a contract with an American firm to move effluents in and out of the States – mostly liquid fertiliser like we're supposed to be carrying today. This is by way of being a job on the side, see?"

"Do a lot like this?"

"Only when the money's right, which reminds me, you got the dough for this little lot?"

318

Albert shook his head. "You'll get it on delivery, Hank."

"Where's that then?"

Albert thought a moment, then shook his head. "North a piece, up beyond Santa Fe." He didn't want to say too much, "Can't say more'n that, off the beaten track a bit. That's why I'm here, anyway, to show you."

Hank nodded and concentrated on getting the best out of his motor. Albert, relaxed by the steady roar of the diesel, drifted off to sleep without realising.

Mile after mile went by; the huge tanker ate up the road steadily. Hank nursed it economically on the upgrades, pushed it on the downs. They were several miles short of Albuquerque when he spotted a cop on their tail.

"Hey!" He reached over and shoved Albert on the shoulder. "We got a cop behind us. What you want I should tell him if he stops us?"

Albert started, reached for the .38 and blanched. Realisation hit him – he'd left it in the car! Now what? The Major hadn't briefed him on this situation.

"What do they usually ask if they stop you?"

Hank shrugged. "See the manifest. Point of departure. Where I'm going. That sort of thing."

"Well do what you usually do."

"I ain't got no manifest, do I? Jose – that's the feller that get's me these jobs, Jose said your lot would make all the arrangements."

Albert shrank back into his seat. He had no manifest.

"Maybe they won't stop us."

"I wouldn't bet on it, buddy. He's moving up; reckon he's going to flag us down."

Kneeling up and looking over behind Hank's shoulders, Albert watched the police car creep up alongside them. On impulse, he seized the wheel and shoved it hard over to the left. Caught by surprise, Hank didn't pull it back until it was too late. There was the crash of metal crushing metal followed, moments later, by the sound of the car grating over rock and a resounding bang.

"What the hell..." Yelled Hank, jamming the brakes on so hard that the tanker slewed to a halt in a four wheeled skid. "Just what do you think you're doing, bud?" He let out a breath in a long, exasperated whistle. "You stupid bastard," he started in again, "you trying to get us both killed?"

"It had to be done. Would you have if I'd told you to?"

"You're ripe for the funny farm, feller. This truck earns me my living and, besides, you just don't run cops off the road."

Albert didn't answer. He opened the door and jumped down, gasping as the stink hit him afresh. He shouted up to Hank before slamming the door: "You'd better straighten her up and take care, you've got maybe six inches from the edge down here – an' it's a good twelve foot drop."

Albert walked around the back of the tanker and looked down at the police car, upside down in the gulley, its roof

320

crushed in almost to seat level. He walked back along the road a few yards and scrambled down into the gulley where it wasn't so deep. Inside the patrol car, the cop was dead; no doubt of it; his head was trapped between the steering wheel and the crushed-in roof. A moment later, he was starting back; a moment after that, he was back at the car again, feeling for his pocket knife. It took a second to decide which the off-side tyre was, a quick stab released the pent up air with a pleasing hiss. If anyone checked now, they would assume the car had had a blow out.

He wondered about setting fire to the wreck but decided against it, smoke would only invite investigation. As it was, below the level of the road, it could be days or weeks before someone spotted it.

Having convinced himself of this, Albert scrambled back up to the highway and trotted along to the tanker.

"Come on Hank," he pulled the door shut, "let's get out of here before someone else comes along, we're fairly close to town."

Hank needed no second bidding and soon had the truck rumbling through Albuquerque. Neither said anything more about the incident but both thought a great deal. Albert's complacence gradually slipped to leave him thinking about Ed's reaction; not only was there the matter of wiping out the cop, there was the gun back in the car at Santa Fe.

As he broke the silence to turn Hank off the main road and on to the track leading up into the hills, the driver asked the question that decided the matter for Albert.

"What you going to tell your boss about that cop?"

"Nothing." Albert snarled. "What they don't know won't hurt 'em."

Hank didn't reply but concentrated morosely on nursing the vehicle over the increasingly rough terrain. He kept silent until one of the wheels jolted against a rock outcropping. "I hope someone'll pay for these tyres, bud. Each one costs a week's wages – you know that?"

"You'll get paid, don't worry." Albert answered without thinking, he was too busy cursing the day he had ever got mixed up with all this, with the Bund – he wasn't even German, not even part-German. The fact that his surname was Gross and that he lived next door to their meeting hall was the only reason he'd ever joined. Albert realised he had done a lot of kidding through the years and now it had gotten him involved way out of his depth. He knew that he could end up very dead. He would get out while he was ahead, maybe even tell the cops about the Major and this little lot – that would see they stayed out of his hair; right out.

The tanker ground up the final slope before the valley in bottom gear. The chassis groaned as it flexed over the uneven ground and Hank slowed down to take it as slowly as possible.

Albert shouted across the sound of the revving engine. "I'm getting out at the top. You've got about two miles to go – far end of the valley. I've got another job to do now."

322

"Okay. See you."

"Keep going."

Albert got out and slammed the door shut as he dropped to the ground. He watched it crest the hill before heading into the woodland on the north side of the track. Albert took off towards the East.

As Hank topped the rise, he saw the full length of the valley spread out before him. Deserted, empty. That crazy mother had brought him all this bloody way to no where!

Cursing bilingually, he let gravity pull the tanker downhill against the low gear, searching for a place where he could turn the vehicle.

The hill was short and steep, he would have to go to the bottom where the long flat valley started before he could stop. Hank only hoped he'd be able to climb the hill with the full load on.

Stopped at last, he started to back up and then forward again. There was a violent banging on the side of the cab and, alarmed, Hank stomped on the brake pedal.

"Hey!" A red face appeared above the right hand window. The door opened and Hank could see the top half of a camouflage tunic; there was no insignia, he assumed the man had bought it at an Army surplus sale.

"Where is Albert?" Asked this individual though, since he asked in German, Hank only understood the name. Hank pointed back up the hill and the other turned and shouted something.

Fachinger turned back and stared at Hank with suspicious eyes as Errol emerged from the trees and trotted across to them. Hank wondered what the hell they wanted aviation spirit for in a God forsaken place like this but stopped himself almost at once; it was none of his business, he was being paid well for the job. In fact, a few more like this and he could buy himself a newer truck and hire a wet-back to drive this one; a couple more years and he could retire.

A quick interchange in German between Fachinger and Errol and the newcomer looked into the cab. "Where's Albert?"

"Albert? That nutter? He dropped off a mile or two back. Said he had some business to attend to first. Where'd you want this lot?"

Errol translated, listened a moment and turned back. "He says you were turning round."

"Damn right. I thought that Albert of yours had taken me for a sucker – brought me out here for nothing. Couldn't see anyone."

Again Errol translated and added: "You take him along to the plane, I'll get on with the work."

Fachinger grunted and climbed into the cab. The Mauser pistol caught him by surprise when he tapped Hank on the knee with its muzzle.

Hank started up and drove along the faintly discernable track, noticing places here and there where wire screening had been stapled into the ground across layers of rocks and pebbles -
324

presumably filling hollows or soft areas. About halfway along the valley, Hank began to realise that the place was, by no means, as deserted as he thought. Up ahead was a curious amorphous shape; it was not quite opaque, Hank could see movement inside.

Suddenly a figure emerged, this time in a leather flying jacket. Hank realised that the mound was camouflage for whatever was inside. They stopped and Fachinger got out, leaving the door open. Hank killed the engine and, suddenly, his ears were assailed by the sound of metal being hammered.

Fachinger saluted and explained the situation to Reinicke who then came across to speak to Hank Garcia. His smile was friendly and open.

"You must be hungry after your long drive, thirsty too. Go with this man and he'll fix you up with something to eat and drink while we unload you."

Pieter Reinicke's English was almost accentless. Hank hadn't realised what language they had been speaking so the first clue he got was the German Eagle glittering on Pieter's breast, between the open lapels of his flying jacket.

Not quite so much at ease now, Hank grinned back and climbed down from his cab.

"Will it take long? I wanna be back on the road."

Pieter kept his disarming smile turned on. "You're going to have to wait a while, I'm afraid. Your money isn't here yet so you might as well take my offer of food. Good trip?"

"Apart from one incident I'd like to forget but which'll jack the price up an extra grand."

"Sorry. An incident?" Pieter's voice lost its friendliness. Immediately, it became that of a German officer.

THIRTY ONE

Ed gnawed at what was left of the fingernail on his left ring finger, spat out the fragments like shrapnel. He examined the surgery minutely – it had been the longest, now it was in the same state of disrepair as the others; the nails chewed down to the quick, even the skin around the half moons was shredded and bleeding.

Waiting. Waiting now, for eighteen hours. He hated waiting, especially when it interfered with his sleep. Sober, Edward was naturally irritable; tired, he was ten times worse.

It was quiet: the heat oppressive. It was fine for the two German officers in the larger bedroom, heads down – the other two were probably sleeping or fornicating. It got on his nerves.

Just ain't right, thought Ed as he considered the talk that the Major – Colonel now – the German leader, Schroeder and Webb had had earlier that morning. He was not supposed to have listened in, Ed knew that, but their voices had carried easily from the living room to the bedroom door where he had eavesdropped unashamedly. Now, he knew why they needed Webb, something to do with bombs inside the Los Alamos government site.

But Webb had told them he did not know the storage areas. The man was lying – Ed was certain and they needed that information. Why? He wondered. Were they planning to blow up a military installation? Suppose he got the information from Paul Webb? If anyone could, it would be himself; he'd squeeze that bastard like an orange and Piekenbrock and the others – would think well of him; he might get more money maybe, the Colonel had plenty…

The thought wouldn't leave him. He poured another cup of coffee but his mind – over active after the countless cups kept returning to the idea. Shock tactics were called for, he smiled.

Paul came tumbling off the narrow bunk bed spluttering and soaked to the skin. There was barely time to grasp what had woken him before he was lifted physically into the air and shaken. A voice was shouting in his ears but so disoriented was he, that it took a long time to penetrate.

Ed was mildly disappointed not to have found Paul and Susan in passionate embrace, it annoyed him the more.

"Where do they keep the bombs, crumb? Come on, spill it or I'll break every last bone in your body. The bombs?"

"Don't… know…" Paul managed.

"Don't give me that. Now tell me before I break your neck."

Susan had been caught by overspill from the flower vase that Ed had used. She came awake at the same moment Ed lifted Paul off the bed. Susan shrank back against the wall, trying to collect her wits. She heard the shouting through a fog of sleep and, only slowly, recalled the thoughts she had had earlier. Should she try it out on Ed?

At the first sound of Edward's voice, both Dietrich and

328

Bergerud awoke instantly. They had been sleeping alongside one another, head to foot on the double bed. Bergerud, closer to the door than Dietrich, was fractionally ahead of the other, Mauser magically in hand as he went out the door and crashed into the small room.

Ed, oblivious of the interruption, dropped Paul heavily to the floor and transferred his grip to his shoulders. He dug his thumbs deep into the other's flesh and began to squeeze down hard on the pressure points.

"Stop it." Susan screamed. "Stop it, for God's sake. I'll tell you what you want to know – just leave him alone."

Bergerud and Dietrich heard her outburst, it was their first clue as to what was happening.

"What are you doing?" Bergerud asked sharply but Ed was still too involved to hear. Leaving Paul in a heap, he turned his attention to Susan.

"So where are they kept?" He snarled.

Bergerud was about to say something further when Dietrich restrained him, a hand on his arm. "Wait." He said in his precise English. "This may be important."

"C'mon bitch. Where are they kept?" Ed was certain that he was on to something and, like a dog with a big, juicy bone, would not let go. "I want to know."

"Okay. I'll have to draw a map – I can't tell you just like that."

"There is no need to draw one," offered Dietrich, "we have

329

maps." To Ed he said: "What is it that she is supposed to be telling us?"

"Something Major… Colonel Piekenbrock and Colonel Schroeder wanted to know. Where the bombs are kept at Los Alamos. I knew this son of a bitch was holding out."

"Perhaps he was not. Perhaps they were asking the wrong person." He turned his glacial eyes on Susan. "And how do you know this, young woman? I understood you to be a doctor in the medical unit."

Susan looked away from those piercing blue eyes. "I'm a doctor but not of medicine. I'm a metallurgist, a doctor of physics. I work on the bomb components."

To Paul, lying unnoticed on the floor, Susan's words were tantamount to her committing treason. Several times, he almost shouted to her to stop but some inner voice counselled him to stay quiet. He could only lie there in pain as the others left the room.

THIRTY TWO

After the beautiful scenery on the run down from the make-shift airstrip in the mountains, Kurt was struck dumb by his first sight of the town of Los Alamos. Much of it had been built up in the late thirties; the grey concrete housing and other buildings reminded him ironically of his visits to the Wolfsschanze, Hitler's Headquarters in East Prussia. It was as though he had been transported back to the Fatherland on a magic carpet. He could imagine what it might be like in another quarter century: crumbling, decaying.

The thought lasted no more than a moment for, as they came nearer, his eyes saw individual buildings, picked out the older adobe structures between the newer and larger ones.

Piekenbrock chose that moment to speak to him. "From this point we start climbing again." Erich pointed out a dirt road on the map, "about two miles from here. It should take us to a vantage point above the target."

His thought processes broken, Kurt returned to the matter in hand, nodded. "Good. Tell me, where are we now in relation to our target?"

"About twenty miles to the south east."

"And there is no shorter route than this? I'm thinking of

331

coming away – not of getting there."

"There may well be, it's something we've not been able to look into yet."

"In that case, it must be given a high priority. If there is pursuit, I don't want to be cut off by road blocks."

"I can use my men for that if you don't need them any longer." Joseph liked the idea – it postponed the decision that he would have to make about what to do with them when their usefulness was at an end.

"Providing Reinicke can finish without them, that is fine. If not, Operation Blondi may have to be put back until I am satisfied that our route out is secure."

"You are aware that there are only two ways out from the 'Hill', aren't you?"

"Two roads, you mean? Yes, that is so. My purpose today is to choose a way in and a way out via the fence – perhaps more than one. I have no intention of trusting to Mister Webb's information in this respect."

The car had climbed through several hundred feet by the time Joseph had brought it to a stop some miles along the dirt road. "As near as I can navigate, we should now be almost due west of the site and above it. From here, we must proceed on foot."

Joseph spoke in German for the first time for Hoeckle's benefit. The soldier had been riding quietly in the back, his eyes as busy as a hawk's.

Hoeckle nodded, shrugging the tight American army uniform straighter and unlocking the door. "Good. It will give me a chance to unfold; I'm afraid my Maker didn't design me to ride in the back of an American car." His eyes sparkled with humor and Kurt, watching the big man duck to avoid the low door frame, had to smile as he agreed.

"I'm sure you're right Feldwebel but he compensated you in other ways, no?"

"In some small ways, Herr Oberst."

"Not so small from where I'm sitting." Laughed Kurt.

Leaving the car, the trio started to ascend a slope from the top of which, Joseph expected to be able to see the target. Walnut trees, pines, and occasional poplar studded the incline and soon hid the car from them and concealed them from any passers-by. Piekenbrock was panting by the time they crested the ridge and envied the evident fitness of his two colleagues; Hoeckle was not even breathing fast.

The view that met them at the top drove all thought of exertion from Piekenbrock's mind.

Below them lay a vast circular plateau ringed by high mountains; a river wove its unimposing way along the base of these mountains, its course marked by somewhat more luxuriant shrubs and trees than in other, more arid areas.

It was easy to identify the 'Hill', it bore the only signs of life in the entire panorama. A flat topped mesa some eight thousand five hundred feet – or rather more than two thousand five hundred metres – above sea level, it was now liberally scattered with buildings ranging from the small to the positively gigantic. The main area of development was still, however, surrounded by pasture and croplands. The site had been chosen partly for its low population and partly because its perimeter would be comparatively easy to guard. Despite the secrecy that surrounded its purpose, Groves, the Manhattan Director, did not want the attention that large scale movements of population would cause. Apart from small farms and a few small holdings, the only concern had been a failing boys' school whose owners were delighted to sell out; farming of the outlying areas had been allowed to continue in order to preserve some air of normalcy.

The three men inhaled deeply of the crisp mountain air as they stood and admired the grandeur below and around them, while the sun shone brightly from a hot, clear blue sky.

"Wunderbar," murmured Kurt, "it reminds me of some parts of Austria in high summer although, even Austria is not on this scale. What are those mountains?" He asked, pointing.

Joseph visualised the map he had committed to memory. "The Sangre de Cristol peaks and the Jemez range, according to the map. The river down there is the Rio Grande, though it is not very grand just here."

Kurt took the Zeiss field glasses from their case and squatted to allow his knees to support his elbows while he swept the area. It was a technique he had learned in North Africa, watching for Allied tanks; it served him well now, as it had done then.

LAST MISSION

The conglomeration of huts and buildings sprang into clarity as he twisted the focus screw; he looked in silence for the few seconds it took him to absorb the visual information spread out for inspection. He then turned his attention to the fence; as far as he could make out it completely encompassed the area containing the military buildings. Kurt's glasses found five pairs of soldiers at various points around the perimeter, there may have been more; some parts of the wire were obscured but, by waiting patiently, he found two more as they came into view. He made a mental note to check the frequency and length of time they would be out of sight of each other.

"It's certainly well chosen." admitted Kurt. "A flat topped hill separated from the rest of the plateau by two deep canyons." He looked around at Hoeckle who was examining their target intently. "Still, that very choice may well be to our advantage." He began to say more, pointing, then stopped. "No. You take the glasses, Feldwebel; pick out the main gates and the guards then tell me how you think you would get in."

Hoeckle accepted the binoculars and, positioning himself flat on his stomach, began his own minute survey. The glasses swept slowly from side to side, stopping here and there to absorb a particular aspect more fully before passing on.

Kurt had chosen the huge Hoeckle for several reasons, not the least of which being the manner in which he had handled himself that day at Berchtesgaden. When the panzers had first appeared, it had been Hoeckle who had taken command and not

335

Dietrich, the nominated leader of the group. Schroeder had swiftly come to respect the man's almost instinctive decisions.

At last, Hoeckle finished his observations, returned the glasses and stood up. "I may presume, Herr Oberst, that we shall not be entering a main gate?"

"It is a safe assumption, yes."

"In that case, the canyon to the right, as we are looking at it, seems to offer the best chance. The distance between the edge and the fence is the shortest; no man need be exposed for more than thirty seconds or so. The interval between guards is about two minutes. Depending on the size of our assault force, I would say thirty seconds to cross the open space and seven seconds per man to negotiate the fence, disappear from.view."

Kurt nodded, then frowned. Hoeckle's analysis corresponded broadly with his own but – "Seven seconds? How do you expect to achieve that?"

Hoeckle shrugged. "A lightweight ladder curved to hang over the fence top."

"Ah, I see. And the last man would pull the ladder over?"

"Yes. The ladder would be put up near a support post, the last man would take a little longer – say thirty seconds at the outside; he would stand on the support and pull the ladder over."

"Provided the fence is not electrified."

"I'm sure it isn't."

He put the binoculars to his eyes again, concentrated on the nearest length of fence. "No. I can see no insulators."

336

"So all we want is a ladder."

"A ladder and practice. And a rock face that can be climbed."

"Mm." Piekenbrock broke into the conversation. "Let me have the glasses, Herr Oberst." He took the field glasses Kurt was just about to use and focussed them in the general direction of the canyon they were discussing. A few moments later, he returned them. "It is as I thought. See those dark areas on the rock face."

Kurt focussed the binoculars.

"Those are Indian cliff dwellings; caves long since abandoned. Now almost certainly, there are narrow paths or steps that will take you that far up. From there, it is not so far."

"Yes. I see them now. I thought they were merely discolorations or shadows."

"It's a pity we can't get closer to see them properly but, with such a tight schedule..."

"It can be overcome." replied Kurt. "Feldwebel; one of your pre-war hobbies was rock climbing, was it not?"

"This is so." Hoeckle's eyes filled with the twinkle of enthusiasm. "Perhaps this was the reason that I was included, Herr Oberst?"

"Perhaps so, Feldwebel. Perhaps so. There are others on the squad with the same interest, no?"

"Yes. Fachinger for one."

"Also, Muller. Another too, though I don't remember which

one, whoever he received training with in his unit early last year. That's three. We shall need three more probably. Can you get them up that face?"

"I see nothing to prevent it. All of them are fit enough and, provided they will listen to advice from the experienced ones."

"Oh, they will, Feldwebel, they will. I shall be one of them."

As the three returned to the car, Schroeder asked Hoeckle about equipment.

"Two, one hundred metre ropes; two, three kilos of pitons thick, strong nails would do – and hammers, preferably rock hammers. You know, the type with a point at one end. The nails may not be needed but we take them in case. Oh – of course, a four or five metre ladder which may have to be worked on."

"You heard that, Oberst?" he asked Piekenbrock.

"Yes." Joseph Piekenbrock was already mentally checking the items off. "We shall have to go to Albuquerque but we'll get it all."

"Why not Santa Fe? I thought it was nearer," enquired Kurt.

"Almost certainly full of Government agents of one sort or another. A project like this has them crawling around like ants. No. I'll send Erich, he's the best procurer I have.

"Where to now?" Asked Joseph when they were back in the car.

"The airstrip I think. I want to confirm that the fuel has arrived and, no doubt, the Luftwaffe could do with a break."

Piekenbrock trod on the starter and turned round. In the

338

front passenger seat, Kurt had already taken a tablet from the dash pocket and was writing. Hoeckle watched, guessing at the notes his commander was making though, since only time would tell, he did not linger on the subject. He would be told at the proper time but, if his surmise was correct, they were in for some action before the operation was through.

THIRTY THREE

As the three men returned to the landing strip from Los Alamos, they were preceded by three other men and a woman.

Dietrich, failing to understand the information that Susan seemed to be willing to give, was taking her to see Neuper who was more technically qualified in the field. He knew that Schroeder would be away from the airstrip and was determined to find out the facts before Kurt returned. He was equally determined that credit for the information should be his; he would seize any opportunity to undermine Kurt's position and thereby displace the man.

As the jeep, with Ed at the wheel, bumped along the uneven roadway, Dietrich imagined the Knight's Cross in gold, with oak leaves, swords and diamonds being hung about his throat. As he looked down at the American uniform he wore, his lips twisted in a mirthless smile. Uncle Sep had refused the Fuhrer's direct order to strip four SS Divisions of their regimental armbands and so incurred Hitler's displeasure: he, Wolfgang Dietrich would wipe clean the family's honor.

Nils Bergerud entertained no such passionate feelings. Calmly, he glanced at Dietrich sitting in front and then across at the blindfolded faces of Susan and Paul beside him. The woman,

340

he noted, seemed surprisingly calm for someone who had
betrayed her country and its Allies. Webb, despite his tan, had
lost a lot of color when the impetuous Edward had started in on
him earlier that morning; he appeared to be a lot better now.

Unlike Dietrich, Nils would have preferred to await
Schroeder's return at the small ranch house. The SS Officer,
however, had noted Dietrich's distress and had decided to go
along with it, making only one suggestion: to hide their German
uniforms. Dietrich had taken one of the American Army
uniforms while Nils wore some of Paul's clothing which, though
somewhat large in the shoulders, was adequate.

Nils Bergerud had observed the tension between Dietrich
and Schroeder. At first he had ignored it as being no more than
the usual antipathy between Wehrmacht and SS but, during the
epic flight they had made, and in the hours they had been on
American soil, the relationship had grown more brittle. Bergerud
breathed a silent prayer that Dietrich's present action would not
cause the flare-up that seemed inevitable – it could jeopardise
Operation Blondi, perhaps fatally.

Susan was thinking about Paul who sat so still next to her.
She tried to put herself in his position; he had made no attempt to
hold her hand since they had been put in the Jeep, he had not
even spoken to her since he had heard her volunteer the
information. Perhaps, after her anger when he had told her about
his amateurish spying activities, he considered her two-faced.
Had he wanted Ed to carry on hurting him? Didn't Paul realise

341

how much she was in love with him, that it would have been easier to take those blows herself than to let him be crippled?

She resisted an impulse to reach out and lay a hand on his knee; he might react aggressively, better that she did nothing at all than to risk a rebuff. Susan knew that there would be a lot more questioning to come, now that she had disclosed her profession; she hoped that Paul would eventually realise what she was trying to do.

Paul ached from head to toe; his shoulders were badly bruised as were his ribs. His arms were still numb from the pressure Ed had exerted on the sub-clavian pressure points and Ed's boots had cut and bruised his fingers – a small price he supposed for Paul's hands had protected his genitals from far greater harm.

Surprisingly, perhaps, Paul's present reaction to Susan's outburst was nil. His mind was filled with thoughts of the brute who had attacked him and how he would like to turn the tables. His mind kept replaying the incident in slow motion; hindsight suggested a half dozen ways in which he could have avoided the ignominy of being hoisted off the bed like a sack of potatoes. The truth was, of course, that Paul had been asleep until that instant; he realised this but, nevertheless, it brought no satisfaction. Ed's time would come, he vowed, and when it did, he would be waiting with a baseball bat; he would take great satisfaction in despatching Edward to meet his Maker.

His thoughts came round to the two German Officers

escorting them; Bergerud spoke excellent English as did Dietrich though the latter's diction was too perfect ever to have been learned outside a high school or university. Bergerud seemed to be a decent enough fellow – far more so than the thugs who worked for Piekenbrock. Dietrich, though, was a horse of quite a different color; it was easy to identify him with Hollywood's idea of a German officer – blond, icy eyes, sadistic enough to knife a prisoner, just to check that his knife was sharp.

Of the two, Dietrich would stand watching.

Edward thought of nothing in particular. His mind was almost wholly visual. He was thankful to be out of that hot little house, thankful that he had thought of taking Webb apart. He felt, in his imagination, the thick sheaf of dollar bills that Piekenbrock would give him for prising the information from the girl, pictured himself counting the bills, spending them. Money was the only way he could think of to express gratitude and Piekenbrock had an unlimited supply.

Maybe they would give him the girl too, when they were finished with her. Ed's colorful imagination started off on this new tack, he licked his lips…

The valley seemed to suddenly erupt with life as they came down the hill. One moment it was empty; the next, men were working as if their lives depended on it – which they did.

Bergerud counted eight men as they stood up from the cover they had hidden behind when the jeep's engine was first heard. Only eight but their energy seemed to increase their numbers.

His observant eyes picked out a score of places where stones and clay had been pounded into soft earth and hollows or where bumps and hillocks had been meticulously levelled.

Dietrich spoke to Ed in German. Ed shook his head and Dietrich repeated himself in English. "Drive to the far end: the plane is up there, camouflaged." Then turning around, he pulled the blindfold from Susan's head and her hair fell free in a cascade of shimmering gold.

Bergerud was captivated by the sight and had to recall what Dietrich had asked: "I'll take her in to see Neuper right away, does he speak English?"

"Neuper? A little. Enough, I think."

The vehicle jerked to a halt and then Ed gunned it in through the webbing as someone pulled it aside. He stopped again beneath one of the wings.

"Come, Fraulein," instructed Dietrich. "There is someone I wish you to meet." Then, shouting: "Neuper!"

The Luftwaffe officer was bent double, inspecting the bomb door release mechanism. He crawled backwards from beneath the fuselage and got up. "Obersturmfuhrer Dietrich?"

"You speak English?"

"Quite well. Why?"

"Because I have brought you someone who knows about the bombs. You are the only one who can understand her and tell if she's lying."

"I see. You said "her," is this the lady?"

344

"It is." Dietrich changed to English. "Doctor – Millar?" Susan nodded. "This is Oberleutnant Neuper. He is our bomb specialist."

"Mister Neuper."

Susan held her hand out to shake Neuper's; she was a little surprised when he bowed and kissed it.

"A pleasure, Fraulein. Let us sit down over here." He indicated some ammunition cases. "I have been briefed on the theoretical aspects of atomic bombs but I may not be able to understand all you are able to tell me. My field is mainly fuses and, of course, conventional explosives."

Dietrich snorted, derision at the Luftwaffe gallantry evident in his voice. "Let us hope that you can distinguish truth from lies, Oberleutnant. That is all I require."

"What about Webb?" Asked Nils who had come up behind them.

"Leave him where he is. Oberst Schroeder seems to think he will be of some use though I do not see how at the moment."

Nils nodded and returned to the jeep and untied Paul's blindfold. He could not unravel the knot and pulled it over the top of his head.

"That was very tight," he remarked, "I hadn't realised. You should have said something."

"Would it have made any difference?" snapped Paul,

Bergerud's lips compressed with annoyance. "I would have eased it, it might have damaged your eyes. Listen, Webb," he added as Paul rubbed his eyes, "don't judge us all by animals like Edward."

Paul realised that he had, perhaps, been unnecessarily rude. "Yeah, I'm sorry. I'd thought I was one of the team until this happened – it makes you wonder."

Nils nodded. "This is a war, Webb. We are here to do a job – a very dangerous one, a very important one. Tempers get frayed and we all act over-cautiously. You'll have to get used to it." He slapped Paul's shoulder. "Afterwards, you will find us very different so stop feeling sorry for yourself. I'll get you a drink."

"Do I have to stay here – can't I go for a walk?"

"Not for the moment. Later perhaps when the Oberst returns."

"Haupsturmfuhrer Bergerud." It was Dietrich, his voice lower now as though realising that Nils was in fact his superior.

"I'll get you something later." Nils looked across to his fellow SS Officer. "Yes Dietrich?"

Dietrich had called Bergerud so he might listen in on the conversation and to help with interpreting. In the event, Neuper's command of English was not up to understanding some of Susan's technical terms and Dietrich's knowledge of the language was even poorer in this respect.

"You are engaged in the making of an atomic bomb?" Neuper was asking.

"Yes – in part of it. I work in the metallurgical section."

346

"And what element is being used in its manufacture?"

"Uranium 235 – that's the lighter isotope – and plutonium."

"Plutonium?"

"It's a synthetic element made from uranium in our atomic reactors."

"And you use both of these in the bomb?"

"No, we are building two types – one for each element."

"And how does it work?"

"I understand the theory but not how it's actually built – that part's not my department's responsibility."

"So, tell us what you can."

"Okay. Basically, it involves bringing together two masses of uranium neither of which is close to the critical mass, until they're together. Together, the whole lot is above that point, it goes 'crit' and detonates."

Neuper was in obvious difficulty and Bergerud translated what Susan had said. Neuper nodded. "It is in line with what I have been told."

"Then continue." Ordered Dietrich.

"How does it work? No, I've asked you that... what I mean is what happens when the two masses are brought together?"

"It goes critical – I told you. Oh, you mean... yes. The neutrons that are emitted naturally by uranium are now enclosed in a large mass of that metal, many of them don't escape but strike uranium atoms which then split up, emitting more neutrons. These strike still more atoms and so on. We call it the

K factor – a sort of chain reaction."

Neuper nodded. "And how is this chain reaction brought about? I know you can't just drop two lumps of uranium into a bucket."

"T.N.T. The bombs are packed with it. When it explodes, the uranium is driven together very fast, very tightly."

"Very dangerous. It seems to me that there is a risk of premature explosions."

"There is a sheet of osmium between the two pieces, we call it a tamper. It stops any neutron interaction until the T.N.T. destroys it. Then - boom."

"I do not know this osmium."

"It's a very rare metal. We mine it here in the States."

"Very well. Now - fuses. What type is used?"

Susan shrugged. "A pressure fuse, I think. An aneroid fuse – does that sound right? I'm out of my depth here."

"Ja. Aneroid. Like the barometer or the altimeter." He turned to his two colleagues, spoke in German. "As far as I can tell, she is speaking the truth. I see no point in continuing with this, she obviously knows far more than I on this matter."

"No, you are right. We need keep you no longer." Dietrich turned back to Susan. "Well Fraulein, it seems that Oberleutnant Neuper is satisfied that you are who you say. I hope you continue to co-operate – it will be good for your health and, also, the health of your lover. We must now wait for Oberst Schroeder's return. You may go back to Webb if you wish."

348

"I'll stay here if I may. Might I have a drink?"

"I'll get you one." Offered Nils Bergerud. "I could do with one myself and I said I'd get one for Herr Webb."

Pieter Reinicke chose that moment to return from helping the runway builders outside. The two SS Officers, despite the American uniform and civilian dress, sprang to attention. Pieter waved a languid hand, signalling them to stand easy. "Did you manage to sleep?"

"We did, thank you Sir."

"You've come to help then?" Pieter swept an outstretched arm around to indicate the long valley beyond the draped webbing. "The men have done well, worked hard but there's still a lot to finish."

Dietrich's face stiffened at the suggestion. "Then Oberst Schroeder will have to delay his plans until the work is complete, Herr Oberstleutnant. The men will have to sleep less and work longer. Perhaps they should drink more American coffee – I am told it has this effect."

Reinicke's customary smile slipped by not so much as a millimetre as he absorbed Dietrich's sarcasm. His voice was like ice water, though, as he replied. "Perhaps you'd like me to issue you with a whip, Obersturmfuhrer? Then you could supervise the job adequately." Reinicke's fury was plain; his own hands were calloused and filthy from helping the others. He turned on Bergerud. "And yourself, Haupsturmfuhrer, does the same go for you?"

Bergerud sighed, his sympathies lay with the Luftwaffe yet he could not afford to be drawn into any argument between his fellow SS officer and the others on the mission, "The men are trained soldiers," he replied at last, "the job you have them doing would be hard enough for experienced construction workers."

"I agree. I'm sure that Wolf has only the Operation's success at heart though. Perhaps the Oberst will order a delay and, if necessary, I am quite prepared to use a shovel."

Nils was perfectly aware that he had said nothing, merely hoping that his conciliatory tones would have the desired effect.

"We shall have to see." Pieter's voice was fractionally warmer. "It doesn't look as though we shall have to wait long, either."

Following the other's glance through the netting – transparent from inside – Bergerud saw Piekenbrock's car returning with Schroeder in the passenger seat. Reinicke left the two SS Officers and went outside; his stride purposeful.

Dietrich had not missed Bergerud's use of his given name; he said simply; "Thank you Nils. I think I may have upset our Luftwaffe colleague."

"I think you did. But then, flyers are a different breed of men from you and me."

Joseph drove in through the gap in the curtain which Reinicke was holding open; he halted alongside the jeep. For a moment, Kurt's eyes and Webb's met. Schroeder thought to detect a trace of malice in the other's expression but the feeling

350

was tenuous, he dismissed it. He climbed out and looked quickly around before greeting Reinicke.

"Hello again, Oberstleutnant. I see there have been developments." He nodded to the fuel tanker, drawn up on the far side of the fuselage with its engine running, pumping aviation spirit into the twelve fuel cells within the wings.

"Yes sir. It arrived about two hours ago. The driver was a little concerned when he realised he was not going to be allowed to leave when his tanker was empty."

"Oh?" Schroeder waited.

"I've told him the money isn't here yet; he seems willing enough to wait for that. However, he will have to stay until the Operation is over."

Reinicke went on to tell Kurt about the incident with the police car and the missing Albert.

Kurt nodded. "You acted correctly, Pieter. The driver must stay here as you say. We can't afford the time or the men to search for this Albert, although his defection worries me. We shall have to hope he will return. "Damnation, Pieter. I thought things were running too smoothly. Now what else? I see that Webb and the girl are here – why?"

"You'll have to ask the SS about that Herr Oberst. They came together and have not deemed it necessary to inform me of their reasons."

"Then I'll find out. Come along Pieter, anything that happens on this mission is your concern as much as mine."

Bergerud and Dietrich had kept their distance while Reinicke and Schroeder spoke together. They waited now as the others came across.

Dietrich made to speak first but Kurt forestalled him. "Inside the aircraft please gentlemen. I'm sure your reason for being here is a very good one, especially since you have brought the woman. I don't want to broadcast it to everybody."

"Both Webb and the woman were blindfolded until we got here, Herr Oberst." Offered Nils, quickly.

"Well, that is something, at least. Colonel Piekenbrock," he called, "a moment of your time, please and ask Feldwebel Hoeckle to entertain Mr. Webb and Doctor Millar."

As Kurt passed Susan, who had remained where she had been questioned, on the ammunition cases, he paused. There was something about her that reminded him of his dead Anna. He could not place the precise feature that struck the chord – her hair perhaps, the shape of the nose? Perhaps only that she was a woman; the first he had been close to since he had last been with Anna. The distraction had been momentary, enough only to nod to the girl in passing before making his way to the nose wheel entrance.

Inside the Liberator's main fuselage – now stripped of its internal fuel tanks – Kurt removed Paul's sports jacket and retrieved the aerial plan of the 'Hill' from its inside pocket. Looking for a suitable place to attach it to a wall, Kurt saw Piekenbrock come through from the flight deck looking curiously about the bomber's vast interior.

"Right gentlemen, perhaps you would care to tell me what happened while I prepare for the briefing."

It was Dietrich who spoke, outlining what Susan had told them and adding that Neuper vouched for the information thus far.

"So, it is not all bad news." Kurt nodded thoughtfully. "But why should Webb have denied her involvement with this Project? Is he trying to protect her or is it that he is not really with us."

"It's more than likely that he is trying to shield her." Suggested Joseph. "Americans tend to be very over protective towards their women."

"No doubt you're right, but, just in case you are not, we must be prepared. It is far better to be over-cautious than to find one's trust has been misplaced. I think we should have Doctor Millar in here so that she can point out the bomb stores again, I may be able to judge if she is lying or not. Colonel Piekenbrock, would you gather my men for me? And you had better post your own men as lookouts while my group is in here."

"You can use the rear hatchway now, Colonel." Suggested Reinicke, silent until this point. "It will be more convenient." A moment later, Susan came in. Like Piekenbrock, she looked around her curiously. Kurt explained what he wanted. Without hesitation, she went to the plan, scrutinised it for a moment and pointed to two rectangles that Paul had drawn in earlier.

"This is it. You see it is annexed to one of the laboratories where the final machining takes place. You won't be able to get to it though!"

"Oh, why is that?" Schroeder smiled at what he supposed was naiveté.

"There are people working there for the whole twenty four hours."

"So? And how many would there be?"

"It could be anywhere between one and ten, Colonel. It depends what is going on at the time."

"There would be fewer at night?"

"Not necessarily. I've been here for over two years, Colonel. I've never known anyone take any notice of the clock." She spoke with pride. It was duly noted by Schroeder.

"Why are you telling us all this, Doctor Millar?"

"I'd have thought that was obvious. I don't want to die and I don't want anything to happen to Paul."

Kurt nodded. "Why should anything happen to Paul?"

Susan saw her mistake immediately. Paul was supposed to be a collaborator, he was supposed to be trusted by the Germans.

"You mean you don't know about that ape you employ as a guard? He nearly killed Paul today – that's why."

Schroeder had not been told of Ed's effort to elicit information. He glanced sharply at Dietrich and Bergerud.

"She is partly right, Herr Oberst. Edward did knock Webb about a bit." Dietrich admitted. "Fortunately, we were there to

354

see it did not get out of hand. Remember though, had he not acted as he did, Fraulein Millar would not now be helping us."

Kurt gave Dietrich a hard look and turned back to Susan.

"Doubtless, it seemed worse to you than it actually was. Herr Webb seems quite recovered now. However, you have my assurance that it will not happen again. I and my colleagues are soldiers of the Reich. We are fighting a war but we are not beasts. You believe me?"

Susan looked up at the saturnine German, saw the truth of what he had said in his eyes. "Yes, Colonel. I believe you."

"Then there is only one more question, Doctor. How many atomic bombs are stored here?" He rapped the plan with his knuckles.

"Two." Susan admitted immediately.

"Two?" Schroeder was, at first, incredulous; then suspicious. "We understood there were hundreds."

Susan laughed. "There are hundreds of casings, Colonel – at least, there have been. They were used for ballistics tests and for training, I think. Only two bombs though."

"And the Americans intend to win the war with two bombs?"

"Colonel, you have no idea how special these bombs are."

"A thousand times more powerful than a normal high explosive."

"At least."

"And how do we recognise them?"

355

"I drew a sketch for you while I was outside. I had nothing better to do and I guessed you'd need to know." She handed a folded piece of paper to Kurt. He opened it and gazed at the excellent free hand drawing of a most unusual bomb; on its forward end, Susan had scribbled the words 'Goodbye Adolf. He looked at it a few seconds longer, committing its detail to memory before passing it on to Reinicke.

"It looks like a small whale." He commented.

Pieter inspected the drawing critically for some moments before speaking. "The square section tail fin is unusual and we know it's big but it's still a bomb." He directed a question at Susan. "What are these loops on the side? Lifting attachments?"

Susan frowned. "I'm not sure. I believe they're radio aerials. These are the first operational bombs, you see, and there's a lot of monitoring gadgets inside. I think the scientists want a recording of what happens inside while they're falling."

"They're ready for use then?"

"Oh yes. They're just waiting for President Truman to decide on the target. There was a rumour that that was why Doctor Oppenheimer and General Groves have gone to Washington. I expect these two bombs will be transported to Wendover air base when they get back."

Kurt's face wore a serious expression. "Thank you Doctor Millar. Will you go back to the jeep now? I expect to be another hour or so and then we shall be returning to Herr Webb's house for a meal."

356

When Susan had left, Kurt rounded on the others. "It seems we may have cause to hurry, gentlemen. What she said about an early decision on targets may or may not be true but we cannot afford to disregard them. I'm sorry about your problems Reinicke but the Operation must proceed tomorrow night, will the aircraft be ready?"

"The aircraft will be ready Oberst. My only concern is the take-off area, and to give those of your men without experience, some parachute training."

"How long?" Kurt's tone was urgent.

"A normal course lasts a month." Grinned Reinicke. "But that is for raw recruits. Since we shall be jumping over sea, they won't have to worry about broken ankles and landing technique but they will have to know about exiting the airplane and falling techniques, how to get rid of the 'chute when they hit the water."

"I think that will have to be sufficient, Oberstleutnant. I too, require time to train them in points related to the mission. I will see how time goes but parachuting will have to come last.

"Now, let us have them in here and I'll go through Operation Blondi from start to finish."

THIRTY FOUR

Albert was tired and dirty and sore enough to ache in every joint. He was also sore as hell at Piekenbrock and the whole German army.

When Garcia moved his tanker over the hill top, Albert had followed the track back a while, staying within the woodland. Then, realising that any pursuit would come back up that trail, he had struck north – away from the trail and away from those bastard Krauts.

At the top of the scarp, he had stopped, already perspiring freely, panting and cursing the God forsaken country he found himself in. It spread, hostile and unsympathetic, in every direction he could see. Almost then, he turned around and went back but the thought of the Major's wrath – for Garcia would have told him about the cop by now – deterred him."

He tramped on, the sun hot on the back of his head. Albert was knee deep in the small stream before he realised it was there.

It was heaven. Ice cold and better than any city bred tap water he had ever drunk. Albert stripped and soaked himself in a shallow pool until his blistered feet were numb with the cold. Hungry but no longer hot and thirsty, he redressed and dozed until mid afternoon, day dreaming about the various forms of vengeance he would wreak on the hapless Piekenbrock. There was really only one thing he could do, when it came down to it: it had to be an anonymous phone call and then get a lift up North to civilisation. An anonymous call to the Police to blow this stupid operation wide open.

Albert heaved himself to his feet and set off to the east. The direction was chosen by estimating where the sun had been at midday and walking to the left of that point. Somewhere out there was Route 66. Somewhere.

By the evening, Albert was suffering badly from dehydration. He had been as sick as his empty stomach would allow, his vision was blurred, his balance – uncertain. The long shadows stretched ahead of him until the sun suddenly slipped behind a mountain and then it was dark, too dark to limp another step.

Albert stopped just where he was and slept like a baby for two hours. There was enough heat in the ground to combat the chill night air for a time and he was almost comfortable. However, he woke in pitch darkness, shivering uncontrollably and frightened. He did push-ups – as low as his bulging stomach would allow, he jogged on the spot, did knee bends until he was exhausted. He cried and licked at the tears until they froze on his cheeks.

Albert was surprised to find himself still alive when the sun came up and started the ground steaming.

Why the hell hadn't he thought to light a fire? Cursing, he

did so, finding some small twigs and dry bark to start it off with. As he warmed through, Albert rationalised his lack of foresight in not stopping earlier and making a fire the night before: he had been ill, it was too dark to see as well; besides, someone might have followed him, seen the blaze. Before the hour was out, Albert had convinced himself that he had acted correctly, that he had suffered purposely to protect himself from pursuit.

And so started the second day in the wilderness. All he asked was a highway where he could thumb a lift. And a pay phone..

THIRTY FIVE

"Our mission, Gentlemen, is to enter an American military establishment and to come out with a bomb." There was a murmur of sorts at Kurt's words. He ignored it.. "A long way for just one bomb, you think? Perhaps. But this is no ordinary bomb; it's an atomic bomb, equivalent to a thousand ordinary ones."

There were several snorts of derision all but smothered by cries of appreciation from the rest.

"Our orders are to return the bomb to this aircraft where Oberleutnant Neuper will arm it ready for dropping on an important target. I shall not disclose this target until we are en route in case any of you are captured. As soon as we are airborne again, I shall take great pleasure in informing you.

"The Fuhrer believes this mission will bring about America's withdrawal from the war and consequent victory for the Fatherland. I am sure we all share this belief."

As Kurt talked, he noted the expressions on the faces of his men, seated in two ranks along one side of the fuselage. Without exception, they were enthused; this was the culmination of their long months of preparation, the marathon flight, the day of backbreaking labor.

"Now we come to the most important part – where the bomb

361

is and how to achieve our first objective." Kurt moved to one side to reveal the site plan behind him. "This plan has been prepared from aerial reconnaissance; it shows the installation known as Project Y which is about forty miles from here – a little over an hour's travel. Project Y is sited on a flat topped hill; it's an extremely isolated place, well chosen with only two access roads: here and here." He indicated,

"The installation has a chain link perimeter fence surmounted by barbed wire. Guard details patrol the outside at regular intervals; mobile patrols inside the fence work on a random basis. The outside patrols consist of two man teams. Dogs are not used."

"Seems sloppy!" Commented a voice. "Is the fence electrified?"

"No electrification. It may seem sloppy but you must remember this: America has never been invaded – before this."

Kurt got a laugh with that. "She does not expect it, cannot expect it. If the authorities were told of the existence of this task force, I doubt they would believe it. Remember this, too – security is tight within Project Y; it's top secret. Not even the local residents have the least idea of what goes on there."

Schroeder continued by pointing out the proposed method of ingress: the rocky canyon, the two hundred metre cave studded wall, and finally, the Tech Area the building containing the bombs and the two guards constantly in the sentry box.

"We shall be going in at night. I am splitting the group into

362

two. Obersturmfuhrer Dietrich, Feldwebel Hoeckle, Giefrauter Weber, Fachinger, Strauch and myself will, make up one team – the team entering the site. The others under the command of Haupsturmfuhrer Bergerud will form the second team." There was some muttering at this which Kurt quickly silenced.

"Both teams," he raised his voice to emphasize the point, "will be engaged in equally important work. It will be team number two's responsibility to create a diversion to draw the internal guards away from our area of interest at an agreed time. They will set a listening tap on the telephone wires and set charges on the access roads. Failure by the second team means failure by the first – and of the mission."

Kurt lowered his voice, the seated men unconsciously leaned forward to hear him. "There is a very good chance that we can enter and leave without being detected before we are in the air again." He raised a forefinger. "If that is not to be, then, when we leave, we shall be leaving at a run. At that time and at that time only, the roads will be blown to cut off pursuit.

"Questions?"

"Only one obvious one, Sir."

"Yes Weber."

"How do we get the bomb out? It's got to be big."

"It is – nearly three metres long. It comes out in the breakdown truck that Oberst Piekenbrock provided for us." Piekenbrock nodded at Kurt's acknowledgement. "That brings me to one more point, Oberleutnant Neuper."

363

"Sir?" Joachim Neuper stood up.

"You are, technically, not a part of my force and, understand, I cannot order you to do this. I need you with me to identify the bomb."

Neuper had considered himself as no more than an observer until the weapon was brought back to the plane. With participation suddenly thrust upon him, he blanched. "I... I'm no good at rock climbing, Herr Oberst." He managed.

"You won't be asked to do any, Oberleutnant. If you come, it will be in style; as a passenger in the breakdown truck."

"In that case, Herr Oberst..." He spread his hands in acceptance.

Kurt nodded. Strange, he thought, that a man who dismantled live bombs should be afraid of heights. Still, every man to his trade. Kurt himself was not overly fond of live bombs.

"There is one question that I'm surprised no one has asked – when is it all happening? I'll tell you, we go in tomorrow night. After listening to a mixture of low whistles and gasps Kurt continued.

"Right? This briefing is closed then. It's damned hot in here so I suggest you all get out into the fresh air; there is still plenty of work for you, and Feldwebel Hoeckle will be selecting certain of you for advice on rock climbing."

There was a round of hurried applause as the men rose to file outside and cool down. When the fuselage was empty, Kurt sat down to discuss his plans in detail with the Officers.

Paul sat in the jeep, aching and disconsolate. His hatred for Ed was still simmering but now his thoughts turned to Susan. Why had she turned traitor, he wondered? What had she been telling them in there? He could understand her initial outburst to save his neck but why had she turned so completely?

Something was stirring, there was no doubt about that in Paul's mind. The tanker had finished pumping the fuel into the B24 and had been driven away into the woods with its accompanying miasma. Now the Germans were arriving in ones and twos to wait outside the plane, obviously a briefing was about to commence.

Susan still sat on the pile of cases where she'd been since coming out of the plane. It was evident that she had no wish to join him or even to speak to him thought Paul though he chose not to dwell on the matter. The fact that Errol had replaced Hoeckle in the onerous task of watching them interested him only in passing. His thoughts were in such turmoil that nothing held his attention for more than a few moments. Thoughts seemed to flit through his head with the impermanence of butterflies and time flew by unheeded.

It was Schroeder himself who finally jolted Paul back to reality. He had taken a carton of cigarettes from the flight cabin and now walked idly across to Paul. He took a pack out and offered a smoke to the American. Paul lit it, took two deep drags before he realised where he was and what he was doing. He looked up sharply as Kurt vaulted into the seat beside him.

"At last we have time to talk Paul." Schroeder seemed relaxed, more human, less soldierly. "We have been talking about you and your part in this exercise. It is an important part, I have to make certain that you understand exactly what you have to do and that it can be done."

"Look Colonel, how the hell do you expect me to do anything if you let thugs like that gorilla Ed attack me – and Sue?"

"Mm. I'm sorry about that. It was very unfortunate but I think you'll agree that you, yourself, were partly responsible for it."

"Me!"

"You killed your brother-in-law, Paul. Carl was Ed's friend."

"Nevertheless…"

"Nevertheless, he will be severely reprimanded. It will not happen again. Fortunately, Edward is not typical of the German peoples. He believes that he is acting like a German because he knows only the propaganda put out by your media. In Germany, he would probably be in an asylum.

"However, Edward is not important. You are. I want you to look on us as your friends."

If this was incongruous, it appeared not to register with Paul. He merely nodded.

"Good. Now this is what you have to do. Go into work as

normal tomorrow, in your car. When you finish for the day –
what time will that be?"

"'Bout seven if there're no emergencies."

"When you finish, leave your car, incapacitate it. Make a
point of telling people that it has broken down and get a lift into
Los Alamos and I'll see you're picked up."

"What about Susan?"

"Susan will stay with us for two days, then she may return to
work."

"But they might send someone to look for her."

"Where would they send someone? I thought she lived
inside the site."

"That's true, but…"

"Is your relationship with her common knowledge?"

"No, not exactly."

"How many people know of it?"

"A couple of Susan's girl friends,maybe. I don't really
know."

"Then we shall meet the problem if and when it occurs.
Now, we shall return to your home for a meal and a good night's
sleep. Tomorrow, you are back at work."

Paul suddenly had a thought. "I've just remembered, that
man Albert took my car."

"Then you will have to take one of the others. I will give the
necessary orders. There will be no problem with an unfamiliar
car, will there?"

Paul shook his head. "I don't suppose so." He smiled wryly at a thought that had just crossed his mind and said. "I suppose as a professional there will always be another mission for you when you return?"

It appeared to take no thinking about. Kurt said, "This will be my last mission; Herr Hitler's last mission and the last mission of the Reich. This is…how do you Americans say it? Ah yes- the last throw of the dice."

Schroeder turned away and called to Piekenbrock, then to Susan, gesturing them over. To Paul, he said, "In a couple of days, it will be all over. Then you can please yourself what you do."

Kurt got out of the vehicle, spoke a few words to Joseph in German and then crossed to where Susan was still sitting.

"It will soon be evening, Doctor Millar. We are going back to Paul's home. Perhaps you will allow me to cook tonight. I cook a very passable schnitzel."

"Couldn't I stay here tonight, Colonel? I don't want to return to Paul's."

Kurt lifted an eyebrow. "Why should you want to stay here? I thought you were in love with the young man."

"Put it down to a lover's tiff. I just don't feel up to sharing a bunk with him tonight."

"A lover's tiff? Ah – a quarrel. Well I'm sorry but I can't permit you to stay here."

Susan nodded listlessly and got to her feet.

368

"I'll be with you presently. I have to speak with Oberstleutnant Reinicke a moment."Together, Kurt and Pieter walked down the valley; the sun, low in the sky behind them shed its golden light along the valley, casting long shadows in front.

"A change from Europe, Pieter?" Kurt swept his arm around to take in the valley, the sky, the sun. "The sun seems to shine more clearly here than anywhere I've been – including North Africa."

Pieter nodded. "It's the clear air, not enough big cities pouring smoke into the atmosphere."

"Nor war to fill the sky with ruin."

The other nodded, then brought the subject back to their immediate purpose. "The work is progressing very well; much better than I had expected. There may be time to give everyone extra parachute instruction."

Kurt laughed, "As you wish Pieter. So far, everything is going better than we have any right to expect. When you told me about Albert running off, I thought this is where it starts – the hundred and one little things that crop up to make a mission difficult if not impossible. I think I was wrong. I have a premonition that everything is going to run sweetly. I feel we should celebrate this evening. Tomorrow is the day!"

THIRTY SIX

Before he even opened his eyes, Kurt knew it was going to hurt. He opened them and, sure enough, there was that nagging twinge across the forehead – symptom of a mild hangover.

Why? He asked himself. Certainly they had indulged yesterday evening but there had been occasions when he had drunk far more alcohol. Then he remembered the bourbon; they had broken into Paul's stock when Piekenbrock's supply of schnapps had ended. He had never had the sweet spirit before and, probably, the mixing of the two had brought on the punishment.

Did the others feel like this, he wondered. Probably not, unless Paul Webb was feeling the effects; he and Paul had indulged most heavily. Of them all, they were the two with the heaviest problems: his – the Operation; Paul's – the woman.

Kurt smiled up at the ceiling and admitted to himself that he had made an uncharacteristic mistake in judging the boy on first impressions. The American had a certain depth to his personality that he had missed at their first meeting.

For a moment, Schroeder considered the possibility of Paul sabotaging the mission. He had the means – or he would have

370

when he reported in for work; yet it would mean the certainty of a trial for his brother-in-law's death – Joseph Piekenbrock would see to that and he would also be putting Susan Millar at risk of the unspoken threats made against her. Again, Piekenbrock would have no qualms about exacting retribution from the girl.

No, Webb would not put the mission in danger.

"Guten morgen, Herr Oberst," volunteered Bergerud from the doorway. He came all the way into the bedroom when he saw Kurt already awake. He carried a tray from which the tantalising smells of fresh-brewed coffee and grilled bacon wafted.

Kurt eased himself to a sitting position, deciding that he did not have a real hangover if food could arouse his appetite like this. Suddenly, he realised that he was, and had been, the sole occupant of the double bed. "Thank you Nils. Why didn't someone share the bed? I wouldn't have minded." Kurt felt guilty.

"No need to worry Sir. Dietrich and I used it yesterday. Webb and his girl slept in the bunks; the rest of us slept in chairs – quite comfortable when you've had to sleep in panzers."

"I agree. What about the flyers?"

"Back to the aircraft, before we turned in. Don't you remember?"

Kurt frowned. "Yes. Yes, of course." He could remember nothing. "You'd better wake Webb up. He has to leave for work this morning."

Bergerud smiled. "Gone two hours. He was concerned

371

because he was late."

"Late!" Kurt looked at his watch and experienced a shock. "It's ten o'clock." He had slept for ten hours. "I wish you'd woken me earlier. There's still much to do."

"Nothing that others can't take care of. Herr Piekenbrock and Erich left before six and Oberstleutnant Reinicke expects us at eleven so you have nothing to do but eat your breakfast before it gets cold. And, I might add, I know that you hadn't slept for three days – you needed the rest."

Schroeder took a mouthful of crisp bacon. "I suppose you're right Nils. This is very good, who cooked it?"

"I did. Although three or four slices of bacon are hardly a challenge, I was a chef in my father's hotel before the war."

"Really?" Kurt always had trouble in visualising a soldier in some innocuous peacetime occupation.

"Oh yes. Our establishment was well known for its Smorgasbord – a speciality of mine. It was in a small village about thirty five, forty kilometres from Oslo; people from the Capital came regularly on Sundays, especially in the summer."

Nils' face had lost the flat planes and angles of the hardened Waffen SS Officer; somehow he looked younger than his thirty seven years.

"And when this is all over, you expect to go back there?"

A cloud covered Bergerud's features. "No Sir. My family was killed in a freak bombing accident. An English Lancaster returning from a bombing mission dropped its last bomb on my

372

father's house. It was so low; witnesses could see them actually kicking it free; it must have been stuck in the rack. My whole family was wiped out in a second."

Kurt could think of nothing to say. The tale struck too close to his own tragedy. He nodded in silent sympathy.

"Crazy." Said Nils. "Crazy, the things that happen in war. That same bomber crashed into the Skagerrak just off Kristiansand. I think they were losing height and they got rid of the bomb before they went down."

"Fate." Schroeder murmured. He had wondered before why a Viking had chosen to join the Waffen SS when Norway was so notoriously pro-ally. He would never have chosen to broach the subject but Nils had just explained a great deal. He was suddenly glad, however, that this Officer was part of his team and, in some obscure way, secretly thankful to the crew of that long dead Lancaster.

He put the tray to one side and threw back the sheets. After stretching his hard muscles, Schroeder began to dress quickly.

"You are familiar with the plastic explosive we brought with us?"

"Yes. PE2 and 808."

"What's the difference?"

"PE2 sticks to anything, explodes outward in all directions. 808 is ideal for blowing holes in masonry or concrete." Bergerud punched a fist into the other palm with a sudden crack.

"Could we use either for the road up to the 'Hill'?"

"808 if you want to blow it away. Or else we could use impact fuses in the PE2; that'll give you similar results to a landmine."

Kurt pondered while he slipped into his pants. "Let's take both then, play it safe for once – if that's the word." He put out his hand. "Thanks for the breakfast Nils, and thanks for being on this mission. With men like you, we have a damn good chance."

Nils accepted Kurt's strong handshake.

"It is my pleasure, Herr Oberst."

Reinicke had already made his preparations for parachute training when Kurt and the others arrived. An area close to the Liberator's port wing was littered with foam rubber pallets from its interior, Pieter was busy arranging them to his satisfaction. He stood up as Kurt greeted him and saluted. "All is ready, Herr Oberst."

Kurt nodded. "Officers first?"

"No Sir. We shall need to go through it together to take advantage of what little time is left."

"Very well." Kurt turned to the two SS Officers who had followed them under the webbing. "Would you round up the men, please?"

Then, as they left, to Pieter: "How is the tanker driver?"

Pieter smiled. "Grumpy and getting grumpier. He has decided to charge you for the waiting time by the hour."

"No matter. This is Oberst Piekenbrock's problem."

"Oh, speaking of him. He was here at seven, he and one of

his fellows – Erich? The intelligent one...?"

"That would be Erich." Kurt nodded.

"Mm. They have gone into Albuquerque. He set the others to discovering various climbing approaches to the 'Hill'."

"Ah, good. Now – parachuting?"

"All is ready."

Kurt nodded, he was about to say something and then thought better of it. A page from one of his men's files had passed before his mind's eye. Never mind, he thought, a smile softening his features for a moment; Pieter will realise soon enough.

Ten men stood to attention in a line parallel with the fuselage of the B24. Still dressed in combat suits, they might have belonged to any army in the world. Neither decorations nor epaulettes adorned the jackets. Instead of the steel helmets or caps, each wore a black woollen balaclava. These were presently rolled up to the hair line but later, in the dark, they would be pulled down to prevent facial glare.

Schroeder viewed them critically and approved. Ten men – the product of what had been the best war machine in the world, unstoppable. Now the balance of history rested on those capable shoulders.

He stood to attention, facing them, then relaxed. "Stand easy. Today is Operation Day." He said quietly, without emphasis. "At 2200 hours we shall assemble into our separate groups and leave for our targets. The one point which has not yet been generally discussed is our returning home."

He raised his eyebrows. "In case any of you are under the impression that we shall be returning the way we came – on a first class air ticket, let me disillusion you. There is not enough fuel."

Schroeder grinned. "Our transport will be provided this time by the Kreigsmarine. Our rendezvous will be by parachute with Die Rache, a small cargo vessel which has run money and supplies to South America since before the outbreak of war. She is now awaiting our arrival in Delaware Bay. Since this arrangement was made too late to include parachuting in our earlier training, Oberstleutnant Reinicke is now going to correct the situation. All of us will be taking instruction."

Kurt signalled to Pieter. "Oberstleutnant Reinicke." He moved across to stand at the end of the rank; Pieter took his place.

"The first thing we have to learn," he started without preamble, "is how to jump and secondly, how to turn our backs to the wind. The actual procedure for securing static lines can be explained on our way out from here.

"Now, since the landing will be in water, I shall not be teaching landing procedures except for demonstrating parachute release. The 'chutes are American Army Air Force issue but, I assure you, they are good. Herr Major Braun has stripped every pack and repacked them personally.

"Any questions before we go on?"

376

There were. Reinicke fielded them and spent the next hour and half on instruction, stopping when the smell of hot coffee took everybody's attention.

As they stood drinking the warm brew, Pieter nodded towards Hoeckle. "I think you have been holding out on me Kurt. The Feldwebel knew exactly what to do and his fitness belies his age; I wondered why you had chosen him to accompany you."

Kurt called Hoeckle over. "Feldwebel, would you care to undo your jacket for the Oberstleutnant?"

Hoeckle grinned. "If you wish it, Sir." He undid the buttons and, so only the two officers could see, turned towards them. On his right breast, beneath the pocket was an insignia; a white plunging eagle within a gold wreath. It was identical to the parachute badge that Reinicke wore except that Pieter's was steel blue.

A wry smile crossed Pieter's features. "You're an old fox Feldwebel, A Fallschirmjager; where did you get that?"

"1936 Sir. The Parachute Infantry Company, I was one of the first at Stendhal."

"So you would have been at Mecklenburg."

"I was Sir. Under Leutnant Zahn but I remustered after that, thinking to see more action."

"Cover it up then, Feldwebel; I can hardly use you as a shining example to your colleagues if they know you're a professional jumper. But, tell me, where did you end up?"

377

"With the Airborn Panzer Corps, It's funny, you know, the way things happen; I would probably have been fighting near my home now but for a dose of food poisoning. My comrades were in East Prussia, the last I heard."

Kurt had listened to the conversation, aware of the places and past actions mentioned only by hear say. "Why are the two badges different?" He asked.

"Your man was Wehrmacht and I, Luftwaffe, Herr Oberst, though the Parachute Infantry Company was eventually absorbed into the Luftwaffe. The Feldwebel must be a lucky man, he is the first live person I've seen wearing that badge. Some of the original battalions took heavy casualties in the Polish campaign and again, later, in Norway."

Hoeckle nodded. "The conditions in Norway were bad, we were not then experienced enough. Crete was the worst I remember though, over six thousand men lost; the divisional staff glider crashed, killed everyone on board." The soldier's face brightened as he remembered. "I was in the western attack, "Papa Ramche took over when Meindl was wounded. Now there was an officer."

"Papa Ramche!" exclaimed Kurt. "I was in his group in North Africa."

"It's a small war," grinned Pieter and the three would have found much to reminisce about had time allowed.

Around lunchtime, Piekenbrock returned with the equipment. He came straight over to Schroeder. "All as
378

requested, Sir."

"Very good. In that case, join me in having something to eat and then Hoeckle can inspect his climbing equipment." Kurt thought how lucky he had been in deciding to bring the man on the mission despite his evident years. He was proving a positive strength, in addition to which Kurt both liked and respected the man.

Most of the group had, following their para-training, filtered away. Some to complete outstanding tasks, others to be alone with their thoughts before the operation started in earnest. Piekenbrock looked around to make certain that no one could overhear his query.

"What chance do you think you really have to pull this off?"

The question came as a surprise to Kurt. He thought about it seriously for some seconds before replying. "Better than I had thought when we first came here. You have heard my plans – what do you think?"

Joseph coughed, bit down hard into his spam. "The plan is a good one, the best for the circumstances. But there seem to be so many uncertainties. For instance, what if there are internal security alarms where the bombs are stored? What if the information we have is insufficient –not necessarily wrong but... well, you see where my thoughts are headed?"

"I do." Kurt stared steadily at Piekenbrock's profile. Mid fifties? He wondered. The man had survived an extraordinarily long time where every other German agent had been caught one way or another. Pathologically suspicious – so the stories went; Kurt was ready to believe them. "Unfortunately, Joseph, these are the vagaries of war; what was it Euripides said...? 'The Gods of war frown on those who hesitate."

"This is one of those cases. Hopefully, we shall be in and out while the Americans are worrying over other things. Remember, they cannot even begin to suspect a German raid into the United States.

"Anyway, we are prepared to fight our way out if necessary. If necessary, too, we shall take hostages."

"But if this were the case, there would be no surprise element. You would not be able to reach your destination, within ten minutes every fighter with shells in its cannon would be off the ground."

"True. But before enemy fighters could spot us, I would have achieved my secondary objective. Mention this to no one; my contingency plan is to destroy Los Alamos itself and head for Mexico." Kurt changed the subject, "Have you heard from your boys yet?"

"Not yet. I expect to before 1800 hours. If they don't get back by 1700, their instructions are to report back to Web

THIRTY SEVEN

Hank Garcia, either sitting in his cab listening to the radio or sitting on the hood, smoking, had spent a boring day. He had wandered over to watch the Germans practising their jumping for a while but his curiosity had waned quickly and he had taken a handful of rough sandwiches and a pail of hot coffee back to his tanker. Came the afternoon, he had spent half an hour watching six men – including the boss Officer with the eyes of an eagle and physique to die for– running up a ladder while one of the others, the pale one with a face like a mountain lion, timed their performance with his watch. This activity too, soon palled and he had spent the remainder of the afternoon figuring what he was due if he charged them a dollar an hour waiting time.

It came as something of a relief when the elderly American came over and jerked his thumb towards one of the jeeps.

"We're going down to Los Alamos, Garcia. You can spend tonight in more comfortable surroundings."

"I don't like leaving my truck here, boss."

"Don't worry about that, guards will be on duty all night."

"Yeah? It'll cost you a bomb if it gets ripped off."

Piekenbrock flinched at the word 'bomb' until he realised it was no more than an expression.

"You goin' ta pay for me hanging around here, doin' nuthin'?"

"I dare say we can work something out. It will all be over by tomorrow."

"What ya doin', anyway?"

"The less you know, Garcia, the longer you'll stay healthy."

*

They were at his house when Paul arrived home. Errol had picked him up, as promised, in Los Alamos and had tried to strike up a conversation but had given up eventually.

Paul was deep in thought, had been most of the day. He had gone up to the 'Hill' that morning with the express intention of figuring out a solution to his problems and had left still no closer to success. The Germans – unconsciously he had started to think of them that way now – held all the aces. Unless something came up unexpectedly he could see no way of sabotaging the mission without endangering Susan and himself. It was a pity in one respect; under different circumstances he could have made a friend out of Schroeder. The man was all that Carl had pretended to be, and more; Paul found himself liking the Colonel against his will. He was doing a job that was right by his own philosophy – the fact that Paul now saw it differently was the fault of neither.

Paul was an American. Searching his conscience, he had come to know this as a certainty. There was no way he could betray his country without feeling guilty. And he was guilty,

382

guilty as hell. He had started this whole damn thing.There had to be a way out..

As he entered, Schroeder looked up from the maps he was studying, nodded and bent his head once more.

"So you are certain the only other way would be too narrow for the truck. What about the jeep?"

Erich spread his hands. "Could be but it's rough. It's the sort of trail you might ride a horse over, no more."

"Still, we must try." Kurt turned to Bergerud. "It could save you a half hour and that half hour would allow us to get well clear of any pursuit. What do you think?"

Nils nodded vigorously. "Oh, I agree Colonel. We must take advantage of it – it would mean us both getting back to the strip at the same time."

"Exactly."

Kurt folded the map and spoke to Paul. "You have done as I asked?"

"To the letter. I've parked it as close to your destination as security would permit. I crossed the plug leads in case anyone starts tinkering with it."

"That's good, because, at ten o'clock tonight you're going to drive the breakdown truck into Los Alamos to pick it up." Kurt waited for Paul to make some comment; when none was forthcoming, he cleared his throat and said, instead, "Then let's eat.."

Paul looked around the living room, crowded again as it had

been the two previous evenings. Tonight though, there was no sign of Susan. He left the room and went down the hall to the bedroom. Opening the door without knocking, he caught Susan in the act of fastening her brassiere. She started, turned her back to him chastely.

Ignoring her gesture, Paul crossed to her side and turned her face to him, putting his hand firmly on her shoulders. "Why Susan?" He asked, low voiced.

"I don't want to speak about it at the moment Paul." Her tone was flat, betraying no emotion. Then, seeing the hurt in his eyes, she stood on her toes and kissed him quickly on the cheek. "Cheer up, I do still love you. Things'll be different tomorrow, you'll see but, for the moment it has to be like this." Agilely, she escaped his arms and picked up her dress from the bed. "I mean it Paul. Don't question me now, just let it rest until tomorrow. Okay?"

Seconds later, dressed, she stepped into her shoes and went out, leaving Paul to make whatever he might of her remarks.

Later, at half past nine, after a dinner of mainly cold meats and salad washed down with great quantities of black coffee, Kurt pushed his chair back and stood up. His gaze swept the men at the table one by one.

"We are ready then?" He asked at last. "We all know what to do?" The mood was sombre though curiously charged. Some nodded, others replied "yes". All were ready.

"Then let's make final checks on the equipment. We leave at

384

2200 precisely." All of the soldiers stood up and Kurt looked down at the still seated Piekenbrock. "Detail a man to stay with Doctor Millar and Garcia, will you? It will be best if Erich and yourself await us back at the strip, we won't be returning here for obvious reasons."

Joseph nodded his agreement and stood up.

"Right Paul? Let me show you the truck. You will be carrying a passenger. Joachim..."

THIRTY EIGHT

Albert peered uncertainly at the vague shapes off to his right. A village? It seemed like it. A village, even an Indian village, would have some sort of trading post, maybe even a phone. It had been the one thought driving him on, a phone booth with a cop at the other end. He grinned at the thought of those Krauts – blooey! Boy were they going to get theirs?

"Hey!" He shouted, or tried to. "Hey! Anybody." A little stronger this time. He broke into a shambling trot, wincing each time his blistered feet touched the ground. The angular white shapes were swimming in front of his blurred eyes now and he stumbled, sprawled full length.

Painfully, Albert got to his knees and then to his abused feet. He lurched on – the buildings swimming as though he saw them through running water, "Hey!" He husked, "anybody there?"

There was, but the old Hopi didn't answer. He rarely spoke to white men, never with drunks, not even to the youngsters of his own people when they drank too much.

"Please," called the stranger, weaving along the street between the crumbling, deserted buildings. "Somebody help."

The Indian sat, as still as stone, on his threadbare blanket and spat a stream of brown tobacco juice into the dust. He

386

watched the drunk come to the kiva in the middle of the old square.

Albert stopped and sat down carefully on the wall. Where was everybody? He needed a phone.

When the wall around the bowl shaped kiva had been built, it had been strong but that was almost a century ago. Since then, the rains and weather had weakened the adobe; Albert's two hundred and thirty pounds crumbled the old wall like so much cardboard. With a cry, he tumbled the twenty feet or so into the Indian assembly area.

The Hopi nodded and fingered his torn and patched pants. Tonight he would go take a look at his new pair.

Miraculously, hours later, Albert was still alive and, to a certain extent, conscious when the old Hopi climbed down the worn steps that hugged the circular wall. He saw the movement though not the shape that made it.

"Help." Whispered Albert. "Got to get to a phone."

The Indian was annoyed that Albert had survived the fall. He picked up a piece of fallen masonry and went across.

"Go – way." He said, searching for the unfamiliar white man's words.

And brought the heavy stone down on the stranger's skull.

THIRTY NINE

At ten fifty five, Paul was at the West Gate into the 'Hill'. The MP came across, giving the yellow breakdown wagon a surprised stare.

"What the hell's this for then?"

"Damn car gave out on me this morning, had to get a lift into town."

"And you're going to tow it out yourself? What sort is it?"

"Buick. Seemed like a good idea at the time." Paul grinned. "There's no way I can get a service man in here and it means all sorts of red tape to get a Site mechanic to see to a private car." He made no mention of the fact that it was not his car.

"Well, I'll wish you luck. Get yourself a Packard or a Ford next time. Got your papers?"

Paul and the guard had known one another for the best part of a year, yet the MP took Paul's pass, checked it, checked the photograph against his face as though they had never met.

"Okay buddy. I'll open the gate wide when I see you coming back in this thing."

"Don't hold your breath, Gus. I'm going to have a go at the bastard myself before I hitch it up. See you." Paul slammed the manual shift into bottom and the truck ground through the gates

388

and into the 'Hill'. He was sweating, it ran down his ribs in cold rivulets; the thought of what he was doing made his hands tremble on the wheel.

What if they had found Neuper in the back? He shuddered, a mental picture of himself standing against a brick wall being shot. He took a side road which would take him around the accommodation blocks, skirting them by a good half mile. Briefly, the humor of a German infiltrator being caught on Bathtub Row – where the Directors and top brass lived – caused him to smile; the moment passed quickly however.

Paul headed into the heart of Project Y, lights at cornices and roof peaks glaring off the dusty yellow hood into his eyes. The second pass in his billfold would enable him to go into the Tech Area; Schroeder had scrutinised it and told him not to use it. He was to remain outside on Trinity Drive until Kurt contacted him – how, was something the German had neglected to explain. As was the case inside Los Alamos, Schroeder believed in telling his men only as much as they needed to know to perform their work efficiently. Paul needed to know very little and, consequently, knew only what he was supposed to do during the next few minutes.

Had Susan been more forthcoming in the few seconds he had spent alone with her the previous night, he might be in a better position to blow this mission wide open, smash the Germans' plans like so many rotten eggs. This way, the opportunity to take action might pass him by without his recognising it.

He halted the breakdown truck, killed the diesel, and switched off the lights. The Buick was five yards ahead. The silence flooded in like a physical presence and minutes went by before his ears could pick up the ever present whine of equipment, the hum of overhead transmission wires.

The minutes lengthened, perhaps the Germans had been captured; what should he do in that case? Drive out with the car in tow and drop Neuper on the highway…?

*

The two jeeps came to a stop two miles short of the 'Hill'. The three officers climbed out and watched the winch truck continue on towards the distant acres of bright light and intense darkness that marked the night time Los Alamos site.

Schroeder took a deep breath. "Right. You have everything straight?"

Bergerud turned the slit of the balaclava in Kurt's direction. "Absolutely."

"And you?" He looked at Dietrich.

"Yes, Herr Oberst."

"We go then." Kurt walked back to the rear jeep. "Pull it off the road and face it in the other direction." He addressed the occupants as a whole. "Good luck!"

Returning to the lead jeep, where Weber sat behind the wheel, Kurt instructed him. "A little further on you'll see a solitary pile of rocks; pull in behind it and turn out the lights. We

390

go in on foot from there."

Each of the six dark shapes carried an M43/1 assault rifle strapped to their backs. Additionally, Weber and Fachinger carried the light ladder, Hoeckle – the ropes, hammer and makeshift pitons. They made their way cautiously over the rock strewn landscape, travelling quietly and quickly with the economy of motion that is the hallmark of men trained in silent warfare.

Schroeder led the file, Dietrich brought up the rear. The group had exchanged their combat jackets for American versions; they wore American trousers and helmets. Most of the men retained their own boots and all wore their own tunic jackets beneath their outer clothing. As Kurt had said to them earlier, "We may seek to look like Americans but we shall continue to think and act like Germans".

The high stone walls of the canyon loomed ahead and Kurt rechecked that his jacket was buttoned at the neck, the wind seemed to blow colder somehow; though, perhaps, it was only his tension that made it seem so.

He adjusted his angle of approach so that they would meet the massive buttresses a little further along; things always looked different at night and he was trying to reconcile what he could see now with the view he'd had through his binoculars the day before. For the first time Kurt could remember, he was wishing the moon would rise quickly and slant its beams down the gloomy rock faces. The light might outline the massive slabs of ancient rock, showing him where the caves were.

In the event it was his feet that located the first flight of stone steps cut into the living rock hundreds – perhaps thousands – of years before. Kurt looked up and then back the way they had come before shielding the flashlight with his hand and risking a closer look.

The quick burst of light confirmed his expectations. The steps, worn and crumbling in places, led upward; a long, long way.

They gathered around him as Kurt halted. He spoke softly. "There are steps here. We use them as far as they go. Take it slowly and keep away from the edge. If I find any steps missing, I'll pause and let the man behind me know. He will pass it on down the line. All right? Let's go."

*

The moon was causing Bergerud some difficulty. Where his group was situated, on the left hand side of the road, three hundred metres from the West Gate.,It was shining brightly. The four men were lying side by side in a shallow depression and could see the movements of the guards quite plainly as they walked off along the perimeter fence. Those at the gates themselves were illumined by floodlights – it was as bright as day and by the same token, those guards would be unable to see a thing outside the immediate circle of light.

"How long do we have?" Whispered Duensing, lying to Nils' left.

"Twenty minutes to midnight but they may change earlier, of course."

"Right, we'll go – see you later."

Duensing tapped Muller on the shoulder. Together they melted away into the darkness.

Bergerud was banking on Kurt's information that he had watched the relieving guards stop to chat at a changeover. For those two minutes or so, a four hundred metre section of the perimeter fence would cease to be patrolled.

It was a situation that would have horrified any German Officer but, Nils could understand its happening here. The Americans must feel far more secure than any European camp guards, the continent had seen no strife since its Civil War. It could not help but unconsciously affect the thinking of every security man in the States. The guards out along the fence sauntered along in pairs, their rifles slung over their shoulders, as if they were taking an evening constitutional – not guarding the most secret installation on either side of the Atlantic.

Nils thoughts turned to Muller and Duensing who had gone to lay charges on the other East access road. Muller would have been with the team tonight but his knowledge of explosives had been deemed more important than his knowledge of rock climbing. Nils had also considered cutting telephone lines as a delaying tactic, but there was certain to be radio communication which they could do nothing about without relatively powerful equipment.

A movement at the entrance attracted his attention. The gates were being opened. It looked as though the changeover was taking place earlier than he had expected. This affected Bergerud's plans. The agreement had been to start the diversion at midnight, giving Schroeder time to scale the rock face; earlier than this could prove disastrous.

Nils inspected the time delay detonators on the three small packages of plastic explosive; checking his watch, he started to set them to a fifteen minute delay.

*

Hoeckle felt rather than saw his way up the rock face. His colleagues were presently sitting in the mouth of one of the higher caves; Schroeder had the lower end of the rope in his hands, awaiting Hoeckle's signal.

So far, they were ahead of schedule, it had gone better than he had planned. The rock face was nowhere near as high as they had originally estimated; the canyon floor had sloped up from their point of entry and this saved them some tens of metres. Too, the stone flight of steps, cut by a long dead race, had climbed a long way.

More important was the face above them, still to be climbed. After the first few metres, Hoeckle had called back reassuringly; the sandstone surface was liberally provided with fissures to use as hand and footholds. If it had not been night time the climb would have been easy, even for the uninitiated.

To those who waited below, Hoeckle's climb into the

394

darkness seemed little short of heroic as they listened to the small sounds that he made on the rock face. Not one of them would have volunteered to change places with him and Kurt heard someone whisper that the Feldwebel deserved a medal. Kurt smiled, unseen – no matter that they, too, had to make the ascent; Hoeckle was first, he was blazing the trail.

Kurt sensed something pass close to his head and the hairs at the back of his neck rose like a cat's. What was it? It happened again and, this time, he heard a twittering at the far limit of audibility which relaxed him. A bird, he thought, someone had disturbed a bird.

"Did you hear that?" someone queried.

Kurt turned back into the cave and risked flashing a light. "Birds?" He offered.

The flashlight caught a flitting shape in its beam and in that split second Kurt realised his mistake: a bat. He informed the men.

"They're bats! Could be dozens of them roosting in these caves although I'd have thought they would have flown by now. Keep still and we probably won't disturb any more, another five minutes and we'll be gone."

"The sooner the better, Sir. This place stinks."

The rope jerked in his hands and Kurt stood up. "Feldwebel Hoeckle has reached the top, we're going. Dietrich – you take the lead, then Weber and me. Fachinger, tie the ladder on the end of the rope and then climb up yourself."

The rope, anchored at the top, made it possible for them to climb up without having to exercise mountaineering techniques. The task was no different from climbing the outside of a building, something they had been trained for both before and after Schroeder had taken over their destinies.

Schroeder reached the edge, Dietrich and Weber assisted him over the lip and, standing up, he saw that Hoeckle was leaning back on the rope coiled about his torso; taking the strain as Fachinger climbed up.

"Quicker, Herr Oberst." He explained, low voiced. "There was nothing to tie it off to nearby."

Kurt nodded and scanned the terrain as the ladder was hauled up. The moon, still too low to illuminate more than the top few metres of the canyon wall, was high enough to show the way. The ground sloped up here to the flatter part of the mesa where the fence had been erected; the natural slope helped to conceal them as they laid flat and waited for the guards to come round.

A few minutes went by before they were rewarded. Consulting the luminous face of his wristwatch, Kurt smiled; the wait at the cave below had put them exactly on schedule. In sixty seconds, provided that Nils had been able to complete his part, they would see some action.

*

The gates opening had been a false alarm; no one had come out, the perimeter guards were still out somewhere on patrol,
396

invisible. Why they had been opened remained a mystery. A phone rang – the sound carrying easily on the night air – an MP went into the gatehouse, came out again seconds later and the gates clanged shut.

Grinding his teeth, Nils checked his watch. Ten minutes had passed since he had set the detonators; should he reset them now that the changeover seemed as though it could be overdue.

The sound of laughter reached him and, moments later, a body of men became visible on the inside of the gates. The new guard, no doubt fresh from their messes, thought Nils. He had no real idea how American troops occupied themselves off duty but supposed it would not be very different from soldiers the world over: a game of cards, a few drinks to keep out the cold, a kiss from those who had wives or local girl friends.

The gates rattled open – no false alarm this time – and the men came through. Nils considered altering the detonators but decided to leave them as they had been set. It meant a five minute delay, no more.

A pair of soldiers came into view along the perimeter fence and ducked through the gate while two fresh men set off in the opposite direction, a second pair came in and two more left. There would now be a few minutes before any more came along. The waiting replacement guards went into the gate house's warm interior and the gate itself was shut.

A few minutes was far more than Bergerud needed. In sixty seconds, he and one other would race forward; fling the plastic explosive over the fence to land on an auxiliary generating shed some metres inside the enclosure and duck back into cover. The remaining two men would cover their action, fingers on sensitive triggers.

*

For the fourth time in as many minutes, Kurt checked the time. Had something finally gone wrong? He was always suspicious of operations that went too smoothly; had Webb turned them in despite the consequences? Had Albert? Should he have sent a search party after the deserter? He wondered.

Seven minutes after the agreed time. The guards must have completed their changeover by now; the off-duty men would all be back inside their barracks. Perhaps he should send in Weber and Fachinger to take out the two nearest guards; they could do it easily enough, silently, without fuss but was it really necessary?

As if in answer to his unspoken question, they heard the muffled explosion that told them Nils had succeeded. It was not particularly loud but to the waiting men it sounded like the crack of doom.

To the guards too, for they came running past – one, two – six pairs of men appeared and disappeared at the double. The entire section of fence was clear.

Yellow and red flames blossomed into distant view, outlining trees and ranked buildings in black silhouette.

Hoeckle picked up the ladder and sprinted across the open ground holding it like a pole vaulter but, instead of digging it into the ground, he threw the hooked end up and over the top of the fence close to the concrete support pole.

He then ducked behind it and held the stiles firm as, one at a time, the men ran, climbed the ladder and leaped from the top in the timed cadence they had trained to do earlier that day. Barely had the last man finished his rolling fall when Hoeckle was climbing. He reached the top, stopped with one foot on the post, the other on the fence wire. He pulled the ladder up, tossed it into the interior and jumped down himself; seconds later, he raced after the rest, the ladder beneath his arm.

*

Paul had decided to play his part to the full. Just sitting there looked too suspicious. Accordingly, he had the Buick's hood open and was peering inside with the aid of a flashlight. This, at least, he thought, would prevent any awkward questions should a mobile patrol come by – as come they did.

The new shift was less than five minutes old when the first jeep appeared and Paul went round to rummage under the dash panel as they stopped.

The first guy, a hard nosed sergeant was unfamiliar to Paul though he recognised the man's partner.

Stepping over the side of the jeep, the sergeant came across.

"Okay then, what's going on here?" His voice was bored.

Paul scrambled back out, smiled wearily. "Blasted car," he aimed a kick at the front tire, "thought I'd give it one last try myself but it needs more than one pair of hands." He looked over the sergeant's shoulder and said "Hi" to the other MP.

"Know him?" The sergeant threw the question at his subordinate without turning his head.

"Sure, Chief Electrician Webb…"

A distant multiple explosion stopped him in mid-sentence.

"Christ!" And the sergeant was back on the jeep's radio without seeming to move. He spoke for several seconds and then listened, nodded, finally putting the mike down.

"They figure the fuel in one of those standby lighting generators has gone up. No need for alarm. Close to the fence but not too close." He came back and looked from Paul to the car and back. "What's your problem then, Mister Webb?"

"Electrical. Must be a short somewhere but I can't find it like this."

"Mm. And you an electrician."

"Yeah – stupid isn't it? But automotive electrical isn't my thing.. Never could understand it.,Completely different from my stuff. Anyway," he jerked a thumb at the breakdown. "If I don't get it this time, I'm gonna lift the front end and tow it out."

The sergeant got out his own flashlight and played it over the engine tracing the wires from the ignition plugs back to the distributor head. Paul watched as it stopped there, wondering how knowledgeable the man was and how he could get rid of him.

"Maybe you got a crack in the cap. You want to crank it while I see if I can see any sparks?"

400

Paul didn't want to but there was no alternative. He got behind the wheel and stepped on the self starter. The engine turned over, coughed and back fired through the carburettor.

"Anything?" He asked. There was no reply. Putting his head out, Paul was just in time to see two black garbed figures lowering the sergeant and his colleague to the road. Moments went by and he was surrounded by what he assumed to be Schroeder's men. The latter's voice confirmed this.

"Drag them out of sight." Kurt ordered in German. "We'll use their vehicle now," then, to Paul: "Hello Paul. Did you think we weren't going to make it?" He spoke in German again, ordering Dietrich to get Neuper out of the winch truck. Two more men vanished into the night at his orders.

"Right then," he addressed the astounded Paul once more, "it is this way to our objective?"

Paul nodded. "Yes."

"Two of us will take the army vehicle, you follow in the truck with Oberleutnant Neuper. Yes?"

Paul drove around the near end of the laboratory complex, heading for the double sliding doors at the rear of the machine shop. Here, he found the jeep halted with the two guards, who had been on duty, walking forward to speak to the German occupants – now temporarily without their balaclavas. As before, the climax was swift and silent. Two shadows detached themselves from the deeper shadow alongside the building; arms rose and fell in unison and the clubbed guards were dragged out of the light, bound and dumped over a low wall.

Two muffled splashes showered water over the assailants and, looking over the wall, they noticed a drainage ditch – the water steaming in the chill air. The channel drained cooling water from machines inside the building, its slow current floated the two unconscious men towards the mouth of a concrete pipe which emptied beyond the fenced Tech Area.

"They'll drown," Paul protested.

"Fortunes of war," answered Dietrich brusquely and tried to strong-arm him back towards Schroeder and the others. "Oh – very well." He ordered Scherf to drag the unconscious men to the bank.

Schroeder was already opening the small door to one side of the larger main ones. He glanced inside, shut it and came back.

"Six of them. Civilians. All working. Go in as though you own the place – take your helmets off, they won't look right for this – go down each side wall as though you're checking something, switches, fire buckets, anything. Understand."

A general nodding of heads indicated that they understood.

"As soon as everybody is covered, round them up. And remember, no shooting, these are civilians, not soldiers." He turned to Paul, changed to English. "When I open the doors, drive the truck straight in."

Finally, he noticed Neuper. "No worse for your journey, Oberleutnant?"

"I've had better, Herr Oberst but easier than your own

402

journey here, I expect."

Kurt chuckled. "Come with me, I shall require your expertise directly." The two men left Paul; Schroeder, with a firm, confident step; Neuper following without hesitation.

Paul went back to the cab, somewhat disappointed that the two guards had not given a better account of themselves; nor solved his own problems in the process. He sighed, the Germans were impressive: the confidence of the sons of bitches, professionals in every sense of the word – the Americans had probably never fired a shot in anger and it showed. It was a sobering thought.

FORTY

At first Susan had been alarmed to find that their guard was, again, to be the hulking Ed. However, her co-prisoner, Hank Garcia was reasonably well built and his presence reassured her. She had watched them playing cards from the comparative safety of the kitchenette – the waist-high counter forming a psychological barrier between herself and the men. They were playing for money and – the big grin spread across Ed's pugnacious face led her to believe that he was winning.

With the last dish dried and stacked in the cupboard, Susan left them to it and headed for the bedroom to find a towel. She had not bathed since her arrival and felt the need badly.

Ed looked up as she passed the table. "Where're you going?" His voice was quite mellow, he certainly must be winning, she thought.

"To take a bath. Do you mind?"

"Mind? Why the hell should I mind? You're too well stacked to think of disappearing down the plughole." Ed laughed uproariously at the joke.

Embarrassed, Susan turned away to hide the blush she felt rising in her cheeks and made her way stiffly into the bathroom. She turned on the faucet, went to get a towel and began an inspection of her face in the mirror while the tub filled. Thank God the rains had come and gone, she thought to herself; back at the site, they had been asked to use Coca Cola to brush their teeth because the wet season had been late. Bath water had been severely restricted.

Ed had two kings; he discarded three cards and waited for Hank to decide on his own hand. Finally, the Mexican-American discarded two and looked up.

"Three, is it?"

Ed nodded and watched as the cards came skidding across the smooth table top. He kept his eyes on Hank's hands until the other had taken only the agreed two before lifting his own cards – an ace and a deuce.

Ed's fingers fumbled over the last card as he turned the end up slowly: a third king. He smiled openly, thirty eight dollars so far and his luck seemed to be running well. He'd take the Mex to the cleaners this time, for sure. He picked up a ten dollar bill and tossed it into the middle.

"Let's make it worthwhile."

Garcia hesitated a moment before responding and adding his own ten bucks. "I'll go 'long with you."

Ed grinned again. "That's the spirit." He threw in another bill.

The bidding rose and, not until he had to reach into his pocket to get more money did he have any doubts. His winnings were out in the center of the table along with forty-two more dollars.

"The hell." He decided to increase the pressure and threw five bills forward. "Raise it to fifty."

Hank scratched his nose and hesitated several seconds, looking from the money to his hand and back again. He muttered something in Spanish and put down a similar amount, "I gotta see what you have."

Ed smiled and turned the kings over, one by one. He watched the Mex's face.

Hank wiped his forehead with his sleeve and tumbled his own cards over in a single motion.

"Three twos and two fives." He smiled weakly. "A full house? This is what you call it?"

Looking at Garcia's cards in disbelief, the smirk fell from Ed's face to leave it looking ugly and thunderous. A week's money gone in a moment. It had happened before – too many times – but he had still not learned to like it.

Scratching his groin, he got up and went towards the bathroom to relieve himself. The sound of bath water reminded him that it was occupied.

"You stay there." He addressed Hank. "Just nipping outside."

"I think I'll bed down now, if that's okay?" Hank's voice was apologetic, conciliatory.

"Sure Mex. You get rested up for tomorrow; I'll be taking that money back in the morning." He banged the door shut.
406

"Yes Ed. Sure." Hank cleared the bills from the table and stuffed them into a hip pocket as he headed for the bedroom. Outside the bathroom door, he stopped, listened a moment and then called out to Susan.

"Miss Millar. I am going to bed, which room are you using?"

"The big one, Mr. Garcia. You use one of the bunks, will you?"

"Sure, no trouble. Goodnight."

"Goodnight."

When Ed returned, he poured himself another cup of hot, black coffee and sat back in his chair. The defeat had left him smarting; he began swearing softly, in a monotone.

The tub started to empty itself and the sound drew his attention to Susan Millar. "Stuck-up bitch." He thought aloud, remembering other women. "All the mother-fucking same."

Ed disliked women. They were good for one thing only and, even then, he generally had to pay a hooker for her services. He could only remember one free sexual encounter and that was some years ago; an old biddy, grateful for anything she could get. Ed had had to be drunk before he went with her back to the squalid little room she lived in; he shook his head – he knew that he had screwed the old bag but his recollection of the event was, fortunately, hazy. He had hated himself the next morning; the old woman had been filthy. For weeks Ed had feared that he had got himself a dose..

He became strangely fastidious after that, paying over the odds to assure himself that the girls were clean.

She was clean, he thought to himself. She was in there now, bathing herself, soaping her breasts... the mind's eye picture brought on a sudden flood of lust. He felt himself rising. Why the hell should Webb have her all to himself? If she'd drop them for Webb, she'd goddamn well drop them for him.

Ed opened the door to the main bedroom – empty. He went to the bunk room. "I'm gonna have some fun with the girl." He opened. "You hear anything, you forget it, right?"

Hank nodded. "Right, I – er, I guess so."

"Damn right you'd better , Mex."

Ed tried the bathroom door, it was locked. He could wait until she came out but, somehow, the thought of her being there, on the other side of the door... naked, excited him. Stepping back a pace, he lifted his foot and kicked out, the heel of his boot landing just above the door handle. The door flew open, the jamb splintered like so much matchwood.

Susan had just finished washing her hair and was stooping to retrieve a towel from the floor. She froze, frightened to look up and confirm what she already knew she would see. She had known all along that he would try something eventually but, with the tanker driver there, Susan had thought herself safe for the moment.

The tableau that presented itself to Ed could not have been more perfect. The girl's skin still gleamed with moisture; her

408

breasts, full and pendant. A second, two seconds and the scene unfroze. Susan stood up slowly, defiant; the silken triangle at her thighs drawing Ed's gaze. The blood pounded through his temples, he pushed the door closed and moved forward.

Making no attempt to cover herself, Susan felt like screaming with anger. Incongruous as it might appear, she recalled the old joke that used to set them giggling at high school: "If rape is inevitable, relax and enjoy it." She considered the idea briefly and discarded it; there was no way that she would submit to this animal invading her body. There were several things she might try – reasoning with him, pleading, fighting, but never submission.

As Ed came forward, he began to undo his belt. Beautiful, he thought; perhaps he should tell her what he was going to do, tell her exactly how he was going to screw her but, at that moment, Ed realised that he didn't know how.

Not yet.

He stopped where he was and slowly pulled the belt out of its buckle. Should he make her bend over the edge of the tub? Take her from behind? Maybe lay her out flat, legs as wide as they'd go. She had luscious lips though, soft, red. Ed let his pants fall and started to unbutton his shirt.

Susan had already made her decision; her eyes searched the bathroom for a weapon – a toothbrush, Paul's safety razor – nothing. She began to sidle around him in what she knew, deep down, to be a forlorn hope of escape.

"Where'd ya think you're going?" Ed's voice was a growl which she ignored.

Her knee touched the large wicker-work laundry basket, was there something in there? To keep him occupied, Susan began to talk.

"Colonel Schroeder and I have an understanding you know. If he hears about this, you're going to be in big trouble."

"Stuff the Colonel; He's got nothing to do with me." Ed stripped his shirt off and tossed it aside; the matted hair on his chest just failed to hide a small gold crucifix and chain.

Spotting this and, unwilling to let her gaze be drawn lower, Susan tried again. "If you're a Christian, you know what you're doing is wrong. You'll be punished."

Ed laughed. "You come here baby, just look what I got for you."

Susan's eyes darted briefly and unwillingly down to his gorged manhood. She shivered and turned away.

"Too much for you, you reckon? You can't get too much of a good thing." And with that, Ed lunged, caught hold of her arm.

She jumped back from his grasp and stood against the wall, holding her nails high. Her tone changed; no more sweet reason, her English temper rose. "Try it and I'll scratch your eyes out. You're filth, you hear me? Filth, not even fit for prostitutes."

The jibe struck home dead center. Ed growled with fury and, suddenly, a fist the size of a loaf of bread caught Susan high on the side of her face. Her head snapped back and cracked against

410

the wall. The world blurred, she could dimly make out Ed saying. "Deliver or I'll finish ya like I did Carl." Then she fainted.

"Christ." Muttered Ed. He eyed her crumpled body for a few seconds. "Still why not?" He seized her about the waist, hauled her up and dumped the unconscious girl, face down, across the laundry basket. Prising her thighs apart, he lifted her flaccid buttocks and thrust forward. He entered her roughly, uncaring, and worked at the lifeless body like a dog. He reached forward and handled her breasts, mauling them, bruising them.

At the moment of climax, he shouted vile names at her, cursing that she would not participate. Finished, he withdrew and left her there. It had not been the satisfying experience Ed had expected.

"That'll teach ya, stubborn bitch." He muttered. "Now you've had a man, you won't be bothering with a boy like Webb again."

Ed started to put on his shirt; he suddenly noticed the frightened eyes of Garcia peering around the door.

"What the hell do you want?"

"Thought you were killing her." Hank replied, looking at Susan's mistreated body. "Shouldn't we fix her up some?"

Ed's rage at the uncooperative girl suddenly found its outlet. He swung a savage fist at Garcia, the man's feet left the floor; he skidded along the hall and burst, head first, into the living room. Still not pacified, Ed followed the other, intent on teaching the jerk to keep his nose out of other people's business.

Susan came to, only dimly aware of where she was. At the first attempt to get up, her legs gave way and she tumbled off the rough basketwork onto the cold linoleum of the floor. She seemed bruised and aching from head to toe. Slowly, her senses cleared and she found herself looking up at the naked light bulb; the nimbus about it pulsed in time to her heart beat, filling the room with millions of shining particles dancing in front of her eyes. She groaned and rolled on to her side, the yellow filament burned into her eyes still, becoming black against an orange corona when she shut her eyes.

The cool floor-covering against her sweat streaked skin was pleasant and revived Susan a little. She tried to reach the edge of the tub to pull herself up, but her arm seemed too heavy. It dropped weakly back.

But not to the floor. The thought penetrated her mental fog, her hand rested on something soft. She turned on to her stomach, wincing as her left breast was momentarily pressed against the floor, compressing the bruises. It took a long time to get up on hands and knees and, finally, to kneel up.

When her eyes were focussed she looked down to see what her hand was holding – Ed's pants. Susan dropped them as though they were red hot. That filthy animal! She pushed them away from her with a quick darting gesture of revulsion and, as she touched the cloth, her fingers felt something hard in the pocket.

412

Overcoming her feelings. Susan explored the shape – the ugly L-shape of a gun! She pulled it out carefully then pulled herself to her feet only to double up with torture as red hot lances of pain stabbed through her groin.

The anguish subsided a little and she opened her eyes again to see a pair of feet just in front of her. She had fallen to her knees again and, looking up, all she could see was Ed's limp penis already beginning to stir again with its own obscene life.

She lifted the revolver and pointed it with both hands at the thing that filled her vision. She squeezed the trigger.

FORTY ONE

The three men returned to the shadow of the embankment beside the road before the sixty seconds had ticked away, Nils leading the way diagonally across the tricky slope, moving fast but with caution.

Phase one was complete. Phase two had now to be commenced: the mining of the road.

*

Four miles away Duensing and Muller began to mine the road leading up to the East Gate. They worked quickly but with caution, laying the small packets of explosive that Bergerud had made up that afternoon.

*

Joachim Neuper followed Kurt in through the doorway automatically obeying the other's gesture to stay close to the wall. Neuper, because of his small size – average for the Luftwaffe – was the only one dressed in borrowed civilian clothing; none of the uniforms had been small enough to fit him.

Kurt nodded to himself, the others were roughly in position; any second now and they would make their move. He angled his way across the main doors towards the heavy steel door leading into what Susan had told him was the area for the final bomb assembly. Neuper was a pace behind. Neither paid a moment's attention to the puzzled glances of the men at the machinery.

Wolfgang Dietrich had crouched behind an untended lathe. He checked the position of each machinist then glanced to where his comrades were stationed. Weber intercepted his gaze, nodded.

Springing upwards, Dietrich levelled the assault rifle to cover the civilians. His movement was so abrupt that the top of his American combat jacket caught on a bracket, the collar and three buttons tore loose; he didn't notice it. "Stop whatever you are doing," he barked, each word sharp and distinct. "Gather here, in front of me."

There were ten men working at various benches and equipment: lathes, a milling machine, one taking careful measurements on a surface plate and a group of three operating some strange but – obviously – micro-metrically accurate equipment. The noise of electric motors and metal forming was heavy in the air but, even so, Dietrich's voice carried over the sound. One by one, they turned and looked at him incredulously.

"Quickly now or I start to shoot."

A couple of the white coated technicians began to walk towards him; several more looked around and obeyed only when they saw the other hard faced men covering them with evil, business-like weapons. Worry, despair, fear; all these were present as everyone eventually obeyed.

Hans Goldstein's face was one that displayed despair. Hans

was a Jew, he had escaped from Berlin a bare two days before the Reichskristallnacht – where thousands of his race had been hounded, murdered, raped and clubbed into unconsciousness. Israel Hans Goldstein – the first name officially imposed to brand him a Jew in anti-Semitic Germany – knew how lucky he had been. He had built his new life in the United States with care, he hated the newspaper and radio reports of genocide and deliberately avoided them when he could. He was well aware of the SS, had seen them rise from obscurity to the hell-force they had become under Himmler's supervision. He both hated and feared them.

Hans took one look at the double lightning flash of the SS runes on Dietrich's collar, exposed by the tearing of his outer uniform. Too proud of his SS rank, Obersturmfuhrer Dietrich had not removed the insignia. Hans' reaction was the blind panic of fear; he began to run.

Weber was nearest, he moved to block off his path but the Jew swerved between a workbench and a tall drilling machine and made for the door.

The foolish attempt to escape surprised Dictrich for a moment and then he screamed across the workshop for the man to stop. Schroeder, who had been walking towards the bomb store, stopped at the sound; he turned and saw Dietrich's rifle track the running man. He shouted to stop the SS officer from firing. The single 7-92 millimetre bullet tore into the back of the man's head as he flung open the door; a scant second before the

416

door frame hid him. The power of the slug's 2000 mph velocity thrust the Jew out into the night.

Schroeder and Dietrich, closely followed by Hoeckle ran to the exit. Hoeckle paused long enough to order Fachinger and Weber to hold their positions and followed his superiors outside.

The technicians, seeing Hans' futile escape fail, sank to their knees; cowering behind metal machine pedestals.

Dietrich was already standing over the fallen body when Schroeder reached him. Dietrich turned the corpse over with his boot; all but the lower jaw had disintegrated leaving a pulpy mass of blood and brains behind.

There was no thought of dignity in Kurt's mind.

"You misbegotten fool." He shouted in Dietrich's surprised face. "I briefed you all before this mission that there was to be no shooting except on my order. Is this the brand of obedience they teach you in the SS? And I thought you to be a combat soldier. Soldier? They should have posted you to one of the Volksturm Regiments. You might be able to cope with looking after sick old women."

Dietrich's surprise changed swiftly to black anger; he stood to attention, every limb trembling with rage.

Paul was sitting, as he had been instructed, in the cab when he heard the gunshot. Waiting to reverse the truck into the building, he looked through the mirror to see Dietrich erupt from the doorway and come to a standstill at the side of a body illuminated by the light from the open door. The engine was running so that he could not hear what Schroeder was saying, even when he stuck his head out of the window. There was no mistaking Schroeder's anger however, nor was there any mistaking Dietrich's reply.

The gun came up and pointed at Schroeder's stomach.

"Take that back." Dietrich hissed through clenched teeth. "I am an SS Officer and not a raw recruit to be treated like a runny-nosed schoolboy. Take that back or I'll kill you."

Schroeder stood his ground. Calmer after his outburst, he wished that he could have withdrawn the words. They had been said in anger and he should not have spoken to a brother officer in such a way. What could he say to improve the situation?

Dietrich's finger tightened on the trigger. "Take it back I said."

Hoeckle saw the movement and moved with unbelievable speed. With one arm, he swept the weapon from Dietrich's hands while with the other seized him about the throat.

Schroeder relaxed, it was now out of his hands. "Get him back inside Feldwebel." He ordered in a tired voice and Hoeckle moved to comply.

For a second or two, Dietrich struggled until he realised that nothing would break that vice-like grip. It added fuel to his anger; he was far closer to madness than to sanity at that moment. He fumbled at his tunic and, as Schroeder turned to see what was holding Hoeckle up, he saw the SS dagger flash as it came free from the scabbard. Kurt recognised the ceremonial but
418

deadly blade that the Fuhrer had presented to Dietrich. With a desperate twist Dietrich's arm came sideways on to Hoeckle, the dagger flashed a second time,

Hoeckle felt the blade slide between his ribs, felt the thrust penetrate his lung, slice through the great pulmonary artery. The life force flooded free as the blood pumped into his lungs. Before he collapsed, Hoeckle swung his right arm with all the force he could muster into a blow that would have pole axed an ox. Dietrich took it on the temple; it knocked him sideways and into the wall at the side of the road. Momentum took him over the top and into the ditch where he sank into the effluent water.

"My God, Hoeckle." Schroeder was on the move even as Dietrich crashed over the wall. He saw the knife, how deeply it had penetrated, where it had entered. Beneath the fifth rib was a killing point.

He knew that he was looking at a dead man. What he did not know was why the Feldwebel was still erect. He looked into the man's glazing eyes. "Hoeckle?" His throat hurt as he spoke the name.

Joseph Hoeckle drew himself to his full height. He opened his mouth to say something but only a great sigh issued. He fell, first to his knees and then, more gently, to the ground as Kurt caught him beneath the armpits and took his weight.

"You are a truly brave man, Joseph… and a loyal friend." Kurt's eyes brightened with unshed tears despite his iron control: he ached with emotion.

419

"I thank you Herr Oberst." The words rattled in Hoeckle's throat and were followed by a rush of bright blood. His heaving chest suddenly stiffened in one mighty effort to breathe and then the giant body relaxed.

Paul saw all of this but it had happened so fast that he was still only halfway out of the cab when Hoeckle fell. He had climbed down and was about to rush across when he saw Kurt open his jacket; he paused and watched as the other reached inside and took something out, place it about the prostrate man's neck. Paul came across as Kurt muttered something in German over the dead man. After long moments, Paul realised what the German words meant: *And they thought me brave. They know not what brave men are.*

"What is that?" Paul queried softly, indicating the medal that now rested on Hoeckle's chest.

"What? Nothing – a piece of metal that men die to possess. It is called the Knight's Cross, my country can make no greater award and it is pitifully inadequate."

As Kurt spoke, the realisation of what this incident had cost in terms of men and relentless minutes came to him. He got up. "Can you help me carry him inside?"

Paul nodded and, together, they carried the body back inside the machine shop.

"What will you do with him?" asked Paul.

Kurt replied without even thinking about the question. "What do you mean? We'll take him back home to Germany, of course."

In the solidly built store room, which adjoined the machine shop, were two bizarre bombs. Almost three metres in length, the best part of a metre wide with a square tail fin assembly and a curious short wave antenna fitted a third of its length from the blunt nose. They lay side by side on two wooden cradles; one of them was still shackled to a chain hoist which ran on curved overhead rails leading back into the machine shop.

"There can be no doubt, Herr Oberst." Smiled Neuper. "These are the bombs described by Doctor Millar."

Schroeder nodded and gave the necessary orders. The bomb already on the hoist was run back into the workshop and loaded directly into the winch truck's cradle without difficulty. They laid Hoeckle's body alongside the bomb and Kurt turned to Neuper.

"Joachim," he said quietly, "you have a choice. You may travel out of here as you came in – with our two friends in the truck or you can attempt to escape via the fence with the men. Which is it to be?"

Without hesitation, the bomb disposal engineer made his decision. "I'll stay with the bomb – and with our excellent Feldwebel."

Paul, who had not seen beneath the truck floor before, found all his unspoken questions answered. Here was the means to remove the bomb undetected and it was he who was expected to drive the vehicle out of the site. His original suspicions of sabotage were unfounded and, for a moment, Paul felt relieved that whatever further plans Schroeder had, they did not involve himself. His worries would be over as soon as they were outside the gates.

But, only seconds later, his fears returned. This was an atomic weapon; he knew, in principal, its destructive potential. What the hell did they intend to do with it? Take it back to Europe disassemble it and copy it? Drop it on an American target?

Paul felt very alone with his fears and very lonely too.

Kurt supervised the incarceration of the machinists in the bomb store and then turned to Fachinger.

"The dead American – what has been done with the body?"

"Thrown him in that ditch, Sir. Is that all right?"

Kurt nodded. "What about Obersturmfuhrer Dietrich? Any sign?"

"No sir. There's a steady current down there; it must have swept him along into the culvert."

Again Kurt nodded, chewing his lower lip. "Very well. Weber?"

"Sir?"

"You will lead the men back down the cliff. Allow me ten minutes to clear the area before you start."

"You are not coming with us then, Herr Oberst?"

"No, I shall have to stay with Herr Webb." His eyebrows rose in query.

422

"I understand Sir, of course."

"Good. You are quite familiar with the route out and the descent procedure?"

"Yes Sir."

"The ropes, the ladder and so on."

"I know where they were cached Sir."

"Then good luck." He checked his watch against Weber's, Weber's was thirty seconds slower. "I'll see you back at the aircraft in just over an hour."

"And Weber..."

"Sir?"

"We cannot wait if you are late."

"Don't worry, Herr Oberst. These Americans are still asleep."

"Don't bank on it."

As the three men melted into the darkness, Paul came forward. He had overheard the conversation and, although his German was rusty from long disuse, he understood the gist of what had been said.

"Excuse me Colonel. Do I understand that you are planning to go by the gatehouse in the truck with me?"

"You do. Do you find problems?"

"Not for me, but you might have some. What about identification?"

Kurt took out a pass card and flashed it in front of Paul's eyes.

"I relieved one of the civilians of this. For the moment, my name is Harry Boyd. We shall tow your motor car out; I shall be at the wheel. The guards are concerned with preventing people getting in, not out. It should all look quite natural."

"And if it doesn't?"

"Then you will hit the accelerator and take us out of there as though the devil's behind you. He will be – and ready to use this at the slightest provocation." Schroeder lifted his machine pistol. "I don't wish to use it but, if I have to, I will."

"What happens to me when we get out of here? Do you intend to use that on me when I'm no more use?"

Kurt frowned. "Of course not. You must agree that you have given us cause to doubt your loyalties, Paul, but I have no intention of shooting you if you follow my orders. Once we are clear of Los Alamos, I shall bid you a civilised "Good Day"."

Their exit went as Kurt had predicted. "Oh sure," said the guard standing in the gatehouse door. "Gus told me to expect you Mr. Webb. Kinda late ain't it?"

"Too right." Paul replied and released the hand brake.

Half way down the roadway, Kurt flashed the headlights behind and Paul drew to a stop. For a few seconds, it seemed that Kurt might have misjudged the spot but then Nils Bergerud's smiling face appeared.

"Everything all right, Herr Oberst?"

"Everything, Nils – and with you?"

"Fine. All of this banking is set to go up if necessary. The

424

charges are ready for seeding the road surface as soon as you are on your way."

"Good. Let's get this car unhitched then. We might as well leave sideways across the road, it'll add to any confusion."

Paul's car was pushed back to block the road and Kurt climbed into the driver's seat while Neuper, who had been released, got in on the other side.

"About an hour then, Nils."

"About an hour, Herr Oberst."

As they turned off the access road onto route 66 for the few kilometres to the trail which wound upward to the landing strip, Kurt explained his intentions to Paul.

"As soon as we get off the highway, Paul, I shall drop you off. It will mean quite a walk for you but, you understand, I must protect myself from any possible interference."

Paul started to reply but Kurt continued.

"Your girl is perfectly safe, by the way. Colonel Piekenbrock issued Edward with appropriate instructions; she and the tanker driver will be released as soon as Piekenbrock sees us take off."

Silence fell as they drove along, the heavy load making for a smoother ride than on the way in. Schroeder turned on to the unsurfaced track which quickly deteriorated to a point where only the two lowest gears were of any use. He stopped the breakdown truck a few minutes later.

"This is where we part company, Paul. I would like to

extend my thanks and those of the German Reich for your help. Hopefully, you will have helped to end the war very soon; the World will be the better for it."

Kurt extended his hand and Paul took it. Schroeder's phrasing was, perhaps, a little trite but his tone conveyed the sincerity in his words, and he obviously believed in what they were doing.

"Whatever happens after today, Colonel, I'd like to call you friend. I admire your convictions. I only hope that you're right."

"Auf wiedersehn, Paul."

Paul climbed past Neuper and out on to the road.

"Auf wiedersehn."

FORTY TWO

Weber, Scherf and Fachinger negotiated the fence without incident and raced to the canyon's edge with the ladder; they flung it into space. Of the guards, there was no sign; the smell of victory was in the air.

The ropes and nails were where they had been left and Weber took the rock hammer and started knocking the nails into the ground. He lost the first three, the earth too soft but he found a rock outcropping a little further along where he tapped two nails into a crevice.

Tying a loop into the end of the rope, he secured it and went back to the edge. "Who goes first? Me?"

"I don't mind but I think we'd better loop the rope through our belts and all go together. Someone's going to find those workmen soon."

"Okay by me. So, Gunther, shall I go first, then you, then Helmut?"

"All right, just let's go."

Weber found the face much as Hoeckle had, plenty of hand and foot holds. It had been many years since he had engaged in climbing but it was coming back to him; he went down quickly, with confidence. Looking up, he could see nothing of the others but the movements of the rope told Weber that they were on their way. He began to hum tunelessly.

Fachinger watched Scherf disappear over the lip and checked the rope as his weight came on to it. It looked fine and he prepared to follow his colleagues.

Corporals Michael Sullivan and Eddie Bonetti, two of the on-duty guard were double timing it back to their posts after helping out with the fire calls when Mike saw Fachinger. He stopped dead, closed his eyes, opened them and looked again. Fachinger's head and shoulders were outlined against the moonlit rock of the canyon's far wall for a second longer, then he was gone.

"Hey. What's going on?" Sullivan shouted.

Fachinger heard the shout and scrambled down the line as fast as he dared.

"What's up Mike?"asked Eddie.

"Hell. Didn't you see him?"

"See who?"

"Some sonovabitch over there, come on."

Mike was already halfway to the cliff edge. Eddie rushed up behind him. "Well?"

There was nothing to see.

"You're a bit jumpy."

"I tell you I saw someone – climbing down. Just about here."

"You'd better let me carry that fifth. You're seeing things."

428

Sullivan's Irish ancestors surfaced and Mike lost his temper. His bellow might have woken General Groves himself, had he been at the 'Hill'

"You stupid…" He flicked off the safety on his carbine and, pointing it down the cliff face, began to fire.

Oskar Fachinger had just found a foothold and was lowering himself down to it. Most of his weight was on his right hand when the bullet smashed the knuckles. He screamed with pain as his fingers lost their grip and he fell. The nails pulled out of the sandstone like maggots leaving an overripe fruit.

Twenty metres below, Scherf was making as small a target of himself as he could. – pressed insecurely against the hard rock. Fachinger hit Scherf, Scherf cannoned into Weber.

One, two, three. Like bottles falling off a wall, they plummeted down. The stone steps, so meticulously hewn by the Indians, acted as no more than a temporary brake to their headlong plunge. Their bodies lay within three metres of each other when all was still again. "Get anything, Mike?"

"Could be. I think that was someone screaming. You get back to Security and report, I'm staying here."

*

Nils finished placing the remainder of the PE2 explosive on the road and signalled the other two to retreat. They backed away from the road, further unrolling the fuse cable as they went.

"You think the others will be back soon?"

Nils checked his watch. Twenty minutes, no more and they

429

would be away. "They'll be here."

*

A bathroom curtain, torn from the rail, covered Ed's bloody corpse. Susan stood in the tub and began to scrub herself all over. She knew her efforts were foolish, that they served only a psychological need yet, as soon as she had rinsed her body thoroughly, she started again.

She persisted for ten minutes and then dressed herself, closed the bathroom door on the dead man and went through to the living room where she found Hank still unconscious. She brought water from the kitchenette and dashed it in his face before bringing him a second cupful to drink.

"I think we should get out of here." She suggested as Hank's eyes began to focus. "There's still a car outside but they've taken the keys."

Hank shook his head and blinked a few times, "What happened to that big gorilla?"

"Gone to meet his maker, I'm pleased to say." But Susan's mouth was tight as his question brought back to her what she had left in the bathroom.

This, more than the water, seemed to revive the driver.

"Let's see this car then. Forget the keys, I can hot-wire the thing with my eyes closed."

Susan nodded, thankful at the prospect of leaving the house at last. Was there anything she had forgotten? She looked around. The telephone – of course; the Germans had used it on

430

several occasions to call outside contacts. She tried it; it was still connected.

"Lieutenant Hartley? This is Doctor Susan Millar."

"Evening, Miss Millar. What can we do for you?"

"There are several German saboteurs masquerading as American troops either on the Site or trying to break in."

There was an obvious splutter of disbelief at the far end which Susan plowed straight through. "Look Lieutenant, I've got an AAA security clearance this is not, repeat not, a practical joke. If you're not going to believe me, get me put through to 'Oppy', I'm sure he's still on the 'Hill'."

"Director Oppenheimer is in bed Miss Millar; I'll listen to you and I'll pass your information on to the duty security people. Okay?"

"Okay." And Susan started to explain. "I don't know but I think they're probably trying to get in through the fence over at the top end of Pajarito Canyon or maybe nearer the Reservoir." She finished.

No sooner had Hartley replaced the phone than another began to jangle insistently. He listened for a few seconds. "Hold it Corporal. Just a sec." He turned to the four security men who had, by now, realised something was in the air. "Get every man we've got into mobiles. I want every inch of this camp checked, send three of them up towards the western end of Pajarito." He put the receiver back to his ear and uncovered the mouthpiece. "Carry on Sullivan." Again Hartley listened and again broke off.

"Forget that last order. Get out there and drive along outside the wire, Corporal Sullivan's reported a definite sighting, he'll meet you, he wants to use the searchlight – it's Pueblo, not Pajarito."

"Got a map reference Lieutenant?"

Hartley looked at the big wall map. "475075 I guess. Anything more Corporal? Okay."

He turned back to the security men again. "Sullivan's just shot at someone going over the edge into the canyon outside the wire and they can see what looks like tracks on the inside. The bastard's have already been in, is my guess; so get some patrols down into the canyon too. We've got to catch 'em fast."

One of the men who were busy making calls over the security PA system, looked up, a grizzle faced Sergeant who had been invalided out of Europe as a volunteer in the British Array. "If they've been in Sir, what the hell were they up to?"

"Oh Christ! Yes! I'd better raise the Director. We'll have to put out a general alarm. Thank God Groves isn't down here."

The Lieutenant was barely into his twenties, his knowledge of security confined to courses at Officer Training School. He started, visibly, to panic. The Sergeant saw the symptoms, recognised them and stepped in as tactfully as he could.

"Flanagan, Doyle, Marcowski. The Lieutenant wants you to take a squad each and cover every security area. Call out the off-duty men and tell them to report to Lieutenant Hartley on the double. Right, Sir?"

"That's, er, right Sergeant. Thanks."

LAST MISSION

"Maybe we should ring Washington, too?"

FORTY THREE

It was pitch black and uncomfortably warm and wet. For nearly a quarter of a minute, he could neither decide where he was nor imagine what had happened. The close, confining darkness brought dim images of cramped Panzer tank interiors; with an effort of will, Dietrich drove these away and grappled with reality.

Hoeckle, the old Prussian and that swine, Schroeder.

He must have fallen down the bank when Hoeckle had punched the side of his head. Odd, Dietrich could have sworn that he had knifed the bastard, the blade must have turned on something.

These thoughts led him to his present situation. He was lying on his back in more than half a metre of warm water smelling strongly of oil and chemicals. A slow current in the water pressed his feet against some solid obstruction.

There was something binding his arms too; had they tied him and then tossed him into the ditch? With considerable difficulty, Dietrich worked a hand free enough to explore the bond which turned out to be the strap on his M43, he would have to move enough to release the rifle which was trapped under his body before he could get free himself.

Dietrich began to twist and splash and succeeded in turning himself over, almost drowning himself in the process. Finally, he was on his knees and stood up; the crack he received on his head practically knocked him senseless a second time.

Dietrich was inside a pipe – he remembered the culvert that the drainage channel had disappeared into. It was about seventy five centimetres in diameter: the obstruction which had stopped him going further was a sturdy grillwork of steel bars. There was no way out from here. He would have to follow the tunnel back to its entrance.

He found that he could crawl on hands and knees and just barely manage to keep his head above water. Dietrich made some progress but he met another obstruction, he put out his hand and discovered a shock of greasy hair; further exploration brought him to a sticky area. His first reaction was to draw away for he knew just what he had found: the man who's face his own bullet had blasted away. However, there was no alternative; the pipe was too narrow to squeeze past, Dietrich had to conquer his revulsion, work the mutilated corpse free and push it ahead of him. It was a macabre situation – one that only Schroeder could have thought of. That it was deliberate, Dietrich had no doubts whatsoever.

There, in the dark, Dietrich fought a grim battle: against the fantasies that his memory wove, against the cold flesh of the body he pushed before him. He had to get out now – to prove that he was the better man.

It was, fortunately, not a long way to the mouth of the culvert, although, on hands and knees, it took a long time to reach the open air. Here, close to the back of the machine shop, Dietrich could hear hurried voices.

"So what have they got away with?"

"A copy of the Little Boy bomb."

"One of the practice models for Wendover?" There was a short bark of laughter.

"Yeah. They cost a goddamn fortune."

"Count yourself lucky." Director Oppenheimer's tall, thin figure was distinctive in the moonlight. "Another few months and it could have been the real thing."

A third voice came to the German's astounded ears. It belonged to Lieutenant Hartley. "What the hell are they going to do with it?"

Oppenheimer shrugged. "What would you do with a few pounds of TNT and three tons of sand?"

"Well, we'll get after them," said Hartley, "they can't have got far with something as heavy as that. Probably still on the Project, the fence wasn't cut where the Sergeant reported the sighting."

A whistle blew and Dietrich watched security guards pour out of the workshop into a number of jeeps parked in the flood of light from the wide open double doors. They moved off east, past the Van de Graff building towards the gatehouse.

436

LAST MISSION

*

Dietrich eased past the corpse, pushed it back into the culvert then climbed out of the ditch and, bending low, moved towards the shadow against the wall.

"You soldier! What are you waiting for? Into the jeeps, I said." Dietrich looked around, saw the man and noted the three chevrons on his sleeve. He came forward into the light, holding his jacket closed at the neck. "Coming Sergeant. Fell in the damn ditch."

"They must have realised what the truck was carrying." Murmured Nils as six jeeps roared out of the main East Gate and down the hill. When he saw them coming, he held a cigarette lighter to the fuse. "Back to the transport." He shouted, waving an arm even though it was dark. The five soldiers began to scramble along the banked shale until they were well clear of any backlash from the explosives. Their only task now was to wait the required time and observe the effects.

The first jeep careered on to the charged area and the plastic explosive went up, lifting the vehicle two metres and then dropping it down the banking. The following jeeps were all travelling too fast and- too close to take evasive action. Four of them ran straight on to further explosive charges and suffered a similar fate; the night was lit by the angry red flashes of detonating plastic. The last vehicle was overturned by the shock wave from the explosion which caught the jeep in front; it skidded off the road in a shower of sparks from steel scraping the

437

hard surface and then, miraculously, regained its wheels as it slipped over the edge.

Gathering momentum, it ran pell-mell down the slope and, in the process, breaking the slower burning fuse to the larger charge and preventing the road going up around them.

Nils group watched from one side of the road; the other two arrived just in time to see the carnage from the far side. They slipped across to join Nils as soon as the last vehicle slid down the bank to stop with its front end supported by a thicket of creosote bush. The luck of the Gods had been with the occupants, all three were moving within seconds. Nils knocked the safety off his M43 and assumed a half crouching stance. The others followed suit and a deadly spray of bullets raked the jeep from end to end. It went up in a sheet of flame as a bullet found the gas tank.

"That's it men. We're late." He added checking his watch in the light from the burning vehicle. "It's time we went back to the strip."

Dietrich crawled away from the intense heat. Blood flowed copiously from a ragged wound beneath his left collarbone where a German bullet had hit his shoulder at the back and escaped at the front. A few centimetres left or right, up or down and, at best he would have had broken bones to complicate things; at worst he would have been dead.

As it was, he blessed his fortune while he looked at the shattered remains of the driver who had taken a whole stream of

438

bullets in a line from head to waist; there was little left to recognise. Of the other two; one, like himself, had been thrown clear but had broken his neck, the second was still roasting in the dying inferno.

Where to now? He wondered. How could he reach the aircraft? For a moment he considered his reasons for wanting to get to it. Was it purely to seek revenge on Schroeder who had left him to die or should there be a more noble motive?

The information he had heard about the bomb. Dietrich was horrified as he remembered. "A few more months," the man had said. Did that mean that the bombs weren't here yet or that they hadn't even been made! In the latter case, Piekenbrock would have to get a message off to Berlin.

Whatever; the bomb could not now be dropped on Washington, it would be futile to try now that Operation Blondi was known to the Americans. Even to drop the useless thing on Los Alamos would be an empty gesture.

Dietrich shook his head. They would probably not be able to make their rendezvous at sea, either. Forewarned, the American Air Force would intercept the Liberator long before she reached the coast. There were going to be no medal ceremonies, no taking tea with the Fuhrer. The whole mission was a fiasco. He, himself – an SS Officer – would be held to ridicule by his comrades.

It was the last thought that moved Dietrich the most. Since his fear-driven action on the mountain above Berchtesgaden, he

439

had become severely self-critical; he censored any thought, any desire which seemed to him to fall short of the ideal. Dietrich knew himself to be a true German, pure Aryan. He had a duty to ensure that the operation, if it was to be of no use to the Fuhrer, would have no propaganda or intelligence value to the Allies.

He tore a strip from his outer jacket to staunch the diminishing flow of blood and went over to the battered remains of the Jeeps to see if any could, perhaps, still be driven.

Jeeps! Of course, the jeep that his own – number one – team had come in. Would the others have reached it yet? It seemed unlikely; at this point, he was probably closer to it than they were; a kilometre perhaps, not much more.

His assault rifle was still slung across his back, it seemed to be an integral part of him now; even in the culvert it had refused to be separated from him. As he walked, Dietrich pulled the weapon around to his front, his hands automatically checking the bolt action, the magazine, making certain that the water had not harmed it. Despite the shoulder wound which throbbed every time his left foot hit the ground, he kept a firm two handed grip on the stock and barrel.

The jeep was as they had left it. Looking across the bare escarpment, Dietrich could see no sign of movement, none of his fellows. He might have been alone on the mountains of the moon that shone down so brilliantly. Captured, he surmised without any real feelings on the matter and climbed in behind the wheel, laying his rifle on the right hand seat where it was instantly available. He spared a glance back up towards the distant glare of lights that marked the East Gate entrance and thought to hear the sounds of more vehicles.

It would take time to clear a path through the pile-up but it was high time for him to move out. Dietrich turned on the ignition and gunned the motor.

*

Kurt nursed the breakdown truck up the last steep incline. The last two kilometres had all been low gear work with the weight of the bomb making the vehicle sluggish. At every bump and jolt the rear suspension hit the chassis with a solid thump.

He wondered about Paul Webb in silence. Had he done right in letting him go? It was a good five kilometres back to the town of Los Alamos. He assured himself that, even if the American did raise an alarm, there was little information that he could give; on his sole trip to the landing strip, Paul had been blindfolded. There were mountains all around, so he would not even be able to suggest a direction. In any case, they needed no more than an hour.

An hour and they would be airborne.

The breakdown's springs bottomed again as they hit a small ridge, the vehicle gathered speed down into the valley. Kurt didn't care now if the suspension snapped; he could almost see the plane where moonlight glinted from glass and metal.

The B24 was ready and waiting. A muted glow on the grass showed where the bomb doors were open; his headlights lit up the narrow track laid across the ground for the bomb dolly to run on.

Pieter Reinicke and Joseph Piekenbrock ran towards them and opened the cab door while Willi Braun and Friedrich Haas went round to the rear to winch the bomb out and on to the waiting carrier.

Pieter's face was wreathed in smiles. "It went well Kurt?"

Schroeder nodded. "Very well though we lost Hoeckle. He's in the back. I want him taken home. To Germany."

Pieter didn't understand why Kurt should be so insistent but, after a glance at the other's face, he nodded.

Joseph grabbed Kurt's hand and shook it briefly, "I didn't think it possible until this moment, Herr Oberst. You must be a very happy man. They will make you a General in the new Reich."

Kurt shook his head and watched the bomb being wheeled across to the aircraft. A depression had been dug into the ground beneath the bomb bay so that the unusually large diameter would clear the fuselage. "It's not over yet." He said. "The important part is still to come." He slammed the door and they followed him across to the Liberator where a chain block and tackle was being attached to a lifting point on the bomb's flank. "We must make haste to be away from here. Everything is ready for take-off?"

"Everything." Replied Reinicke as vehicle headlights approached. They were switched off for a moment and then on

442

again.

Either Nils or Weber thought Kurt and spoke to Reinicke again. "You had better get the engines turning over."

The jeep swept round in a wide circle and came to a stop facing the aircraft, its lights showing the lower tail fin on the bomb just disappearing into the plane's interior. Neuper was already inside, waiting for it to be clamped firmly so that he could loosen the cover plates ready to assess the fusing mechanism later.

It was Bergerud who stepped down from the jeep. He came running across the turf. "You caused some sort of a stir-up back there, Herr Oberst. It didn't take them long to discover something was wrong. No less than six jeeps came hurtling out about twenty minutes after you left."

It couldn't have been Webb's doing then, Kurt thought, and smiled slightly. "What happened?"

"They were dealt with. We didn't blow the break in the road, one of the vehicles went down the side and snapped the fuse line but it'll take them the best part of an hour to clear the wreckage."

"Did you see anything of the other team?"

Bergerud shook his head. "No. It's worrying me a little. I'd have thought they would be back before us."

Kurt frowned. "Five minutes. I'll give them no longer. Even if they clear the mines off the road from the East Gate, we can expect no more than thirty minutes grace – forty five at the

443

outside. The other vehicle might even unwittingly lead them here if they haven't already left."

"Obersturmfuhrer Dietrich is leading them, of course?" Bergerud queried.

"No." The clatter of the donkey engine starting up in the nose compartment drowned his words and he had to shout. "No, another casualty. Dietrich and Hoeckle." The starboard outer prop began to turn and the whine of the electric motor made further speech impossible.

Piekenbrock came forward, and tapped Kurt on the arm. Kurt pointed to the aircraft, Nils nodded and ducked into the bomb bay while Kurt and Joseph moved a little further away from the increasing thunder as, one after the other, the big radials fired.

"I shall have to leave, Herr Oberst. I have certain problems concerning the dispersal of my men, also I have an important radio call to arrange."

"Yes Joseph – I appreciate your problems. Go now, it is urgent that the ship knows the plane's on schedule And, Joseph; thanks."

"A pleasure Herr Ob... a pleasure Kurt." They shook hands. Piekenbrock walked into the darkness behind the Jeep's headlights. He backed the vehicle up and then started off along the valley.

Kurt went back to the plane and ordered the bomb doors closed behind him.

444

LAST MISSION

FORTY FOUR

Paul considered heading back to the Los Alamos site but it was not much further to go on home; he decided to go home, Susan was there with Garcia and Ed and he wanted to assure himself that she was all right. He broke into a trot, estimating that he could make it within forty five minutes.

Back on the highway, Paul kept an ear open for traffic; it was very late but there was always the possibility of a trucker driving through the night. As he ran, he tried to concentrate on what he could do to frustrate the German's plans – whatever those might be.

It seemed hopeless, if they were not already airborne, they would be very shortly. Paul could guess fairly accurately where the landing strip was located, he had deduced more than Schroeder had given him credit for. Despite the blindfold, he had a good idea of the general direction, the turns taken and the duration of the journey. The time had been less than an hour which meant no more than thirty miles on the kind of terrain they had travelled over and – he suddenly realised – Kurt had just now taken a turn-off which must lead to the valley! A slip-up on the Colonel's part.

If only he could secure a lift, even then though, he knew too much to safely tell the authorities. Give too much away and they would suspect his collaboration, there was also Carl's murder to think about as well. Paul sat uncomfortably on the twin cusps of his dilemma.

The twin beams of headlights came into view just as his chest was beginning to ache from the unaccustomed exercise. Too bad the car was heading the wrong way. Paul stopped, waiting for it to pass while he drew in lungfuls of cold night air; to his great surprise, the car stopped a few feet past him.

"Senor Webb." Said a face at the offside window.

"Paul! Paul!" A girl got out of the passenger side – Susan!

"Paul. Oh, Darling, are you all right?"

Dumbfounded, he stood there as she rushed across and huddled against his panting chest. "What are you doing here?"

Susan pulled away, caught hold of his hand and tugged him towards the car. "Looking for you of course. Come on, get in the car, we'll go back to the 'Hill'."

The three of them sat on the broad bench seat, Hank Garcia at the wheel.

"So you got away from Ed?"

Susan's vivacity suddenly drained away and she stared through the windscreen at the trees on either side of the trail.

"She killed him, Paul." Offered Garcia and reached across to pat Susan's hand. "She is a very brave girl."

"Damn right." Paul put his arm around her and bent to kiss her mouth but Susan turned her head at the last moment. "No."

She muttered. "Not just now. There're other things we've got to talk about – when there's more time."

Puzzled. Paul had to accept the situation and was silent for a while as they drove towards the still dark western horizon.

"I don't really know what we're going to do here." He said at last. "How can we stop them?"

"Isn't there someone you can talk to?"

He shook his head. "There's no way I could raise the security alarm – the Germans know too much about me and Piekenbrock will tell them about Carl, too."

"Oh Paul – I'd forgotten about that. Ed told me before… before he died. Edward was the one who killed Carl, not you. You hurt him maybe but it wasn't you that killed him."

"What? You're sure about this?"

"Absolutely. Ed was boasting." Her voice dropped again, the recollection was too recent to be anything but painful.

"That bastard Piekenbrock. He's been bloody well blackmailing me all this time."

Garcia grunted. "He's out on a limb, Paul. He can't drop you in it without implicating himself even further."

"You sure?"

The driver dropped the car into low and took it off the road. "The site's that way, folks. Five minutes' He looked at Paul. "I think your car's there, that right?"

Paul nodded. "Don't know what shape it's in, mind you. What're you going to do now?"

448

"Me?" Garcia shrugged. "Piekenbrock paid me my money last night. I've got a car." he smacked the steering wheel with his palm and bounced up and down on the seat as far as his stomach would allow. "And I'll put my Mex hat on until this lot's over."

Susan opened the door and they climbed out, she slammed it shut again.

Hank Garcia wound the window down. "Have a good war."

Paul grinned. "You too. And thanks."

"Me? Ain't done nothin'."

"For looking after Sue." Paul tightened his arm around her shoulders.

*

Piekenbrock's jeep climbed out of the valley as the B24s engines were run up to full power one by one and then allowed to idle again while the pilot went through his pre-flight checklist.

He had decided that Errol and Fred would have to be disposed of; it was the only safe way. Erich could see to that. There were also the cases of Edward and Albert to decide upon. Albert would have to disappear when he turned up, Joseph was certain that he would return to his old stamping ground up North; it was the only place he knew. Edward, too, might have to go; he would assess the situation when he spoke to the man.

The number one priority, however, was a call to the Mexican newspaper offices and he would do that as soon as he reached Webb's house. The ship had to be informed that 'Blondi' would rendezvous on schedule and a coded message had to go to Berlin.

Piekenbrock was within a mile or so of the main road when he saw the car approaching him at the bottom of the incline. It was the old Ford – Erich's. He slowed, anticipating the other's halting. Erich was supposed to collect him from Webb's place in the morning, why this early?

The car's driver ignored him. He recognised Garcia behind the wheel, Garcia must have seen him...

*

Kurt took one last look at his watch before securing the rear hatch. He regretted having to leave Weber and his two colleagues but he would be imperilling the mission's objective if he waited longer.

He made his way to the flight compartment, past the enormous weapon suspended over the bomb bay doors on a thick wooden pallet. Neuper was running possessive hands over the casing. "You'd better strap in Joachim. We shall be moving very soon." Then, putting his head through into the cabin; "We go." Pieter's upturned face nodded and he turned back to his instruments.

Reinicke switched on the two underwing floods and the airplane began to follow the twin beams along the valley. Kurt strapped himself down next to his men and, unconsciously, started to count the cost of Operation Blondi so far: Hoeckle, Weber, Scherf, Fachinger, Dietrich – all gone or, at least, not here, alive.

450

LAST MISSION

Realising the morbid direction of his thoughts Kurt deliberately stopped the flow. What were a few men set against the lives that would be saved by a cessation of hostilities? Probably the three missing men would be apprehended if they had not already been caught and would spend a short time imprisoned as POW's for, if Bormann and the Fuhrer had calculated correctly, the end of the war was near – nearer still now that the mission seemed about to be crowned by success.

Across the central aisle, Nils Bergerud had his eyes closed; trying to relax a little. Kurt smiled: at least he had come through alive and had fulfilled all that was expected of him.

The aircraft shuddered and vibrated as though in imminent danger of coming apart while the engines howled at full throttle, only the brakes holding it back. The atom bomb, which reminded Kurt even more of a whale, hung from its hooks and rattled against its braces; an ominous yet pleasing sight.

*

Dietrich swept up the slope in the second jeep, his foot hard on the gas peddle despite the tremendous jolting and hammering from the rough track. Eyes glued to the ground in front of him, he never even noticed the two stationary vehicles off to the side. Two objectives lay before him: to get the mission changed from the Washington target and to exact his revenge on Schroeder. If the second proved the means to obtaining the first: so much the better.

Errol and Fred were still, nominally, on guard duty at the

head of the valley. They were to remain until Erich came back to pick them up. They stood now, just within the tree line, watching the B24 roar towards them, the echoes from the engines thundering up and down the valley. It was Errol who saw the jeep's headlights first, pale in the growing light; he nudged the other and pointed and they moved out to stop the vehicle.

"We'll have to hide them," offered Fred. "They aren't going to stop that plane now."

Errol nodded and waved his arms to attract the driver's attention.

Dietrich saw the two men, he could also see the Liberator travelling along the valley, its lights flickering as it hit the many small irregularities. The swine were leaving him behind! The thought swelled, squeezing every other consideration aside.

Belatedly, the two Americans realised that the jeep was not going to stop, not even slowing. They scrambled for safety; Fred leaped aside at the last moment but the heavy metal bumper caught Errol squarely at knee level, breaking the joint and tossing him contemptuously into some bushes.

Without pausing, mouth set in a grim rictus of hate, Dietrich shot down the valley; all four wheels occasionally leaving the ground. His left arm was just strong enough to hold the wheel although his shoulder seemed to be on fire. With his right hand, he felt for the M43.

It was doubtful that he fired it merely to attract attention. The results, however, were not at all doubtful.

LAST MISSION

Pieter Reinicke sensed rather than saw the oncoming jeep; he saw the brief flashes where bullets hit the aircraft and ricocheted and realised that they were being fired at. There was nothing he could do; the ground speed indicator read seventy miles an hour – over a hundred and ten kilometres an hour and the landing gear was finding every bump and hollow that they had labored to eradicate.

He strained forward and just made sense of the approaching lights.

"God in Heaven, Willi. Hang on to your seat." He cried. "One of them's back and he's shooting at us."

The windscreen glass starred as a bullet came through it.

"Weber?"

"God knows."

Firing an assault rifle one handed is dangerous enough, firing from behind the steering wheel of a bucking jeep is senseless. Nevertheless, Dietrich squeezed off burst after burst; the slugs dispersing in a wide cone. One shell found a target in the plane's left hand tyre; most whistled harmlessly down the valley but that one hit was critical.

At seventy five miles per hour, the aircraft slewed a little to the left; Pieter strained at the controls and the huge momentum already built up carried them through. The B24 was virtually airborne, a handful of seconds later its bumping, lurching gait suddenly smoothed. It rose, leaving the cursing, gesticulating Dietrich firing the last of his ammunition at the aircraft disappearing into the false dawn of the last day.

FORTY FIVE

Up, up, sweeping around in a steeply banked curve, the B24 climbed out of the valley and settled on its course. It was later than they had planned for and Mexico was two hundred miles to the south. Reinicke stayed low, stayed to the west of the mountains that were the biggest landmark on Willi Braun's chart. They crossed the southern end using the same pass as route 70, a handful of trucks below then raising dust along the way.

Under Willi's guidance, they crossed into Mexico south of El Paso and flew towards the coast with the border a comfortable fifty miles away. Reinicke slowed right down, they had the time and if spotted, he didn't want to draw unnecessary attention.

They flew almost due east aiming between Cuba and Florida, crossing over water for two hours without seeing another aircraft. Nor did they see the fighter whose shadow suddenly fell across them. The radio challenge made Freidrick jump.

"Ambulance aircraft number 42-7467, please report your origin and destination."

Friedrich Hass looked up and around. "Sir…"

"Yes, Friedrick?"

"We've got company and he's asking awkward questions."
Hass pointed upward.

"What questions?"

"Where to and where from."

"Nosey bastard. Tell him we're on a secret mission to
recover – I don't know – yes," Pieter Reinicke made the story up
out of whole cloth, "the crew of a German U-boat beached on –
Willi, somewhere well away from the Bahamas?"

"Tell him Santiago."

Friedrich told him, in his best imitation American accent.

"Okay, 42-7467. Will give you protective cover for the time
being."

The control team on the flight deck cursed collectively while
the radio operator thanked the fighter pilot for his help. They
flew on, bearing further south as they neared Cuba , Hispaniola
could be seen through the haze.

"What do we do when we get there?" Asked Haas.

"We can all make suggestions and vote on it. In fact Willi,
on that note, you'd better let Colonel Schroeder know the
situation if you would."

*

Over a thousand miles north of the B24, in Washington,
Lieutenant John Fryers had already finished his breakfast. The
day had started better than most.

Fryers made his way briskly across Twenty First Street and
456

into the War Department entrance, taking the steps three at a time.

Spring seemed to have come to Washington at last; the thin April sunshine promised to strengthen later on and infected his mood. He smiled, touched his cap to the small crowd of office girls and stenographers, and, scorning the elevator, took the stairs up to the fifth floor. He went along the corridor and unlocked the door to room 512, one of the two offices assigned to the Manhattan Engineer District.

John was normally first in but, from long habit, he opened the interconnecting door to see if his boss, Lansdale was already here. It was deserted and then he remembered that the Colonel had left for a conference at the White House.

He opened the window so that the morning breeze would drive the stale smell of yesterday's cigarettes away and reached for the coffee pot. It was as far as he got, the telephone jangled insistently.

From there, the day went downhill.

"Fryers." He said and smiled as he heard the other's name.

"Why, hello Pete. Long time no..." The smile faded and he listened in silence.

"A what? A B24 ambulance... Okay. Let me check." Fryers put the phone down and unlocked his filing cabinets. He checked the contents of several manila folders."

"No," he said into the phone a few seconds later; then, "Hold on." Something stirred in his memory. "You got a registration?" He listened, wrote it down. "Rings a bell. I've had something recently, from the coastguard and also from... back in a sec." John Fryers *was* back in a sec. "Tell them to stay in touch with it. This is the third report I've seen on this aircraft and it's not from round here, I'll get back just as soon as I've got more info – and some orders."

With Lansdale gone, Fryers went in search of someone else which turned out to be Major Lockhart, a career officer looking forward to retirement 'just as soon as we get these fucking krauts cut down to size."

"Tell me again." Lockhart put his hands together beneath his chin.

There's a B24 air ambulance flying across the Mexican Gulf, Sir. It's number is 42-7467. That number has been queried twice before in the last thirty hours, no one seems to know anything about it – or the captured German U-Boat crew it is supposedly picking up from Santiago."

"Well, can't we contact its base?"

"Its base, in 1943, was in Burtonwood, England. It crashed on a test flight on 27 August that year. It was a transport, never was and never will be an air ambulance."

"Then tell it to land, there must be plenty of airbases near enough. Make sure there're guns pointing at it."

"And if it won't land?"

"Shoot the swine down."

*

The fighter plane peeled off and big breaths of relief were taken all round. Reinicke banked and turned north. Their reprieve was short lived: a quarter hour. Two more aircraft were back to shadowing them; one on each side.

"We're being instructed to land for inspection at Hurlburt Field."

"Where the hell is that?" Reinicke had been getting worried before, now he was alarmed.

"Not the faintest," said Willi.

"Play radio problems again." And Pieter Reinicke began move the plane about as though they had steering problems.

The US Air Force instructions were repeated and then turned to threats as Grand Bahama Island crept up over the horizon. The pilot on their right hand side was making stabbing motions at the ground.

Reinicke continued the erratic flying and feathered one of the props. "Tell them we have electrical trouble, lost an engine." There was insufficient power in the three engines to maintain height with the bomb load but that didn't matter, they were going to be forced into landing soon anyway...

Their subterfuge was not believed. There was a final *land or we fire* warning followed by a spray of canon fire hitting the tail. A few holes in the tail fins made little difference to the handling but it brought home their escort's serious intent.

"Fredrick, tell the Americans we're going to have to ditch in the sea. You Willi, tell Schroeder, I'll jettison the fuel and the

459

wing tanks'll keep us afloat quite a long time. When you've told the Americans, see if you can raise U-683 and advise them. I want a pin-point location from them, I intend to ditch as nearly on top of them as I can."

Still losing height, the pilot followed the approaching coastline counter-clockwise and when Fredrick Haas had the U-boat's position, he jettisoned his fuel, lined up along the waves and brought the aircraft down in a long shallow glide with undercarriages still up.

"Brace." Reinicke lifted the nose ten degrees at the last moment and the fuselage hit the water, braking them as if God's right hand had reached down and taken hold. The B24 skipped once, came down again and stayed down. It was nothing short of miraculous but he had no time to dwell on it.

Reinicke went back into the fuselage. "Sorry there was no time to consult." He said to Schroeder as soon as he had identified the other. "Trying to make the best of a bad job. Blitzing Washington is out but we might be able to save the bomb for another time." He looked at his watch. "Three hours to darkness, I'd say. I'm asking the U-boat to come up underneath us; we'll open the bomb doors and winch the thing down onto the submarine's deck. Okay?"

"Okay." Schroeder was a little uncertain. "And?"

"Come full dark, they'll surface and take the bomb down their torpedo loading chute. Looks like we're all going to South America."

LAST MISSION

It wasn't as easy as that of course. The Little Boy bomb was twenty eight inches in diameter, a standard torpedo is twenty one inches. The bomb weighed in at four tons, a torpedo at less than one ton. But it happened. The surveillance aircraft remained unaware of the feverish activity taking place below them, they waited for the high speed MTB's to arrive by which time B24 42-7467 was completely empty with bomb doors open to the sea.

FORTY SIX

"I want the fuse de-activating," said Franz Busch, the sub's torpedo engineer.

Neuper laughed. "Give us a break, Franz. Look at my hands…" Neuper held up both hands, both were shaking from exhaustion. He'd just spent the past three hours helping to manhandle the American bomb down a temporary chute into the torpedo storage room. The sub's remaining fish were now in the torpedo tubes to make room for the ugly, oversize creation.

"We don't move until then. Kapitänleutnant Keller's orders."

"Fine. Okay. Do me one favour, will you?"

"What's that?" Now that the brief contest of wills was over, he felt more friendly.

"Mug of coffee? Strong, sweet. *Very* strong."

Neuper borrowed a screwdriver and a small crescent wrench and got to work. Since he'd already made certain of the inspection plate fastenings it came off quickly. There were two fusing mechanisms: a pressure fuse, activated by the external air pressure change as it fell and a time fuse which would trigger after a preset time. Both would set off the detonation of conventional explosive which would compress the fissile material in the bomb.

Franz Busch returned with the coffee to be met with the pale, sweating features of Neuper peering out from under the bomb casing. The framework they had put together from bunk frames had buckled and the bomb had moved, rolled off the hastily rigged rack and onto Joachim Neuper's leg. His hand, at an awkward angle, was jammed inside the inspection opening.

"Mein Gott! What happened?" Asked Busch, his voice a whisper.

"Abandon ship." Said the munitions expert also in little more than a whisper. "I can hold it for a while but not forever."

"We've go to get you out of there first," Franz bending, prepared to peer under the huge casing.

"No." Neuper shook his head. "Daren't move anything or the fuse goes off."

"But your leg..."

"Get me some morphine if you have it, just a little, just enough. I have to stay here, though, got to stay conscious."

Brusch shook his head. Took a last look at Neuper's grey visage and hurried aft.

The medical officer arrived and knelt in the two inches of dirty water on the floor of the torpedo compartment. He used a flashlight to gauge the extent of Neuper's injuries.

The U-683 included a full medical officer in its crew rather than making do with a first-aid trained radio operator. "We need to get that off you with a block and tackle before we can do anything useful." If Brusch had conveyed what Neuper had told him, Franz Rasche had ignored him.

"Doctor," Neuper whispered. "I am a dead man already. Move this bomb and the ship goes up, then we are all dead men."

"*Boat*," said Rasche, he licked his lips. "How do you mean, dead?"

"If I take my hand off the fuse, Doctor, the bomb explodes. My leg is broken, if you don't get rid of the pain I cannot answer for my actions for very much longer."

"Well..."

"Give him what he asks for, Franz. Now. This is an order." Keller had entered unheard and was looking down at Neuper's rigid form.

"Ja, Kapitänleutnant."

Moment's later, Joachim Neuper relaxed as much of the hurt was submerged beneath the morphine's gentle touch.

"Watch over him Franz. Make certain he does not fall asleep. I now have to speak to Oberst Schroeder and find out just what our guest has brought into my boat."

Five minutes went by and the klaxon sounded between repeated orders for Gefechtsstationen – *combat stations*.

"So we have three tons of unstable explosive in the bows of my boat? Do I have it right, Oberst?"

"More or less, Kapitänleutnant. The explosive, for want of a better word, is powerful enough to demolish a whole city. So we must abandon ship, there is no other recourse."

464

"And suppose it doesn't go off? Suppose it is a dud or the fuse fails to work?"

"I don't follow you, Kapitänleutnant. Surely it is better to abandon ship than to hope for it not to work?"

"No." Keller, a 28-year-old on his first U-boat command, drummed his fingers on the small table between them. "We were heading out into the Atlantic in February, from Bergen, trying to steer clear of convoys and patrols before making as a fast a run as possible to Japan."

Schroeder looked surprised.

"We intercepted a British signal saying we had been sunk." Keller smiled bleakly. "A little premature. However, we carry four Enigma coding machines and almost seven hundred kilos of specifications and blue prints for aircraft. These are a part of an accord with the Japanese to help with their war effort but we were diverted by Reichsleiter Bormann's direct order."

"For us?"

"For you. To take you to Paraguay. We were already en route for Japan around Cape Horn – away from the conflict, so we were convenient. Imagine what would happen if the Americans got hold of what we carry?"

"I understand." Schroeder nodded thoughtfully. "I understand."

"When I agreed to save your Götterdämmerung device, Oberst, I exceeded my orders. Without even being set off, it has put an end to our larger mission."

"So..?"

"So I must scuttle the boat against the possibility of its *not* being destroyed and very much against my wish and my will." He sighed deeply then gave the order.

There were persistent clangs and bangs as seacocks were opened all along the hull, except where Schroeder knelt next to Joachim Neuper.

"What can I say, Joachim? This is my fault, my arrogance."

Neuper frowned and was about to say something.

Schroeder cut him short. "If I could take your place, Joachim, I would. You know that?"

The other nodded.

Schroeder kissed him on the forehead. "Go with God." He placed a revolver in Neuper's free hand then headed for the torpedo hatch.

Soon, there was only the sound of rushing water and the quiet hum of the electric motors.

EPILOGUE

Kapitan Reinhardt waited on station for ten hours after the agreed time before signalling Germany. The message read:

Blondi missed her date. Stop. Am returning to agreed station.

Bormann left the Fuhrer's birthday celebration to take the message. He read it through three times without showing emotion then began to make his plans. Admiral Doenitz was in the party. They had conferred briefly on the position regarding the new electro-U-boats. He, Martin, had put it casually that the Fuhrer might need to leave for the North as he was determined not to go to the National Redoubt in the Alps. That such a U-boat might be an excellent means of salvation, Doenitz had agreed. Now all he needed to do was to press for one on the basis of this message. The boxes could be transported there in hours probably even sent along with the Admiral when he left later that same day.

Content with these thoughts, the greatest manipulator of the Reich went to work his schemes. He would have to tell the Fuhrer about Operation Blondi, but first things first.

END

JACK EVERETT & DAVID COLES

Also at Acclaimed Books

Rachel's Shoe by Peter lihou

Soon to be released
Jihad by David Coles & Jack Everett
The Abbot and the Acolyte by David Coles & Jack Everett
Passage to Redemption by The Crew
The Causeway by Peter Lihou
Book by Peter Lihou
Druid's Bane by Phil Gillanders
Stretch by Brian Black
North Slope by Michael Parker

Lightning Source UK Ltd.
Milton Keynes UK
29 August 2010

159172UK00001B/1/P